Light At The End Of The Tunnel

BOGGY MARSH

Best wishes Jeanette from Trevor 'Boggy' Marsh xxx

Any similarity between the book's characters or their names and real people is purely coincidental. Anyone still alive at the time of writing or publishing has not been used as the sole basis of any characters. Locations, however, are real and most are in the Bolsover area.

The right of Trevor 'Boggy' Marsh to be identified as the author and illustrator of this work is asserted in accordance with the Copyright, Designs and Patents Act 1988 et seq.

Copyright © 2013 Boggy Marsh

All rights reserved.

ISBN:1493542001
ISBN-13: 978-1493542000

DEDICATION

This book is dedicated to my late wife Lynda, my son, Hugo and my 95 year old mum-in-law, Joan Plevey.

CONTENTS

1. Sound The Alarm! The Olly Wood Gang Is In The Woods.
2. Mam, A Weasel's Bit Our Willie's Willy. (It Was A Stoat, Stupid.)
3. Sorry Sir, The Dog Ate My Homework.
4. Flinty's Flying Bedsteads & A Mob Of Stampeding Stags, Other Animals & Birds.
5. A Robin Flew In, All Brave & Fiery, So Neville Wrote It In His Diary.
6. Watch Out Wally, You're In My Way – An Everyday Tale Of Crashley Ashley.
7. Another Rat, Just A Stone's Throw Away.
8. The Sons Of The Source Of The River Poulter.
9. Sergeant Sensible and Corporal Punishment.
10. This Train Is Bound For Dudley, This Train.
11. The Sting.
12. The Plaza Plan.
13. The Masked Ball's Up.
14. A Bit Of A Fuss On The Back Of A Bus.
15. The 1812 Overthrow By Tchaikovsky The Cat.
16. Eye Of Newt And Toe Of Frog – Double Trouble, Pile Of Rubble.
17. Willie Wood In Eastwood Ward.

- 18 Get Me Three Jets And Send Three And Fourpence, We're Going To A Dance.
- 19 Gunfight At The Sookholme Corral.
- 20 Join the Navy, See The World. What If You Can't Swim ? Doesn't Matter, They Give You A Ship.
- 21 On The Slopes Above The Sheepwash In Scarcliffe Wood.
- 22 Wicked William, The Pirate Captain, Brings The House Down.
- 23 Ready, Steady, Go ...

ABOUT THE AUTHOR

I was born at home in the village of Scarcliffe near Chesterfield, England in 1950.

When I went to Grammar School, I was christened 'Boggy' Marsh by friends - my mum hated that but the Boggy-ness stuck with me.

I 'worked' as a civil servant and later I became an Intelligence Analyst. I'm now retired, the whole nation will be relieved to hear. I also spent many happy years as a part-time youth worker, 'giving something back'.

My son Hugo was born in 1988. When he was about 7, he asked me to 'tell me a story from your mind'. Thus the tales of the 'Olly Wood Gang' were born which are the subject of my writings.

I still live in Bolsover as I love the place and its people. My interests include politics, reading, poetry (especially Percy Shelley), writing and football (I must get out more).

Visit my website at www.boggymarsh.com

ACKNOWLEDGMENTS

I would like to pay tribute to my late wife, Lynda, and my son, Hugo, for their support for the stories, as it was their suggestion that I should someday write them down. I could not have finalised and published them without Hugo's help.

My own brother Roy and the three Wrath brothers, Rob, Paul and Will, also made massive contributions and their late brother, Andy, was a great friend and inspiration to us all and similarly contributed.

There are many others, too numerous to mention, but their help is appreciated.

1

SOUND THE ALARM! THE OLLY WOOD GANG IS IN THE WOODS.

As the two Heath brothers and the four Wood brothers lived next door to each other on Castle Green, it was easy for them to call for each other. Eric 'Jasper' Jones lived literally just a stone's throw around the corner and, instead of calling for him in person, they usually threw small stones or pebbles across their back gardens at his windows. His mother would jump out of her skin and storm outside angrily to shout at the boys but they would run and hide as soon as they had 'knocked on Jasper's door' to come to Scarcliffe woods or to play football.

There was an eerie silence in the air, frightening to anyone on their own. As they approached the tall trees at the end of Poulter Well Lane the seven boys sang their favourite songs, alternating between and sometimes oddly combining them together, producing a strange mix of such as The Beatles and Rolf Harris.

A loud screeching arose from the rooks, which flew up from their nests in the treetops. The boys' gazes followed the birds' flight towards Little Wood at the edge of Scarcliffe village.

Willie, as usual, lagged behind until something brought him up to the others through either fear or curiosity. No-one saw the young rook, which had been exercising its wings high up in the safety of its nest, plummet like a bomb. It landed, still flapping and screaming with alarm, smack on top of Willie's head and the boy cried out and slumped to the ground. The gang gathered around the two prone casualties.

"Could be dead," said Balsa, sounding matter of fact.

"Yeah, let's hope not, it'd be a terrible shame," added Newt.

"It's a baby rook, isn't it ?" said Giggsy, trying to impress, having been reading Whitlock's Birds of Derbyshire in the school library.

"Well, as it fell out of a nest in a rookery, it's hardly likely to be a bloomin' pheasant is it ?" said Olly, laughing and putting his brother's nose out with his cruel words.

At that Willie burst with laughter and opened his eyes, saying, "Don't worry, I'm all right, I was just tricking you."

"It wasn't you we were worried about," replied Balsa, "It was the rook chick."

He picked up the bird and held it close to his chest like a baby, stroking it. The chick opened its eyes but was somewhat worse for the collision than Willie, having fallen much further. It neither struggled nor made any sound at first.

"Should we take it to Tarzan ?" suggested Mac, knowing this would be a popular idea.

"Yes," said Balsa, "Put the dive-bomber pheasant rook-chick in your bag now, Newt and we'll see what he's got in at the minute, shall we ?"

They all agreed enthusiastically so Balsa carefully put the chick in Newt's gas mask bag. These bags were popular with children at the time and Newt always took his to the woods for carrying any equipment they might use or 'prizes' they might find. He also used it to carry drinks, sweets, food and a notebook and pencil for recording anything of interest.

As the others marched off to the strains of two currently popular songs, Willie bent over and washed the bird-muck from his hair in the River Poulter. He ran after them shouting, "Hey, wait for me."

Tim Harman was well known in the village for nursing sick animals and birds. Though only just turned thirteen, he had already cared for around a hundred such patients which he had either found himself or other villagers had brought to him. The gang were regular visitors to his home. The door on the side of the house was open. Olly cautiously shouted in.

"Are you there, Tarzan?" He deliberately used Tim's nickname, knowing that his mother hated it. Her instant reply as she angrily stomped out of the kitchen into the hall made them all jump back from the door.

"He's round the back, and what have I told you about calling him that ?" she boomed.

They scurried to the back garden, laughing at their success in provoking Mrs Harman. To call it a garden was a great compliment. There were hardly any plants left and the large 'lawn' had been trampled and eaten almost bare. A brick outbuilding housed a toilet and a coal-house. There were four assorted sized sheds at the bottom of the garden. An aviary was attached to one of the sheds and there were also some hutches and wire runs dotted around.

"Hello Tim," "All right Tarzan," "Ay up Tim," they variously called to their friend who was kneeling beside a run unravelling fishing line from a mallard. Willie ran forward, excitedly asking, "What've you got there Tarzan?" As he neared Tim, Willie, in his haste, slipped on a large splat of bird-muck (from the mallard, to be precise). He then lost his footing and fell headlong into an old tin bath, half filled with cold water awaiting the duck.

The youngster jumped out of the tin bath, drenched and spluttering. He cursed his misfortune and everyone there for laughing at him, to their great amusement. Newt knew that Tim's mother was helping the Vicar to organise the Church Summer Fête. His own mother had given some of his better old clothes, which no longer fit him. He suggested to Willie that he therefore go and ask Mrs. Harman if he could borrow some, on account of his being drenched, but to make sure that he asked her properly and politely. So off he trotted, practising his words, knocked on the door and when the glowering, threatening Mrs Harman appeared, delivered his speech as nicely as he could.

"Excuse me Mrs Harman, the others say you're planning a fight with the Vicar this summer. I wondered if I could borrow some of Newt's old clothes that his mother gave to you to sell at the fight, as mine are drenched?" He thought 'fight' sounded more appropriate than 'fête'. Without a word the lady stepped back into the kitchen, making Willie think he was in luck. Tarzan's mother returned with a frying pan in her hand and a blood-curdling scream on her lips and proceeded to chase him along the side of the house and into the street. She turned and saw the other boys, including her own son, Tim, all staring open mouthed at her crazed and hysterical display as she whirled the frying pan through the air. Letting out another warlike cry she chased the seven stunned onlookers back down the garden.

"Mam, Mam!" Tim screamed, in a panic stricken attempt to halt her advance, as he clung to the now disentangled but equally panic stricken, quacking, flapping mallard.

The Wood and Heath brothers and Jasper Jones had youth, speed and agility on their side as they negotiated different routes over the sheds and the six-foot wooden fence. Olly and Mac ran straight at the fence, leaping to grab the top and hurling themselves up and over. Balsa and Newt lifted Giggsy and Jasper onto the shed roof then climbed up after them, before all four jumped over the fence. Newt first threw down the gas mask bag, containing Bomber the rook chick, to his brother, Mac. Tim meanwhile wasn't so quick, carrying the frightened mallard, which slowed him down. His mother was gaining on him, exerting every muscle in her blind rage. Suddenly he turned round and launched the luckless duck at her bright red face, knowing that she didn't like birds, particularly large ones. That she had just thrashed one way with her weapon prevented the duck from suffering a mortal blow with the frying pan and ending up on the table. It then managed to beat its wings to a hasty and lucky getaway.

Putting his mother in a flap and losing his duck gained Tim precious seconds, in which he managed to clumsily clamber on to a shed. He then jumped over the fence to join his friends' race to freedom down the field, where they were later rejoined by Willie.

When they reached Gang Lane, they collapsed from their efforts and the relief of escape. Though none of the boys made a sound a loud announcement was heard from among them.

"Caw, caw," it began, to be repeated even louder, "CAW! CAW!", as Newt's bag began to rustle and jump about as though alive itself.

"What are you doing with a baby rook?" asked Tim, recognising the call.

"That's why we've come to see you. It dive bombed our Will on Poulter Well Lane so we've called it Rook Chick The Dive Bomber," said Giggsy, "It must've fallen out of its nest".

Tim opened the bag himself, carefully inserting his hand. He gently stroked the bird rather than lifting the flap when it was so frightened. He then reached in with his other hand to bring Bomber out in a supportive but secure grip. The calm and reassuring way he spoke to it showed why he was so successful and highly regarded in his dealings with animals and birds. He performed a careful examination, before passing comment.
"It should be alright, it's just been bashed about a bit. I'd best get it settled in the aviary quick though." He got up and set off down the lane towards the village, turning to add "Oh, and don't come round for a bit, especially you Willie. You've seen how upset Mam can get."

They watched Tim disappear from view and the gang heard him exchange greetings with a group of other boys and they were relieved when they realised who these newcomers were, as Paul Morley and the two Tupac brothers came around the bend in the lane. All three lived on the Moorfield Estate in Bolsover. They were all friendly and exchanged greetings. Paul had an air rifle over his arm, which he bore with pride.
"New gun?" asked Olly admiringly.
"Yeah", said Paul, "It's a Diana 2.2 shooting standard pellets, but it's got a good range. Here, have a go with it." He loaded the air rifle and passed it to Olly. "See if you can hit that Holly tree down the lane towards the village."
The other members of the gang protested in panic.
"No, not that way, not towards the Vicarage," said Balsa.
"No" added Mac, "the Vicar's a Cambridge Blue at running and he can't half go. He'd catch us easy."
"We're not frightened of any Vicar, are we ?" said Paul defiantly, so Olly shrugged and aimed at the tree. It was a good shot, but it glanced off the trunk and they heard a crash of glass, which was the parlour window of the Vicarage shattering.
"Run," shouted Olly and he gave the gun back to its owner, as his brothers, along with Mac, Newt and Jasper, all turned and sprinted towards the Little Wood and the Sheepwash, a walled section of the River Poulter which flowed through the wood. Paul and his friends laughed and shouted "Chicken" after them but their faces dropped however as they turned back to face the Vicarage. Reverend Woolley hurdled his four-foot garden

fence and ran across the field next to the lane, bursting through a gap in the hedge and on to Gang Lane itself.

The three boys headed for the woods where their friends had already hidden. Paul was no slouch and despite the handicap of his air rifle was twenty yards up on his friends by the Sheepwash. The vicar also overtook the other two, brothers Jan and Mario Tupac and was clearly after the one carrying the gun. The Reverend rugby tackled him as they neared the Cedar of Lebanon in which were hidden Olly and his gang, high up on a platform they had made. From there they saw and heard the ensuing struggle and exchange.

"What's your name boy?" demanded the vicar, while holding Paul in a vice-like grip in a very un-Christian like manner. "And where do you live?"

"Paul McCartney, Father," he said, smirking, "and I live at Bolsover."

"Oh, do you know the Heaths and Woods?" asked the Reverend in a worried tone, looking around nervously as if he half expected them to fall out of the nearest tree. Which they nearly did at this question.

"Heathsand Woods?" repeated Paul cheekily, "Is it part of Sherwood Forest?" This humour served only to anger the vicar even more. He dragged Paul to his feet, frog-marched him back to the vicarage and telephoned the police to inform them of the crime.

The policeman who came fortunately did not know Paul Morley and had never heard of Paul McCartney either, but he took down the boy's particulars and said, "I'll take him home to face the music from his parents."

Meanwhile Olly and the gang had climbed down from their hiding place. It had been too close for comfort with the 'Revved-up-Reverend' as they called him.

"We're not out of the woods yet," said a smirking Mac to his friends who jeered his humour. As they were about to leave, Olly spread out his arms and stood still, then pointed into the wood towards a Common Ash beyond their Cedar of Lebanon. Only Mac saw what he meant and, with his mouth wide open in shock, he walked forwards with Olly to investigate. The smooth, stout trunk of the tree had been carved with the word

'MAC' in four inch high letters. The others followed, still unaware of what they were looking at until they were all stood next to the offending tree.

"What did you do that for, Mac ?" asked Willie, breaking the silence of their astonishment.

"Well for a start, I didn't do it and for another thing, somebody probably did that to make people think it was me," replied Mac. "And last of all, from the angle of the letters, whoever did that is right handed and I'm left handed. So who did do it and why ? Either somebody else called Mac, or they're trying to get me into trouble."

Olly picked up the pieces of wood and bark that had been cut and dropped at the base of the tree and pushed them into the crevices of the letters until they were almost filled and hidden.

"There, that should cover it up for a while," said Olly confidently. "Come on, we know it wasn't Mac but there's nothing we can do. Let's just look round for any clues before we go."

They crawled around on the ground, most of them just pretending to search for clues, when really they were looking for creepy crawlies to avoid. Only Mac and Olly looked for clues and as they stood up, they both saw the strands of long black hair attached to a branch at their head height. Olly pulled it off and showed it to Mac, then held it up as the others gathered round to look.

"Who do we know with black hair that long?" asked Mac uncertainly although he knew that they did know someone but he did not want to say who, as she often followed Olly about.

"There's that stupid Stubley-Stanhope lass but she'd get lost in the woods like that woman who found her way back when the church bells rang," said Giggsy. "Her called Lady Constantinople de Fresheggsville, or whatever it is."

"No, it's Lady Constipation de Frogslegsville, isn't it ?" joined in Jasper.

"What about Lady Consolation de Cominglastville ?" suggested Balsa.

"Or Lady Condescension de Phil the Greek," joined in Newt. The others gave him a puzzled look. "My history teacher calls Prince Philip 'Phil the Greek'," he explained and they all shook their heads.

"Lady Constantia de Frecheville, you dopes," laughed Mac along with everyone else.

"Come on, let's get going, we can ask her when we see her sometime," said Olly, taking advantage of the light hearted moment to deflect the unwanted attention from the 'spoilt little rich girl', Hannah Stubley-Stanhope .

They wandered on past Foxes Den, which they usually visited, though not on this occasion. Along the track out of the plantation they hurried, before they came to the fishpond. This was always a favourite place where they would stop to watch the wildlife and even swim in the pond if it was a nice sunny day. The other main attraction of the fishpond was to sail in Bush-a-Vella, or Bush-Fella, an old but buoyant tin-bath.

"They shouldn't fence off our Billabong," observed Balsa, climbing the fence, "We should be free to roam where we want, live off the land and sail Bush-a-Vella, like Aborigines."

"True," said Mac, "but I bet they don't have Father Woolleys or Mrs Harmans in the Australian outback."

"Our Will was right though, you know," said Olly, "we do get picked on by grown-ups and we're always getting into bother with the police, farmers, gamekeepers, landowners, the vicar, the Duke of Devonshire, teachers, station masters, that Torchy woman at the pictures, shopkeepers and Mr Palfreyman."

They all laughed at Olly's inclusion of Mr Palfreyman, the Superintendent of Bolsover Swimming Baths, where they went to swim and meet friends. His enormous, bushy, handle-bar moustache was both scary and comical to them. The ex RAF man would often shout at them as though they were on parade and so they called him 'Wing Commander Palfreyman' or 'Wingco'.

"Bus conductors," added Jasper to the list.

"School bobbies," said Giggsy.

"Nit nurses ? They pick on everybody," suggested Willie, straight-faced.

"Nearly everybody picks on US, even when we've done nothing wrong," added Mac. "We ought to join their scouts or youth club and, sort of, pretend we're on their side. There's only Frankenstein who treats us as though we're human or at least a friendly species."

"Yeah Mr Finkelstein's nice to us, we never have any problems with him," said Balsa.

"It'll look funny if we all turn into angels and join the church choir and scouts with our Newt and everybody calls us the Good Wood Gang," laughed Mac, bringing raucous agreement. They walked purposefully and noisily around the pond singing 'O For the Wings Of A Dove'[i] to poke friendly fun at Newt and at what they thought about being angelic. Balsa and Giggsy dragged Bush-a-Vella out of the bushes on the boggy side of the pond, but only to check that it was still there. They were on a secret mission to which they had all agreed and nothing was going to interfere with it. They hung it up a tree to hide it again. "Come on," urged Newt, looking at his watch, "We're supposed to meet Mick in ten minutes at the Station."
"We Bush-Fellas," said Balsa, "Not use watch - use Sun tell time."
This prompted a full and hearty rendition of Rolf Harris songs from all the would-be Aboriginals.

The gang clambered through the hedge and into the Brook Field. Here they walked, sometimes alongside the stream, at other times in it, as they were all wearing their wellies. When they reached the wooden bridge they ignored it, wading across the stream. Then up the path to the railway cutting, alongside which they walked for just over a hundred yards. They simply slid down the steep sides in to the cutting itself at a point where the Woods' dog, Joss, had done the same two weeks before when he was chasing a rabbit.

The railway line had been part of the Lancashire, Derbyshire and East Coast Railway, closed in 1951. It was announced at the time that the 9½ miles section between Chesterfield and Shirebrook North would be closed to passenger traffic on December 3rd and the 2,625 yards of track running through the Bolsover to Scarcliffe tunnel would be removed.

In fact the track along the whole section had been fully removed before ever Doctor Beeching used his axe on the railways. The sleepers, the buildings at the nearby station and many other features still remained along the route. Scarcliffe Station marked the summit of the main line at 521 feet above sea level. The stretch of cutting leading to this end of the tunnel, like the tunnel itself, had always been troubled by water.

Thus it was that seven noble savages in their wellies marched along the cutting through the many puddles of water. They sang their marching chant, announcing their arrival at Platform One to Mick Furness who stood there as if waiting for a train.

He was a classmate of Newt's at the local grammar school at Shirebrook. He was known and liked by all of them, and many others, for his spirit and bravery in the face of adversity.

Mick had a false, rigid, plastic right arm from his elbow down and this was held on through a system of straps around his shoulders. Despite this he would try almost anything, just like the other boys and they were fiercely protective and supportive of him. He always said a crazed, giant crocodile had bitten off his arm in an Australian swamp, which served only to fuel the awe in which he was held by the gang for the explanation he gave. They knew it was not true but did not mind.

They tramped back along the swampy cutting and told exaggerated stories about the old tunnel they were heading towards.

"They reckon Army trucks have been heard at all hours of the day and night," said Olly.

"Yeah and carrying H-bombs and missiles," added Balsa, "to store them underground in a secret place where the Ruskies don't know about them."

Water poured over the tops of their wellies as they went through a particularly deep puddle.

"Are you sure they brought them on trucks and not boats ?" said Mick. The water got deeper still for a while but then largely disappeared due to a slight incline as they reached the huge imposing metal door, which barred their way at the mouth of the tunnel.

"I expect they meant us not getting in, as well as the Ruskies," observed Newt with a disappointed air. Although the gang had been here many times it was the first time they had gone with the intention of getting in.

"Come on," said Olly encouraging, "we're not packing in now. Look, the little access door might be locked but there's the window at the top. We can get through there. All we need is a load of branches to use as ladders."

Mac took his machete out of its leather sheath attached to his belt and they each took it in turns to hack large branches off trees. Willie and Mick waded back along the cutting and found their own, already cut, and they all reassembled by the great metal door.

"Right" said Olly, as usual taking charge, "I'll climb up. Newt, give us a torch."

Newt duly produced a triple-battery torch from his gas mask bag,

"Our Will, give us your rope," added Olly.

Willie uncoiled a thick rope from around his shoulders. Olly climbed the makeshift ladders that leaned against the door, to fifteen feet above the ground and reached up to the window. Either side of it were thick metal bars. He tied the rope to the first bar and used it to climb through and lower himself down the inside of the door. One by one the others did exactly the same in the order decided by Olly.

First Newt, with the other torches, then Giggsy, Jasper and Willie. Mick was next, helped up by Balsa and Mac, who were the last ones still on the outside. He got to the top of the branches on the outside but he could not lift himself into the window as his plastic arm could not bend. Olly climbed back up the inside of the door using the rope. He found Mick stood on the branches with both arms outstretched and both hands clinging to the rim of the window. His plastic hand, shaped as an immovable claw, had become stuck on the rim.

Despite his own and Olly's best efforts it could not be freed. Instead, the great energy used succeeded only in Mick knocking all the branches to the floor. He could hang on no longer with his good hand and the shoulder straps gave way, sending him crashing to the ground with a splash into the shallow water and cushioning, fallen branches.

"Aaaargh," he cried, leaving his plastic arm clinging to the window frame.

"Mick's arm's come off," reported Olly solemnly.

"Which one?" came the mischievous reply from Newt, bringing fits of uncontrollable laughter from all of them, including Mick.

Olly unhooked the claw-like grip of the plastic hand from the window. Holding the elbow end he leaned down and pointed the hand towards Balsa, on the ground, saying,

"Here you are, I'll hand you this." Yet more wild mirth then came from Balsa, Mac and Mick on the ground and Olly himself. He then dropped the arm, in his laughter, on to the cushioning branches. After many minutes of repeated falling about laughing until they cried, they eventually regained their composure. Balsa and Mac set about refitting Mick's arm so they could continue. Finally they managed to haul their friend through the window safely. They lowered him down on the inside, using the rope, before Balsa and Mac also completed the entry along with all of the branches. Olly had insisted on taking their makeshift ladders to ensure their safe exit at the other end at Carr Vale.

They checked their equipment before they set off down the 1 in 20 incline. The sounds of the woods, the chattering and calling of a multitude of birds and animals, had been replaced by a near silence. The only noise in the whole length of the tunnel was the constant and frightening sound of dripping, splashing water. Though they did not know it, the tunnel had always been in need of attention during its use, on account of its excessive dampness. Indeed, towards the end of its useful life, it was believed that this caused parts of the brick lining to give way. This probably explains why some railwaymen had been reluctant to pass through it and may also have contributed to the tunnel's and the line's closure.

The boys walked nervously in tight formation, the front four's torches lighting their path – Olly, Mick, Jasper and Willie. The other four were close behind, torch in one hand, dragging branches with the other. Though none would admit it, they were all scared stiff. By a hundred yards in, they began to sing to relieve their fear, - not their marching song, as might have been expected, but a selection of songs with 'Sun' in the title, with a hint of irony in the total darkness. The tension lifted and they began to relax and enjoy themselves.

Olly, as well as leader, was often chief fun-maker. He pretended to stumble but secretly picked up a piece of broken brick as he fell and carried it in his hand for a short distance. Shining his torch to the right, Olly saw a large rat frozen in the glare before it ran off into the distance. While the others stared at the rat, he threw the brick hard over his left shoulder against the wall of the tunnel, which at that point was weakened by the water. A loud crack was swiftly followed by a fearsome rumbling. The eight of them literally ran for their lives as five yards behind them a section of the brick lining of the wall and roof caved in. The great pile of rubble which fell was so close that it trapped the trees they had been towing. Immediate survival was, at that point, more important than saving the trees to use as ladders.

They ran for fifty yards without stopping, then turned to see how close they had been to tragedy. A large cloud of dust and rubble was settling where they had nearly come to grief. A cloud of silence settled on the boys as they turned and continued quickly towards Carr Vale. Their fear was now such that no one wanted to walk too close to the sides of the tunnel or to be bringing up the rear. There followed much scrambling and jostling for positions. Olly showed his customary bravery and leader's example by volunteering to be at the back but then no one wanted to lead the way at the front, without Olly there, which brought more pushing and shoving. This at least lightened their spirits again and they gradually spread out and began to talk and enjoy their adventure once more, as they approached the halfway point.

Up on the surface, a great mound of blueish-grey shale over a hundred yards in diameter and fifteen feet high marked this halfway point. It had been excavated from the tunnel when it was being constructed and brought up through what became a ventilation shaft. A thick concrete and metal cap, in which were cut a number of two-inch diameter air holes, covered the shaft. Here the Tupac brothers were messing about and still waiting for Paul Morley (who, by now, was already at home), unaware of the gang's progress through the tunnel below them. They sang down the shaft and listened to it echoing downwards.

The tunnel travellers were at the very bottom of the shaft and responded by making train noises, which of course echoed their own way back up. When they heard this, the Tupacs were petrified and left the Blue Hills as fast as they could. They ran across the fields to Hillstown where they met Babs Nelson, recently escaped from detention at home, courtesy of his eldest sister, who he'd asked to help him escape from his 'curlew', to her amusement.

Babs might have gone with the gang had he not been kept in

'as a detention and curfew', his mother had said, for stealing a neighbour's bike and crashing it the previous day. The Tupacs told him about hearing a 'ghost train' at the Blue Hills. Babs of course realised what this 'ghost train' really was and began to dance and make the same train noises.

This was just too much for Jan and Mario and once again they ran off in fear and puzzlement. Babs wanted to be there to greet his friends from the tunnel exit but how would he get there in time and which end of the tunnel should he go to, he wondered?

A group of boys playing football on the Rec had left their bikes behind the goals and Babs saw his chance. He leapt on the bike belonging to Steve Maude, another local boy, and pedalled away as fast as he could towards Carr Vale and the Western end of the tunnel. Within minutes Babs was speeding down the steep New Station Road, pursued by Maudey, Robert 'Froggy' Frost and Colwyn Holness 'The Pope', along with the twelve others who had been playing football. A hue and cry soon developed with shouts of "Stop thief", although some of them had an idea that it could be Babs from previous experience.

Others joined in, including some young men who came out of the West View Hotel, slightly drunk, a passing policeman on his bike and a dozen cyclists from Bolsover Wheelers. Before his leading pursuers had turned the dogleg bend in the road, Babs had already reached the path near the 'Big Girls School' leading to the footbridge over the railway cutting. Here he got lucky as, crossing the footbridge, he met a youth about his own age.

"Hello," said Babs, lying, "I'm Colwyn Holness. What's your name?"

"Pietro Vitaly Polczynski," replied the youth, to Babs' surprise, "But people call me Pete," he added, to Babs' relief.

"Do us a favour Pete," said Babs ever so nicely, "Ride my bike around will you, I'm meeting my girlfriend for a walk – I'll see you back here in an hour."

Pietro Polczynski, also known as Pete, was most excited by this show of friendship and he straddled the bike. Babs hurtled down the bank into the cutting before turning with a laugh to shout,

"See you later Pete," and did a double take at Pete's reply, "See you later Babs."

Off cycled Pete back on to New Station Road where he turned down the hill and past the entrance to the girls' school. He was just opposite the public swimming baths when he heard the commotion behind him of the chasing hue and cry and their cries of "Stop thief". Pete turned and stopped in curiosity to watch them go past, wondering who they were chasing and why. The Bolsover Wheelers came first and struggled to stop as they were going so fast. Eventually they came to a halt and pedalled furiously back to Pete who was astonished to be dragged off the bike and wrestled to the ground on the green opposite the baths. Constable Stagg on his police bicycle was next, followed at intervals by various footballers and the rest.

When Maudey, the bike's owner, arrived he took one look at Pete and announced loudly,

"That's not who took my bike. It was Babyface Nelson, not Pete Polczynski. Alright Pete ?"

"Babyface Nelson ?" scoffed the constable. "You've been watching too many gangster movies, young man. I've better things to do than chase film characters even if it was a good film, with Mickey Rooney I believe. I reckon you lot have had me on a wild goose chase."

The Bolsover Wheelers let go of Pete, remounted and cycled off down the hill towards Carr Vale, shouting "Which way now, Wheelers ?" at each junction they came to. The police constable began pushing his bicycle back up New Station Road which was a long steep hill. It was hard work on a heavy police cycle not built for speed, unlike the Wheelers' bikes. When Constable Stagg was far enough away Maudey spoke quietly to his friend.

"Ok Pietro, how did he get you to have my bike ? Where the devil's he gone now ? What's he up to ?"

"I met him at the footbridge over the railway cutting. He told me some rubbish about meeting his girlfriend and he said his name was Colwyn Holness. He's a laugh, isn't he ?"

"He's not just stolen a bicycle then," observed The Pope. "He's stolen my identity as well."

"Well, at least I've got my bike back," said Maudey. "Let's go finish the game, it's 19-all."

LIGHT AT THE END OF THE TUNNEL

The footballers wandered back up the hill to the Rec to decide their game. Next goal won it, scored by The Pope.

The now forgotten bike thief, Babs, ran along the cutting towards the tunnel as fast as he could. At the same time the tunnel travellers were beginning to lengthen their stride towards the light at the end of the tunnel, some quarter of a mile to go. Soon they broke into a trot, excited at their achievement. With whoops of joy they abandoned their earlier caution, leaping in and out of the cavities built into the walls and doing jigs and twirls in wild excitement and relief. All of this changed dramatically as Willie, in the darkness and hullabaloo, ran headlong into a water-filled trough near the wall. Measuring twelve feet long, four and a half feet wide and over four feet deep, it was big enough to swim in, at least for Willie.

For several seconds he trod water until his fellow explorers, trying not to laugh, hauled him out. The air in the tunnel may have been warm, but the water was cold and took his breath away.

"Come on," urged Olly, smirking, "we'd better get out before anything else happens."

At that moment the light at the end of the tunnel went out, accompanied by a loud clang.

The shocked and scared boys ran the short distance to the large metal door, thinking that their escape window had been closed by National Security officials or someone thinking they were Russians. They feared that the cave-in they had witnessed, and now the exit being blocked, meant they were entombed in the tunnel. Panic and hysteria quickly spread amongst them.

"Olly, what are we going to do?" asked the thoroughly wet Willie.

His eldest brother, used to taking charge, quickly responded, "HELP! HELP! HELP!" and the others immediately joined in.

As if by magic the thick, metal cover, which had earlier been slammed over the window, was slowly opened.

The grinning face of Babs appeared, accompanied by the words, "The Cavalry's here!"

A stream of abuse, catcalls and massive relief was hurled at Babs who enjoyed every minute of it. An old ladder he had found outside the big door was passed backwards and forwards through the window, with the help of Willie's bull rope, until all of them were safely on the outside. The laborious process took them more than fifteen minutes. They then climbed up the steep sides of the cutting, hauling Mick and Willie up with the rope, and set off up the fields and lanes belonging to farmer, Pip Hill. They took the direct route home, avoiding the roads and the vigilantes' presumed search for the bike thief, on the advice of Babs. There would have been singing, despite their tiredness, but Babs wanted to know all the details of their adventure. The gang, or most of them, were only too pleased to tell him. Babs bubbled with excitement at every word. Only Olly and Mac looked unhappy and did not join in.

The inevitable question from Babs was not long in coming.

"Can we do it again next weekend so I can come?" he asked of the two leaders.

"No," said Olly, unexpectedly, "it's too dangerous. The tunnel's not safe, especially after a roof fall. We're not taking the risk again. Living dangerously is ok if you can cope with it. Dying dangerously is for idiots and if the roof falls in, on your own head be it, so to speak."

Mac nodded his agreement and smiled at Olly's pun. The others all stopped and stared open mouthed at them. They were not used to considering danger and risk. They were used to climbing trees, going up and down cliffs, exploring caves, sailing in tin baths and getting into scrapes. And evading capture by gamekeepers, farmers, the vicar, policemen and people like Mrs Harman. Grown-ups talked about danger and safety. The gang did all of these things, while others talked about the dangers of doing them.

"Awww heck," moaned Babs. "I always miss out on things, it's not fair. Go on, I'll blow up the school if you want. I could make the explosives with my chemistry set. BOOM !!"

The others all looked at Mac and Olly, expecting either an agreement or an argument but they would not be drawn.

"Come on," said Olly, "let's go home."

They trooped wearily up Darwood Lane, in silence and deep in thought, wondering what it all meant. As they neared the top of the lane where it took a left turn they usually ran past Pip Hill's bungalow but on this occasion they could not be bothered if he saw them.

"Oi you lot," shouted the smallholder from his yard. "Where do you think you're going?"

None of them spoke and they simply stared at the old man and carried on walking, straight up Poly Fields and round on to Castle Green. Olly put an arm round Babs' shoulder to try and make him feel better, which appeared to work. He did not push his luck however and said no more about the tunnel, although all of them were thinking about it.

"Another place we need to have a look at," said Babs, changing the subject to make everyone feel a little easier. "Is that Aroma Free Group site because something funny's going on down there, I reckon. The place stinks cos I was there yesterday."

"So that's what that awful smell is," laughed Olly. "I'd always wondered Babs..."

"Yeah and there's even some American Army geezers involved and sniffing around as well," replied Babs. "I've seen them in their uniforms and big cars with two posh English blokes while I was hiding up a tree and you'll never guess what I heard them talking about."

They were all too tired to have more than a half-hearted interest in the American Army's arrival at the Aroma Free Group so when no-one else spoke, Olly decided to humour Babs. "What they talking about, Big Chief Babs Sitting Up Tree Watching Yankee Invaders?"

They all loved adopting the characters of their heroes that they had seen at the Saturday Matinee at the local Plaza Cinema and Babs happily joined in.

"Big Yankee General, him say to posh English bloke that him call Baron Rothschild that they watch Olly Wood Gang and Scarcliffe Woods but big lorry go past and Babs not hear any more and they disappear, so Babs disappear as well and fly home like eagle. They could be spying on us now."

The trouble was they were so tired that no-one could be bothered with this.

"See you later," they all said as they entered their houses on Castle Green, while Babs went on home to Pleasant Avenue.

"Where do you think you're going my lad?" shouted Mrs Nelson as her son tried to sneak in. "You were told to stay in.

Where have you been ?"

"Sorry mam, I fell asleep in my chair in the shed," said Babs. "Can I help myself to bread and jam, mam ? And would you like a nice cup of tea, mam ?"

"Oh, alright then, Bab," said Mrs Nelson, mellowing.

That large group of companies, located on the outskirts of Bolsover, specialised in making smokeless fuels and chemicals out of coal. Known as the Aroma-Free Group, producers of Light Aroma-Free Fuels (LAFF) and the locally disliked and distrusted Chemicals From Coal (CFC), they also had their own road haulage depot and garage on site, under the name of Derbyshire Aroma-Free Fuels Transport (DAFFT). Although the group was undoubtedly popular with some people from outside of the Bolsover area (customers, suppliers and certainly investors), it was decidedly unpopular with local people who were wary of the company's processing plants and effects on their health and the environment. It created some smells even worse than the ones Babs made. Babs himself was suspicious of them and, with his enthusiasm for chemistry, he knew more than anyone about the dangers of chemicals. This was why he had acquired a large number of World War Two gas masks that he would use when performing what he knew would be dangerous experiments and processes. Accordingly, the rest of the family kept out of the wash-house when he went in and put up the 'No Entry' sign.

He took one of his gas masks, along with some borrowed 'Aroma Free' overalls, when he went investigating again, the day after his observations of the US Army 2nd Cavalry Regiment, Military Intelligence Top Brass, to see what might have brought them to Bolsover. He walked alongside the River Doe Lea from the bridge, where Station Road meets Chesterfield Road and benefited from the cover of the riverside trees and vegetation that formed the western perimeter of Bolsover Colliery, upstream from his target.

He collected various samples of water from the river, soil, dust and flora from the banks, all of which he labelled with description, date and place. He took photographs using the interesting Minox B miniature camera that he had borrowed from a friend. He marvelled at the sophistication of the wonderful little piece of engineering. Focussing was not a problem, once he had been shown how and operation was easy for him. No wonder spies used them, he thought.

Finding a newly built red-brick building with warning signs and 'Keep Out' notices, he was naturally inquisitive and approached the door to try and see through the small pane of frosted glass. Leaning lightly against it, he was surprised when the door swung open and he cautiously crept inside. There was lots of strange equipment that seemed to be in operation. He particularly noticed two charts headed '2,4-dichlorophenoxyacetic acid (2,4-D)' and '2,4,5-trichlorophenoxyacetic acid (2,4,5-T)' that were displayed on the wall, beside a typed page headed, 'Top Secret - Agent Orange' and another headed 'Top Secret – Agent Purple'. Babs grabbed the sellotaped charts from the wall and in their place left a home-made calling card bearing the name 'The Chemistry Set'.

Scared of being caught, he left as soon as he had taken photographs of all the equipment and, when he heard voices and footsteps approaching, he hid behind some nearby bushes. Two men went to the mystery building.

"Hey up, Bash, you left the reactor lab door unlocked, we could have been in big trouble there if anyone had come along and seen all that stuff inside, especially the Shift Chemist."

"Come on, we were only gone a few minutes for our cup of 245-Tea," laughed his mate. "Nobody else would have known what it was, even if they'd got in and read all the papers."

"Blimey," said Babs to himself. "I'd like to be a Special Agent named 'Agent Orange' with all this top secret stuff going on. How fab does that sound, more colourful than 007 ? No wonder the Yanks were here with that Baron."

He sneaked away carefully and headed home unseen, clutching the miniature camera tight. Minutes after he had left, the two young men realised the charts were missing from the wall and after a search they reported it to the Shift Chemist, lying by saying that they had locked the door while they went for a cup of tea and not mentioning the calling card. The angry supervisor called the Head of Security who called the Company Chairman who called an old friend with the news of the break-in.

Later that morning Babs visited his friend Nigel who had loaned him the small Minox camera, one of several that the young man owned. These were originally made in Riga, Latvia and later in West Germany. Because they were so small they became known as and were actually used as, 'spy' cameras. Nigel extracted, processed and developed the film and produced two copies of each of the photographs that Babs had taken earlier. Nigel was seventeen years old, a few years older than Babs, worked at the National Coal Board Area Headquarters in Bolsover and was interested in photography, books and politics. He had recently become a member of the Young Communists League, like his father and grandfather had been in their youth in Latvia. The communist, book-loving amateur photographer felt his pleasure at the quality of the developing, while Babs, the bicycle and chemistry-loving rogue, was even happier with the images of the 'chemical plant plan' that were depicted, as he described his secret mission.

In the afternoon he 'borrowed' a bike again and cycled to Palterton to show the photographs and tell the story of his morning's expedition to his other friend, Colwyn Holness, who knew his chemistry. Being the son of a farmer, The Pope also knew his agriculture and his herbicides and the ingredients and processes used in their manufacture. The pair soon realised that what Babs had found was intended to kill all vegetation.

2
MAM, A WEASEL'S BIT OUR WILLIE'S WILLY (IT WAS A STOAT, STUPID)

Stoats (mustela erminea) are particularly curious animals. The Latin name is derived from mustela (weasel) and erminea (Armenia, from where they were thought to originate). It is not widely known that stoats have been observed to form large packs although why this should happen is not certain. The gang have speculated that it could be for protection, for attacking larger prey, as a social aspect of the species, while Babs said it could even be a trip to see his home-made fireworks.

On Saturday 15th of June 1963 a motley crew gathered outside the adjacent semi detached houses of the Heaths and Woods. They tried not to look like they were already guilty of every wrong-doing they would be accused of that day and of course deny.
They did not deliberately get into trouble or do something wrong. It just sort of happened. Olly and Mac, as always, planned today's journey. Their main objective involved avoiding the vicar and the gamekeeper, and hence Scarcliffe Woods but they often had outings to other places anyway - Carr Vale Clay Hole, Clumber Park, Sutton Hall, Hardwick Hall.
"We're going over the fields to Port-ton, where we'll pick up Trapdoor, then over the Crow Fields to Glappy, and through Rowthorne to Hardwick", said Olly. There was no arguing. Well, there was only a little and you could not really call it

arguing. As they set off Babs was moaning because they were not going to Scarcliffe to go through the disused railway tunnel again. This was the great adventure he had missed out on, except for his part in the great escape from the tunnel at the Carr Vale end. When they arrived in Palterton village their friend Trapdoor appeared, as if by magic, from the terrace where he lived on Main Street. Continuing noisily along the road they sang their marching song, "Ah-yee-oh-ko, yer-ger-der". This was really 'The Canoe Song'[ii], a traditional African native song that was sung by Paul Robeson. He was one of their heroes, even though they knew little about him, other than that he was a friend to Welsh miners, had a deep voice and sang this funny song, ideal for singing if they were marching or paddling.

Palterton village must have been very different before its present two main streets were first built, since Back Lane now seemed to be the main thoroughfare, while Main Street was now at the back of the village and, in fact, at one time, the main part of the village was located further down the valley.

They went, as planned, across the Crow Fields to Glapwell, on their way to Hardwick Hall, the Elizabethan house built by Bess of Hardwick and renowned for its large and numerous windows. 'Hardwick Hall, more glass than wall', as the saying went.

Playing games and listening to Trapdoor's jokes along the way, they also climbed the odd tree, sang the odd song and were unconcerned about anyone else knowing they were there, since they stuck to the footpaths and did nothing wrong. Well, nothing much wrong for them anyway.

Unusually, no-one noticed that they were being followed. The carrion crows that inhabited the rookery in the woods, and after which the Crow Fields were named, tried to alert them but to no avail. Olly and Trapdoor, particularly, could talk to these birds and interpret their responses and the flock always followed them across the fields as far as Glapwell village. On this occasion however, Babs was leading a raucous discussion on the 'Light at the end of the tunnel' that everyone took part in and the crows' warnings were ignored.

After passing through Glapwell they soon reached the Rowthorne Lane entrance to Hardwick Park, with its cattle grid on the road and large wooden gate. Then Willie noticed something apparently playing or jumping in the long grass at the side of the road leading up to the hall.

"It's a weasel, isn't it?" asked Giggsy, unsure as they could not get a proper look at the animal as it playfully leapt up and down.

"No, it's a stoat," said Olly. "See the black tip to its tail. It's not fully grown though so, other than that black tip, you could mistake it for a weasel. They do that crazy jumping to sort of hypnotise their prey so there must be something it was after nearby." He was like a walking wildlife encyclopaedia but they all respected his knowledge.

Olly knew that it was perfectly possible for the little predator also to be hypnotically attracted by either of two similar methods.

"You can usually call a stoat by sucking on the back of your hand, or blowing on a blade of grass between your two thumbs to make the squeal of an injured rabbit." He sucked once on his hand then blew once on some grass and the young stoat appeared and stood still and they all instinctively froze in the same way and stood motionless. Olly deftly grabbed the animal with one hand holding the back of the neck and the other extending the hind legs and tail so it wouldn't be able to bite him. He handed it to Willie who had spotted it first and the boy knew to hold it the same way as his eldest brother.

As they gathered around to look at the captive, Olly noticed out of the corner of his eye, two male figures about a hundred yards away, walking towards them. It was their least favourite gamekeeper, William Hitchcock. He seemed to turn up everywhere that the boys went. They mischievously called him

'Wild Bill' Hitchcock, after the lawman 'Wild Bill' Hickock, known to them from the cowboy films they saw on TV and at the 'Saturday Matinee' pictures.

"Nobody move or look round, Wild Bill's coming. Newt, get your book out about Hardwick and start reading about trees or something. Will, put the stoat down your trousers and let it escape down your leg into the grass," unaware that his little brother's trousers were tucked into his wellies, so the animal had no way of escaping. Both boys did as they were instructed before the gamekeeper and his assistant arrived.

"Hardwick Park contains a variety of indi..., indig... err, local farm animals - sheep, goats and cattle, as well as a herd of indig..., oh stuff it, blooming deer," read Newt, like his very serious history teacher from school, Mr L.F.W. Webber, who would carry on reading from his text book even if a bomb went off in his classroom.

"What are you lot up to ?" asked their tormentor, Wild Bill. Newt carried on reading as if he hadn't even noticed Mr Hitchcock.

"There are a number of lakes, Miller's Pond and the Great Pond, and seven smaller snakes and ladders, I mean lakes and ponds that don't have names."

"Just enjoying a day out and a picnic in the park, Mr Hancock," said Mac cheekily, glaring at his brother's reading and they all stifled a laugh at Mac's deliberate mistake of Wild Bill's name.

"There are fine gardens and fine walks and the fine Hardwick Inn and lots of fine windows in the Hall which give it its nickname, Hardwick Hall, more glass than wall," said Newt.

"Shut up Neville and it's Mr Hitchcock, as you all know full well," said the angry gamekeeper. "Ninety-nine times out of ten you lot are up to no good. I know that, oh yes, I do. Alright, go and have your picnic but don't let me hear that you've been up to any more mischief or that anything's gone missing or got broke in the park or you're for it. I'm watching you, I am."

Mr Hitchcock turned and angrily began striding back towards

his Land Rover, parked behind the park gatehouse. His assistant, his son Kevin, a few months older than Mac, just stood smirking at the boys, and wished he was part of their exciting world instead of his father's. His dreams were shattered by more shouting from his menacing father.
"Kevin, get over here, we have work to do. WE'RE not on a bloody picnic."
"See you at school on Monday, Kevin. You can come with us next time if you want," said Mac quietly, thinking that they might use Kevin's desire to be part of their gang.
"What do we want him for ?" Giggsy complained after Kevin had gone out of earshot.
"No, it's good thinking Mac," said Olly. "We can use him to find things out about Wild Bill, like where he's working and for cover if we have any problems, that's why we want him."
"Aww, yeah," said the others with varying degrees of understanding on their faces.
Olly and Mac were often one or more steps ahead of the others.
"What's that rubbish you were spouting, our Newt, asked Mac, grabbing the book his brother had read from. "Ian Allan's Combined Volume Trainspotter's Guide ?"
"I got the wrong book off the sideboard this morning," replied Newt. "So I just made it up as I went along and hoped they wouldn't notice what book I'd got." They all laughed heartily. As they went on their way towards the hall, Willie declared that "Weasley the stoat is still stuck down my trousers and it's bit my tail. It couldn't get out cos my trousers are tucked in my wellies and I couldn't get it out while Wild Bill was there, could I ?"
They all managed to conceal their laughter but no-one wanted to look.
"You'll probably have to go to hospital to have it examined and you might even have to have it indicated," offered Balsa, bringing strange looks from the rest. He was immediately

reprimanded and corrected by the other boys.

"You mean amputated !" said Giggsy to great laughter from everyone except Willie, who was not amused and expected more sympathy.

"I don't know what you're all talking about," said the victim sniffily, bottom lip wobbling.

"It's alright our Will, they mean inoculated but you don't need an injection," said Olly, putting a supportive arm around his little brother.

They persuaded Willie that swimming in the lake would help so Weasley the stoat was retrieved from his trouser bottoms and put in Newt's gas mask bag-haversack, in the company of their sandwiches, which were wrapped in the waxed paper from sliced bread loaves. Newt's mother would often say to customers in Lawman's shop where she worked that these wrappers were the best thing since sliced bread. The only other person who had brought a similar bag was Babs and the contents of his bag were too dangerous, he said, to put the young stoat in. They accepted Babs' excuse, even though no-one knew exactly what was in his bag. He appeared to have acquired a healthy interest and thirst for knowledge in explosions and fires since he had been given a chemistry set for Christmas two years ago, so they knew his bag would contain something dangerous.

His mother had recently taken his chemistry set off him, since the explosion in their house one Sunday morning had given all his family blackened faces and left his baby sister scared of loud bangs. He had got it back with promises not to do it again but he was banished to the wash-house or the garden shed for future experiments.

They sang loudly as they marched off to the park lakes where they all stripped off their clothes and had a swim and played about in their three Hardwick tin baths. They had these old tin baths hidden at every lake and pond in the area. These were known only to them and each one was called Bush-a-Vella or

Bush Fella, partly because they thought they were would-be Aboriginals and partly because they always hid the tin baths in the bushes. As usual, they played in the largest of the lakes, the Millers' Lake which they liked because it was big and open, though shaded by trees in places and they kept more Bush-a-Vellas at Hardwick because they were big lakes.

Babs and Mac didn't fancy swimming and instead climbed a large willow tree on which was a thick rope swing that swung out over the lake. Babs sat astride the branch that held the swing with his "fire can", an old tin can, which was pierced with nail holes, around the sides and the bottom. A length of thick wire was strung through the top of the tin in two places to make a handle. He would stuff rags into the tin, lit by a match and left to smoulder, with the lid pressed back on. An occasional twirl of the tin on the end of the loop of wire kept it smouldering. When he lit it that is, which he hadn't done on this occasion. Being self confessed 'quite interested' in fires, he'd doused the rags in paraffin and included a piece of coal to make his version of a Molotov Cocktail, which he called the Mooracre Cocktail, after the street where his school was located. Babs was thus occupied with his pyrotechnic devices and Mac whittled a piece of wood he was carving with his long bladed 'Bowie knife'.

While the other boys were a-swimming and a-sailing, some girls who lived near them at Hillstown, Irene Howard, Annie Roberts and Jessica James, known as Jessie James, came sneaking through the trees, trying to avoid being seen. The boys would never let them join in anything and so the girls had followed them at a distance. Thinking they had not been seen, they stole the boys' clothes, their bottles of water, and their gas mask bag, containing not only Weasley the stoat but, more importantly, their sandwiches. Babs and Mac watched them but made no sound or movement and the girls sat down on a small knoll about thirty yards from the lake and loudly and merrily provoked the boys by having the nerve to sit and shout that they were going to eat the sandwiches that they had found in the gas mask bag.

"Let's get the sandwiches out and have our picnic girls. The seed ye sow another reaps[iii]," said Irene quoting from her favourite poet, Percy Shelley. The girls all laughed madly, gloating that they were more literary and studious and closer to the picnic than the boys.

"The wealth ye find another keeps. The robes ye weave another wears. The arms ye forge another bears," responded Jessie and their laughter rang even louder. Their shouts about eating the boys' picnic also attracted the attention of a tramp well known in the area, Wandering Walt, and he came silently through the trees behind the girls, picked up Willie's bull rope and tied the girls up with it, to their screams of panic. Walt was so busy tying up his frightened prisoners and then searching for the sandwiches that he did not see the naked boys come out of the lake and pick up large sticks. They then crept around in a pincer movement and encircled the man and the shackled girls.

"Don't turn round and if you do turn round, you're dead," warned Olly.

Suddenly they heard a shrilling noise, a chittering of many tiny voices, exactly the same noise that the young stoat was making in the bag but much louder. They turned and looked towards the wood and saw a pack of some forty or more stoats emerge about seventy yards away, and begin to move quickly towards them.

"Untie the girls, quick," said Olly, nodding towards Newt and Balsa who did what was asked as the three girls tittered at their state of undress while Weasley the stoat protested from the gas-mask bag.

Olly shouted to them all to run and get into the three tin baths, a girl and two boys to each bath, and push them out onto the lake. However, first, he also quickly opened the top of the gas mask bag before sprinting to the last 'boat' and getting in himself. Even Walt dived into the water to escape the animals

and swam fast across the lake in panic - and in his clothes. As they frantically paddled out onto the water, Olly shouted to Babs, hidden up the tree.
"Babs, you got any of that bomb-making stuff with you ?"
"Yeah, why ?" replied the tree, to the girls' surprise, as they had not realised he was there.
"Make an explosion at the water's edge to keep the stoats from swimming after us."
Babs set to work and in seconds produced his home-made bomb from his own gas mask bag which he hung on the next branch up, its contents and his ingredients closely guarded secrets. Just as the first of the angry, chittering stoats were starting to enter the lake he threw the bomb into the water below, in front of the stoats, to avoid harming them. He and Mac hugged the tree tight.
The boom shook everyone and everything, both in and out of the water, including Babs' tree as the explosion was like that from some war film action on the sea. Miraculously, Mac and Babs managed to cling on to their branches. Immediately after the blast, Babs did a dance of celebration and whooped in triumph on the branch on which he stood. Not surprisingly however, he lost his footing and fell out of the tree with a loud scream, landing in three feet of water and causing almost as big a splash as his bomb had.
The startled stoats turned and ran back to the woods as fast as they could and the Woods- on-water gang and the girls began their return to the shore, while Wandering Walt-on-water swam across the lake to the other side and ran up the road towards Heath village.
As Babs struggled to his feet, very soaked and a little stunned but more or less unhurt, Trapdoor turned to the girls and sarcastically said,
"See, if it hadn't been for Babs and his Big Bad Bomb scaring the stoats, your tomorrows would never have been your yesterdays and your seeds would never have been reaped."

"Don't talk daft, Trevor," said Irene, "It wasn't his Big Bang Bomb that scared them off, it was him falling out of the tree into the water and you lot in the nuddy."

"Ah-yee-oh-ko-yer-ger-der. Ah-yee-oh-ko-yer-ger-der." sang the boys, to the puzzlement of the three girls, who all thought this was a very strange world.

"Come on, let's get out of the lake and get dressed," said Olly, to smirks and embarrassed giggles from the girls.

"Who's Boss of Hardwick now?" roared Babs, looking like some bedraggled pirate in his wet and torn clothes.

"That's Bess of Hardwick, you mean Babs," corrected Mac, climbing down from the tree. "Not any more it isn't. Babs is Boss of Hardwick," chuckled the boy and they all laughed with him.

Trapdoor stood up in his tin bath and danced and sang 'Ah-yee-oh-ko-yer-ger-der' again. He was followed by all the other boys making the girls scream and grip the sides as the boats rocked dangerously. Inevitably and dramatically, the baths one after another capsized and the boys crashed overboard, while the girls rolled into the water with the sinking wrecks. They all swam, struggled and spluttered to the lakeside where Babs and Mac were creased with laughter at the sight of their emergence and the boys' flight to their clothes which they took behind some trees to put on. The girls now stood drenched and bedraggled.

When the boys came from behind the trees, all dressed and ready to go, they set off in silence up the fields towards the entrance to the park where they had come in earlier. Olly voiced what all the boys were thinking. "Stay alert and look and listen and no talking. Any sight or sound of a stoat and we climb a tree and use some of Babs' bombs against them."

Irene, Annie and Jessie James were petrified and wetrified. Wandering Walt was already up the road, halfway to Heath. Babs was 'Boss of Hardwick'.

3
"SORRY SIR, THE DOG ATE MY HOMEWORK."

Holness The Pope asked Newt how to attract a girl that he liked and invite her out on a date.

"How the hell should I know ?" replied his friend. "I suppose you should find something that you have in common to talk about. Anyway, who is this wondrous goddess and object of your desire ?"

"Good idea," whispered The Pope. "It's Jane Pearson and she likes Chemistry, same as me."

"Ok, there's your solution," laughed Newt, pointing to the test tube rack in front of them, just as the blackboard rubber flew through the air across the Chemistry Laboratory and hit him on the side of the temple, knocking him off his stool in shock. He climbed warily to his feet and sat back on his perch, wiping the blood from a cut.

"Heath, boy," shouted Foxy, the Chemistry teacher. "Why ever did your parents Christen you Neville Newton Heath when you have absolutely no interest or ability in sciences ?"

"Sorry, Mr Fox sir," apologised The Pope, realising he had caused his friend this aggravation. "It was my fault, sir. I asked Newt, I mean Heath, how to spell 'lipophilic' that you just mentioned in relation to making soap, sir. And I suppose Mr and Mrs Heath didn't know what he would be interested in when he was Christened, sir. Not at under three months old, sir."

The whole class erupted into laughter which did not amuse Reynard Fox. He never used his full Christian name and was known only as Ray Fox, even to the Headmaster. He wrongly thought that Neville Heath would curse his parents as much as Reynard Fox cursed his own.

"A hundred lines for the pair of you, 'I must not talk in class, other than to the teacher', on my desk, first thing tomorrow morning," said Foxy. "And quiet everyone," he shouted. "And I wrote the word on the blackboard, Holness, which you would have seen if you had been paying attention, boy."

"Sorry, Mr Fox, sir, but I couldn't read your writing."

"Then you should have asked, Holness," shouted the increasingly irate teacher.

"I did, sir and Newt was just telling me," replied The Pope with a faint smirk on his face and the rest of the class had to pull faces to hide their amusement.

"Rubbish ! Is there anyone else who cannot read my writing on the board ?" asked Fox of the whole class. Everyone put their hands up except those on the front row who were too close to dare risk angering him. He shook his head and swore under his breath as he re-wrote it in large capital letters. When the lesson ended The Pope accompanied Newt to the First Aid Room where a plaster was administered to his wound and he told the nurse he had banged his head.

"Why don't you tell her you're starting a secret society called 'The Chemistry Set' and all the members get a code name ? Agent Red, Green, Blue, Purple and so on. Or the names of scientists, only don't let anyone be Agent Newton though, eh ? Foxy would go mad if he found out."

"Brilliant idea, Newt" said The Pope. "I'll be Agent Blue, she can choose her own colour. Come on, I'll ask her now."

"I can't," replied Newt. "I'm in trouble for letting that live rat loose in Assembly this morning and I'm up before the

Headmaster. It was funny though, did you see everybody jumping up on their chairs and Miss Povah fainting ? Bellum omnium contra omnes, as the saying goes."

"What's that mean ?" asked The Pope. "You know I'm no good at French."

"Not sure, 'For whom the bell tolls', or something," said Newt. "But it's Latin, not French."

"Languages are all Greek to me," quipped The Pope. "I'm going in to dinner and ask Jane."

While The Pope went to the dining room to invite Jane Pearson to join his two-person secret society, 'The Chemistry Set', Newt had already received an invitation to visit the Headmaster in his study. He ran up the stairs with the carefree, unconcerned air of a thirteen year old boy and knocked on the door. Neville almost enjoyed his visits here, because of Mr Smith's collection of railway engine prints that adorned the walls, even though such visits were for him to be, at the worst, caned, or at the least, reprimanded by the Head.

"Enter," came the stern instruction and Newt went in. "Sit there, Heath," he continued, pointing to a chair next to his large, leather-topped desk. "We need to talk, you and I."

"Why, sir ?" enquired the puzzled youngster. "Aren't I just going to be caned like normal ?"

"No, boy, you are not just going to be caned," smiled the Head. "I'm concerned about your apparent willingness and even eagerness to come to my office for punishment. I watched you in Assembly this morning and, if I did not know better, I would say that you released that rat deliberately so that you would be summoned to my study, for the seventh consecutive Wednesday. That is something we need to discuss urgently, boy. I know that you are a train enthusiast because I have seen you at the out-of-bounds-at-lunchtime engine sheds when I've been there."

"Oh, so you can go but I can't," observed Newt sarcastically, knowing the Head liked trains.

"Do not argue with me, boy. I often take tea with the station master, as I do with other local officials and dignitaries," came the unexpected reply.

The Pope managed to get on the same table as Jane Pearson and could not believe his luck when he was also able to sit next to her. If only school dinner of stew and dumplings was as attractive, he thought. He nudged her and put his index finger to his lips, then passed her the invitation on a scrap of paper that he had prepared before going in to the dining room. Jane's eyes lit up at the idea of being a member of a secret society and she nodded happily.

"I'll talk to you after dinner about that chemistry experiment, Popey," she said affectionately and he blushed so much that all of the pupils at the table laughed at him.

"Oooh, Popey," said Philip 'Slacker' Lowe playfully. "You look like you've just reached melting point in your Chemistry experiment."

Jane gave Slacker a playful slap on his head as she went round the table to clear away and they sat and ate their semolina pudding and prunes, still smirking and laughing at 'Popey'. When they had finished their dinner and the Prefects allowed them to leave the dining room, Jane grabbed The Pope's hand. She led him off to the school playing field, instead of the opposite direction where he had been heading to play twenty-plus a side football, on the drive behind the classrooms overlooking the British Rail Staff Association sports ground. School blazers were used for goalposts (by the boys, not on the BRSA sports ground).

"Come on you," she said. "I want to know more about this secret society you're starting, you little rebel, you. I never knew you had it in you. We'll talk on the school field."

"Watch out for spontaneous combustion, Popey" shouted Slacker after them.

When they reached the bottom of the field the Pope's blazer was used as a pillow for Jane.

"Tea, boy?" asked the smiling Headmaster, as Newt uncomfortably thought that this should not be how he was to be treated if he was in such trouble. "I'll be mother," added Mr Smith.

"Err, no thank you, sir," said the confused boy. "I don't drink tea. I only drink coffee."

"Well then, coffee you shall have, instantly," came the reply, as the Headmaster left his study and went into his small kitchen. He quickly returned with Newt's coffee in a china cup.

"There you are Neville and help yourself to chocolate fingers," the boy thought he heard. "Your rat certainly caused a stir, but not to worry, some people needed waking up from their daydreaming. And Miss Povah has recovered. Faints at anything, poor woman."

Neville thought he was daydreaming, himself. He pinched his own leg in disbelief.

"Now, you're wondering why I haven't given you your usual six strokes of the cane and dismissed you, aren't you Neville? Well, that's because a friend of a friend is undertaking investigations about a problem in the area and it's known that you frequent the Duke of Devonshire's woods around Scarcliffe. It is also known that you are a very talented singer in the Church Choir - another of my friends, of course, is your good Reverend Vicar, Father Woolley."

"It wasn't me, sir, I never touched the gun and anyway, it was an accident. It just glanced off the tree and broke the vicarage window," jumped in Newt, thinking he was in for it now.

"Oh dear," said the Head. "I didn't know you were anywhere near when that occurred. Bully, sorry, Father Woolley, said it was some boy called Paul McCartney. It isn't the Paul McCartney, I'm sure, is it? No matter. Anyway, Neville, some friends of mine, Peter Wright and Victor Rothschild, want you and your little gang to look out for anything strange or unusual happening in the woods. Peter and Victor can't do it themselves, being outsiders, but no-one would suspect you because you're always in Scarcliffe Woods from what I hear."

"Well, what are they looking for and why ?" enquired Newt. "And who's telling them what to do, who are we up against, what's happened to create suspicion about ... the suspects ? Who, what, when, where, why and how, to quote Rudyard Kipling's 'The Elephant's Child' ?"

"Neville Heath, your levels of knowledge of Latin and Literature, when set beside your levels of behaviour and exam results are at times surprising to say the least. Anyway, someone appears to be attempting to undermine important work being done by the Chemicals From Coal people in making a herbicide that will not only protect crops against ALL insects and disease but will also produce rain at any time in any part of the world, even in a desert."

"Is that what's making that awful smell and killing all the plants, animals and fish in and around the River Doe Lea ?" asked Newt angrily. "And who are these two friends of yours, Rotterdam and White ? Are they policemen or who are they working for ? Somebody must be paying them for whatever they're doing. Those stinking CFC folk, I guess. Or is it those U.S. Army blokes that have invaded the place ? One of my mates saw them from up a tree."

"Go to lunch now Neville," said the headmaster patiently. "Think about what I've said and I will send for you at the start of your double games period this afternoon when our two friends will be here. Not a word to anyone about our conversation. Dismissed now boy."

Neville left and went to lunch, arriving late for the second sitting which got him a telling off from the duty prefect. He was made to sit next to Pinky, who had been 'sent to Coventry' by everyone in their class, 4B, for his disgusting habits. Although Pinky tried to make conversation, he was too concerned with what Mr Smith had said to him to respond.

After dinner Neville made his way to Room 11, where a single period of History was due to start in fifteen minutes time. This would be followed by Double Games, involving athletics for the athletic and a variety of other games for the ..., well, everyone else. Room 11 was Newt's form room and his form teacher, L.F.W. (Lenny) Webber, who taught him history, was already at his desk preparing for the lesson.

Newt knocked politely and peered through the glass panelled door instead of walking in.

"Come in Heath," shouted the teacher, adding quietly. "Not like you to wait to be asked."

"I can't get in sir. The door's locked, as usual," shouted the boy. Mr Webber stood up nervously, looking for booby traps or attacks from behind. He unlocked the door and glanced beyond the boy for his cronies but none appeared.

"Excuse me sir, can I ask you something about that Thomas Hobbes you told us about last week ? Him that wrote that 'Levitation' book."

"The Leviathan[iv], Neville, not Levitation and no, you can NOT have a further extension for those lines I gave you for that fake dog dirt incident. Henry Ford only said 'History is bunk' to sell motor cars. You will learn to treat History lessons seriously or pay the consequences."

"But sir, that's why I wanted to ask you about Hobbes and anyway, it was real, not fake." Lenny curled his lip with acute displeasure and felt decidedly sick, having picked up the allegedly real dog dirt at the time and put it in his desk, where it still remained.

"What about Hobbes ?" said Len, choosing to change the subject from the mess in the desk.

"Sir, you know you said that any abuses of power by higher authority are to be accepted by the people as the price of peace but in severe cases of abuse, rebellion can be expected ?"

"Absolutely correct, Neville," replied Lenny, proud of his own teaching skills. "That is the social contract between the sovereign authority and the people in a nutshell. Well done." Newt knew that this gave him Brownie points with Lenny, who he also knew would break his neck to tell the Head the full details of this exchange. And then, he wondered, if Mr Smith would tell the mysterious Mr Wright and Mr Rottweiler and, although he was unsure what effect that might have, he thought that it might put him in a good position. As his classmates began to arrive they all looked in surprise at their friend who was sat quietly at his desk, studying his text book. His tie and blazer were unusually immaculate. Last to arrive were The Pope and Jane Pearson and they were jeered noisily by everyone except Newt who simply smiled. Even Mr Webber was shocked by this new found good behaviour of Neville Heath.

"Please open your text books at Chapter 6, page 85 and we are going to look at some more interesting facts about Bess of Hardwick and Thomas Hobbes."

The whole class groaned as one as they turned to the appropriate page, again except for the smiling Neville Newton Heath who did an unlikely impression of the class swot and was already at the right page. Mr Webber turned to write the subject and chapter on the blackboard with a new piece of chalk and expected the usual hail of paper aeroplanes and missiles to be thrown at his back. Instead, they were all thrown at Newt, whose smile remained fixed and unchanged throughout the lesson. Most of the class were glad when the period was nearing the end.

"What did Hobbes mean when he said life is nasty, brutish and short?" asked Mr Webber.

"He was anticipating the effect questions like this would have on us," quipped The Pope. "And what have you done to Newt, sir? He looks as though he's been hypnotised. He's not the same lad who let the rat out of the bag."

"Oooh, that's poetic, 'not the same lad who let the rat out of the bag'. Ahhh," gushed Jane.

"Quiet, class," shouted the hapless Mr Webber, as the lesson erupted in uncontrollable mirth. "That is your homework then. I want a full page."

Everyone tore a page from their notebook, screwed it up and threw it at the teacher's back as he wrote the question in chalk on the blackboard. Well, everyone except Newt, who wrote at the top of his next page - 'Homework – What did Hobbes mean when he said life is nasty, brutish and short ?'

He stayed at his desk waiting for a signal from Mr Webber while his classmates filed out noisily but then they stopped and stared at their friend's continued unusual behaviour.

"Who do you prefer, sir ?" said Jilly Robinson, on her way through the door. "Elvis or Cliff, on a single sheet of paper for the next lesson."

"Class dismissed," said the teacher with new found confidence at having won over one pupil, at least, as the boy's friends broke into an irreverent version of the National Anthem.

"God save our gracious Newt, Long live our noble Newt, God save our Newt."

They all made for the changing rooms for the beginning of the double games period. Mr Galloway, the boys' Games master, had sellotaped up lists of who was to do what.

Anyone deemed totally useless or disinterested in athletics was entered in Pool B of the Shot Putt to be located in the bottom corner of the field. There the teacher thought they would be out of the way and play bowls with the shots or a crafty game of cards.

Newt was to do twenty minutes of High Jump, followed by twenty minutes of Hurdles, not that he was any good at these but his height made him look as though he might be.

The Pope was to spend the whole double period, after a suitable warm up, throwing the Javelin. At thirteen he had already broken the School, Area and County records for under sixteens.

Some of the girls did high jump, long jump, hurdles or sprinting on the railway side of the field while others played tennis and netball. Jane kept going over to where The Pope was warming up and she distracted him so much that Lawrie Galloway shouted at her scarily.

"Miss Pearson, unless you are also able to throw the javelin a long way, go and play netball. And Mr Holness, take that silly grin off your face and get on with your Javelin practice now."

"Yes sir, Major Calloway," laughed the boy as he took his javelin and winked at Jane.

"I have to go into school for a moment," the teacher announced abruptly after a Fourth Year boy appeared and handed him a piece of paper. He turned and walked away in his usual quick stride: Mr Gallopaway, as some of the pupils called him.

Seeing the games master disappear, some of the 'athletes' took the opportunity to do some stretching exercises lying flat out on the ground. Newt wandered across to the shot putt bowling game.

The Pope was trying to impress Jane who had returned to watch him. He took his run up and launched his javelin which soared and flew further than he had ever thrown before.

In the bottom corner of the field, over twenty non athletes and holders of excuse notes from their mothers were enjoying their game of bowls with the shot putt balls, while six others sat playing cards on the grass. They were all well out of the normal range of the Hurling Holness.

The last to go, Gerry Davies, bowled his shot really hard to knock all of the others out of the way but his aim was poor and he over-shot his shot, by quite a lot. The boy wandered lazily across the field to fetch his over-hit shot putt ball.

"GERRY," shouted The Pope. "LOOK OUT!"

Meanwhile, over at Moorfield School in Bolsover, it was quiet as most of the first year had gone on a combined Science, Geography and History field trip to Hardwick Hall. Flint's Buses of Carr Vale had taken ninety children on the trip, eighty-seven of whom had made fun of the three of them that had gone in their wellingtons and were also carrying gas mask bags, Barry 'Balsa' Wood, Trevor 'Trapdoor' Appledore and David 'Babs' Nelson.

"Check the evacuees for ricketts, scurvy and nits," shouted someone cruelly.

"Right, we'll try the stoat call when we get to the lake and we'll show them, eh!" said Babs quietly. "And if that doesn't work, I'll lob a few stink bombs around. That'll shut them up."

They had to put up with lots of similar taunts from their classmates as they went around the hall and then the park. Although Balsa and Trapdoor responded with their own humorous jibes, Babs became increasingly irritated by it. Even before they reached the lakes, he began blowing a piece of grass and all three of them were doing it by the time they reached the Miller's Lake. Trapdoor led them in a rendition of John Philip Sousa's marches, with Balsa playing bits that he knew but what Babs played sounded more like songs by The Beatles that he had heard on Radio Luxemburg than Sousa.

As the children gathered around the three teachers, Mr Saint (Science), Mr Cooper (History) and Mr Butt (Geography), the wellington booted boys continued their grass-blowing calls beside the lake while looking east, up the hill to one side of the hall. Instead of a gang of hypnotised stoats that they expected to appear, behind the group of pupils and teachers, a large flock of angry Canada Geese came flying down from the skies, attracted by the boys' intended stoat calls, and landed on the lake nearby.

The crazy-eyed geese cackled and honked as they left the water and chased the frightened children and teachers. Babs, Balsa and Trapdoor had been standing at the shallow water's edge and they rushed with everyone towards the nearby trees which overhung the lake.

"Quick, climb the trees before they arrive as we can't be sure if they will attack," said Babs.

"I'd say those mad geese are already attacking us, thanks to you three," scoffed Mr Saint, as he and the other teachers began helping the children to climb into the trees.

"It isn't the geese we have to worry about," replied Balsa solemnly. "It's that enormous pack of stoats coming down the hill over there," he added, pointing up the grassy slopes towards the north-east gate of the park, having been in this situation before with the stoats.

They all turned and looked in horror at the moving carpet of the brown-coated and white-fronted little killing machines heading their way. The three boys helped the teachers to climb the trees before they too miraculously ascended one of the trees like monkeys, despite the disadvantage of wearing their wellingtons. Everyone was hushed with fear.

Babs opened his gas mask bag and took out his bomb making materials. He secretly and swiftly made and primed five 'exploders'. He never liked to share his skills with anyone else, especially teachers and he hissed to Balsa in the next tree and held one up for him to see.

"Water," he mouthed to his friend and gestured throwing them down to the lake. "Catch."

He threw one to him, then a second one which Balsa nearly dropped as he had not expected it. As the stoats neared the lakeside and a confrontation with the geese appeared certain, Babs and Balsa silently counted to three with their fingers. With the sleight of hand of a card sharp so no-one else could see it, they threw the secret weapons unnoticed into a space in the water where no geese or stoats were gathered.

The deafening explosions sent plumes of water into the air and drenched the trees and terrified all of those that had not expected them - geese, stoats, teachers and eighty-eight children alike. Trapdoor, who had been leaning out of his tree,

too far it turned out, was trying to get a good look at the wildlife fight, if and when it happened. He lost his grip on his branch however and fell into the water as geese and stoats fled, ran, flew and made a mess in terror. The geese noisily took off into the air and flew in groups across the sky and the stoats ran off in small packs and headed back up the hill.
"What the hell was that?" shouted Babs.
"Yeah, what the hell was that?" echoed Balsa and they climbed down from their trees and helped the soaked and shocked Trapdoor from the lake.
No-one else would come down from the trees and a few of the girls became hysterical and screamed fearfully, even though they could see the boys below them, looking relaxed.
"It's ok," said Balsa. "You can come down now, they've gone. There's no need to be scared."
This did nothing to reassure at least one pupil, who was obviously so afraid that she wet herself on to the three boys on the ground.
When the tree dwellers saw this happen it lightened their mood and there was barely concealed laughter as they began to climb down. Mr Saint and Mr Cooper decided that they would all cut short their field trip and immediately return to the hall where Flinty's buses should be parked.
"Get into pairs, children," shouted the Science teacher. "We are marching back up to the hall. If anything attacks us again, just run as fast as you can."

Everyone exchanged worried looks except the welly-wearing ones who simply smiled silently.

4
FLINTY'S FLYING BEDSTEADS & A MOB OF STAMPEDING STAGS & OTHER ANIMALS & BIRDS.

Some of the pupils on the school field at Shirebrook held their breath as others shouted their frantic warnings.
"GERRY, LOOK OUT !"
The boy stood up and half turned to look up the field towards The Pope. The javelin flew deep into his leg, just above the knee. Gerry was rooted to the spot in shock and pain as concerned pupils rushed from all around to help him. Mr Galloway was returning from the Headmaster's office where he had been summoned and asked to fetch Neville. The teacher was most unhappy at being what he thought was a messenger for one of his pupils. As he rounded the changing rooms at the top of the field he saw a crowd gathering at the bottom and heard the hysterical wailing of some of the children. He also thought he saw a javelin sticking out of a boy's leg.
"Bloody hell, The Pope, look what you've done to my trousers," said Gerry Davies angrily. "Me mam'll kill me, she only bought them for me on Saturday. She'll have to stitch them."
Having seconds earlier been in a state of shock, panic and distress at what they were witnessing, the crowd of bystanders burst into fits of laughter at Gerry's unlikely comment, just as Mr Galloway arrived on the scene at the worst possible

moment.

"This is not a time for laughter," came the booming voice of authority. "Go and report yourselves to the Headmaster and tell him what has happened. You deserve to be caned for your shameful irreverence and irresponsibility. Two of you, stand one each side of Davies and hold him steady and upright. No, not you Heath, the Headmaster wants to see you anyway. Two visitors, policemen I would guess, are with him. I don't know what the world is coming to when I have to act as your messenger. Move, everybody. Now!" he shouted.

The Pope and Robert Reynolds adopted the positions either side of the casualty, while twelve other boys and two girls began to walk up the field to report to the Headmaster.

"What have you been up to, Wayward Heath?" whispered Anita Bliss, who seemed to always speak knowingly about any subject. Newt simply shrugged, having never heard of Haywards Heath and therefore not understanding her stupid grin. A group of girls wandered down the field from the netball game to investigate the uproar. Jeanette Harrison fainted and several others were physically sick as they neared the scene. Robbie Price saw a chance to avoid reporting to the Head and left the group in trouble to tend to Jeanette.

"Leave her alone Price, she'll live," instructed Mr Galloway. "And Price, run and tell the nurse and whoever's in the Staff Room to call an ambulance and then get down here quick."

"What, me get down here quick, sir?"

"No, you idiot, the nurse and teachers. You can then follow the others to the Headmaster's study. You, at least, should know where it is by now."

"Yes sir," said Robbie, defeated, and ran up the field as instructed while Newt led the 'shameful, irreverent irresponsibles' to what they all expected would be some kind of punishment. Newt secretly thought that he might hold a strong hand from his earlier exchange with the Headmaster. He alone was quiet and pensive while the others chatted noisily about what had happened on the field and what could happen to them as a result. The group of sinners walked past the four classrooms along the corridor leading to the stairs to the Head's study. They were watched intently by all the pupils that were supposed to be studying hard and who wondered what must have happened in double games as everyone knew where they were going and that they were probably going to be disciplined. They stopped talking as they began to climb the stairs, fearing that they were in enough trouble already. Newt knocked on the door and they all leaned forward to listen for a sound.

"Enter," shouted the Headmaster and Newt went in, followed too closely by ten other boys and two girls, causing Newt to stumble forward before regaining his balance.

"What is going on here ? What are you doing in my study ?" asked a surprised Mr Smith, looking over Newt's head at the others.

"You shouted 'Enter', Mr Smith, sir," said Anita Bliss, "So we thought we'd better obey and come in sir."

The pupils heard a muted laugh from the corner of the study and turned to see two strange men in suits attempting, without success, to conceal their laughter.

"Yes, I know I shouted 'Enter' but I was expecting only Heath, not a crowd scene from 'Spartacus', Miss Bliss." There was more stifled laughing from the corner of the room.

"Anyway, what is the reason for the rest of you turning up ?" the Head continued.

"Unfortunately we laughed at something someone said and Mr Gallopaway, sorry, Mr Galloway, said we should report to your office, sir but laughing isn't a crime is it sir ?" said Anita, casting a glance at the two men who by now were in stitches.

"Dismissed, Miss Bliss," said the exasperated Head, to more tittering from the corner and the pupils.

"Everyone is dismissed, except Neville Heath, if you would not mind staying, Neville."

The three teachers and ninety pupils from Moorfield School began walking up the grassy slopes of the park in the direction of Hardwick Hall. They started out in pairs in a snake formation but every movement of a sheep, a cow or a deer that inhabited the park made them go a little faster. Before long they were all so scared that they simply broke formation and ran like hell, everyone for themselves, despite the hill being steep in places. Their own stampede served to create just the same among the animals and birds of the park, both farm and wild, as the aforementioned sheep, cows and deer plus rabbits, goats, stoats, squirrels, rooks, crows, magpies, geese, ducks and all, scattered with cries of fear.

The two drivers of Flint's Coaches of Carr Vale had been having a drink from their flasks while they stood beside their buses, or 'Flinty's Flying Bedsteads', as they were commonly known.

"What the heck?" exclaimed one driver when he saw the hordes of excited and disturbed animals and birds, pupils and teachers come hurtling over the summit of the hill.

As the stampede neared the hall the resident peacocks began their alarm call which added to the already noisy sounds of widespread panic. Both men leapt on to the nearest bus as the rampage passed by and were quickly followed by the equally scary human beings, or almost human-looking beings. Trapdoor was still soaked and dishevelled from his fall in the lake, while many other pupils had trod or fallen in varying amounts of animal droppings.

Instead of passing by like the animals, the children and their teachers leapt on the buses and closed the doors behind them for fear that the animals would get on after them.

"Take us back to the school immediately please, driver," asked a clearly stressed Mr Cooper, not realising that both drivers were on the other coach, until this was pointed out to him.

"Excuse me sir, but we don't have a driver, sir and he's too scared to get off the other bus."

"Sir, shall me and Balsa and Babs shoo all those cows and sheep away from the other bus ?" asked Trapdoor, opening the door to get out. "We're used to dealing with animals, sir."

"Yes. No. Oh, please yourself. I've lost the will to live," replied the distressed teacher.

"Excuse me Mr Cooper, can I go and get a wash somewhere before we set off, please sir ?" asked a cow-pat encrusted, smelly boy that no-one recognised in the state he was in and no-one would go near and consequently had the whole of the back seat of the bus to himself.

"Please sir," said a pale looking girl standing in the aisle nearest to the boy on the back row. "That cow-pat pong is making me sick." She threw up over a girl next to her and Mr Cooper. Suddenly there was a rush to get off the bus and help Trapdoor and his friends herd cows. Within minutes all of the animals were dispersed by a mixture of shoo-ing and calming talk by the three original cowhands, along with hysteria and mayhem from the ones that had got off their bus to escape from Cow-Pat and Sicky Vicky. The drivers and the other children and teachers were freed from the buses to their great relief.

"In the light of events, I'm afraid that we must abandon our trip and return to school," announced Mr Cooper seriously. "Those who need to wash can go to the cattle trough or the toilets along the road at the top of the hill. Trapdoor, I mean Appledore, could you get Cow-Pat and Victoria off the bus and take them to the cattle trough to clean them up, boy."

"Aye aye, Captain Cooper," said Trapdoor as he trooped off to retrieve the great unwashed and sick to refresh them in the stone drinking trough, one hundred and fifty year old but common on local farmland and here in Hardwick Park.

"Come on you two," he said gently as he boarded the bus. "Let's get you both cleaned up so we can get you back to school, eh."

Unlikely though such tenderness might be from the boy, they climbed wearily from their seats and left the bus for some nearby cloakroom or toilets where they would get cleaned. Cow-Pat, as he would forever be known, walked awkwardly with both arms and legs splayed, as if the mess was his own rather than a cow's. He insisted on being within inches of Trapdoor while Sicky Vicky stayed ten yards behind the pair, holding her nose to block the smell. Even as they approached the trough neither realised it was intended to be their bath. Then, as they seemed to be going past it, Trapdoor grabbed the back of Cow-Pat's trouser waistband and the top of his jumper and lifted the slightly built boy straight into the trough of cold water, submerging him horizontally. He held him under for several seconds before lifting up the shocked and spluttering figure and standing him up straight in the trough.

"Right," said Trapdoor. "Get yourself clean enough to travel on Flinty's Flying Bedstead cos you can't get on like that. Or you stay in the trough and I'll duck you in the water again."

Cow-Pat did as he was asked but poor Sicky Vicky was heard to scream hysterically and shout, "No, no, no! You aren't putting me in that deep ship or sheep dip or whatever it is."

"It isn't a sheep dip, it's a drinking trough for horses and cows," said Trapdoor, trying to pacify her but she turned and ran back to the buses, which most of her classmates were already on. Her friends managed to quieten her and get her sat down. She told everyone on the bus about Trapdoor throwing Cow-Pat in the trough and they all laughed, especially the driver.

"That lad deserves a medal," he said. "The bus gets dirty enough as it is without cow-pats."

Trapdoor helped the now much cleaner Cow-Pat out of the trough and persuaded him to run around to try to dry himself and also to warm up. The driver and Mr Cooper got off the bus and shouted for the pair of boys to hurry up.

"He's trying to get dry so he doesn't make any more mess on the bus cos he's soaking wet," shouted Trapdoor.

"Tell him he can wear my spare overalls that I keep for doing

any repairs. They're clean," said the bus driver.
When the boys returned to the bus, Cow-Pat went behind a bush and changed into the overalls which buried him. As he boarded the bus and took his seat near the front next to Sicky Vicky, he was jeered affectionately. She secretly held his hand under her cardigan which she'd placed on her lap and no-one noticed him blushing. Friends through adversity.

Flinty's Flying Bedsteads returned the children to Moorfield School where Mr Cooper asked Trapdoor to accompany him to the Staff Room so that he could be thanked for his help.
"Thank you, Mr Appledore," began the teacher. "Your help at Hardwick is appreciated. However, your creation of explosions of such size as I saw is very worrying indeed but, of course, you were hoist by your own petard, blown off your branch by your own bomb and, of course, a petard is a small bomb but you will know nothing of such things. I intend reporting the matter to the Headmaster. Empty your bag and your pockets please."
"Fart !" came the retort from the boy.
"I beg your pardon, young man ?" exclaimed Cooper. "You will pay for your insolence !"
"The word petard comes from the French word for fart, sir," explained Trapdoor in triumph. "Mr Saint told us that in Science, sir. A fart is a small bomb, sir."
"Pockets !" said the angry History teacher who felt he had been made to look foolish.
Trapdoor did as he was told and started emptying his pockets. There was a small amount of money, two Oxo cubes in their wrappers, a tube of Spangles, a box of matches, a ball of string to which was attached a three inch long door key and a white handkerchief that appeared to be wrapped around some items that Mr Cooper thought would incriminate the boy. Everything was still wet from his unfortunate fall into the lake.
As the teacher began cautiously opening out the handkerchief, Trapdoor realised the metallic wrapping on the Oxo cubes

would have kept them dry and he peeled one open and put it in his mouth as both of them watched the hanky unfold.

"Aha," exclaimed Mr Cooper when the Oxo, five snobs and rubber ball were revealed and which he thought were the ingredients for a bomb. "What have we here, young man ?"

"Snobs, sir," said Trapdoor, chewing his Oxo cube.

At that moment the Headmaster walked in to the room.

"Ah, Mr Cooper, just thanking young Appledore for his assistance, I hear and over a game of snobs as well, I see. Haha. Well done. Now then, Trevor, you run along and have a cup of tea with everyone else and Mr Cooper can come to my office and fill me in on what's happened. Haha, snobs eh ?"

"Thank you Mr Scott, sir," said Trapdoor who picked up his snobs in his handkerchief, stuffed them back in his pocket with his other things and left with a smirk on his face.

Mr Cooper resolved to ask Curly Johnson, the Sports Master, who had been a navigator in the Dam Busters operation during the war, if he knew anything about Trevor Appledore and his bomb making abilities and whether snobs were ever used in their production.

The Headmaster was also a former military man in the war but Cooper thought better of sharing any of this with Mr Scott, who would explode himself if he knew the whole story.

Trapdoor, Balsa and Babs became the school heroes with all but a few of the older boys and most of the teachers, who eyed them suspiciously. A few even began searching Trapdoor whenever he arrived for the start of a lesson, on the advice of Mr Cooper, who still believed that Trevor Appledore was an agent of the devil or communist Russia or both. Of the teachers, Mr Smith (Mathematics) publicly doubted that any of his pupils could carry out any of the things that were being said.

"You're adding two and two and making five. Talking to animals, making explosions ? I think not. Have they ever shown such levels of skill before ? No."

In truth, he also ran the after-school youth club and hoped to get the three accused to come and to bring all of their friends. He could handle them, he boasted. The three boys were besieged with invitations from girls to nights out at the Plaza Cinema, the school youth club and the Diamond Horseshoe Café, in some cases with the girls often offering to pay. One girl even asked all three of them to go to the pictures with her together. Being treated like pop stars did not affect the ways of Trapdoor and Balsa. Babs, however, grew his hair, used Brylcreem, started shaving, had a bath every other night and cleaned his own shoes for ten minutes every morning before he went to school. Strange behaviour this, for a twelve year old, which had the opposite effect to what he had desired. When he arrived home from school one day he asked his sister, Ann, why the girls seemed to have started liking him, so he tried to make himself more attractive to them and, as a result, they all seemed to stop liking him which he could not understand and could she help.
"What did they say when they started liking you?" said Ann, with a sister's arm around him.
"They said I was a loveable rogue and a likeable little devil, things like that," answered Babs.
"Well, likeable rogues and loveable devils don't bath and clean their shoes that much, do they?" she said.
"Brilliant," replied the enlightened hell-boy turned heartthrob.

5

A ROBIN FLEW IN, ALL BRAVE & FIERY SO NEVILLE WROTE IT IN HIS DIARY.

The two strangers pulled up chairs and sat in a relaxed and informal way beside Newt.
"Neville, can I introduce my friends, Baron Rothschild and Mr Peter Wright," said Mr Smith.
"Victor Rothschild, please," said the older of the two. "I'm a biologist and chemist, Neville."
"And I am a scientist by training, working for Marconi Electronic Systems," added Wright.
"If you're wanting help with some homework," said Neville. "I'm not very good at science subjects and anyway, cribbing isn't allowed."
The men raised their eyebrows and smiled.
"Neville," said Mr Wright seriously. "What do you know about the Cuban Missile Crisis?"
"Ok, it's true," replied the boy. "I just tried them on and sat with my feet in them, then I forgot all about them, so I went to the flicks with The Pope to see The Alamo and I didn't realise I still had them on."
Hearing mention of The Pope, Pricey, who had just arrived outside the Headmaster's study and was straining to listen, knocked and ran straight in, thinking he was late. He fell on to the lap of Mr Wright who was sat too close to the door.
"Sorry I'm late Mr Smith sir," said Robbie. "The ambulance is on its way, sir."

He patted the strange man's sleeve in apology and stood up, embarrassed.

"What are you talking about Price ? Why is the ambulance on its way ?" queried the Head.

"For Dai Davies, sir, he's been spared by The Pope, sir but he's standing up now. I just saw down the field."

Pricey was now red in the face as he wondered why the Head did not know.

"I hope we will all be spared, boy but what part has The Pope played in this little miracle ?"

"Sorry, sir, I mean he's been SPEARED by Colwyn Holness, 'The Pope', sir, with his javelin, sir. Accidentally like, of course, in Double Games, sir. It flew that far, sir and stuck in Dai's leg. Gallopaway told me to come and tell you, sir."

The Headmaster rose from his seat and the colour drained from his face as the story sank in.

"Excuse me gentlemen, I should perhaps go to the sports field and investigate. You may use my office to continue your discussions with Neville as I may be absent for some time. Price, follow me."

Mr Smith left without waiting for a reply from anyone and his black, sleeveless teacher's gown wafted after him, as did Robbie Price.

"Sorry Neville, may we return to what you were just saying about having your feet in something when we asked if you knew anything about the Cuban Missile Crisis ?" resumed the slightly older of the pair, somewhat curious as to what the boy was talking about.

"My brother has a pair of Cuban-heeled boots that are all the rage and I accidentally wore them when I went to the cinema with Colwyn Holness, known as The Pope, to see The Alamo. He's Holness The Pope, get it ?" said Newt slowly and deliberately, to bemused looks on the two men's faces.

"Then when we got home my brother hit me for wearing them so I took them off and threw them at him. Mam said I'd used them as missiles and threatened to tell dad we'd had a Cuban Heels Missile Crisis when he got home from the Miners Welfare later. John Wayne was brilliant. Get off your horse and drink your milk. Did you see it?"

"No, we're more The Third Man than The Alamo," said the disagreeable Mr Wright.

"Oh yeah, Horson Welles instead of 'Horse and drink', I suppose," joked the boy.

"And what do you know about the Duke of Devonshire's woods at Scarcliffe?" asked the posh and smarter dressed one who preferred to be known simply as Mr Victor Rothschild.

"Why do you want to know that?" queried Newt, visibly irritated at this question.

"Why do you question everything?" said the unfriendly one, who had either lost weight or bought the wrong sized suit, Newt thought.

"Well, first because my mam told me to question everything when I came to Grammar School and second, because you're wanting my help with something and you're questioning me, so I've every right to ask questions, which is three reasons really," replied Newt calmly.

"And anyway, why are they the Duke of Devonshire's woods? Does he ever visit them? Does he live in them? How did he get them? My mam says his ancestors stole them off the villagers whereas our family, the Heaths, have lived in Scarcliffe for a thousand years. And my dad was in the Coldstream Guards with him in the Second World War when the Duke ..."

"Listen, you little commie sod, shut up and do as you're told for once." said wrong-sized-suit.

"Get lost then," shouted Newt, jumping to his feet and running to the door. "You can't bully me. You're too big for your boots and not big enough for your suit, as my mam would say."

"Alright, Neville, come back. I know that the Duke was withdrawn from the fighting at the front in Italy," interrupted Baron Rothschild. "But it was deemed for good reason at the time although it was perhaps a bad idea in retrospect. Now, would it help if we just called them 'Scarcliffe Woods' and recognise that you have a 'right to roam' in them, as it were? I shall personally agree that with Andrew, the Duke of Devonshire, with whom I am acquainted."

Newt returned to his chair, more curious than frightened, but glared at Peter Wright.

"Your mum sounds very astute," said the Baron reassuringly. Newt was now confused. "Astute?" he added, unsure of its meaning. "Like The Stute at New Houghton?"

Now it was Victor's turn to look puzzled.

"I think it's short for Institute," Newt explained. "And that's short for Miners' Welfare Institute, I reckon. What does yours mean?"

"It means smart and perceptive and I think you are too, Neville, but you are quite correct to ask questions and want answers," continued Rothschild warmly. "Would you mind leaving us alone Peter and I will take it from here, if that is acceptable to you and our young friend."

Wright left, clearly unhappy but without speaking.

Rothschild described how information had been received from inside the GRU, the Russian Foreign Intelligence Agency, that 'spetsnaz' or special forces operating here in Britain were obtaining and supplying intelligence to Moscow from either a location or an agent named 'Scarcliffe Woods'. Newt's eyes widened on hearing this, which the man said was top secret. Nathaniel Mayer Victor Rothschild, 3rd Baron Rothschild, was a biologist by training, a cricketer and a member of the prominent Rothschild family of very rich bankers.

He was the son of Charles Rothschild and Rozsika Edle Rothschild (née von Wertheimstein). Rothschild was educated at Harrow School and at Trinity College, Cambridge, where he studied French, Physiology, English and Partying. He played first-class cricket for both the University and Northamptonshire.

At Cambridge he was known for his playboy lifestyle, driving a Bugatti sports car and collecting art and rare books. He was recruited by MI5 during World War 2 and became a Major in the Intelligence Corps.

Whilst he was unable to use any of this to try and persuade Newt, the boy would have been unimpressed anyway, which the Baron realised, although he didn't know that he had done some digging in the school library and in his History lesson about the Rothschild family. No, Newt was persuaded to spy on principle alone. Well, that and the twenty pounds Rothschild gave him, with the offer of five pounds each time he reported the gang's observations of the woods.

He quickly decided however that there was no way he would split on any of his close friends as none of them would be up to anything, he was quite certain. Well, nothing out of the ordinary anyway. And he would make sure that only the immediate members of the gang, Mac and the four Wood brothers, knew about this. It was agreed that they would meet at church every Sunday morning and take coffee in the vestry after the service.

"See you in church," sang Newt as he strode across the room, opened the door and left. Rothschild heard his carefree footsteps bounce down the stairs two steps at a time until, half way down, Neville missed the step and shot to the bottom where he noisily and painfully landed in a crumpled heap.

The baron heard the commotion and dashed to the top of the stairs just as the boy rose to his feet and brushed himself down. All Newt could think of was Saturday's party at Wiggy's.

"Neville, are you alright ?"

"Err, yes sir, I'm fine. I must go, 'Tough of the track' and all that." He turned and limped away to go and change out of his athletics gear, hoping the weeks spent practising singing and dancing to 'Twist and Shout' in his bedroom would not be wasted because of injuries from falling down the stairs.

Gerry Davies was speared but spared, taken to hospital and

made a good recovery although, as he predicted, his mother was none too pleased about the whole affair and his trousers. Everyone asked Newt about the two policemen but he said that they were from the National Association of Choirs and would be attending Scarcliffe Church on Sunday to hear him sing in the choir and any of his fellow pupils were welcome to come and sing as well. This put them all off, just as he intended but, of course, a Mr Victor Rothschild or whatever his name was, would truly be there, in case anyone did turn up to check on him.

When he arrived home from school, he called a 'council of war', at which he told the rest of the gang, including Trapdoor and Babs, what had happened. They all agreed that they would do what had been asked of them and keep an eye on the woods, as they did that anyway.

"I told you all that I'd seen these two blokes at Aroma Free Group with some American soldiers and one of them was called Baron Rothschild but you took no notice," said Babs.

"We heard what you said, Babs but it didn't mean anything at the time as none of us knew who they were," said Olly to reassure their hurt friend.

"I've heard of this Baron," announced Trapdoor. "He was a German fighter pilot in the war."

"We've all read about that Baron in the Victor comics," said Newt. "Baron von Richthofen, who was known as the Red Baron in the First World War. This one's Baron Rothschild, Trapdoor."

His friend shrugged and they all laughed.

"But what about this Peter Wright ?" asked a concerned Mac. "I don't like what you've told us about him and his name sounds a bit too much like Sergeant Pyewright for my liking. Anyone with Wright in their name has got be wrong."

6
WATCH OUT WALLY, YOU'RE IN MY WAY – AN EVERYDAY TALE OF CRASHLEY ASHLEY.

Gang Lane, Scarcliffe, was named after the gangs of Irish navvies who lived in wooden huts there while they were constructing the Lancashire, Derbyshire & East Coast Railway's Bolsover to Scarcliffe tunnel in the 1890's. The boys knew the true origin of the name but nevertheless liked to tell everyone that it was named after their own gang. Many people, especially of their age, believed their version of the story. Neville Newton Heath, also known as Newt by the Olly Wood Gang, was named Neville by his mother after her favourite novelist, Nevil Shute. Or to give him his correct name which he continued to use in his other world as an aeronautical engineer, Nevil Shute Norway, (1899 -1960). That's Nevil Shute Norway, not Neville Newt's Sure Way. And she named him Newton after Sir Isaac Newton (1642-1727), mathematician and physicist, one of the foremost scientific intellects of all time (Isaac Newton, that is, not Neville).

On Friday 21st June 1963, the day after Neville Newton Heath's 13th birthday, Lynda Marshall, also 13, had invited Newt to meet her on Gang Lane after school and from there they proceeded along the lane to the large clearing in Little Wood. Lynda had told him that the sun shone romantically into the clearing during the afternoon and there was cover in case anyone passed by while they kissed passionately. Such words had shocked Newt and he had kept them to himself. He could not and dare not begin to think of telling anyone else. "What comics do girls read ?" he'd said to himself curiously. As they entered the wood, Lynda had eyes only for Newt, whereas he had eyes only for the large fence that had been erected around the clearing and the brand spanking new wooden hut that had appeared inside it since he'd been there three days earlier with the other boys. Newt silently stared in disbelief at the fence and hut in their wood but Lynda simply shrugged her shoulders as if it was not there.

"We can climb over the fence and go behind the hut. It'll mean that we won't be disturbed," she said, not understanding the reason for Newt's silence and adding, "They were just finishing it yesterday when I was here after school with Mal Snead..." She stopped abruptly as Newt turned and ran out of the wood. "Come back Newt, nothing happened and it's you that I want to be here with now, honest," she shouted after the departing boy, thinking that she had upset him and he was jealous.

In truth he was on his way home to tell the others about what he had found in the woods and it was nothing to do with kissing Lynda and everything to do with the new fence and wooden hut that had been constructed in their wood. Who should come walking along the path from the middle of the wood towards Lynda, having been watching, but the very Mal Snead who she had been here with yesterday. 'Sneaky Snead', as the gang knew him, had been hiding among the trees, with his little home-made bow and arrow, watching the unfolding scene. Although she was disappointed that Newt had taken it so badly, she decided to take advantage of Sneaky's appearance. "Fancy a snog ?" said Lynda, laughing. "The plan didn't work so we'll have to think of another way to use that lot."

"Yes on both counts," replied Mal, still unsure of Lynda's intentions and motives in respect of either himself or the gang. When Newt left the wood and ran towards the village he saw

Harry Marshall, Lynda's dad, and the family's Jack Russell dog, Doo-Doo, coming around the bend of the lane a hundred yards away. As the boy neared them, the dog barked at him aggressively, as did Mr Marshall.

"Neville, have you seen our Lynda ? She should be home by now."

"Yes, I saw her coming through the Little Wood just now, I think, with Malcolm Snead," replied the breathless Newt as he sprinted past them. He hoped Harry would catch her with Sneaky who he'd spotted hiding in the undergrowth as he fled.

"Hey, wait a minute, Neville Heath, I want a word with you," shouted Harry impatiently and unsuccessfully, as Newt disappeared around the bend and was gone.

Lynda heard her father's shouting and Doo-Doo's barking and sat up with a start, pushing Sneaky off her and into some nearby nettles which stung his hands and made him cry out.

"Ouch," called the boy and was quickly hushed by her.

"Quick, it's my dad and Doo-Doo, our dog. If he finds us here, we're both dead. Come on, we've got to head for Mansfield Road."

She pulled him up and dragged him along the path deeper into the wood and away from Gang Lane and they tore through the undergrowth making more noise than a mob of Stags.

Even for Sneaky, being caught by a dog called Doo-Doo was bad enough, but being caught by the renowned for being protective of his daughter, Harry Marshall, was even worse.

Running as fast as he could, Newt reached the end of Gang Lane in quick time and saw his fellow church choirboy, Ashley Crawshaw, riding his bike, also very fast, down Main Street. Ashley rang his bell, tried to brake and even shouted out loud when he saw Newt but, although he'd had the bike for several months, he still had not properly mastered either steering or stopping. Everyone therefore avoided Ashley like the proverbial plague, especially when he was on his bike. Even his own family had labelled him Crashley Crawshaw, which had been universally adopted in the village. He collided spectacularly with Newt and careered up the banking and into the fence surrounding the field next to the vicarage. Ashley then crashed through the fence and into the field, the bike falling on its side with the back wheel spinning around dramatically.

"Crashley !" shouted Newt in anger, pain and rebuke, although he did not feel that he was too badly hurt. Ashley meanwhile groaned and was physically sick in his greater pain, having broken his leg.

A man wearing green overalls, that were tucked into similar coloured, green Hunter wellingtons, came running like a blur out of the garden gate of the house opposite the lane, Manor Lodge, 23, Main Street.

Newt was half scared to death before his jaw dropped as he recognised the man's face. The 'green man' took one look at Ashley's leg, then ran back inside and rang George May, a local doctor in Bolsover. Mr and Mrs Crawshaw, Ashley's aunt and uncle, were working down at the bottom end of their garden, near their chicken coop, which was much further away from the scene of the 'accident' than the 'green man' had been.

"What was that noise, Martha my dear ?" asked Eric Crawshaw of his wife, stopping work.

"Well, I can't be certain," replied Martha. "But it sounded as if a bicycle has crashed again."

"Oh crikey, not Crashley again," sighed Eric. "Did we ought to go and see what he's done ?"

"Yes, come on Eric, the red mites in the chicken coop can wait. Let's investigate."

The couple downed tools, took off their gloves and walked back up the garden path and out of the gate on to Gang Lane to find Crashley crumpled beside his bicycle.

"Oh Ashley," said his aunt. "Why can't you be more careful ?"

In truth, although they had not witnessed what had happened, they had already made up their minds in seconds that it was their nephew's fault. The crumpled heap that was 'Crashley' Crawshaw just moaned. The lady heard a noise behind her and realised that they had left their garden gate open and their goats, Billy The Kid and Nanny Neenah, had come out to join them and eat nettles and other green growth beside Ashley. Mrs Crawshaw grabbed the goats and dragged them back through the gate and closed it quickly to prevent their escape. Seeing Newt getting to his feet and dusting himself down, Mr Crawshaw went to Ashley's assistance and calmly instructed him to lie still and told him he appeared to have broken his lower leg, which was clear from the angle at which it stuck out below his knee. The 'green man' came running back out of his garden gate and came to an abrupt halt.

"Ah, hello there," said the man in a warm, cultured voice. "My name is Victor Roth, I'm staying at Manor Lodge here. Shall we move things from around the injured boy to make it easier for the doctor when he arrives ? I've just rung Doctor May who is on his way here."

Eric was reassured by Victor's well-spoken tones and knew that there were several families called Wrath in other local villages and presumed that he was related to them and that Neville must know him from the look on his face.

"Hello Victor, I'm Eric Crawshaw. Shall we remove the fence from around my nephew, Ashley, or 'Crashley' as everyone now calls him since he got his bicycle ?"

The Manor Lodge lodger smiled and they began to move parts of the broken fence. They both turned to see whose were the footsteps they could hear coming along the lane.

"Victor, what are you doing out here ?" said the Reverend Woolley, sounding to Newt as though Rothschild was severely contagious with a dangerous disease.

"Look Jeremy," replied Victor. "The boy has clearly broken his leg. I couldn't just ignore him and I have rung George May who is on his way so I thought I should stay."

"Come on then," said the vicar. "Let's get him inside so that we can get you off the street. Perhaps we should take him into Manor Lodge if you have telephoned George. Do you agree Eric?"

Mr Crawshaw nodded his agreement, despite feeling puzzled. Newt tried very hard not to be seen to react in any way, but the watchful Mr Crawshaw nevertheless looked for and saw his reaction, a slight movement of the eyebrows as the boy concentrated to hear anything else of this strange and interesting conversation. Eric was just as intrigued as Neville appeared to be at the secret nature of this Victor Roth. The three men continued their demolition of that section of the fence which Ashley had begun so that they could attempt to lift him. Victor called to Newt to come in with them as they then carried Ashley into Manor Lodge, a large detached cottage, surrounded by an enormous, impenetrable hedge of mostly Hawthorn.

On entering the house Newt was struck, as when he had been here before, by the smell of the old books which appeared to cover every wall in both the hall and the first room on the left which they went into. Here Ashley was laid on what Newt thought was a very old looking red leather settee and which he seemed to remember was, strangely, named after the town of Chesterfield, eight miles away.

"Jeremy, I'll talk to these boys while you wait outside for Doctor May," said Rothschild in a way that Newt had never heard anyone speak to the vicar, not even the Dioceson Bishop, and Reverend Jeremy Woolley quietly did as he had been told.

Mr and Mrs Crawshaw said that they would go and tell Ashley's parents what had happened. Victor escorted the vicar outside and Newt heard the two of them in conversation.

"Be careful what you say in front of that Neville, Victor" urged Reverend Woolley. "He's big trouble along with the rest of his gang and they're truly meddlesome. They all have weird nicknames, they call him Newt."

"Well, well, Woolley Bully, how people love having their aliases and nicknames. Besides, his middle name IS Newton," smirked Victor and he hurried back inside.

Once again, Newt tried to conceal his reaction to all that he had heard, which was scrambling around his brain searching for understanding. In the same way that Eric Crawshaw had done earlier, Victor observed the boy's facial expression which gave away his discomfort.

"Why aren't you allowed to go outside, Mr Rothschild ?" asked Newt, trying to deflect attention away from himself, "Are you ill ?"

"I suffer from a Bipolar disorder although it doesn't stop me going out but let's not talk about my cyclothymia, let's look at the injured boy here," countered Victor, succeeding in confusing Newt even more with this response, as the Baron had been hoping.

"Now then Ashley," said Victor gently, "Doctor May will be here soon. How do you feel ?"

"Terrible !" moaned the victim, intent on milking his situation. "I was just on my way to choir practice when that 'Neville the Devil' ran out in front of my bike without looking."

"You must be concussed, Crashley", said Newt, laughing dismissively. "I was at choir practice which was last night and you missed it because you were in Little Wood with Jessica James. You were at kiss practice, not choir practice, you lying little leg breaker."

"No I wasn't, I was ill and unable to go out," protested Ashley, lamely changing his story.

"I think I hear Doctor May's car Neville, would you mind meeting him and showing him in ?" suggested Victor as a way to defuse the situation.

Newt cast a look of contempt at the hapless Ashley then did as he was asked and went outside to meet the doctor who was just getting out of his car by the front gate. The Doctor's reaction to Newt's presence was much the same as the vicar's.

"Neville, what are you doing here ? Have you been in Manor Lodge ?" Newt was puzzled by this. Why was the place he had been in before, now thought to be out of bounds to him?

"What's up, do you reckon I'm going to catch his Polar Bear cycling thingymajig ?" said Newt sarcastically. "The vicar didn't think I should be here either. What's going on ?"

"Nothing boy, of course not, now come into the house please and show me to the patient," said the doctor icily, wondering what the hell 'Neville the Devil' was talking about.

George May strode in purposefully, followed by Newt who pointed to the first room off the hall, that he knew would be called the Drawing Room where guests were received.

"Wait in the hall a moment, Neville while I examine Ashley, then you can come in and tell me what happened," barked the doctor.

"But doctor ...," began Newt as the door was closed in his face.

"Don't be taken in by that Neville Newton Heath boy outside, Victor," whispered the uneasy doctor. "He may have an angelic voice in the church choir but he's the devil-child in every other way and will have made mental notes of everything he's seen and heard. Then he furtively writes everything down as quickly as he can and uses it with the rest of their gang against people. I've seen him do it myself and Bully will tell you the same."

"Oh, Mayday, leave the boy alone, he's an injured party as well, although it's Ashley here who needs your attention, not 'Neville the Devil'. He's playing at spies that's all," laughed Victor, though intrigued by the boy's reputation and knowing what he had agreed to do.

"Come in Neville," shouted Rothschild to the boy who opened the door and came in smiling.

Newt and Ashley were able to describe to the doctor what had happened although their accounts varied a little. Then, while the patient was examined, Victor asked Newt to take Ashley's bike home and then go home himself, which Newt was by now glad to do.

"Come and drop in next time you're passing and bring your friends as well," suggested Rothschild as he walked the boy to the gate.

Newt was pleased to find that the bicycle was still rideable and he smiled and waved as he rode away. Instead of taking it home to the Crawshaw's, he pedalled home furiously to tell the others about the newly constructed fence and hut in Little Wood, about Crashley and about the strange way that the vicar and the doctor had reacted to the Baron's presence. As he reached the Recreation Ground he found the gang playing football with their jumpers for goalposts and the teams lined up. They never had set positions other than the goalie and even he would join in with attacks.

<u>Goalie</u>

Robbie 'Froggy' Frost

Trapdoor	Olly	Mac	Jasper

Jack	Babs	Willie	Balsa	Giggsy

Colwyn Holness 'The Pope'

<u>Goalie</u>

He cycled through the gap in the hedge in the corner of the 'Rec and shouted, "Hey!"
"Come on choirboy," called Olly, in slight leg-pulling of his friend. "We're a man short but only 6-3 down." Froggy had also been in the church choir till his voice broke and was now somewhat difficult to control for the boy. Newt decided his news could wait and he dashed on to join in the game to a chorus of singing from his friends in mock boy soprano voices

which they often sang to him in fun.
"Oh, for the wings, for the wings of a dove."
The newcomer rushed enthusiastically up field to attack the ball just as Babs launched a powerful clearance that struck Newt full in the face from three yards away, knocking him out instantly.
The ball rebounded like a rocket straight past the unprepared Holness 'The Pope' into the 'net'..
No-one seemed to notice that Newt was unmoved by the goal. His own team celebrated, dancing and singing, and pretending the winning goal was scored by their favourite player.
"And Denis Law scores the winner for Manchester United in the FA Cup Final at Wembley."
While the other team squabbled amongst themselves and blamed Babs and 'The Pope' for the freak goal, only when the ball was brought back to the centre for the game to restart did they all see the bloody-faced, motionless goalscorer and gathered around.
Olly knelt down next to the casualty and spoke seriously,
"Okay Newt, just lie there and take your time. Are you alright now?"
An air of concern spread amongst them when Newt did not move or respond.
"Get your trolley Babs so we can take him home. Giggsy, get over the fence and run and tell his mam what's happened," said Olly.
Babs fetched his home-made wooden trolley from the side of the pitch, the best wooden trolley ever seen, made by a neighbour who was a 'chippy', a carpenter. They lifted Newt carefully on to the trolley, then gently pulled it off the Rec and round the corner to the Heath boys' house where their anxious mother waited. He nearly fell off several times but the bumpy ride home brought him round a little. The pale and bloodied boy was carried in through the front door, placed carefully on the settee and covered with a blanket.

"Olly, go and look," Newt mumbled numbly. "They've built a big fence round Little Wood." Olly gave Mrs Heath a puzzled glance and shook his head sadly.

"He must be hilarious," suggested Willie seriously, to a critical glare from his eldest brother.

"Sorry Mrs Heath," apologised Olly, "He means delirious, he's always getting his words mixed up like that." Newt's mum was used to this from all of the gang and smiled at them.

"Alright you boys, let's have you all out now, leave our Neville to have some peace and quiet please but thank you all for bringing him home."

As the boys trooped out of the Heath house, Newt tried to sit up and said painfully, "You've got to go to Little Wood, Olly and see what they've done."

The doctor wasn't called for this accident but Mrs Heath still insisted that her son spent the rest of the day in bed and she would see if he was well enough to get up the next morning.

"Aww, Mam, " protested Newt as he lay back down and smiled about Willie's earlier wrong choice of word.

"Hilarious," he laughed. "Ouch," he added. He forgot all about developments in Little Wood and fell asleep.

7
ANOTHER RAT, JUST A STONE'S THROW AWAY.

Hannah Stubley-Stanhope, the eldest child of a local gentleman farmer and landowner, Hector Stubley-Stanhope and his wife Letitia (known to everyone as Lettuce), was in her study in the Manor House. The Stanhope family name is thought to have begun in these parts in the early 13th Century and indicated someone who lived on a stony (Stan) ridge (hope). Clearly the family had a long history but then, so did the Woods and Heaths.

Hannah attended the Mount St Mary's College private school a few miles away as a day student, only boys being taken there as boarders. She liked to walk in Scarcliffe woods with her friends from the college when they came to visit and they walked her dogs. She was fourteen, the same as Olly, who she idolised but who considered her too spoilt, stupid and selfish. He was also uncomfortable with, and critical of, her wealth and privilege. Olly had an even greater dislike for her younger brother Peter who, at twelve, already irritated most people in the village with his superior and snooty attitude and telling everyone that he will own the whole village and the woods surrounding it in due course.

The last time they met when Peter was home from boarding school, to shut him up, Olly challenged him to a race through the woods and to even things up he would be blindfolded with his hands tied behind his back. Peter's response was that if Olly was caught in the private, out-of-bounds area of the woods he would be prosecuted for trespass.

Olly was a woodsman and he knew everything about his surroundings and the wildlife and could run or walk through Scarcliffe woods without making a sound. He knew how to find birds' nests and how to call and attract every bird and animal in the wild. He was known as the best poacher in the area but had proved uncatchable, to the anger of Hector and Lettuce Stubley-Stanhope, who owned a small amount of local land and woodland, and the Devonshire Estate which owned the rest.

After the gang had first met Hannah, they had looked into the history of the Stanhopes in a book that Newt had found in the school library. This told him that historically they had been descendants of a Jarl (Earl) of Norway, Halfdan Olafsson, and were later landowners, hunters, Earls of Chesterfield, Sheriffs of Nottinghamshire and Derbyshire, Members of Parliament, supporters of kings, Royalists but most importantly, as far as the boys were concerned, they were oppressors of ordinary people, even if they were now widely viewed as pillars of the community.

Hannah appeared to know nothing of this which Olly thought was even worse. Newt had even found, to his own and the rest of the gang's great amusement, an ancestor of hers named Wotten Stanhope. She, however, did not see the joke.

Olly told Hannah that she was not interested in looking at the world or history around her - she was only interested in herself and the rest of the world looking at her, she was so vain and selfish. Strangely this philosophical observation only served to make her more interested in him, seeing him as "The Noble Savage", a concept she was studying at school in Dryden and Rousseau, literary types that they like in posh private schools. It was Friday evening and she was bored by her studying and instead was daydreaming of being carried away by her hero riding on a flying, wild stag. She was staring out of the window when she saw Olly zoom past on what she knew to be 'Crashley' Ashley Crawshaw's bicycle. Hannah watched him disappear up Malthouse Yard, jumped up from her desk and threw her school books on to her bed. She dashed downstairs, tip-toed out of the back door and quietly got her bicycle out of the 'bike shed', one of their outbuildings. She did not notice her younger brother who followed her out of the house to see what all the rush was about.

By the time Hannah reached the bottom of Malthouse Yard, Olly had disappeared and the bike had been left there but which house he might have entered, she was not sure. As she studied the various stone cottages dotted around the lane, a voice piped up behind her.

"Whoever you're looking for and I'd guess it's him, Olly Wood just ran past the bowling green and headed towards Wood Lane," said Jimmy Clarke.

Hannah blushed as she turned and got back on to her bike, before she broke into an embarrassed grin and cycled away. Jimmy carried on walking and saw Peter Stubley-Stanhope creeping around the next corner while almost clinging to the wall of the nearest house as though he was standing on a precipice. The kids all called him Stubby Stonethrow due to his nasty habit of throwing stones at wild animals and birds and even at pet dogs and cats when their owners were not looking.

"Alright Stubby, I can see you so it's no good trying to hide in the wall," said Jimmy jovially. "And if you're looking for your sister, she's just gone up past the bowling green, cos she's following Olly Wood to Wood Lane."

Before Jimmy could say any more, Peter began running after his sister who by now had reached the stile at the top of Wood Lane. She could not get over it with her bike, so she just abandoned her transport, vaulted the fence, clipped the top bar and painfully fell flat on her face. She dragged herself up, dusted herself down and ran on towards the woods.

Olly crossed the old wooden bridge over the brook into Brook Field and, although he had not made a sound, a group of rabbits hopped away into the wood. He had decided to come this way to go in a circular route to Little Wood so that no-one would think he was checking out the wooden hut and fence that had been erected.

Without stopping, he turned and ran two hundred yards upstream alongside the River Poulter to the trees that bordered the body of water known as The Fishpond. As he entered the undergrowth, he cocked his head to one side as he heard the sound of footsteps running over the bridge above the railway cutting that he had crossed minutes earlier. The boy quickly climbed a tree on the west side of the pond where he could both hide and from which he could observe the bridge over the cutting and the footpath down to Brook Field.

He smiled and shook his head when he saw the slight figure of Hannah Stubley-Stanhope running down the dusty path beside the hawthorn hedge at the edge of the corn field. Olly was just about to jump down and carry on towards Little Wood when he heard a strange sound in the distance like large pebbles scraping and cracking together as they bounced around. Around the same time as Hannah came into view after crossing the old wooden bridge into Brook Field, Olly also saw her younger brother Peter come round the bend of the footpath after the stone bridge over the railway cutting. Unsure whether these two were chasing him, each other or someone else, Olly edged further up the tree for even greater concealment and camouflage high up among the branches.

Within a few minutes, as Hannah squeezed into the undergrowth that bordered the pond, she too turned and heard the sound of footsteps running and the strange clanging and scraping, a noise she knew meant that it was her own brother, his pockets full of the large pebbles and stones which he liked to cruelly throw at animals, birds and humans.

Hannah moved a couple of yards away from the thinned out

run used as a path by everyone and found a leaf laden branch that she could pull down in front of her for even better cover. When she heard her brother arrive at the other side of the thicket she jumped up and grabbed the branch and it took all her strength to pull it down enough to hide her. It was a birch, tall and slim but with lots of leaf that provided the protection from view she wanted. The top branches of the birch tree were also moved by her effort towards Olly's own tree and he was forced to change position as a result although it did at least conceal him even more.

When Stubby emerged from the undergrowth he could not see anyone and his frustration was clear as he turned and threw a large, smooth stone into the branches. It hit his sister directly on her forehead and she let out a faint cry as blood gushed instantly from the wound. Hannah let go of the branch which flew outwards and crashed into her brother's face just as the boy cautiously walked forward to investigate, knocking him backwards into the water. Then Olly, who had leaned forward to see what was happening, was catapulted from his tree as branches flew about wildly. The smooth stones in his pockets did not help as the stunned Stubby sank slowly in the water although help quickly came.

Olly had flown out of his tree to fortunately land on his feet on the path around the lake but his momentum meant he could not avoid shooting headlong into the water. Luckily, his outstretched hands touched, then grabbed, the sinking Stubby. He steadied himself and dragged the unconscious casualty to the side, lifted him on to the path and climbed out beside him. He didn't wait to check on the boy but went straight into the trees and emerged moments later carrying the senseless Hannah who was bleeding badly from the gaping wound in her forehead where she appeared to be either hatching an egg or growing a horn. With the girl hanging limp in his arms, the rescuer walked back to the boy who was now spluttering and coughing and not as badly hurt as his sister. Olly kicked him in the stomach.

"I'm taking your sister back to the village. You can go and jump in the lake for all I care."

He started to go through the trees to get back into Brook Field until he realised it would be very difficult for him to go that way carrying the girl so he turned and walked past Peter who was just getting up. Olly also remembered his original plan to observe what Newt had seen.

"I'll take her home through Little Wood, it'll be easier and quicker, there's less obstacles," said the wet and bedraggled Olly, as if to himself, and he set off briskly while the similarly soaked Stubby Stonethrow stumbled after him looking guilty. There was no chance of the miserable boy keeping up as Olly ran up the woods path past the Foxes' Den and then down another path past the gang's Cedar of Lebanon, in which they often hid, and across the wooden bridge, just yards from the Sheep Dip.

As he went up the slope from the river valley he noticed new signs on the trees – one pointing to the outside of the wood, indicating 'Footpath' and another bearing the notice 'Scouts Wood - No Entry'.

"Scouts Wood," he spat dismissively and went up the path through the out of bounds Little Wood that local people had used for generations.

"So this was what Newt was trying to tell me about."

He was even more disgusted when he saw the wooden hut in a new clearing that was surrounded by a large perimeter fence. A group of fifteen scouts and two scout leaders, all in their immaculate and well pressed uniforms, approached the inside of the fence.

"Where do you think you're going?" asked one of the adults, who both looked somewhat strange in their khaki shorts and knee-high socks. "Scouts Wood is out of bounds to you."

"Would you mind doing your good deed for the day?" said Olly straight-faced. "And go back to look for the brother of this apparently invisible casualty. Family fall-out at the fishpond. I think she knocked him into the water when he hit her. He might need the doctor as well. I'll get her to the Vicarage and ask the vicar to call the doctor. You hurry up and get Stubby."

Olly turned and continued on, out of the wood and along Gang Lane. When he neared the Vicarage he noticed the Vicar in the garden and shouted over the hedge to him.

"Vicar, err, Father Wooster, or whatever, can you help please ? Stubby Stonethrow has thrown a big stone at his sister and knocked her out and she needs the doctor, I think."

Reverend Woolley rushed around the side of the large house and met Olly on the drive. "Come into the drawing room, boy. Crikey me, whatever has happened to the poor child ?"

The Vicar helped Olly to lay her on one of the two large sofas, then fetched a pillow and a towel which he gently placed under her head, not wanting blood on his precious furniture.

"Wait outside, boy, while I ring Doctor May," said the Vicar gruffly. "Mrs White," he shouted towards the kitchen where the housekeeper was cleaning up after dinner. "Come to the drawing room please and watch Hannah Stubley-Stanhope who's had a nasty accident."

Olly dutifully went outside and the door was rudely closed in his face. Mrs White obediently went past the Vicar in the hall and into the drawing room, where she gulped at the sight of Hannah and Reverend Woolley closed the door behind her. He picked up the shiny, heavy, black Bakelite telephone and carefully dialled four numbers. After three rings his call was answered.

"Victor, I have an emergency at the Vicarage," he whispered furtively. "Is George still there ?"

"Yes, we're having a wee dram of the good doctor's favourite tipple. What's happened ?"

"Just tell him to get over here quickly."

Olly decided that he had had enough of being kept outside and started to go home, having done his own good deed in carrying Hannah all the way back from the scene of her accident.

He sauntered off along the lane, passing Doctor May, carrying his black leather doctor's bag, and another chap walking alongside him. They exchanged greetings with him and Olly made his way up Budget Lane towards the footpath and over the fields to Hillstown.

George May knocked on the Vicarage door which was opened almost instantly by the Reverend.

"Come in," he said. "Where's that boy? Did you see him? I knew he was guilty. He's made off to avoid answering questions from the police about his role in the young lady's injuries."

"Well he didn't look guilty when he passed us on the lane, if that was who you mean, the Olly Wood laddie," replied the doctor. "Anyway Jeremy, if there is an injured girl, shall we investigate the effects and let someone else investigate the cause?"

The doctor tended to the casualty who shortly regained consciousness and gave a brief account of what had occurred, making no mention of Olly. Her story was then confirmed by her soaking wet brother Peter who was accompanied by seventeen members of the local church scout troop who upset the Vicar by trooping into his drawing room in their dirty footwear, several of which had trodden in Doo-Doo the dog's doo-doo. Letitia Stubley-Stanhope was summoned and, when she arrived and was told the full story, she blamed Olly for the whole thing.

"My Peter would not do such a thing, whereas that horrid gang of boys from Hillstown are clearly guilty, leaving the scene of a crime is an admission of their guilt."

Her son beamed inwardly and kept silent while he faked a sorrowful look on his face.

Newt quickly recovered from his injuries which had loosened

one of his top front teeth although it did not affect his ability to eat, drink, talk, sing and whistle. His face just ached for a while.

Hannah's recovery took a few weeks longer before she was able to go out again but with warnings from Lettuce.

"Do not associate with that horrible Olly Wood lot. I do not know what has got into you young people today with those Telly Boys and Mobs and Robbers."

"Mummy, it's 'Teddy Boys', not 'Telly Boys' and 'Mods and Rockers', not 'Mobs and Robbers' and it was my nasty little brother, not Olly Wood, who caused my injuries. Oliver rescued both Peter and myself, as I have testified."

When Newt next went to scouts on a Tuesday, Mr Phillips, the scout master made a speech to his charges outlining the new rules barring entry to Little Wood by anyone other than scouts in their full uniform. Twelve boys sat quietly taking this in and intending to obey the order.

"That isn't fair," said the thirteenth, who was Newt. "People have walked through Little Wood for hundreds of years so why should we stop now? We should write to the Queen."

"Neville, we are not going to write to the Queen. Now, quiet everyone, can we get on?" said Scout Leader Phillips.

"My mam says it's something called a 'right of way', so that obviously means we can write away to the Queen," said Newt, unwilling to let the matter rest. "I'll write to her myself."

"I've already told you Neville, you will not write to the Queen and you will stop arguing," shouted the exasperated and red-faced man.

"I don't need your permission to write to anyone, so I'll write to her when I get home," countered Newt. "And my mam says I should question everything."

"Right!" shouted the now foaming at the mouth, angry scout leader, jumping up.

"Yes, I am going to write," said Newt, thinking this was what he was being told to do.

"I meant R-I-G-H-T, not W-R-I-T-E, you insolent, rude, disrespectful, little brat," yelled Phillips. "I've had enough of this. You are expelled from this scout troop. Go home, Now !" Newt shrugged his shoulders and left with a look of resignation on his face.

"What's the point in having a Queen if you're not allowed to write to her ? What does she do for us, anyway ?" he said as he left the hut and ran off through the wood towards Gang Lane. When he arrived home and told his mother, she was not happy.

"Oh, Neville dear, all that money I've spent on your scout uniform and that wiggle thing," she complained.

"You mean 'woggle', mam," said Newt. "And don't worry, I'll still get my wear out of it. I'll wear it for Church."

On Sunday, Newt duly wore his full scout's uniform and walked over the fields to Scarcliffe in plenty of time for the Sunday church service, at which he was to sing Mendelsson's 'Hear My Prayer' (O For The Wings Of A Dove), to be followed by him giving a reading of 'The 23rd Psalm'. He arrived early and went straight to the vestry, where he immediately put on his Cassock, Surplice and Ruff over his scouts uniform and began warming up with his usual vocal exercises. After around quarter of an hour practising singing tonic sol-fa, scales and arpeggios while making faces in front of the mirror, Newt heard what he recognised as the vicar's footsteps crossing the stone flags of the church, apparently followed by another man. Sure enough, seconds later, the Reverend Woolley and Victor Rothschild entered the vestry. The Baron playfully waved an imaginary baton and pretended to conduct the choir of one while the vicar gave scornful looks to both man and boy, then began his own preparations for the service.

Newt moved effortlessly into 'O For The Wings Of A Dove' and Rothschild conducted with great enthusiasm, to the obvious disapproval of Jeremy Woolley who glared at them both.

"Victor, please don't encourage the boy," he said. "We have enough trouble from him."

"Encouragement is just what such talent requires," replied Victor. On seeing the look on the vicar's face, he added, "I'll go and find a comfortable pew and see you afterwards, Neville." When Rothschild had closed the vestry door behind him the vicar turned to the boy and said, "Mr Phillips has told me all about your behaviour at scouts, Neville. The church will not accept such indiscipline and disrespect for our Queen. He was right to expel you forthwith."

"Does that mean I'm expelled from the church and choir as well, Reverend Woolley?" asked Newt defiantly.

"Ah well, no, that's a different matter all together," said the vicar, not wanting to lose his star chorister, the only member of his choir who could actually sing. Not just sing, in fact, but sing quite beautifully and be so undeserving of his ability, in the vicar's honest opinion. The rest of the choir only sang the last three words of each line as they spent too much time looking around and not concentrating on their hymn singing.

"No, punishing you twice would be considered as double jeopardy and we must avoid that," he added, realising how this would look to the Dioceson Bishop, besides the congregation. "Good Lord, no," he whispered to himself.

The church service was fairly routine until Newt gave his solo performance of 'O For The Wings Of A Dove', at which most of the congregation cried, as they usually did when he sang. His own mother tearfully mouthed the words along with him, as did every mother and even some fathers in the place. Even the vicar was moved, which he would be again shortly.

When the boy finished singing he went and climbed up the steps to the pulpit and began.

"On Tuesday I went to scouts and was told that only scouts in their uniforms are now allowed to walk through Little Wood. I said this wasn't fair as Scarcliffe people have walked through that wood for centuries and I wanted to write to the Queen to complain. Because of this I've been expelled from the church scouts, but not from the church choir, obviously. I was supposed to read the 23rd Psalm but I'm sorry, I don't think I will now. I'm leaving now."

He started to take off his surplice and cassock and hang them over the pulpit. As he turned to descend the steps he trod on his cassock, tripped and fell to the cold stone slabs, on which he landed with a loud smack.

He jumped up and shook himself to prove that he was not hurt and handed his ruff to his astonished mother as he walked unsteadily out of church, leaving everyone else open-mouthed in shock and some in admiration. Not for long though, as first, his mother, then virtually the whole congregation, stood up and left the building.

"Can't walk through Little Wood, eh ?" said Mrs Heath. "We'll see. Come on, everybody."

Only Victor Rothschild, an old lady who had fallen asleep and the verger remained, along with the vicar, the organist and the rest of the choir.

The Baron shook his head with a smile, wide-eyed amazement and even a little admiration at the boy's brave actions.

Newt continued to go to church every Sunday in his suit or his scout uniform so that he could meet the Baron. He also went so that he could sit in the congregation and continue to sing along beautifully and loudly, to the great embarrassment of the vicar and the choir and the amusement of his supporters who gradually returned to the Sunday service to watch the fun.

8
THE SONS OF THE SOURCE OF THE RIVER POULTER.

The gang continued to walk through Little Wood, or Birch Hill Plantation, to give this part of the woods its true name, as though the 'No Entry' signs and fence did not exist and, if the scouts were there, the two groups stared but largely ignored each other. Newt reminded his friends that the Baron had said he would arrange with the Duke of Devonshire for them to always have access to the woods and this must be the result. They all nodded in agreement and stuck out their tongues at the scouts in mockery and derision.

Today they were first going to measure the depth of the Sheepwash. The boys had noticed that the water levels had begun to fall dramatically over a period of several weeks. In both the River Poulter in general, and the lake upstream from Brook Field, it appeared that there was a drought. This puzzled them however, as there had been a lot of rain during the recent winter and spring.

They walked the short distance upstream to the source of the river on Poulter Well Lane and found that at various points the stream appeared to split and go underground. When they were undertaking this assessment Trapdoor, being from Palterton, voiced his theory that, as it was known as the River Poulter then at some point it must flow through or from Palterton village.

Otherwise it would have been called either the River Scarc or the River Liffe, if the source was thought to be near to Scarcliffe, he had asserted.

"That's in Dublin anyway, isn't it, the River Liffe, or River Liffey, or whatever?" said Mac.

"The source may be on Poulter Well Lane but from there it flows UP the Lane to Palterton before turning round and coming back down Port Well Lane," announced Trapdoor, ignoring the attempted diversion tactic. "Palterton, Poulter Well, Port Well Lane, River Poulter. Ha!"

Olly thought about this. "Ok Trapdoor, tell us this then. How can a river flow up a lane, uphill, oops a daisy? Closed the trapdoor on your theory. Ha!"

"Consider this then," countered Trapdoor. "When a river first comes out of the ground, the water comes up in a spring, after being underground. The River Poulter travels underground in a downward direction up Port Well Lane to Palterton, where it comes up to the surface in a spring, as usual, to claim its name, River Poulter. Then it goes back underground, travels back down Port Well Lane and comes up again as a spring. Ha, Ha, see, spring is sprung!"

Everyone waited for Olly's reaction.

"He's right you know. Where do you think it comes to the surface then Trapdoor?"

Great excitement spread among them as this more or less dawned upon them all.

"Dunno," said Trapdoor, "but we can search for it, can't we?"

In previous times they had been able to swim in the fishpond and sail Bushevella, by building a dam in the brook to give a depth above the dam of up to four feet.

Trapdoor was in full flow now, even if the River Poulter was not.

"Right, now here's another thing I'm going to tell you," he said, chancing his arm some more. "We've all been studying that

Thomas Hobbes, the philatelist, at school ..."

"Philosopher," interrupted Olly. "A philatelist is the name for a stamp collector. Thomas Hobbes was a philosopher."

"Yeah, yeah, Phil Officer," agreed Trapdoor. "Anyway, he's written some famous books. There's one called 'Tractor, Bus, Octopus', which I think must have been about things you could ride on and another called 'The Levitation', which must be about how to lift things."

Although the others all listened seriously and intently, Olly, Mac and Newt rolled around laughing so much until they cried.

"What's funny ?" asked Trapdoor.

"He wrote a paper, not a book, about optics, or the properties of light, called 'Tractatus Opticus' or 'Tract on Optics', not 'Tractor, Bus, Octopus' and his book was 'The Leviathan', which is a biblical giant sea creature, not 'The Levitation', about lifting," said Mac, barely able to speak as he and Olly almost burst with laughter.

"Ok, so I got the titles a bit wrong," said the smiling Trapdoor. "But Mac mentioned the River Liffey and Thomas Hobbes wrote in The Leviathan that the Liffey is nasty, British and short, so that shows that rivers could be affected by droughts hundreds of years ago too."

This was too much for the two older boys and Newt and they became totally incapable of speech for several minutes.

"He said 'LIFE is nasty, BRUTISH and short', not the 'LIFFEY is nasty, BRITISH and short', you dope," Olly was finally able to say. "Go on Newt, read it out."

Newt had not only studied Hobbes, as they all do, because the philosopher was employed as a tutor by the Hardwick/Devonshire families and is buried locally at Ault Hucknall. The boy had also become interested in some of the theories in The Leviathan, Hobbes' major work and had torn some pages from a school text book; from Mr Webber's, his History teacher's copy, that is.

"Beginning from a mechanistic understanding of human beings

and the passions," quoted Newt from the page lifted from his teacher's school text book, "Hobbes postulates what life would be like without government, a condition which he calls the state of nature. In that state, each person would have a right, or license, to everything in the world. This inevitably leads to conflict, a 'war of all against all', or bellum omnium contra omnes, and thus lives that are "solitary, poor, nasty, brutish, and short".

"See," said Olly. "It's life is nasty, brutish and short, not the Liffe is nasty, British and short."

"To escape this state of war," Newt continued in his usual unstoppable way. "Men in the state of nature accede to a social contract and establish a civil society. According to Hobbes, society is a population beneath a sovereign authority, to whom all individuals in that society cede their natural rights for the sake of protection. Any abuses of power by this authority are to be accepted as the price of peace. However, he also states that in severe cases of abuse, rebellion is expected. In particular, the doctrine of separation of powers is rejected: the sovereign must control civil, military, judicial and elastic powers."

The others pulled puzzled faces at these strange words being read out.

"Shut up Newt," they all shouted but he had finished reading anyway as it was the end of the chapter.

"Elastic powers ? Isn't that stretching it a bit ?" said Olly to groans from all his friends. "Okay, let's go up Port Well Lane to look for the source of the River Poulter. There are some Hazel trees up there as well where we can get some water-witching dowsing twigs."

Newt flattened out the creased page. "Oops, ecclesiastic powers, that should read," he smirked.

Just over two hundred yards from the Scarcliffe end of Poulter Well Lane was the spring from which the boys thought the

River Poulter emerged. On the opposite side of the lane stood a row of large trees and below them was a broad, dense hedge of smaller saplings, shrubs and low trees of various types. Trapdoor suggested that they should each climb one of the big trees which stood across the lane from the stream so that they could all have a good view of the surroundings.

He rose to his vantage point over thirty feet up the tree immediately opposite what they thought was the source of the River Poulter, in fact, at that point, the tiniest of streams. Trapdoor could hardly see the flow downstream, let alone evidence of his theory upstream. Not wanting it to be disproved so easily, he climbed to the very top of his tree and signalled to his friends to do the same, as each one occupied a different tree.

When he was thinking, Trapdoor often chewed an Oxo cube, and he reached into his trouser pocket for such a beef stock cube that lubricated and fed his thought processes, strange though this seemed to everyone. As he did so, a man's voice, raised at someone he was with but kept low to avoid being heard, caught his, and his friends', attention.

"Stop struggling," was clearly heard.

They all raised a finger to their lips to each other and leaned forward to try to get a look at the figures on the lane below. They were all shocked to see that one of them was Hannah Stubley-Stanhope, who was gagged with a dirty rag, had her hands tied behind her and was being dragged along at knife-point by a scruffy, well-built man. Holding his Oxo cube in one hand and trying to hang on to a branch with the other, Trapdoor lost his footing. He dropped twenty feet before his fall was broken by the lower bushes below. Here he bounced on the cushioned growth which threw him up and out over the bushes and into the lane.

This human missile then landed forcefully and feet first on the head of the apparent kidnapper who had just looked up in the direction of something he had just sensed and heard and he was instantly knocked senseless. The rest of the gang saw how Trapdoor had descended and one by one took the same route down to the ground, landing beside Trapdoor, except Willie who unfortunately landed on the other side of the hedge in the field.

They quickly untied the girl and used the rope and some of their own to tie up the unconscious captive since he was so much bigger than all of them and he began to come round as they finished.

Seeing the boys and realising that he was tied up, the man swore and spat at them, "Let me go or I'll kill the lot of you," he roared threateningly.

"Shut up you, you're too tied up to start killing a flea, never mind the lot of us," shouted Olly fearlessly.

"Hannah, what's happened?" he said more softly to the girl.

"I saw you in the village and decided to follow you again to see what you were doing. Then this brute grabbed me in the woods and tied me up," replied the sobbing Hannah.

"Come on, let's get you home and your dad can call the cops," he told the girl.

He then turned to the gang and said, "All of you get big sticks and if he looks like getting free, everybody lay into him and hit him really hard around the head. That should keep him quiet. You lot stay here with him."

Olly led Hannah along the lane towards the road to take a short cut through the woods. The boys meanwhile left the group one by one to get themselves a good hefty stick with which to stand guard over their prisoner.

"Don't worry everybody," said Babs, laughing, "I've got a bottle of chloroform here that I made at home. This'll keep him quiet if he starts any trouble."

The boy waved the little glass bottle and a rag in front of the man, who shrunk back and lay very still, watching Babs warily. They all laughed but kept their sticks ready should they need them.

Meanwhile Olly and Hannah were just about to cross Mansfield Road when a big black car came thundering along and screeched to a halt just past them.

"Oh no, it's mummy," said Hannah as the car reversed alongside them and she opened the passenger door.

"What do you think you're doing out here with this boy? What did I say about their gang?" growled an angry Mrs Stubley-Stanhope, who then noticed the blood and marks on her daughter's wrists and face and the dirt on her clothes. Lettuce jumped from the car and examined her daughter.

"Has he interfered with you? You will pay for this you wicked ruffian," she shouted at Olly.

"No, he hasn't mummy but he and his friends have rescued me from a man who kidnapped me, and the others have him tied up just along this lane. Come and look."

Hannah ran back up the lane, followed by her screaming mother and a bewildered Olly.

"You've left your car engine running," he shouted after them, to no avail. He saw no reason to stand guard over their car, even if it was a 1957 Jaguar Mark VIII.

"Not my blooming car, gang of flash Harrys," he muttered, walking after them up the lane.

When Olly arrived at the scene Letitia was venting her fury on the prone prisoner who was clearly more scared of Babs and his chloroform than he was of Mrs Snotty Posh, as many people called her. Even the boys did not take kindly to her Headmistress manner.

"Well do something then," she screamed impatiently as they stood watching the captive.

"We've done what we needed to and tied him up," said Olly, "And I was taking Hannah home so that you could call the police while the others kept watch on him. Oh, and you've left your Jaguar's engine running," he added, nodding down the lane towards the car.

"Come along Hannah, we'll sort this out. This lot are clearly in league with this criminal," declared her mother.

"But mummy, they saved me from that beast," she protested, running after her mother.

"Don't worry," Babs shouted after them, "We'll look after him while you go and have tea." He waved his bottle and rag in the man's face again, scaring him almost to death.

Spotting an opportunity to gain information out of the man, Olly prodded him with his stick.

"Ok, mate, you tell us who you are and where you're from or Babs here will persuade you with his chemistry set and home-made bomb kit. He doesn't half make good explosions."

"I'll tell you and I'll not lie either," he said, clearly petrified. "I'm Malcolm Snead and I've escaped from Rampton Mental Hospital near Retford and I'm walking it to Shrewsbury where I'm from. I was in Ashworth Mental Hospital in Liverpool but they transferred me to Rampton and I didn't like it there so I just escaped like. I've been to see my brother who lives in the village here but he wouldn't help me at all. I spotted Miss Posh Pants and thought she might be loaded with money so I captured her like and I was just going to see if I could nick anything off her."

"Watch him Babs," said Olly, "And any excuse put his lights out."

He walked up the lane and motioned the others to follow. As soon as they were out of earshot and sight around the bend he gathered them round.

"It sounds like he's Sneaky Snead's uncle. I don't care what he says that we might agree with, he's escaped from Rampton so we let the cops sort him out. It's too dangerous for us and we don't know if he's telling the truth about anything."

No-one disagreed and they simply walked back and stood in silence, watching Malcolm Snead, until Willie remembered something from when he had come down from his particular tree on the wrong side of the hedge.

"Hey," he exclaimed. "I reckon the stream starts on the other side somewhere 'cos, not only did I get my feet wet over there, I could hear running water as well."

They had never been over the other side of these bushes and trees, since at this point on the lane they were always interested in other things just ahead of them. Willie began to walk up the lane until Trapdoor suggested the alternative route they had recently found.

"Hey up Willie, climb a tree and do a parachute jump again." They all looked at each other then there was a mad rush to the trees, accompanied by laughing, pushing and good natured wrestling as they fought for the best tree. As usual Balsa seemed to just run up a tree, so skilful was he at climbing, while Willie got pushed to the back and complained and swore the loudest, despite being the youngest. Balsa was easily the first to make his jump, shouting Geronimo as he launched himself from the top of his tree before bouncing off the lower undergrowth down to the ground.

As the others followed and shouted their Geronimos they were all playing parts in their favourite war film, The Red Beret, about The Parachute Regiment, although each one imagined that he was Alan Ladd playing the leader, 'Canada'. It is doubtful however, whether the stuntmen in the film, never mind Alan Ladd, would have undertaken these jumps quite so eagerly, they were so dangerous.

Sure enough, Willie had been right. Where they landed, the ground was dry immediately opposite where the River Poulter rose on the other side of Poulter Well Lane. However, ten yards further west there was a stream of water on this side that bubbled and gurgled where it went underground. They excitedly began following this 'new' stream and it now appeared that Trapdoor would be proved right about the source of the River Poulter.

"Aaaargh, coppers, get off me, I haven't done anything. He has," Babs cried out, pointing at the captive, as he was taken by surprise but also to alert the gang to what was happening.

Olly peered through a gap in the trees and saw that two policemen, a Sergeant and a Constable, had grabbed Babs from behind. The Constable was in the process of handcuffing him, while the Sergeant was looking suspiciously at the boy's bottle and rag and his apparent victim laid on the ground.

"Well now, young Babyface Nelson, what have you done to this poor fellow and why've you got him tied and trussed up ?" asked Sergeant Pyewright.

"Yes," joined in the Constable, his excitement to be in on some enquiries evident as he said, "Why have you got him tried and trusted ?"

The sergeant sighed at his junior officer and barked at him angrily.

"I said 'tied and trussed up', you flaming idiot, not 'tried and trusted'. Why would he be tied and trussed up if he was tried and trusted ? And stop repeating my questions. I'm in charge of this enquiry."

"It's that stupid Sergeant Pyewright and Constable Stagg. They're arresting Babs," whispered Olly to Mac. "Do you think we should try and explain what's happened ?"

"Yeah come on," said Mac, "We can't allow him to get taken in on his own."

Mac and Olly climbed through the undergrowth into the lane followed by the others. The senior of the two police officers spotted the gang coming towards them, gave a nervous laugh and said, "Well, well, well, look who's here. Wouldn't you just know that where there's trouble and Babyface Nelson, the Olly Wood All Stars wouldn't be far behind."

"Yes sarge, I saw Babyface Nelson recently but I think there was only one big Hollywood star in it that I knew and that was James Cagney. Good film though. You dirty rat^v," said Stagg.

"It was Mickey Rooney in Babyface Nelson," said Babs. "James Cagney said 'you dirty rat' in another film, Blonde Crazy, I think it was called."

"No, you're wrong," said Mac. "It was James Cagney but he

never said 'you dirty rat'. He said 'take that, you yellow-bellied rat', I think."

"Look you fools," shouted the angry sergeant, "We aren't talking about film stars here and who said what in which film and anyway, it was from the film, Taxi, so no more discussion."

"Sorry sarge," replied Constable Stagg meekly.

Olly and Mac walked right up to the Sergeant as the other gang members lined up silently behind them. Learning from Stagg's and their own earlier mistake, Mac said respectfully,

"Sergeant Pyewright sir, could I try and explain what's happened ?"

Shocked by an unlikely show of respect from one of this gang of youths that almost everyone locally believed to be the biggest source of trouble in the area, Pyewright very nearly choked on his own breath. Unable to get his words out, the bemused fat policeman nodded for Mac to go ahead.

The boy began with an account of the falling water levels, Trapdoor's theory on the source of the River Poulter, the gang's visit here to investigate the source, them climbing the trees to get a better view, the arrival of Hannah Stubley-Stanhope being dragged along by her kidnapper, who said he was Malcolm Snead from Shrewsbury, who was now tied up before them, Olly starting to take Hannah home to safety, the arrival of Lettuce, that is, Mrs Stubley-Stanhope, her misunderstanding of the situation and then, the last Act of the drama, the subsequent arrival of the police officers, led by Sergeant Pyewright, to sort out the matter.

Mac gave every last minute detail of what had occurred and more besides.

"All eight of us are more than happy to accompany the police to the station to help you with your enquiries, sir and we hope your car is big enough to get all of us in, as well as Malcolm Snead here who reckons he's escaped from Rampton Mental Hospital," concluded Mac.

Pyewright had just begun to get bored of this apparently

endless story and was having to stifle his yawns, when this last nugget of information made the policeman take notice. "Rampton Mental Hospital ? We know where you all live so we don't need to take you in," said the distrustful and disbelieving Sergeant. "Stagg, bring the car along the lane so we can get this escaped offender taken in, alleged escaped offender, that is."

"Sarge, do you want me to reverse down the lane so we can go out forwards or come down forwards, then reverse out ?" asked the Constable in all seriousness.

"Just get the flaming car, Stagg," screamed Pyewright hysterically. "It doesn't matter which way round you do it, you'll have to reverse one way and go forwards the other way, you stupid boy. You haven't got the brains you were born with."

Stagg stumbled along the lane, his allegedly absent brain under pressure from the verbal missiles his boss had just fired at him and his legs went to jelly as a result. The car was positioned where he had reversed it into the end of the lane from the main road when they had arrived. He started it up first time and, still in panic from the sergeant's words, proceeded to reverse straight into the river, the sound of which was clear to the waiting group thirty yards away up the lane. They ran to the scene to find the hapless Constable standing scratching his head beside the police car in the twelve inch deep and twelve feet wide river.

"Stagg," shouted the red-faced, bulging-necked sergeant, "You're more trouble to me than this lot put together and that's saying something. Get out of the damned water and go and get another car or go back to the station and get the Mariah."

"Where am I going to get another ..." began the Constable.

"Just use your damned initiative if you've got any !" fumed his enraged superior.

The poor young man ran out of the river and along Mansfield Road towards the village. Panic-stricken, he decided he would

go to the Horse and Groom public house. There he would seize the landlord's Rover car and bring it to Poulter Well Lane to transport the offender to the police station and try to calm down the sergeant, or at least stop him shouting so much.
As for the Olly Wood gang, they would be allowed to go, told not to leave the country and be visited and interviewed later, although after hearing Mac's story, personally he thought they should be rewarded, not arrested, for saving Hannah.

Once at the pub he tried to persuade Tom Payne, the landlord, to lend him the car but he was not very willing - until Stagg told him that the police car was broken down and they needed to transport the suspected escaped prisoner, or rather Rampton Mental Hospital patient, to the police station for questioning over the kidnapping of Hannah Stubley-Stanhope. It being a Saturday lunchtime, the place was quite full and all the customers, along with Mr Payne, ran to the windows very quickly when the young officer dropped out this information, a little too loudly he feared, given the reaction. Three customers took advantage of the distraction to go round the bar and re-fill their beer glasses without paying.
"You had better all stay here till you see us leave the village," said Stagg.
Mr Payne now handed over his car keys and ushered out the constable, then proceeded to lock and bolt all the doors, to the delight of his customers.
Back at Poulter Well Lane, Sergeant Pyewright had decided that guarding the suspicious looking Malcolm Snead was more important than guarding the police car and went back along the lane to where Babs' torture tactics had been doing the job better than anyone else could have done. Only Willie stayed at the entrance to the lane, supposedly to wait for Stagg, but really to take the keys from the police car. He then hid them in the knot of the rope swing hung from a tree that stood next to the river.

The young policeman was soon back at Poulter Well Lane and was disappointed to find only Willie waiting for him but was pleased to see him dance with delight, not realising that this was nothing to do with his return. Willie set off and dashed up the lane, with Constable Ian Stagg chasing after him.

"Come on," shouted the boy, "Your Sergeant's waiting for you."

Sure enough, the impatient Pyewright was indeed waiting and appeared to be in a worse mood than before.

"I've borrowed Mr Payne's Rover, Sergeant Pyewright, sir," said Stagg fearfully.

"Keys!" replied his boss, now clearly in a bad state of mind. "You wait here and watch Snead. And keep an eye on this lot as well. They're being too helpful, I don't trust them." He strode away angrily.

"Don't take it personal Staggers, he wouldn't trust the Queen, old Pyewright," said Mac supportively, as the officer freed Babs from his handcuffs and put them on Snead instead.

The constable thought better of making any comment, fearing that his superior would be even angrier with him if he knew what he was thinking, that these boys were good kids, just a little misunderstood and in need of support and direction. Before he could think too much, the Rover was reversing towards them at great speed and they all jumped aside in fear for their lives, except sneaky Snead's uncle who was tied up, so he could not jump at all and the car stopped inches from his prone figure. Pyewright leapt out and single-handedly manhandled the tied and trussed-up suspect into the back seat.

"Get in the back, Constable Stagg and handcuff Mr Shrewsbury Snead to you," he barked.

In seconds they were gone and the gang wandered to the lane end to watch them go. As Willie climbed the tree, the others checked the police car and its position in the river.

"We could drag it out with the ropes," said Olly, standing pondering what they should do. "Pity we haven't got the keys.

We could have had some fun."

Willie slid down the rope and began swinging backwards and forwards over the river.

"We could still have some fun with it," he shouted and let go of the rope with one hand as he waved the car keys at everyone below. They all cheered him, at least until he lost his grip and fell towards the river bank where Mac, Newt, Balsa and Trapdoor broke his fall, but all five of them ended up falling backwards into the water.

"It's our Willie, the Flying Water Lily," laughed Olly uproariously.

Willie and his four wet friends who had broken his fall pulled themselves out of the water and Balsa gave his little brother a playful slap as they all saw the funny side of the soaking they had received.

"Let's get the car out of the water then," urged Olly drily, still amused. "Get in the car and start it up our Will, then when we've got the ropes on the bumper we can give it a pull out." Two thick ropes were tied to the front bumper and two boys held each rope while Willie started up the car, struggling to reach the pedals in this vehicle. Despite being the youngest, Willie was already the best driver in the gang. When he was only five years old, the police had brought him home, having caught him driving a JCB digger he had 'found' at the bottom of the Polyfields. They soon had the police car out of the river and everyone climbed in, Olly and Trapdoor in the front with Willie driving, perched on the edge of the seat, the five others squeezed in the back, packed in like sardines in a can. Willie could hardly see or be seen over the top of the steering wheel but his driving was smooth and accomplished. They went up the hill into the village and approached the crossroads, beside which stood the Horse and Groom public house. Olly told everyone to get down except Willie and, to the people in the pub who were still looking out of the windows for more escaped prisoners, it appeared that there was absolutely no-one in the car as it sped along Rotherham Road.

"Where should we go ?" asked Newt. "Cos Mr Payne at the pub will ring the Police Station and tell Sergeant Pyewright he's seen the car going past with no-one in it."

"Good point," said Olly. "Old Payne in the neck always has it in for us anyway. What do you reckon Mac ?"

"Well, if I were the sergeant, I'd think that we were heading to Four Lane Ends, where he'd then think we would go to either Boser, Shirebrook or Clowne. Constable Stagg, on the other hand, he's from Mansfield and, somehow, he's both clever and stupid at the same time and he'd think we'd be just as likely to turn round and go back the way we'd come. Pyewright will tell him he's stupid and they'll search the places he thinks we'll be."

"That's it then," decided Olly. "We'll turn left at Four Lane Ends as though we're going to Boser, then we'll turn left again at Hillstown crossroads on to Mansfield Road so we can go round in a circle back to Scarcliffe. All in favour."

As usual, this was a statement, not a vote.

"Can we just call at our house and show our mams and dads me driving the car ?" asked Willie seriously.

"And can we call at Palterton so I can get some more Oxo?" added Trapdoor.

"No," laughed Olly. "You lot are stupid. If we start stopping everywhere, people will see us and be able to tell Sergeant Pyewright. We might as well stop at Lawman's Newsagents and ask them to put it in the Derbyshire Times where we're going."

As they drove past Lawman's they stared at the sectional concrete wall opposite the shop as someone had painted, in red three foot high letters, 'MAC' and Willie nearly crashed the car into the wall in shock.

"What the hell ... ?" cried Mac. "Somebody is trying to get me into trouble and I don't need help, I manage quite easily on my own." No-one else spoke.

They carried on towards Glapwell, a couple of miles north-west of Mansfield, then turned left to Stoney Houghton and back towards Scarcliffe. They stopped just fifty yards short of Poulter Well Lane, from where they had started out in the Police Car, so that they could check that the coast was clear to return the car to the river.

Balsa fairly ran up a tree that overlooked the lane and signalled the all clear. Everyone except Trapdoor got out of the police car and Willie drove to the lane entrance and reversed it back into the river in one apparently seamless movement and in exactly the same place as it had stood previously. The boys all ran up the lane a little way and climbed trees in which to hide from the police when they inevitably returned, as Mac had said they would, or at least Constable Stagg would, Mac had guessed. Sure enough, they both came back in Mr Payne's Rover, within ten minutes, at Stagg's suggestion. However, they could see no sign of the gang, only the car.

"That idiot Payne has had us on a wild goose chase. If you weren't so soft with everyone, Stagg, we'd get more respect laddie. Car's been here all along, look," said Pyewright smugly. The constable stepped into the river to get into the car and, putting his hand on the bonnet as he walked around it, he noticed how hot it felt, but he said nothing to the Sergeant. He then had a good look around the inside of the car as he got in and saw that the floor was wet in the front and the back, and there were leaves and 'sticky buds', the heads of those thistles that stick to your jumper especially, on the seats and the floor. The keys were in the ignition and the engine started first time. He got out and tied one end of the rope around the police car's front bumper and the other end around the rear bumper of Mr Payne's Rover, which was being driven by Sergeant Pyewright. The police car was easily pulled out of the water but the brakes seemed not to work fully, either through being in the water or the driver, Stagg, not paying enough attention, and it crashed into the back of the Rover and dented the bumpers of both vehicles.

"Oops," said Stagg quietly and steam could almost be seen

coming from the Sergeant's ears.
And even some nearby trees appeared to shake with laughter. As soon as the two policemen left Poulter Well Lane in the two cars the gang descended from their perches high up in the trees and ran across the road and into Little Wood at planned ten second intervals. They quietly passed through the wood and emerged on Gang Lane which they walked along cautiously. Olly and Mac said that the vicar might either be watching them or they could bump into him at any time as the vicarage was at the village end of the lane. There were no such problems or surprises but, just before they reached Main Street, Olly sent out two 'scouts' to check whether the coast was clear.
Trapdoor crawled along the outside of the vicarage hedge towards the tunnel head, then around past Malthouse Yard and Chambers' Farm Machinery onto Main Street.
Balsa went through the hedge into the field on the opposite side of Gang Lane, then walked along the field and into the back gardens at the rear of Stone Row, which stood further up Main Street from the lane.
Once in position both of them carefully peered along Main Street and signalled to the others on Gang Lane by whistling their 'all clear' signal, whereupon the six did their earlier procedure of crossing the road at ten second intervals, followed by Balsa and Trapdoor. They then ran up Budget Lane and across Rotherham Road on to the path over the fields to Hillstown and home.
Willie was unable to keep up as they hurried across the first field and he complained loudly.
"Wait for meeeeeeee. I'm not running if you leave me behind. I don't care if they find us." Olly told the others to go slowly and dropped back to run at his little brother's pace which cheered him up and they slowly reached Hillstown Rec. There, two of their friends had just arrived with a football, Robbie 'Froggy' Frost and Colwyn 'His Holness The Pope' Holness.

Mac climbed over the wall and went to the shop where his mother worked while Olly told the others to put down pullovers as goalposts and sit down. No-one spoke again for several minutes.

"What's up ?" said The Pope. "Is it cos we're here ? We don't know anything about you pinching Sergeant Pyewright's police car, do we Froggy ?" He blushed at what he'd said.

"No," replied Balsa. "We're waiting for Mac coming from the shop with frozen Jubblies."

"Right," instructed Olly. "If anyone comes, especially Sergeant Pyewright and his Constable, it's half time and the score's 10 - all and we've been here nearly an hour. Now you two, what's this rubbish you've heard about a police car being stolen ?"

Mac returned and handed round the frozen, triangle shaped Jubbly cartons to everyone. They all bit open the wrapping and sucked on the frozen orange drink.

"We've just seen Babs' dad biking up Pleasant Avenue," reported The Pope. "Said he'd borrowed a bike from the Top Pub at Scarcliffe. That sounds like you Babs. Anyway, he said that when he was in the pub, a copper came in and borrowed the landlord's car cos their's was stuck in the River Poulter. Then about fifteen minutes later, just as he was getting on the bike, he reckoned he saw the police car go past with no-one in it, not even a driver. Obvious who was in it cos we knew you'd gone to Scarcliffe and it sounds just like you."

"I'm not saying whether it was us or not but we've got to be careful cos everybody's trying to blame us even when we haven't done anything wrong," observed Mac. "When I just called in the shop, mam asked me what I'd been doing to get these marks on my arm so I just told her about us climbing trees and jumping down on to the hedge below, far enough to kill ourselves and do you know what she said ? 'Well, don't you go damaging anybody's hedge, our Malcolm'. I could have come home with two broken legs and she'd have said she hoped I hadn't made a hole in someone's hedge doing it !"

They all laughed as they sucked on a Jubbly.

"Do what Tom Paine did," said Holness The Pope, remembering something he'd learned in school. "A Declaration of Independence somewhere else till the fuss dies down."

They all looked puzzled at this until a look of enlightenment flashed on Balsa's face.

"Look, The Pope," he responded. "Just because Tom Payne's had some Decorator in Attendance at the Horse and Groom, it doesn't mean we can do the same, does it ? Anyway, we aren't even allowed in the pub, especially after this morning."

"No Balsa, The Pope means this other bloke called Tom Paine, P-A-I-N-E, of the American revolution, not Tom Payne, P-A-Y-N-E, of the Horse and Groom pub. We're doing about the other one at school. He left England cos he kept getting into trouble like us," said Newt.

Everyone now nodded agreement that the principle was a good one, even if they did not fully understand it, although they all knew that no-one seemed to like them very much.

"Even our mams are more worried about people's hedges than they are about us," said Mac, returning to his earlier theme which made them all smile again. "What we could do with is something that's going to make us look really good, not having to leave the country."

"I've got it," said Babs excitedly. "We could make a 'bull roar' up a drain pipe by using rags and newspaper soaked in paraffin, and then get some dog muck soaked with paraffin as well and set fire to it on their doorstep. We'd knock on the door and run away and when they came to the door, they'd stamp on the dog muck to put it out and get it all over their feet."

"Are you stupid ?" asked Olly in disbelief. "Do you really think that what you're suggesting is going to make us look good, you idiot ? We'll get deported to Australia for that !"

Babs shrugged at the rejection of his idea, which he'd thought was really good and he felt would certainly have increased his reputation and standing amongst his friends.

"Anyway," added Mac. "We need it to be dark when we do a 'bull roar' so we can get away and then get a good view of the flames. Mischievous Night's the best for bull roars, along with 'hedge hopping', gate stealing, smearing treacle or Vaseline on car door handles, lighting bonfires belonging to people you don't like, writing someone's name who you don't like in chalk on the side of someone's else's house to get them into trouble. You know, like somebody's trying to get me into trouble. In fact, everybody tries to get us into trouble."

They all tried to look like they were thinking of what they could do when The Pope spoke.

"What about cleaning up the old folks' gardens and outsides of the bungalows on Mansfield Road and Pleasant Avenue? We'd get medals for that and it wouldn't take long with the ten of us."

"You know, The Pope's come up with the big idea of the century that could just make us into local heroes," exclaimed Olly. "This'll change the course of history, not that Cuban Heel Crisis they keep on about on the news. Come on everybody. You've never had it so good."

9
SERGEANT SENSIBLE AND CORPORAL PUNISHMENT.

They walked towards the sectional concrete wall and nine of them ran the last few yards and jumped at the six feet high obstacle, pulling themselves up and over with ease. Willie, however, was too small to make it this way so he simply approached the wall, lassoed a fence post with his bull-rope, pulled himself to the top, untied his rope and jumped down on the other side. As he jumped, his loaded cap bomb bounced out of his pocket and landed perfectly on its nose, making a loud bang. Willie sprang back against the wall in shock, then laughed along with the others.

When they reached the first of the bungalows on Mansfield Road, Olly, Mac and The Pope went up the garden path, having sent the rest of the gang to their homes just round the corner on Pleasant Avenue and Castle Green to fetch garden tools and equipment.

Olly and the advance working party walked along the path nervously, each one trying to stay at the back and make the others take the lead. Mac stopped this game and whispered. "Holness, Mrs Walters knows you cos she's from Palterton, like you and you go to Grammar School with our Newt so you know how to talk proper and it was your idea so you'll know what you're talking about so you can go first and do all the talking."

"Aww, bloody hell," exclaimed Holness, realising he'd been

out-manoeuvred by his friends.

Mrs Walters appeared around the corner of her bungalow with a stern look on her face.

"Colwyn Holness, your father will hear about your bad language after I've been to church tomorrow. Now, what is the reason for your visit and bad language, young man?"

The boy tried to hide his embarrassment and distress at the prospect of his father finding out that he had been swearing and, as with all the boys, any confidence he had was shattered by what he thought of how his father might react to hearing about this.

"We're sorry, Mrs Walters," cut in Mac in his best voice to save The Pope's blushes and stuttering. "We were just sat on The Rec doing nothing and talking about doing something to help our neighbours and His Holness The Pope here suggested we should ask pensioners if they would like us to tidy up their gardens for nothing. We don't want paying or anything, we're just doing it for our community, for anyone who needs help because we're communityists and helpers of the common people like Robin Hood, not communists."

He bit his tongue, realising that he had said too much and that the last bit was a big mistake, as was using Colwyn's nickname, 'The Pope'.

The old lady was now even more puzzled and suspicious, as their reputations did not suggest that the gang were the kind of boys that pensioners or anyone else would let loose in their gardens.

"I didn't realise your family were Catholics, Colwyn," she said, looking over her glasses.

"It's his nickname, Mrs Walters," smiled Olly, pointing at the red-faced, dumbstruck Colwyn. "We call him 'His Holness The Pope', like 'His Holiness The Pope'. See?"

"Yes I see," she replied, curling her lip in distaste. "But I do not appreciate such disrespect even though I'm not a Catholic either. However, if Colwyn suggested helping local pensioners and it's free, then of course, you can do it as it's a mess. I'll put the kettle on."

It was said that putting the kettle on was Polly's reaction to any event, good or bad. She did the same thing at both the start and the end of the war. Because they loved nicknames, the boys knew Mrs Walters as 'Polly Wally Kettle All The Day', from 'Polly Put The Kettle On'. They just dare not let her hear of this as Polly was also known to be a fiery old bird.

While Polly Wally was making tea, which she thought was for just these three nice boys, the seven others turned up armed with spades, forks, a scythe, two push-along lawn mowers, two pairs of shears and Babs with his flame thrower.

The overgrown garden looked a daunting task for them and they all stood open mouthed, except Babs, that is.

He fired up his flame thrower and aimed it at the jungle before them. In seconds it destroyed weeds, bracken, brambles, hedge, flowers, fence, clothes prop, clothes line, clothes post – all went up in flames. Babs danced around in front of the embers and waved his flame thrower above his head.

He was still shouting triumphantly when Mrs Walters came out with three teas, a spoon and a bowl of sugar on a tray and did a double take when she saw that half of the kids in Hillstown seemed to have appeared at her back door.

"I'd better go and put the kettle on again," she announced in surprise. "I didn't realise the Land Army was on the march again." She handed out the three teas, making sure The Pope got one and, as she turned to go back in, sniffed the air and added. "And what's that awful smell, is someone having a bonfire ?"

Olly took a sip of his tea and, although he enjoyed it, he threw most of it on the burning fence. Mac did the same and The Pope drank half of his before similarly emptying the rest. The others finished dousing the fence in a different way that left the whole garden hissing and an even stronger smell than before. They quickly set about digging the ashes into the garden with care, as some of it was still hot but they soon had it looking neat and tidy, with a totally new look to it. The burnt fence appeared to have been painted black or creosoted and it would be several days before the forgetful old lady began to wonder where her line post, clothes basket, clothes line and prop had gone.

After considering the results of their efforts at the back, particularly Babs' handiwork, they picked up their tools and hurried around to the front garden. There, however, Babs was only allowed to use his flame thrower in short bursts and then, under strict control by Mac. Balsa first cut the grass shorter with the scythe while the others attacked the borders, during which time Mrs Walters turned up bringing a tray full of teas which they drank quickly to ensure an early departure. Olly and The Pope mowed the lawn with the two push rotary mowers, both with rollers that made perfect stripes. When the borders were dug it looked a picture and Mrs Walters was so pleased that she said that she would put the kettle on again.

As soon as she disappeared inside, the boys picked up their tools and ran from the garden and round the corner on to Pleasant Avenue, just in case Mrs Polly Wally Walters realised what they had done to her back garden.

Olly and Mac decided, in their version of everyone having a say, that they should next give their help to someone who did not live too close to Mrs Walters but anyone who disagreed could do the garden next door to her. As it was, they all went to number 12, Pleasant Avenue, where Mrs Roberts lived. The same advance party of two scouts and one spokesperson went up the garden path while the others waited on the pavement outside. Once again, they roped The Pope into delivering their message of hope, offering help in clearing and tidying the old lady's overgrown garden. This time he was better prepared and delivered a perfect speech in his opinion.

"Ay up Mrs, want your garden tidying up ? We'll do it for nothing. We're doing all the old people's gardens on the street."

The cautious look on her face was quickly replaced by a broad toothless smile as she hardly ever wore her false teeth, unless she went out. The charming looks on the boys' faces betrayed their reaction to turn and make a run for it away from the wrinkly old lady.

"I'll put t' kettle on for a brew," she said through her scary gums but the boys stood bravely and not daring to refuse, in case she turned nasty. You didn't upset these old ladies. Like Mrs Walters before her, she disappeared inside and they heard the sound of the kettle being filled and the whistle cap being pushed down before she set it down on the stove. Olly beckoned the waiting, patient-on-the-pavement, gardeners to come in and make a start.

"What did she say?" asked Babs enthusiastically and excited about using his flame thrower.

"She said she'd put the kettle on for a brew. At least we won't have any trouble putting out your fires Babs, drinking all this tea," laughed The Pope.

As Babs gleefully started up his Dragon-Fire-Spitter, as he called it, three girls were listening to records on Annie Roberts' Dansette record player in her bedroom on Castle Green. Looking out of her bedroom window, they saw the boys gathered in Annie's granny's garden, fifty yards away.

"What are that lot up to now?" said Irene Howard admiringly. "Let's go round and see."

"No let's stay here, we can watch them without them knowing and have a better view and besides, we might miss something while we're on the way there," suggested Annie.

The three girls giggled as they bounced up and down at the bedroom window, making the needle jump and scrape across a popular Twist record by Sam Cooke going at 45 rpm. This time they took the clothes line down and moved the clothes prop and anything else in the way, before Babs quickly reduced the overgrown garden to ashes, with Mac standing over him directing and trying to make sure that nothing was incinerated that shouldn't be. With the garden cleared the others set about digging and tidying and after the kettle was heard whistling, Mrs Roberts soon brought out three teas. Like Polly Wally she realised that three cups were not enough so she said 'sorry' and went back into her bungalow, then returned with a large jar full of gob stoppers, which she left for the appreciative boys.

"How come she keeps all these blummin' gob stoppers in the house ?" whispered Willie.

"Don't look a gift horse in the mouth," replied Mac, taking a massive one from the jar.

"I wouldn't dare look her in the mouth," said The Pope. "I reckon I'd have nightmares."

"Do you reckon Mrs Roberts eats them ?" asked Willie, puzzled by old people's behaviour.

"No, course not," added The Pope. "All she can do is suck them, she's got no teeth."

Having finished the back garden, they trooped out to do the front, enjoying themselves now. Mac, who was at the back, turned to close the gate and shouted in total shock at what he saw. "Everybody, quick, the fence is on fire again."

The three girls in Annie Roberts' bedroom were just about to stop looking out of the window and go back to their dancing when the boys returned to the back garden and extinguished the burning larchwood fence as only boys can. Annie, Irene and Jessica screamed and shrieked with great hilarity at what they saw. The girls fell on the bed in hysterics as the boys finished their action in the back garden and left to let the fence dry.

"Put that flaming thing down Babs, we're not using it again, she's got a big hedge and a rose bush in the middle of the lawn," said Olly, worried that they would get into trouble.

Babs did as he was told and they tidied, dug the borders, mowed the lawn and snipped the privet hedge without further incidents.

"Thank you boys, I'll tell your parents how grateful I am and you've even painted my fence round the back, I see. I don't know how to thank you enough," said a tearful Mrs Roberts as she walked down the path towards where the Land Army had gathered outside on the pavement, ready to run if she realised what had really happened to her fence. They muttered uneasily, unused to being thanked by anyone and drifted along to the next house, as their previous lucky customer returned to her house, wiping her eyes on her pinafore.

Next door was the home of Mr Leo Finkelstein, an old Latvian, Jewish man who came to live in the area in the early 1950's. He liked the boys although he would sometimes tell them they were cheeky and disrespectful. As if to prove his point, they would ask him what was the difference between them being disrespectful and him loudly criticising everyone from the prime minister to the postman to Prince Philip.

"Ah, the innocence of youth," he would always say. "They must question everything."

He would also tell them, and anyone else that would listen, stories of his survival and escape from what he called the 'Bikemieki Massacre of Riga' in Latvia in late 1941. Then there was his flight across Europe to avoid both the Russians and 'Mr Hitler and his evil, fascist gang' and their concentration camps, where many of his family and friends sadly ended up. They admired the old man but sometimes avoided him, since his stories occasionally went on a bit too long and they could also be a bit too scary as well. Olly pulled Mac away.

"What do you think, Mac, should we do Frankenstein's garden as well ?" he whispered.

"Yeah, come on, we'd better," replied his friend. "We can't leave him out, we'll just have to hope he doesn't start talking about those camps and people being gassed and piled in mass graves while we're digging."

Despite them being the two oldest in the gang, they both shivered as always at this thought.

"Frankenstein's garden next everybody," said Olly, as matter of fact as he could. They all hesitated. No-one moved.
"Come on Balsa, The Pope, everyone, it'll be ok," he continued.
They were just about to go through the small, slatted front gate when they heard shouting from inside, Mr Finkelstein in his own language, which he only used in anger. Suddenly, the figure of a tall young man with long black hair came running out of the bungalow.
"Alright mate, is Frankenstein ok ? We were just going to do his garden for him," said Balsa, standing next to the gate.
The young man stepped over the low wall and smiled at them all, then swung the heavy shopping bag he was carrying. It struck Balsa across the temple and knocked him to the ground with a clang of heavy metal. The attacker ran off down Pleasant Avenue and around the corner on to Mansfield Road while the gang were rooted to the spot in shock. The Pope was the first to react and picked up two cricket ball sized stones that Mr Finkelstein used as gate stops before running after the fugitive, with the others behind him shouting at the top of their voices, "Get him !"
They all gave chase, only to find that an accomplice had been waiting near the telephone box on Mansfield Road, with a motorbike as a getaway vehicle and was heard to shout, "Come on Val, hurry up." The fugitives headed down the road towards Bolsover.
The Pope was Derbyshire Under Fifteens Javelin Champion and was as good a cricketer as any that his school's sports master, Mr Maggs, had ever seen. He threw his stone with unerring accuracy and it travelled about thirty yards before striking the pillion passenger on the back of the head, knocking off his wig.
The missile caused a deep gash to the man's scalp and nearly unseated him but he managed to cling on as the motor cycle sped away. Moments before, who should have come out of

Lawman's Newsagents but Sergeant Pyewright and Constable Stagg and they witnessed the whole incident.

"Oi, you gang of thieving, no good, layabout delinquents," shouted the angry, red-faced, bulging-necked Sergeant Pyewright.

"What the 'eck are you miserable lot up to now, assaulting innocent, law abiding motorists going about their business on their motor cycle?"

The junior officer stepped into the road and retrieved the long black wig. With an enquiring look on his face, he held it up to show Sergeant Pyewright, who regarded it scornfully.

"Strange," said the constable. "Why would a young man wear a wig on a motor cycle?"

"Constable Stagg, we are not interested in a wig," shouted his irritated superior. "This lot have committed yet another crime and we're taking them in this time. Get after them boy."

"But Sergeant Pye...," began the young policeman who was not given the opportunity to finish.

"Get moving, Stagg and arrest those criminals or I'll arrest you instead," shouted Pyewright.

The constable did as he was instructed and set off, wig in hand, in a half hearted walk, trying to look like he was running, though clearly not, the lumbering sergeant behind him, out of breath from shouting. The boys stared in disbelief.

"Not again," said Olly. "Just what has that idiot Pyewright got against us, we haven't done anything. Come on, let's go and see how our Balsa is, before Waddle and Twaddle get here."

They ran back round the corner to where Balsa was still laid on the pavement while Mr Finkelstein and a gathering number of locals looked on.

As the boys disappeared from sight, Constable Stagg was concerned that they were attempting to escape arrest, so he drew his whistle and gave three loud blasts that could be heard all over Hillstown, before he shouted, "Stop thief, err thieves, err, criminals, attackers, juvenile delinquents, err, STOP!"

Within seconds, people came out of every house in the vicinity to see what was happening.

"You stupid boy," complained the exasperated sergeant.

"You've just made our job nigh on impossible and we're going to have hundreds of people, including their parents, watching our every move. And why did you shout 'Stop thieves'? Who said they were thieves?"

"Err, I think you did sarge. You called them a gang of thieving, no good, juvenile delinquents. No, that should be layabout delinquents, you called them, sorry sarge," said Stagg, as if reading from his notebook in court.

Pyewright hit his constable on the back of the head, knocking his helmet to the ground and walked away muttering at the young man.

By the time the two policemen arrived outside Mr Finkelstein's bungalow, where the old man was tending to Balsa's injuries, watched by the rest of the gang, a crowd of over a hundred, and rising, locals had gathered, including Jack and Mary, Balsa's mum and dad. They were astonished and angry at the distressing sight of what had happened to their boy and even angrier when they heard the older officer clear his throat and announce loudly,

"Right can I ask everyone to go back to their homes so that I can proceed with my enquiries? All except these ... err, boys, who have assaulted an innocent motor cyclist, as witnessed by myself and Constable Stagg here. And it is our duty to question them about the assault."

"Just you hang about a minute, Sergeant Sensible and Corporal Punishment, or whatever your names are," complained Mrs Wood. "What about you investigating this so called innocent motor cyclist who attacked our Barry here and laid him out with a bag of heavy metal objects stolen from Mr Finkelstein? Isn't that right Mr Finkelstein? So just watch your mouth or you can use it to investigate my own metal objects on my knuckles."

The ever increasing crowd also became ever increasingly hostile towards the policemen who made a sensible withdrawal and moved a little distance away from the throng. Olly took advantage of the policemen's departure to speak to Mac so he could not be heard.

"Did you notice what the bike rider called 'heavy metal man'? He not only called him 'Val' but he was also wearing a wig. Or it was a she called Valerie wearing a wig? Anyway, I thought it was that Ringo with the long hair at first. What's going on, do you think?"

"I don't know but you're right, something's going on and it's almost as if they're trying to get everyone to blame us. We can get ourselves into trouble without their help," said Mac.

"Hundreds of years ago we'd have all run away to sea to escape all this. Perhaps we should ask our Newt to tell that Rothschild fella. I know we said he shouldn't tell him anything that looked bad on us but this is getting out of hand."

"Good idea. We won't say anything to the others till the crowd and the cops have gone."

They rejoined the crowd just as Stagg, the junior of the two policemen also returned.

"Listen please, everyone," announced the constable. "The immediate priority is to see that young Master Wood receives proper medical attention and my sergeant has gone to the telephone box to call for medical assistance."

Mrs Wood looked a little happier at this considerate speech.

"Can we therefore carry the injured victim to his home to await arrest?" continued Stagg.

The lady's face changed as she swung her right arm and gave him a slap across the face that almost knocked the big, strong officer off his feet.

"Sorry," he said, as he shook his head in shock. "I meant to await assessment. By the doctor."

Balsa was duly carried home and the crowd dispersed in small groups that wandered back to their homes discussing the unpleasant events on Pleasant Avenue. The gang, minus Balsa, went straight away to play football on 'the Green', the central grassed area of Castle Green, where a large metal sign proclaimed 'No Ball Games', by the authority vested in Blackwell Rural District Council. Mac went in goal, two jumpers acting as goal posts, while Olly told everyone what the pair of them had decided, that Newt should tell Rothschild about these events, so that the others could vote for it.

"All in favour?" asked Olly.

"Why do we bother voting?" asked Willie. "When you two have decided what's happening."

"Good question, our Will," agreed Newt, as this one affected him more than anyone else.

"Alright then you two, you can come up with a suggestion that we can all take a vote on," said Mac, coming out of his goal to join the discussion.

There were lots of shrugs of shoulders but no suggestions.

"Those in favour of the original proposal?" said Mac and every hand appeared to go up.

"Those against?" he continued and no hands went up.

"Motion carried. Quick game?"

Jumpers were thrown back down, teams were picked and the serious stuff started. As play got going, Annie, Irene and Jessica came walking back from Pleasant Avenue, where they had been with the rest of the village to watch the fun that seemed to follow the boys.

"Oi Newt, you look tired. You need arrest," shouted Irene, distracting the boy as he swung a leg at the ball and sliced it badly. He was further distracted by Dr May's car arriving outside the Woods' house. The ball flew off fast up the street, not in the intended direction. As he got out of his car, the doctor was struck by how quiet it seemed despite the evil gang's presence on the Green. He was then struck by the football and swore loudly.

Gritting his teeth he turned to bellow at them.

"YOU …" he began but the boys had all disappeared over the hedges and walls of gardens that surrounded 'the Green'. Only the three girls remained and they stood frozen, just staring open mouthed at George May who himself did a double-take when he realised that the attackers who had scored a hit had now escaped. The doctor turned and hurried angrily down the garden path as he reluctantly must attend to the patient, 'another member of their flaming gang', he thought. Newt told everything to Baron Rothschild, codenamed 'Mr Roth', at church on Sunday.

Ten pounds was handed over, both of them assuming this could be very valuable information.

10
THIS TRAIN IS BOUND FOR DUDLEY, THIS TRAIN.

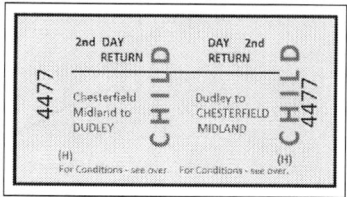

Because they kept getting into trouble wherever they went, the gang decided that they would do some odd jobs for people, to make it look as though they had a legitimate source of income. Then they would use some of the money from 'Mr Roth' to secretly go places. And they had a mission, a plan, this one so secret that no adults must find out about it, so Willie, in particular, being the youngest, was told repeatedly that he must tell no-one.
"Where are we going on Saturday 27th of July, our Will ?", asked Olly.
"Blooming 'eck," said the boy, "We've only just been talking about going to ... Oh no, you don't catch me like that. We're not going anywhere. Haha! Oh no."
They all praised him and slapped him on the back and he beamed with pride.
"How long will it take us to get to Chester ?" asked Mac.
"No, we're going to ..." said Willie helpfully. "Oops, I nearly said it, didn't I ? Stop trying to trick me, everybody, please."
Eventually the day came around for their 'big adventure' and the boys all rose at 7:00 am, a little earlier than was normal for a Saturday's trainspotting, which they had told their parents and friends they were doing. Strangely, they also all dressed in their smartest casual clothes, as though they were meeting girls which, of course, their mums thought they were. Trapdoor had declined the invitation to go, saying that he refused to get up

early on the first Saturday of the school holidays, unless it was to go to the seaside.

Babs, as usual, was being kept in by his mum for his latest bike theft, or for his next one, as she used to put it.

Apart from taking bikes, gamebirds and their eggs, and making fires and explosions, Mrs Nelson quite rightly pointed out to everyone that he was a good lad and would help anyone, and this did not have to involve any of the aforementioned activities. He also regularly 'ran errands' for anyone in the old folks' bungalows although some people unfairly commented that he only did it because it gave him an excuse for stealing a bike.

All the boys had their trusted Army Stores Gas Mask bags, containing sandwiches, bag of crisps and notebook and pen or pencil. Mac was the only one who also had a copy of a 'Trainspotter's Bible - Ian Allan's ABC British Railways Motive Power: Combined Volume Spring 1963'. Just before 8 o'clock in the morning Mac and Newt came out of their back door at the same moment as Olly led Balsa, Giggsy and Willie from their house and they met up on the road out front. No-one spoke as they set off smiling, walking, laughing, breaking into a trot, then whooping, cheering and running towards the Corporation bus stop half a mile away. When they reached the bus terminal opposite the Water Tower, they did not stop, but continued running down the long straight of Portland Avenue towards Bolsover, past each subsequent stop. They were strung out just about in age order and reached Bolsover Market Place as the bus came along on the other side of the road, heading for the terminus at the Water Tower.

They barely had time to get their breath back before the bus came thundering back into the Market Place and they were ushered on by the surly bus conductor.

"Right you horrible kids, downstairs where I can get your fares and keep an eye on you." boomed the large, lady bus conductor.

As Willie went to his favourite long back seat and she followed him to get his fare, the others all shot up the stairs.

"Oi, you lot, what did I tell you?" she shouted after them to no avail, as she spun around. Ignoring the smallest one, who she resolved to get later, she climbed up the stairs surprisingly quickly, after the five older boys. She was closely followed by Willie who then dived unseen on to the floor under the front seat.

Babs had been standing under the awning of Meadows' grocery shop, watching the rest of the boys. He was forced to wait outside the shop while his mam was inside talking to the manager about a job for him as a Saturday bicycle delivery boy. She had thought of this as a means to keep him out of trouble and because it meant he would get a bike with the job.

He knew where the gang were going because they had asked him to go but his mam still had him on a short leash for stealing the vicar's bike. Reverend Woolley admitted that his bicycle was returned cleaner and better running than before it was stolen which had surprised and pleased him. Mrs Nelson was deeply embarrassed by her son's theft from a local dignitary and she had wanted him punished so she was keeping him under close watch. Babs, that is, not the 'personage from the parsonage', as she called the vicar.

Not close enough however. Babs sneaked down to the bus stop and lobbed one of his home-made, delayed action, rotten eggs stink bombs in through a wide open downstairs window. Willie failed to notice it as he was just beginning to follow the conductor upstairs. The bomb cracked open as it landed on the metal floor but the foul smell did not begin until the bus was over a mile away, several minutes later. By this time Babs had returned to his place outside Meadows' store, just before his mother came out.

"You've got the job, David, start next Saturday," said Mrs Nelson proudly.

"Mam, can I go to the Saturday matinee to celebrate ?" asked the cunning boy, knowing that she would not allow him to go, and not really wanting to. He knew if he asked for much more than he wanted, his mother would give him some leeway. The first principle of bargaining was known to Babs; ask for much more than you want, as an opener, then you might get what you want when a compromise is offered.

"No but here's a shilling," she replied firmly. "Go and buy some spice. Ah, here's Mrs Wood. And bring me the change."
Babs skipped innocently across the small market place which was already busy with market stalls, traders and shoppers. He was soon out of sight of his mother who in any case was now distracted by chatting with her friend, Mary, the mother of the Wood boys.

If she could have seen him, she would have realised that he had ignored the sweet shop and ran straight up Cotton Street and turned left on to Church Street, then past the back of the Plaza cinema, where kids had to queue for the popular 'Saturday Matinee flicks'. This week's main feature was advertised as 'Zorro', with support from 'The Little Rascals' which were both favourites of his. Pietro Polczynski, who Babs met a few weeks before on his way to the tunnel entrance at Carr Vale, was offering his crisps to a girl as they passed the Caledonian Indoor Market Hall.

Irene Howard was equally as impressed by Pete's generosity as with his handsome features.

"Oh look," said Irene, looking into the crisps at the little blue bag containing the salt. "You haven't put the salt on yet."
As she was handing the crisp packet back to her fellow film fan, Babs ran past and snatched it out of their hands, to the amusement of everyone in the queue except Irene and Pete.

"Stop thief," shouted Pete in his best public voice.

"Oi, Babs Nelson, you thieving bugger," screamed Irene angrily, bringing "Tut tuts" of condemnation at her language from adult cinema staff and passers-by.

Within seconds Babs had sped through the churchyard and was at the bus stop at Town End just as a bus arrived that was going to Chesterfield, where the rest of the boys were clearly heading. He knew that they were on their way to the Midland Railway Station.

He got on, paid his fare downstairs then quickly ran up the stairs and slid as low as possible on the front seat to avoid being seen by anyone in the Market Place, his mum particularly. As the earlier bus carrying the gang stopped at the Gasworks at the bottom of Bolsover Hill, the people who got on were not aware of the impending assault on their senses from Babs' stink bomb. Nor were the group of miners who got on at the next stop at Bolsover Pit, having stayed late on the night shift. Nor the people who got on at Markham Lane End, a mixture of miners from Markham Pit and workers from the nearby Aroma Free Group.

There was always a pungent smell that was carried along with the LAFF, DAFFT and CFC workers from the Aroma Free Group, so when the home-made bomb started to release its ugly vapours the other passengers sniffed and looked down their noses at the AFG lot. The bus passed the next village of Duckmanton, then travelled to Arkwright Town, with its rows of terraced houses, built by and named after the industrialist and original owner of the village pit, Richard Arkwright.

The smell from the stink bomb soon spread and became unbearable on the lower deck, and the driver was asked to pull in to the bus stop near the village school where he leapt out, quickly followed by the conductor and the passengers. A Corona lorry that had been delivering 'pop' in the village came around the corner off Sutton Lane and the driver was astonished at the scene in front of him. He parked up and got out to help. Every person who had been on the bus had streaming eyes and was coughing and spluttering but no-one thought that this was a 'Babs special', except for the Olly Wood gang who all recognised their friend's evil work.

They looked around for him but were surprised when they could not find the suspected creator of this mayhem.

"I bet he threw it in through the window, probably in the Market Place, cos he couldn't come with us," said Mac, who did not even mention his name but they all knew it was him. After the Corona man and his van-boy gave everyone free drinks from his lorry he began to worry how he would explain all of this to his boss but he would cross that bridge when he came to it. Meanwhile the bus carrying Babs arrived at the bus stop and its driver and conductor both got out to enquire what had happened. Following a conference between the drivers and conductors, they decided that the passengers would all get on the second bus, where Babs sat on the front seat upstairs worrying that he was about to be rumbled. However, the conductor only allowed people upstairs until all the seats were filled and the gang had to stay downstairs, unaware that he was so close.

The bus sped through Calow and Hady without stopping, despite there being people at every stop putting their hand out in the normal way to request it to stop, then swearing angrily when it just sailed past them. And when it stopped for people to get off, no-one was allowed to get on and they soon arrived in Chesterfield.

As often happened, the bell was rung for the bus to stop opposite the Bridge Inn, just before Hollis Lane, some four hundred yards from the bus station on Vicar Lane. People struggled to get through the crowded lower deck and Babs saw that the gang were among the first to land on the pavement and they were able to file across the road before the bus set off again. He slid down into his seat to avoid being seen and watched them as they ran up Spa Lane towards Eyre Street and with the famous Crooked Spire up the hill to their left.

Babs got off the bus on Vicar Lane and took his time, unconcerned about his friends as he knew where they were going. He walked up town and looked in Swallows'

Department Store window. The boys by now were running and skipping down Corporation Street, past the bottom of the Civic Theatre, then the dingy little tobacconists and alongside the big, once red, now black with smoke from the trains, brick wall opposite the Station Hotel. As they reached the railway station itself, Olly told them all to slow down and to avoid attracting attention by splitting into two groups of three until they were safely on the platform. Olly queued for the first of the Ticket Office windows while Mac went to the queue farthest away and the rest spread amongst other travellers in the building to try and look as innocent and inconspicuous as possible.

Since the recent closure of the nearby Central Station to passenger traffic, the Midland Station was now much busier so it was easier to hide on a busy Saturday morning. Unless someone recognised any of them, that is.

"Neville Newton Heath !" shouted a loud, high pitched voice when its owner spotted Newt across the ticket hall. Everyone in the place turned to look, first towards the origin of the shout, then searching for its target who pulled on a balaclava and hid in the crowd.

"Hannah Stubley-Stanhope, shouting in a public place is embarrassing and unladylike," said Mrs Phillipps, her Guide Group Leader, quietly but forcefully. "I am shocked at you. Remember your standards, you girls. Proceed to the platform, gracefully please, Hannah."

Newt had immediately ducked amongst a group of people who were on their way out of the station and quickly found his way outside to avoid being identified by anyone else. The other boys all took similar evasive action and spread out. Strange to see six boys wearing knitted grey balaclavas in July but they had brought them just in case they met anyone they knew. It proved unnecessary as Mrs Phillipps led her Girl Guide Troop through the ticket barrier and onto Platform One, to await their train taking them camping in the Peak District. Balaclavas were removed when the gang saw the girl guides had gone.

With a nod from Mac they all went outside to the front of the station to join Newt. When they reached their friend there was a tension in the air and they were alert and cautious. A flash of light suddenly swept across Olly's face and he dropped to the floor.

"Get down everybody," he said urgently and each one followed suit and sat on the ground behind a parked car as if they were resting there.

"Our Balsa, you look the most different to normal. Stand up and go quickly into the station then come back out with a family or other people and pretend to talk to them as if you're going up town with them. Have a gander across towards that Land Rover that looks like the one Stubley-Stanhope drives. Somebody's stood behind it with binoculars either watching the station or watching us."

"Yes sir, Sergeant Stryker," came the reply. "Private First Class, Balsa Wood, advancing on The Sands of Iwo Jima. Search and deeeestroy, Sir."

He crawled back into the station, to the amusement of the rest of the boys and all the other passengers. Once inside, he stood up and saw a family coming through the barrier off the platform. He accompanied them outside and joined in conversation with their boy, about the same age as himself, as they headed towards the Station Hotel and Corporation Street.

"Ay up Jack, I didn't realise it was you. Want a bubbly ?" asked Balsa, offering a paper bag containing the pink bubblies so hated by adults.

"Yeah !" said John William Bradshaw, cheeky as ever, taking three to Barry's disgust. "Thanks Balsa, what are you doing here ? I didn't know it was you. Was that the others from the gang, sat outside the station ?"

"Yeah, we're going to ...," began Balsa but realised he was revealing the gang's secret. "Err, we're going to trainspotting," he added, rescuing himself. "Anyway, are these your family ?"

"Noooo, " replied Jack, laughing. "I just latched on to them to avoid looking as though I'm on my own, like you do, same as you did, in fact."

Balsa had been chewing his pink bubbly and blew an enormous bubble which burst all over his face in apparent surprise at Jack's words. He stopped, unable to see through the disgusting stuff, as his mam called it, and said cheerio and waved goodbye to his friend. Jack could not understand exactly what Balsa had said but he got the general idea, said goodbye and turned and continued up town.

The bubbly-plastered boy peeled the pink mess from his face as he walked back towards the gang. As he passed the Station Hotel he saw, on the other side of the road, Hector Stubley-Stanhope peering out of the Land Rover's window, watching the train station, while William "Wild Bill" Hitchcock leaned on the front of the vehicle and aimed a rifle towards the gang. The pair then appeared to turn and look directly at Balsa just as several showers of stones came up and over the wall behind them that stood above the court and police buildings. The two men jumped into their vehicle and drove off down Crow Lane while Balsa took the opportunity to run back to the station. He waved to the others to follow him inside and they dashed in, curious to find out what was happening, having witnessed the urgent departure.

"It was Wild Bill and S-S but they've scarpered now," said Balsa, breathless from his sprint. "They had a gun that Wild Bill seemed to be aiming at you lot but something scared em off."

"Come on, let's get on the platform," suggested Mac. "Our train's due soon and we can talk about this some more when we're safely sat down. Two groups again."

They duly separated into two teams of three, in which they went through the barrier a minute apart. Olly led his group up and over the footbridge to Platform Two. When he saw that the first group had reached the platform, Mac led his group after them. A uniformed Station Guard appeared, with buttons that shone like mirrors, a similarly shiny pocket watch on a chain and a moustache like Adolf Hitler's. He grabbed Olly by the collar.

"Off my platform, I don't allow trainspotters. This is a railway, not a holiday." he growled.

"Hey, get off," said Olly, standing firm. "We're not trainspotters, we've got tickets for the next train."

He shoved them in front of the eyes of the bullying Guard who was clearly irritated by his very public mistake but was saved any further embarrassment by the toots and billowing smoke from the approaching train, The Cornishman, pulled by Royal Scot Class Engine, 'Sherwood Forester'.

"It's a Royal Scot," shouted the boys, further angering Mr Hitler-Guard.

As the train came to a stop beside Platform Two, Willie, as instructed, slipped through the door before people had even got off and he dashed along the side corridor looking for an empty compartment, which he soon found. He threw his pullover, a bag of sweets, an old newspaper and his haversack on to four of the six seats and sat on the sixth by the window. Several people came and opened the door of the compartment but withdrew awkwardly when the boy told them his parents had taken his three brothers to the toilet. Olly and Mac climbed the steps on to the train and both turned and looked each way along the platform. Towards the back of the train someone caught their eye, getting on with a last minute dash to the rear carriages.

"It feels like we're being watched and followed, Mac. Do you think that was Wild Bill ?"

"I'm not sure, I didn't get a proper view of them," said Mac. "First that outside the station, now this, it all seems a bit strange, doesn't it ? Why's he following us ? "

The two older boys looked serious as they arrived in the compartment won by Willie and the others knew something was wrong.

"We don't know for sure and we don't know why," announced

Mac. "But someone seems to have rushed on to the train at the last minute. It could have been Wild Bill. We aren't sure."
A discussion followed and it was decided that two of them would search the train when it went through Clay Cross tunnel. A few lights always came on for tunnels. Balsa and Newt stood ready to go along the corridor and the rest of the gang hung out of the corridor windows looking for the tunnel's approach. In the opposite direction, towards the rear of the train, another head was poking out of a corridor window, shouting.
"OLLYYYYYY, MAAAAAAC, EVERYBODYYYY !"
"He's seen us, get in," said Balsa, the only one with his head still inside but he had heard the shouts.
They all quickly pulled their heads back through the windows.
"Hang on, that can't be Wild Bill. He wouldn't shout to us like that," said Mac. "And anyway that was a younger voice than his."
They put their heads out again and looked from their windows to the back of the train.
"It isn't Wild Bill Hitchcock," shouted Olly excitedly. "It's Babs."
They all pulled their heads back in just in time as the train entered the tunnel, and they ran along the corridor to meet their friend who they met coming the other way and returned to their compartment with him. The buzz of mischief and excitement that always seemed to follow Babs was evident again.
"How did you manage to persuade your mam to let you come, Babs ?" asked Olly.
"She doesn't know," laughed the rascal. "I sneaked away from her in the Market Place, threw a delayed action stink bomb through an open window on to your bus and caught the next one, the one that you lot got on at Arkwright."
"We knew it was you ! Why didn't you get off the bus with us on Hollis Lane ?" said Mac.
"Well, I knew you were going to the station and I wanted to

surprise you so I went to look in Swallows' window first." Everyone roared with laughter at the thought of Babs going window shopping.

"So what did you do then Babs, did you just go down to the station and get a ticket?" asked Olly, moving on the questions.

"I walked through the Crooked Spire churchyard, then down Tapton Lane. Then, as I came across Malkin Street, I saw Balsa talking to Jack Bradshaw further up Corporation Street," he said.

"I didn't know where you lot were but I saw Wild Bill aiming a gun towards the station and S-S watching you with binocs. I went on to Brimington Road and round the back of the police station so they wouldn't see me. Then I stood behind the car park wall and threw a shower of stink bombs and stones over the wall which made them swear and scarper dead quick."

They all laughed again about Babs' famous evil-smelling, home-made stink bombs.

"Then I ran back round on to Malkin Street and across to the station but, instead of going into the ticket hall, I just went through a gate on to the platform and came over the footbridge as the train arrived. I haven't got a ticket."

The laughing stopped as Babs' words sank in. He hadn't got a ticket. Balsa stood in the open doorway of their compartment and they all heard the dreaded words from along the corridor spoken loud and clear.

"Tickets please," announced the Ticket Inspector to the next compartment.

"Quick Babs," said Olly. "Lie down along the seats. Right everybody, jumpers, haversacks, that newspaper, anything we can cover him up with, then the three biggest sit down and hide him. Me, our Balsa and Mac, you sit by the door with all the tickets. Newt, get that book out and start reading to us again, that '4ft 8½ And All That', history of railways book [vi] you've got." This was a pre-print edition of the book, given to him by the Baron.

They got into position and Newt took out his book and began reading aloud just as the Ticket Inspector opened the door and announced his usual 'Tickets please' request. Mac handed them to him and everyone focussed on Newt as he read, even the ticket man.

"What is the Englishman able to do which lesser breeds find impossible, apart from watching cricket matches? Why, of course, he can laugh at himself! Though I must warn anyone outside the pale that it is permitted for him to laugh at us!" The Inspector punched the tickets, smiled and closed the door and left to sighs of relief.

"Keep going Newt, in case he can hear us from next door," whispered Olly. "And just stay there a bit, Babs."

"Well now, Railways," continued Newt theatrically. "Those pieces of steel which snake over the green island in ordered parallels, and only occasionally go mad and get knotted up at places like Clapham. They are our national nerves, and if you have nerves, you must expect headaches."

They heard the ticket man leave the next door compartment and he went into the next carriage whistling Colonel Bogey's March. A very quiet rendition followed from the boys of their favourite version of this tune -

"Hitler has only got one ball, Göring has two but very small. Himmler has something sim'lar, but poor old Goebbels has no balls at all"

Giggsy was sent to check that he had definitely gone and soon returned nodding and smiling. Babs was allowed up from his hiding place.

"What I'd like to know is how that Jack Bradshaw gets his hair to stand up like that," said Babs, to hoots of laughter and agreement.

The subject of Jack's hair and whether it stuck up naturally or with the use of a stiffening agent occupied them until their train pulled in to Birmingham New Street, with speculation ranging from Brylcreem (Newt) through sugar and water (Mac) to electric shock treatment (Babs). The more pressing matter to occupy them was the issue of a ticket for the ticketless one among them. However, Newt suddenly remembered that he had his James Bond book and spy kit in his haversack and this included a passport forgery set. He used this to peel apart his own ticket and duplicated both blank sides to create a barely passable forgery.

They had expected that getting past the barrier and out of the station at Dudley would be the trickiest moments of the journey.

In fact, it proved relatively easy for the resourceful gang, thanks to Newt's forgery kit and Babs and his stink bombs creating a distraction that saw all the passengers disembarking from the train whisked through and out of the station. Olly and Mac led them out on to Station Drive and curbed their desire to laugh in case anyone noticed and became suspicious of their guilt.

Two young men in dark suits followed them out of the station and one of them smiled and addressed the boys.

"That was a good trick you lot played. Was it just for fun or don't you have tickets ?"

All seven of them stood paralysed and unable to speak, not just since they appeared to have been found out, but also because they had never seen a black man in real life.

"It's ok boys, don't worry, you're not in trouble, we aren't the police. We're just on our way to our church. Are you having a day out ?"

"Yes," replied Mac taking charge. "We're going to the zoo. Can you tell us the way please ?"

"You could get a train from the Lower Level Station over there," replied the elder of the two. "Or it's about a fifteen minutes walk, in which case, turn right at the end of this street and it's signposted look. Ah, here comes my mum and my little brother, Lenworth. Hello mum, we're just giving these boys directions to the zoo."

"Thanks very much," said Mac, which was echoed by his

friends. "Yeah, thanks mate."

"Goodbye, Mrs ... err," added Mac politely.

"Mrs Henry," replied the lady, smiling graciously, which was similarly followed by the three boys in her charge as they all waved goodbye and were gone.

11
THE STING

The gang followed their new friends' directions and the signs pointing towards 'Zoo' and 'Dudley Canal'. There was excitement about the boys they had just met with their mother. "Why do people make it sound as though there's something bad or dangerous about blacks, when really those we've just met are nicer than the people that call them bad ?" asked Newt, conscious that his own father sometimes made such cruel remarks, while his mother always said you should treat people as you found them.
"I think it's just that folk have never met them, so they just repeat things they've heard, like we've done before, in truth. They were really helpful people, seeing as we're the foreigners to Dudley and needed help," observed Mac, to which the others nodded their agreement.
This serious discussion occupied them for several minutes, until they realised that they were now walking on a towpath beside the canal, the other side of which were the railway lines.
"Have we come the wrong way, do you think, Mac ?" asked Olly, when he nearly walked into the water, prompting Willie, Babs and Giggsy to sit down beside the canal and take off their haversacks while the others decided whether they had taken a wrong turning.
Willie, as usual ten yards behind the next last, saw that an ants' nest appeared to be in the canal bank and proceeded to kick at it to dislodge and send it in to the water. However, immediately

beneath where the ants' home had been, a wasps' nest was also built and the wasps were most unhappy with the destroyer of their own and their ant hosts' nests. Several thousand angry female worker wasps took to the air and attacked the unsuspecting boy, covering his whole body in painful stings. Willie leapt to his feet screaming loudly and dived headlong into the water, to the shock of both the wasps and the gang. There was also another person who was both shocked and angry and he walked quickly along the same side as the rest of the boys from the West Bromwich direction of the canal.

"Hey you lot, what the hell do you think you're playing at and what's that kid doing in the canal ? We're fishing here for fish, not sprats , brats or prats like you."

"Hey mister," shouted Willie, as he pulled himself out of the water on to the other bank. "Watch out, there's a wasps' nest in the bank near my haversack. That's why I jumped in the water cause they all ganged up on me and stung me."

"Don't be stupid sonny, who do you think you're kidding ?" replied the fisherman but he approached the haversack tentatively and gave it a tap with his toe-end. He then wished he hadn't gone anywhere near it as, once again, thousands of wasps appeared from nowhere and the fisherman was also covered in stings. He took the only course open to him and, like Willie, dived into the murky canal. Unlike the youngster however, the effects of the stings and the cold water hit him like a heavyweight boxer and when he came to the surface he uttered a weak cry for help as he struggled to stay afloat.

"Come on everybody. Will, get ready to grab hold of him when we get him to the bank," shouted Olly, throwing off his haversack and kicking off his shoes as he ran back along the towpath.

As Mac was taking off his things he shouted further instructions.

"Willie, go up that banking and shout for help from the station. Babs you go down this banking and shout for help from those houses. Giggsy, go back round to the station so you can bring help back. There was a policeman outside."

"Why have I got so many things to do when everybody else gets just one thing?" grumbled Willie as he turned and ran up the banking. He climbed on to the wall, waving his arms about and shouting.

"Help, Help. We've all been stung by wasps and a man's jumped in the canal and might have drowned. Heeeeellllllpppppp !!"

The wet and bedraggled boy had not been affected by the stings as badly as the fisherman but his appearance certainly attracted the attention of the stunned onlookers, especially when he slipped off the wall and rolled back down the banking. He came to a stop just before the canal bank and luckily avoided rolling into the water.

Balsa, Newt, then Mac followed Olly and dived into the canal and they too got stung before entering the water, though not as much as Willie and the fisherman.

Olly reached him first, just as he was going down and dragged him back up to the surface with some difficulty as he had gone limp and heavy. The others arrived in quick succession and the four of them managed to get him to the canal bank adjacent to the railway lines. Willie grabbed his collar and helped to hold him steady.

Mac and Olly climbed out on to the towpath and, as Balsa and Newt pushed the man as far out of the water as possible, he was pulled up and out by his clothes. Once all four boys were on the bank they carried the unconscious fisherman fifty yards away from the danger of the wasps and laid him on his side in the recovery position. Passengers, railwaymen, guards, the station master, taxi drivers, two police officers and an ice cream man jumped off the platform, dashed across the track and while a nurse who had been travelling to Wolverhampton tended to the highly-stung Willie, the others gathered around the four boys and the prone fisherman.

"Move back please, I'm a doctor," said another passenger who knelt down by the man and examined him. He found that the man was alive and commented that he had helpfully been put in the recovery position by the boys.

Giggsy ran back round to the railway station but everyone seemed to have disappeared, including the policeman. The only person around was a taxi driver sat in his cab peering dreamily from his open window.

"Where is everyone ? It's an emergency," said the boy.

"You're out of luck," replied the man. "There's been some kind of accident the other side of the tracks, a load of kids have been hurt."

"Yes, I'm one of them. We've all been stung by killer wasps," he exaggerated, showing the stings on his arms and neck. "They've sent me round to find the policeman and send for an ambulance. Have you got a radio in your taxi ?"

"Yes, I'll radio my base and get them to send for it."

The man duly performed the task and passed on the message, emphasizing the killer wasps, and as he finished he saw a single wasp on his windscreen. He frantically wound up his window, then drove quickly away from Station Drive and away into town to the bewilderment of Giggsy who stood open mouthed and hands on hips.

Meanwhile, Babs ran down the steep banking towards the houses on the opposite side of the canal to the railway and was followed by a swarm of wasps. He ran so fast to escape them that when he reached the bottom of the slope he could not stop and crashed through a hedge and into the garden of the first house. There, a large Alsatian guard dog called Fritz had been dozing in the shade of the privet bushes. The shocked and frightened Fritz whimpered and backed away from the invader, before slinking to his large kennel beside the house. Unfortunately the dog-house was already occupied by the large, fluffy family cat, Muffin, who would prove to be a much better guard dog than the cowardly Fritz.

Muffin screamed, howled, spat and swiped sharp claws at the luckless dog and the noise brought Mr and Mrs Bricknell out of the house from their cups of tea.

"Bloody hell, Muffy," shouted Mrs Bricknell.

"Bloody hell, Muffy," mimicked the family's parrot, Polynesia Pasionaria, known as Polly.

When they saw the dazed Babs struggling to his feet the puzzled couple wondered what the hell had happened here.

"Are you alright young man ?" enquired Mr Bricknell.

"And what exactly are you doing in our garden ?" added his wife.

"I'm sorry," struggled Babs. "I'm looking for help cos we've been attacked by killer wasps on the towpath and everybody's jumping into the canal to get away from them and a man might have drowned and they've chased me and I crashed through your hedge running down the slope from the canal and they've stopped on the other side of your hedge and ..."

Mr Bricknell dragged his wife and Babs away from the hedge on hearing this news.

"You go in the house dear and close the windows and doors. Come on son, we'll go a different way to avoid your wasps," he said.

"Be careful John," his wife said.

"Be careful John," repeated the parrot.

"Oh bloody shut up Polly," said June angrily.

"Oh bloody shut up Polly, haw, haw, haw," said Polly, laughing.

As they ran past the end of the hedge through which Babs had crashed, they both glanced around warily but they ran too fast to see anything. They safely reached the canal side and Mr Bricknell shouted across to the group on the other side.

"Anything I can do ? The boy came for help."

"Go down to the road-side by the bridge and wait there and make sure no-one comes up," shouted one of the policemen.

"And you, young man, can you back up a bit to the next bridge and stop anyone coming that way."

The two of them did as they were told and the situation began to be brought under control as shortly, two ambulances arrived and half the local police force, it appeared.

The boys were all made to go to hospital, very much against their wishes, as they saw it as a danger to their staying together. When they arrived at Emergency, Olly and Mac did all the talking and they refused to be split up for their stings to be treated. Thus, seven boys crowded into one cubicle and were made to undress so that two nurses could paint their bodies blue which they said would reduce any pain. Mac told them all to say the pain had gone.

"Forget their treatment," he said. "I know how to get rid of the pain. We need to borrow a bit of cotton wool and get some vinegar when we go out."

They were all given gowns to wear while their clothes dried and they took every opportunity to grab a handful of cotton wool and stuff it in the pockets. Olly asked if his train ticket, which had been in his jeans pocket, remained intact. It was, but it was now barely legible.

"Don't worry about your tickets," said a pretty nurse. "You've all become heroes. There's a reporter from the Express and Star waiting to interview you and take your photographs. The man whose life you saved is the brother-in-law of the Police Inspector who's also waiting to thank you," she continued. "Inspector, you can come in now," she called.

A fearsome looking brute of a man entered the room and scared the boys half to death.

"Don't worry, boys," he said reassuringly. "I've only popped in to thank you for your public spirited display of bravery by visitors to our town willing to risk their own lives to save the life of someone they don't even know. Invariably these days we see young people being castigated and vilified as Teddy Boys and delinquents so it is indeed refreshing to find young men who are deserving of public thanks. I thank you on behalf of the people of Dudley."

"Castigated ? Isn't that when they take your b...," began Willie, only to be interrupted.

"That's right William," cut in Mac. "They take bad behaviour and criticise and castigate it."

Willie looked suitably puzzled but kept this to himself as the Inspector smiled appreciatively.

"Now then, I heard that your train tickets have been damaged or lost in the commotion so we'll fix you up with new ones. My brother-in-law who you rescued is going to be all right but is resting now and cannot speak properly, so you'll be unable to see him at the moment and be thanked personally by him."

"Thank goodness for that," whispered Olly to Mac.

Eventually, the boys were given their dried clothes and a lift to the station in a 'black maria' police van, to be provided with new tickets, which solved a problem for Babs, who had never had one in the first place. Three people from the Wolverhampton Express and Star followed them as though they were pop stars. They were photographed as a group on the station but only the cautious Mac and Olly would be interviewed and they made the others keep quiet and say nothing. They decided to forget the vinegar and the Zoo and leave town on the next train, just in case the Inspector's brother-in-law regained his powers of speech while they were still there. It was a mostly uneventful journey home, not counting the uproar when they boarded the train.

They got funny looks from everyone that saw them and comments about them being 'The Bumblies' from Michael Bentine's television programme of that name about three little aliens from the planet Bumble, all due to their similar blue appearance. Some passengers left the carriages in panic and waited for another train. They did not wash it off however, since it ensured that people kept away from them so that they had a compartment to themselves and also because the stings that they had all received still caused some irritation and pain.

Babs sat smugly clutching his ticket, obtained under false pretences, as he had pretended that he had lost his ticket in the canal. He, along with Willie, who was both the youngest and the most stung, fell asleep after their train left Birmingham. Olly and Mac talked on the way back home of whether their 'Dudley Day Out' would come back to haunt them and they decided they should all swear to secrecy over their experience. Babs sleepily sucked his thumb and, unwittingly, his ticket as well, so that when he awoke as the train pulled in to Derby Midland Station, his mouth was dry from the bits of cardboard from his ticket and his lips were black from the ink off the print.

When the ticket inspector came round, the situation was easily explained however and he could just make out that the ticket being sucked by Babs appeared genuine. The man accepted the story as he did not want to get too close to this bunch of blue children who were covered in spots. He told his colleagues to avoid them too.

They alighted from the train at Chesterfield and people walked as far away from them as possible. Their journey up town was the same and they discussed whether they would even be allowed on the Corporation bus to go home to Hillstown. Fortunately, they knew the bus driver although their explanation of their appearance was not accepted by everyone on board. Some passengers got off to wait for the next bus and the conductor would not approach them to take their fares and issue tickets.

The Inspector got on at Calow and said, "Tickets please." He too would not approach them and instead tried to eject them from the bus but other passengers protested that they had offered to pay so they were allowed to stay on.

"Alright then," conceded the Inspector. "But you'll have to go upstairs and be quantified in strict desolation or whatever it is and send any other passengers back down here to safety."

"Sorry boys, I think he means quarantined in strict isolation," said a smiling fellow passenger.

When they went up to the top deck, the dozen or so passengers up there, all smokers belching out their smoke, stubbed out their cigarettes and dashed down the stairs in fright, as the boys opened all the windows to get rid of the clouds of cigarette smoke.

"They say every cloud has a silver lining," laughed Babs. "We get stung and a free bus ride."

"And 'Do unto others as you would have them do unto you', mam says," suggested Newt.

"What about 'There's some good in everybody' as well? That's grandma's usual," said Mac.

"Our mam says 'Waste not, want not' and 'Share and share alike' to us," offered Balsa.

"There's 'As you reap, you sow'. Mam's always saying that to me and our Bill," said Babs.

"We get that one a lot as well but shouldn't it be 'As you sow, you reap', Babs?" queried Mac. They all snorted at this but stopped as Will cleared his throat to speak.

"An apple a day ...," He was the only one that realised they had arrived at Hillstown and was first off the bus.

As the bus had approached Hillstown crossroads the passengers on the lower deck rushed to alight and get away from the scary looking Olly Wood Gang. Any new passengers that had boarded after the boys were banished to their 'strict desolation' of the top deck were warned about the highly contagious, foaming at the mouth, rabid dogs upstairs. Even the bus driver, conductor and inspector got off the bus and quickly moved a safe distance away, where they watched the boys cross the road and walk up Mansfield Road towards their homes.

"We'll have to remember this, I think," said Olly. "We can paint spots on our skin and people will leave us alone. What do you reckon, Mac? Think it would stop us ever getting into trouble again?"

"Nah," laughed Mac. "We'd still get the blame for everything but they'd just say 'a plague on both your houses', like whatsisname in Romeo and Juliet. Portfolio, or someone, it was."

"Was it Domino ? He would have had spots like us," replied Olly, to groans from everyone.

When they reached Pleasant Avenue they stopped abruptly, as one, on seeing the police car outside Babs' house.

"It must be serious Babs," said Olly. "What have you done that's so bad to bring them out in the car ?"

"Which day ?" Babs laughed.

They cautiously walked along the avenue and saw Constable Stagg came down Babs' garden path.

"Hello boys, we were wondering where you were. Your house appears to have been broken into, David, so we may need to interview all of you as to your movements today."

"Have they taken anything, do you know, Staggers ?" asked Babs, using their name for him.

"We're not sure yet," answered the young policeman. "You can perhaps assist us with that."

"Let's hope they didn't steal your bike, eh Babs," said Olly mischievously and they all followed the officer up the garden path.

As they entered the house they could see Babs' family sitting in the living room, while Sergeant Pyewright and another man, not in a uniform but built like the proverbial brick outbuilding, appeared to be interrogating them, or at least addressing them.

"The suspects are back, Detective Sergeant Poppleton. Shall I bring them in ?" said Stagg.

Hearing themselves described as suspects, the seven boys ran back outside and made off in all directions, each one shouting a different location: "Blue Banks", "Gang Lane", "Parks", "Hornscroft", "Sherwood Lodge", "Clay Hole", "Back Hills". This was not a random selection of suggestions but a means to confuse pursuers in such circumstances. Each of them had two alternative destinations they could shout but only Olly's were the real options so the others all listened for "Parks" or "Mill Field".

Three ran down the garden, Willie and Giggsy squeezing through the hedge and Newt hurdling it, into the corn field opposite.

The other four went back along the front garden path and split into two's on Pleasant Avenue, one pair turning left, another pair turning right then left on to Castle Green. Within minutes all seven were gathered at the top of the 'Parks', a large steep field used by Tommy Turner of Elm's Farm at Palterton for sheep and cattle grazing.

"What do you think, Mac ?" began Olly. "Do you think we're going to have to go back ?"

"Definitely," said his friend, without hesitation. "We don't know what we're suspected of but we haven't done anything wrong. Well, like Babs said, not today. Well, not much."

"All in favour ?" asked Mac and, without having a vote, they set off back to Babs' house and agreed that they would explain that they realised that they had lost Newt's trainspotting book and had left quickly to find it. Willie was also given some lines to say if prompted. They walked down Babs' garden path and as they filed past the kitchen window, the police and the Nelson family did a double-take at the sight of the gang returning. Both family and constabulary shrunk away when the boys came in bearing their wasp stings and blue skin.

Newt explained about the loss of a book as he'd got off the bus and waved his 'British Railways Combined Volume 1961' to show that they'd found it.

"Oh, I've got that that one and I'd hate to lose it," said Stagg. Hearing the two sergeants tutting, he added, "But we have more serious issues to address. Err, ton to you DS Poppleover, sir. Oops, I mean over to you DS Poppleton, sorry sir," apologised the blushing officer.

"Hello boys," said the smiling, brick outbuilding. "Did you

spend the day in Chesterfield?"

"Why are you interested in what we did today if Babs' house was broken into?" asked Mac. "We'd never do anything like that and Babs doesn't need to, seeing as he lives here."

"I'm tired," complained Willie on cue, when pinched. "I haven't eaten all day with doing that stupid train-stopping or whatever it's called. I want to go home." He started to cry convincingly.

"You should perhaps all go home and get some rest and we'll talk to you tomorrow," said the man in charge, DS Poppleton, who clearly had no desire to remain close to the gang that everyone thought looked highly contagious and blue with something.

"See yer, Babs," they all chorused as they filed out of the kitchen. The boy himself had sneaked out when Willie began his speech and was soon hiding behind Alex 'Bow' Evill's garden wall at the bottom end of Castle Green. Babs felt a warm glow when he saw his friends walking towards their homes on Castle Green, only to realise that this was mainly due to the Evill's two dogs, Hector and Lysander, having cocked their legs and peeing on him as he lay behind the wall.

Sergeant Pyewright was irritated at being sent by DS Poppleton to interview the Olly Wood Gang at 8 o'clock on a Sunday morning about the theft of Babs Nelson's socks and pants. "They have to be guilty of something, they're always guilty of something," said Pyewright. "We'll establish their movements for yesterday, Stagg and check their alibis," he added.

"Sarge, aren't we supposed to be investigating a theft of clothes from the Nelson house?" queried Stagg. "Shouldn't we keep open minds until a lead and some evidence are found?"

"Listen laddie," spat his superior. "This so-called theft is just a distraction from some crime they've committed, a red haddock. Your mind is so open, the wind is blowing away any sense you might have once had." He laughed loudly at his own humour.

"Red herring, sarge, not red haddock, with respect sir," corrected Constable Stagg, as they both climbed out of the car in front of 4, Castle Green, the home of the Wood family. Next door at Number 2, Mac was on his bed in the front bedroom, reading his comic, The Victor. Hearing the car's arrival, followed by the policemen's voices he knelt on the bed and spied them from behind the curtains. He leapt off the bed and ran along the landing and burst through the bathroom door where he found his brother Newt sat on the toilet reading the Sunday Mirror sports pages, minding his own business before going to church.

"Oi, get out," complained Newt, suit trousers round his ankles, jacket hung on the airing-cupboard door handle.

"Quick," urged Mac, opening the bathroom window to climb out on to the flat roof of the outbuildings. "Pyewright and Stagg are at Olly's front door. Hurry up !"

He jumped through the window and half-shouted, half-whispered to Barry Wood next door, who was sat on the outside toilet doorstep whittling a stick.

"Cops are knocking at your front door, Balsa. Get the others so we can escape across the gardens onto Mansfield Road."

"Too late, I think," said his friend. "Constable Stagg's stood by your dustbin waiting for us, look.."

Mac peered over the end of the outhouses and met the smiling gaze of the constable.

"Alright, Staggers," said Mac ruefully as he climbed down on to the dustbin and jumped to the ground.

"Hello Malcolm, can we get you all together please so that me and Sergeant Pyewright can interview you about yesterday's events," said the constable, as Mac's mother came out of the back door to see what was going on, having heard the policeman's comment to her son.

"What do you mean, sonny, interview them about yesterday's events ?" said Mrs Heath sharply. "And it's 'Sergeant Pyewright and I', not 'me and Sergeant Pyewright', young man and you need a haircut. You're supposed to set these boys a good example and please don't slouch and pull a face when I comment on your poor standards. You're worse than my boys."

The young officer stood to attention and blushed guiltily. He hoped to be saved any more embarrassment by the arrival of Sergeant Pyewright at the Woods' back door, having walked angrily around from the front of the house as no-one had answered his knocking.

"You're absolutely correct, Mrs Heath, my constable is slovenly in his dress, his speech and his haircut. Young people eh ? May we come in and talk to your boys, with you present of course and would you mind if we talked to the four Wood brothers and that David Nelson at the same time ? They may know of someone who might have a grudge against them that led to the strange break-in at young Nelson's house."

Stagg shook his head at this change of tune.

"Of course, Sergeant Pyewright, just tramp through the house with the cast of Ben Hur, why don't you but if you want a list of people who might have a grudge against them, I just hope you've got a blooming big notebook that's all," said the lady of the house sarcastically. "Barry, get your brothers please and everybody in our front room. Sergeant, get your constipated constable there to fetch Babs, I mean David, Nelson. Let's get this over with."

Stagg did not wait to be told but simply scuttled around the outbuildings and ran up to Pleasant Avenue to bring back Babs. The boy was in the middle of eating a large bacon sandwich in two slices of bread as thick as doorsteps and washing it down with a mug of tea the size of a bucket. Nevertheless he accompanied the constable back to the Heath household but brought his bacon buttie and bucket of tea with him. Everyone else was there when Stagg and Babs arrived and the boy was ushered to a dining chair by the door, while the other six squeezed into the three-seat settee, Sergeant

Pyewright occupying one armchair and Mrs Heath the other. "David Nelson, you can't eat bacon butties with ketchup while juggling a mug of tea in my front room. Go in the back and get a plate and finish eating in there," said Mrs Heath in a firm but kind manner, to smirks from the others, jealous of his doorstep bacon sandwich. Blushing, Babs did as he was told but returned within a couple of minutes, having quickly finished off his breakfast although ketchup and crumbs were evident on his face and shirt.

"Can we make a start then please ?" said Sergeant Pyewright. "So that we don't take up too much of Mrs Heath's valuable time. Stagg here will make notes if no-one minds that. Ian ?"

"No sarge, I don't mind," said the constable.

"I wasn't asking you if you minded, you incompetent nincompoop. I was asking you to commence making notes, in your notebook," replied Pyewright through gritted teeth. Constable Stagg frantically patted his hands over all his pockets before he eventually found his notebook and quickly realised he had no pencil or pen.

With everyone's laughing eyes on him, he cleared his throat and pulled a face as if expecting to be hit over the head, and said, "Sergeant Pyewright, sir, could I borrow something to write with please ? I appear to have lost my pencil."

The room erupted in uncontrollable mirth from all present barring the two policemen. The red-faced-with-anger sergeant took his own pencil from his top pocket and rapped his underling over the knuckles with it, only to see a large piece of lead fall out of the sharpened end, producing even more hilarity from their audience.

Mrs Heath got up from her chair and stood in front of the fireplace requiring silence. She walked to a small writing desk in the corner of the room, opened the drawer and pointed Stagg to the pens and pencils inside. He gratefully chose one and indicated his readiness.

"Thank you, Mrs Heath," said the constable and the sergeant

together, to Pyewright's irritation.

"If I may begin by saying that we are investigating a burglary at number 23, Pleasant Avenue, Hillstown yesterday. First, can I ask you boys if you know of anyone who might have a grudge against any of you that would make them want to steal some of David's socks, underpants and stuff from his chemistry set?"

"There'd be plenty of people with a grudge against us but they'd have to be mad or wear a mask to go anywhere near his underpants and socks or any of those other things of Babs'," said Mac. "I haven't got a clue about this." The others all nodded agreement.

"Next, David, a chemistry set isn't the sort of thing many boys play with. Why do you have one?" read Pyewright from a prepared list of questions.

"It was a Christmas present from a relative," replied Babs. "I wanted a bike really but you don't always get what you ask for, Sergeant Pyewipe. Sorry, I mean Pyewright, sir."

"Everyone will know that you have socks and underpants David but how many people will know that you possess a chemistry set?" recited the questioner from his list.

"Well let's see," said Babs thoughtfully. "There's me mam and dad, me older brother and sister, these lot and, I suppose, their mams and dads. Then there's me Auntie Betty who bought it for me. Who else?"

Stagg was furiously writing down details of the people concerned at the same time as adding them to five-bar gates to count the numbers. The boys all scratched their faces trying to think of other people that could possibly know.

"What about The Pope, doesn't he know as well?" suggested Newt.

"Yeah, The Pope knows," agreed Babs. "Next door's cats, they know. They were sat on the fence when I blew the roof off the shed that time and I think the neighbours either side must know cos they came and complained about the explosion once the smoke cleared. And Mart Ward knows cos he was just

going out on his bike and the bang made him fall off it."
"Irene and Annie know as well, don't they Babs ?" mused Olly.
"We told them at Hardwick."
"Yeah and Jessie James," added Babs.
This latest name proved too much for Sergeant Pyewright.
"Look, stop messing about laddie, we've heard The Pope, next door's cats and now Jessie Bloody James. Who next ?"
Mrs Heath stood up menacingly and everyone fell quiet.
"Sergeant, if you think you can swear in my house you've got another think coming. You can ask your questions and write down the boys' answers, then go and solve this crime and leave them alone. They've done nothing wrong, unlike you with your bad language."
"Yes, I'm really sorry about that," said Pyewright, trying to rescue the situation. "I'm just anxious to catch the criminals. Alright boys, where did you go yesterday and who might have known where you were going and take advantage of your absence ?"
They knew that they would be asked this question so everyone had practised the answer. Olly looked around as if to ask if he should answer.
"Go ahead then," said Pyewright.
"Obviously, lots of people knew we were going to Chesterfield cos we'd told our mams and dads, we told Irene, Ann and Jessie. Trapdoor knew as well cos we asked him to come but he wanted a lie-in with it being the first day of the holidays. The Pope knew, that's Holness The Pope. We call him 'He's Holness The Pope', don't we ? Like 'His Holiness The Pope', get it ? Anyway, The Pope couldn't come either cos he's got cricket stuff and he has to do jobs around the farm for his dad as well. He works hard, doesn't he ? Who else ? I heard Newt telling Mr Hempsall on Thursday night when he came round with his cart selling vegetables, didn't you Newt ? And Titch Davis knew, Jasper knew but he was going out with his dad. Ashleys knew, Lawmans knew. Mart Ward knew but he was

going out on his bike."

"Yes, I think we get the general idea that it was no secret," interrupted the sergeant. "Don't bother with all the names Stagg. Now, where did you go in Chesterfield and did you see anyone that you knew and did anyone follow you that you knew of ?"

"Well, it's funny you should say that," said Olly with the practised look of a sudden realisation that it all meant something. "We did see someone watching us outside the station where we went train-spotting, didn't we everybody ?" The others all nodded and said "Oh yeah" accompanied by similar looks of an explanation dawning on them.

"And who was this mysterious person ?" asked the impatient and dis-believing policeman.

"Well, it was two persons, not just one, and they were that toff Stubley-Stanhope from the Manor House and 'Wild Bill' Hitchcock, the gamekeeper, and they were watching us with binoculars and aiming a gun at us, until they knew that we knew, then they jumped in Wild Bill's Land Rover real quick and drove off."

Although he knew that Stagg was writing down all of this, Pyewright could not help pausing to consider if this could be true but he tried to make sure that no-one could tell what he was thinking from the look on his face.

Eventually he looked at his list of questions again.

"Now, where else did you go and did you see anyone else who might have been watching or following you ?" he asked, but was still distracted by thoughts of the previous answer.

"Anybody remember seeing anybody else ? No, I don't think we did," said Olly, as the others all shook their heads and pursed their lips in concentration.

Sergeant Pyewright went to Scarcliffe to see Hector Stubley-Stanhope and William Hitchcock, both of whom he knew from the Hardwick Masonic Lodge that met in Chesterfield. Stagg dealt with Chesterfield itself to check the boys' story of their journey to and from the town and whatever may have happened while they were there.

The sergeant went first to the Manor House, where he was told by the housekeeper that all the Stubley-Stanhope family were at church but it was the normal Sunday service so he could just go in if he wished. He walked back down the long drive from the house and then up the slope to the church and went in through the large front doors. Everyone turned round in their seats to look at the latecomer and most were surprised to see it was a uniformed police officer, especially Newt who thought he was spying on him.

Pyewright bowed towards the altar as he crossed the aisle and sat in a pew at the back, behind the Stubley-Stanhopes, who were themselves in the row behind Neville Heath. The boy was sat with a man who the officer felt looked familiar but he could not recall from where or when. He made a mental note to ask Hector later.

When the next Hymn was sung, the sergeant also thought to himself how could that young devil Neville sing 'Onward Christian Soldiers' so beautifully and wondered why he was in the congregation rather than the choir which sounded worse than bad, even to him. Pyewright wrote a message in his notebook, 'Can I talk to you after the service?' and showed it to Hector and the whole congregation turned around at just the wrong moment when Hannah Stubley-Stanhope sneezed and giggled at herself immediately afterwards. Everyone saw the two men, one holding a notebook and the other reading it.

Constable Stagg had telephoned Chesterfield Police Station in advance and reported there as a courtesy and to ask if they wished to conduct the inquiries, knowing that they would not. He then drove across town to the Midland Station, where he had arranged to meet the Assistant Station Master and one of his staff, Mr Skirrey. The Bolsover police officer was

astonished by the story that unfolded. That the boys had indeed been to the station, that they had bought return tickets to Dudley and had returned later that day, all of them apparently covered in blue war paint with pink spots on. The two railwaymen gave him a number for Dudley Train Station with which he obtained more information about the boys' day out that he found truly amazing and unbelievable.
Stagg dashed out of the station waving his notebook, jumped into his car and sped back to Bolsover and his own base and desk so that he could telephone Dudley Police Station.

Hector Stubley-Stanhope sat wondering why Sergeant Pyewright had turned up in uniform to see him at church on a Sunday morning. Was it something he had done ? The kids ? Or even Lettuce ? Hector hoped that it was nothing to do with those 'hooligans from Hillstown' that he and Hitchcock had followed. He tried to think of possible questions from his brother Fellow Craft Mason. Strangely, Selwyn Pyewright was thinking exactly the same thing and decided that, first, he must tell Hector the reason for his visit and that he did not suspect a brother Mason of any crime or improper behaviour but that it was the Olly Wood Gang that was under suspicion. As soon as the service ended the two men left and went straight to the Manor House, where Mrs White prepared a pot of tea for them and they retired to the study. Pyewright gave his prepared introduction and was surprised by the anxious look that flashed across the face of his host. Stubley-Stanhope confirmed that he had been waving off his daughter and had seen the Olly Wood Gang outside the station and that they did not appear to be misbehaving. He seemed mighty relieved when he was asked no further questions, thought the sergeant, as he finished his tea, voiced his thanks and left.

Back at the police station, Pyewright was visibly deflated by the news from Stagg's enquiries about the gang's movements, especially the revelation that they had been hailed as heroes. Since his constable was busily writing up notes, the sergeant said that he would get them both some breakfast as neither of them had eaten yet, even though this was usually the junior officer's responsibility. He went to the kitchen, cut four thick 'doorsteps' from a loaf of bread, fresh from the day before and lit the grill of the gas cooker and put two of the slices under the flames. The cook stood and watched after getting the butter dish, a dish of dripping for himself and a jar of marmite that Stagg liked, for some reason Pyewright could not fathom. "Disgusting stuff," he muttered.

"What I think we're looking at here, sarge," shouted Stagg, "Is someone trying to shift blame for something, trying to implicate someone in some crime, either the Olly Wood Gang or Mr Stubley-Stanhope and Mr Hitchcock. Perhaps we're dealing with Hitchcock's Psycho. Do you get it sarge ? That thriller 'Psycho' by Alfred Hitchcock. What a film, scared me to death !"

Pyewright came through to the office from the kitchen.

"Stick to police work, constable, your jokes are terrible. You'll never get on Sunday Night At The London Palladium," he said. The young man had not expected his sergeant to come back from preparing breakfast for a good while and had been transferring information from his notes on to a 'Link Chart' on the back of a roll of wallpaper, in the manner that he was learning from the Intelligence Analysis Correspondence Course he was doing.

He was taken by surprise when Pyewright walked in.

"What's this lad, decorating the office ?" laughed Pyewright at the wallpaper. Turning his learning folder, open on the desk, to see the title on the front he tormented him mockingly, "The Use Of Intelligence ? You've got to have some in the first place lad to be able to use it."

Stagg audibly sniffed the air several times.

"Sarge, did you put some toast under the grill ?"

"Damn," shouted Pyewright as he ran back along the corridor into the smoke-filled kitchen, pulled the grill pan out with its handle and tipped the burning slices into the sink and turned on the cold tap to extinguish them. The 'lad', as his sergeant called him, rolled up his wallpaper and put it away in the protective cardboard tube he had found to keep it in.

Stagg went dashing into the kitchen and said, "Blooming 'eck sarge, no wonder it set on fire, putting doorsteps that thick under the grill."

"Listen, lad," replied the embarrassed, incapable of any kind of cookery skill, Pyewright. "Would you mind taking over preparing breakfast so that I can look at your wallpaper?"

"Actually, it's called a link chart, sir as it shows the links between everyone involved and it's in the cardboard tube on top of the cabinet."

The pair swapped jobs and one made breakfast while the other examined the 'chink-lart', as he called it, which his junior corrected him on, to no avail.

Stagg brought the tea, toast, dripping and Marmite.

"It's disgusting, I don't know how you can eat that stuff," said the sergeant, curling up his lip to illustrate his dislike for it. Give me toast and dripping any day. Wholesome is dripping."

"Yes," laughed Stagg. "I suppose you couldn't mention Pyewright and Marmite together."

"Are you trying to be funny lad?" enquired his boss. "Anyway, tell me about this chink-lart thing. I've been planning something like this to use in our investigation of those hoodlums."

"Ok sarge, the Link Chart shows the links or relationships between the people and other factors involved or present at any time prior to, during or after, criminal activity – suspects, victims, witnesses, locations, vehicles, telephones, bank accounts, stolen goods, journeys …"

"Look laddie," interrupted Pyewright impatiently. "Just cut out that poppycock and let's see what we've got about this gang of juvenile delinquents on our doorstep. What they need is some discipline but parents and teachers have gone soft, not like in my day when I got the cane from teachers and a thrashing with a belt from my dad and it never did me any harm. We need more capital punishment in schools. That's what's needed with kids today !"

Stagg smiled and explained all of the symbols and links to his superior who interrupted constantly and questioned every item that did not support his view of the Olly Wood Gang.

"Alright, it may be useful," conceded Pyewright. "But it can't beat good old fashioned police work, getting in the car and pounding the beat. Ninety-nine times out of ten it works best. Right, I'm off home for a read of the Sunday paper, then down the Blue Bell before dinner."

The constable shook his head as he took the dirty pots to wash in the kitchen sink.

The Annual Village Cricket Match between Scarcliffe and Palterton had been at the top of the two villages' sporting calendars for generations and was the one time that each village came together and united against the other. Bets were entered into involving money, real or hypothetical amounts, and possessions, even those belonging to other people.

"I'll bet you any money you like ..." was a typical opener for a bet.

Scarcliffe had won the match for the past five years, largely due to the amazing batting exploits of William 'Welly-It' Elliott and this year they thought they were in line for a record breaking sixth win in a row. However, Palterton had unearthed its own secret weapon in the shape of a thirteen year old bowling sensation, Colwyn Holness, 'The Pope'. Though a slightly built and skinny boy, he was surprising anyone who had not seen him bowl a cricket ball before with how powerful, accurate and venomous was this missile launched by his long arm. Even the Derbyshire County Cricket coaches had been and observed him with unconcealed astonishment and excitement at what they had seen. In the week before the match, The Pope was disappointed to be told by his father that he could not venture off their farm, not to the village shops, not to his friends' houses, not to the rope swing on the big tree on Main Street, not to the bus stop and certainly not to Hillstown or Bolsover, whether on the bus or over the fields. And the name of their village rivals could not even be spoken. Some people whispered it – Scarcliffe – which was usually followed by "Shhh !"

The Pope's mother was less concerned about the result of the village cricket match than with the effects of keeping the eldest of her three sons under virtual house arrest, while the two youngest were not only allowed out, but tormented The Pope endlessly.

As his frustration at this situation increased as the week wore on, so did his mother's sympathy and willingness to allow some leeway. The boy always worked hard to help on the farm.

"If you practise your bowling and do all your work on the farm," she said kindly, "you can go to the shop and maybe even go to Hillstown or Bolsover one evening to see your friends."

Colwyn set up his practice wicket in front of a brick wall and began bowling with both great power and unerring accuracy, hitting the stumps with every ball. He did not place the bails on the stumps, however, as it would have been too much trouble finding them all the time. After almost half an hour of constant demolition, the bowler began to tire, both physically and mentally. It would have been better for him to have a batsman facing him but no-one who had seen him bowl would volunteer for the job. So instead, Colwyn called the wicket keeper Brick Waller.

12
THE PLAZA PLAN

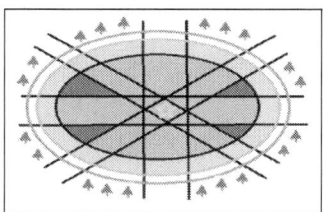

The nursery-rhyme 'Rock-A-Bye-Baby' is thought to possibly derive from the story of Luke and Betty Kenny or Kenyon, charcoal burners in Shining Cliff Wood, Sherwood Forest. They were said to have lived with their children in a tree with a turf roof and legend has it that they hollowed out a bough (large branch) of the tree in which they would rock the babies to sleep – Rock-a-bye-baby, in the tree top ...

William Hitchcock was the grumpy Gamekeeper employed by the Duke of Devonshire's Chatsworth Estate to patrol Scarcliffe Woods and was known to all the local children as 'Wild Bill' Hitchcock. He often visited the local schools, supposedly to give talks about the woods and their wildlife, while in truth he was simply lecturing all the children to scare them from entering the woods. As a School Governor he had various responsibilities but he ignored these and used his visits for his own purposes.
The boys from the Olly Wood gang disliked anyone in authority but Wild Bill seemed to invite unpopularity and even enjoy it.
Whenever they saw him in the woods, if possible they would quickly head for their hideout tree, the Cedar of Lebanon, into which they would retreat and hide high up in the cover of the branches, where they had made a platform. This prevented anyone seeing them from below and they figured that there would be little chance of anyone seeing them from above.

The gang were in the woods when Olly heard footsteps that he quickly recognised as Wild Bill's coming up past the Foxes' Den. As Hitchcock approached the Cedar of Lebanon tree he took out a hand drill and used it to make a small hole at the base of the trunk. He then used a tape measure to measure exactly 5 feet 3 inches, or 1.60 metres, above the first hole. Here he drilled a second hole into which he appeared to place something. The gamekeeper looked around to check if anyone was watching him before he set off up the path and back down past the foxes' den, whistling 'O For The Wings Of A Dove' very loudly, which brought puzzled looks from the boys. Being the best climber amongst them Balsa made to descend from their platform in the tree to retrieve the canister but Olly stopped him.

"No," he said quietly. "He's whistling a message to someone. We don't want to get caught."

They waited until the whistling could no longer be heard before Balsa gave a look and raised his eye-brows to ask his brother if he should now get it.

Olly put his finger to his lips then mouthed "Someone's coming through the Little Wood."

They all strained to listen but Olly had finely tuned hearing and it was a while before the others heard the footsteps crossing the wooden bridge by the Sheepwash. They could now tell it was a woman who was light footed and made little noise. She came directly to the tree and they could smell it was Letitia Stubley-Stanhope from her excessive use of perfume. She first located the lower hole, climbed up to the second one and collected the canister, then jumped down and quickly sprinted back the way she had come, clearly attempting to avoid being seen. The gang waited several minutes before they descended, even more puzzled by the behaviour of Lettuce Stubley-Stanhope. They walked cautiously down towards the Sheepwash to see where she had gone. Just before the wooden bridge Olly bent down and picked up what appeared to be the shell of a slim bullet.

He quietly said "Teatime", their code word for the Cedar of Lebanon and ran back to the tree followed by the others. When they reached it, he changed his mind.

"We can't hang about here, Lettuce might come back when she realises she's dropped her bullet, or she might get Wild Bill to come back, which would be even worse. We can't hide here if they're using it as a hiding place."

"Why has she left a bullet, Olly ? What does it mean ?" asked a puzzled Willie.

"I think Wild Bill's left a message for Lettuce and she's just dropped it near the Sheepwash," said Olly. "And we need to open it but not here. Come on, let's go to the big trees on Port Well Lane, through the top field, then down into the Little Wood. Quick, one at a time, wait here up the tree till the one in front is out of sight, then move when the coast is clear."

Olly then set off up the path to the top field while the rest of the gang all climbed the tree. Once he was through the hedge and gone the others took it in turn to climb down and follow as instructed.

When they arrived on Poulter Well Lane they scaled the tall trees with ease and waited for Olly to get the bullet from his pocket.

As he fiddled around with it, sure enough the head came off to reveal a piece of paper rolled up like a Rizla cigarette paper. He opened it and held it out to show everyone that there was writing on it and he proceeded to read it in a whisper.

"Lettuce, Lynda says he will be at Plaza on Fri 9th Aug and she will get him to sit at back and smother him with kisses. Mac will create a diversion in front of stage at 8 o'clock. Ringo and his mates will straight after create second diversion in middle, then you use Babs Nelson's hankie and smother him with either kisses and take him out through back exit to where we'll be waiting with a van to take him to ..."

The person who had written the note seemed to have run out

of space and not been able to include where they were to take the person who was apparently being kidnapped.

"Look," protested Mac loudly, "This is getting stupid. I'm the only Mac round here and this has definitely got nothing to do with me. Honest."

"Calm down, Mac," said Olly. "We know it's not you but we can't know everybody, can we? There must be somebody else called Mac and anyway, there's two other people besides you and Babs named in this note – Lynda, with a 'y' that is and Ringo."

"Ringo with an 'i', that is," added Willie, which caused them to laugh so much they nearly fell out of the trees.

"Shhhh! Somebody's coming," said Olly bringing them back to seriousness and they peered through the treetop leaves and branches to try and see who it was. Again, they nearly fell out of the trees when Lynda Marshall and Malcolm 'Sneaky' Snead walked along the path beneath them, hand in hand, whispering secretively.

"Shhh!" said the girl and she stood still and yanked Sneaky to a halt. "I can hear someone."

"Could it be your dad again?" said the worried boy, looking around. "I don't want him to catch me with you. He's crazy."

"Shut up Mac," said Lynda, looking up and down the lane in fear and suspicion.

"How many more times, my name isn't Mac," replied Sneaky. "It's Mal." Above them there were knowing looks, mixed with surprise, exchanged between the gang at this interesting piece of information.

Lynda dragged him back along the lane but before they reached the road she pulled the shocked youth into the River Poulter, through which they quickly walked and emerged on to the other side. They pushed into the undergrowth and then hid behind the large upturned base and roots of a fallen tree.

Olly put his finger up to his lips to indicate silence to everyone and spoke in hushed tones.

"They've gone into the jungle to hide from someone. She must have sensed we were here. We'll have to stay up here till they've gone. Don't move or speak at all anyone."

After the gang spent ten minutes silently perched high in the branches of the three adjacent trees they heard the splashing of footsteps coming back through the river, followed by the sound of feet running along the lane towards Mansfield Road and the Little Wood.

"What the hell is going on ?" asked Mac. "And why is Lynda Marshall behaving so strange and calling Mal Snead 'Mac', especially as he clearly doesn't want to be and, more to the point, who is being kidnapped ? And if Wild Bill, Lettuce Stubley-Stanhope, Lynda Marshall and Sneaky Snead are in it together on one side, I know which side I'm on and it isn't theirs."

"Come on, we're all on your side, Mac," said Olly. "Let's take the quick way down and we can start thinking of what we're going to do about this note, whatever it is that's going on."

He leaned out from his tree top perch to check his flight path, before leaping out and dropping the thirty feet to the next level of thick vegetation of the hedge below and then bounced off the hedge and into the field. The others all followed suit but as they had gathered fairly close together in the tree top, they ended up similarly close together on the ground and they all bounced in a heap on top of Olly in the field. No-one was really hurt and they simply dusted themselves down and set off to walk along the lane to Palterton. The note was repeatedly passed around to be read out very loud by each one and analysed and discussed at length.

"Lynda must be certain of going to the Plaza with whoever is being kidnapped, so she must have already arranged it or she is sure he'll go with her," said Olly. "I reckon it must be someone like Newt, or at least someone his age. What do you reckon, Newt ? You know her better than the rest of us. She's at school with you and is she still in the church choir ?"

"Well, I can tell you she's left the choir and she's getting a devil with the lads," replied Newt. "But other than that I don't know any more about her than any of you do. What does puzzle me though is the bit about Babs and his hankie."

"Use Babs Nelson's hankie and smother him with either kisses?" said Olly. "Yes, either kisses or something else, but what ? You're right Newt. Sounds odd, doesn't it ?"

"Can you remember when somebody had broken into their house when we got back from our 'Day out in Dudley' and the burglars only seemed to have gone in his bedroom. Even stranger was that all they seemed to have pinched were all of his underpants, socks and hankies and some bottles of ether he'd been making in their wash-house ? It could mean use the ether on Babs' hankie to knock someone out," said Newt.

"They could knock somebody out with his underpants, the trumping they've had in them," said Olly to roars of laughter from everyone.

"Our Newt is right, I reckon, " exclaimed Mac. "Come on, we've got to talk to Babs and everyone else. We're going to have to fill the Plaza with our mates and stop them from whatever it is they are planning."

They all agreed and rushed home to Hillstown, where they went straight to Babs' house on Pleasant Avenue. None of them were sure what they had agreed to but it sounded good fun. As they trooped down the path and round to the back of the house, Babs's mother shouted harshly at them through the kitchen window as she was preparing some food.

"He's in the garden shed with that blooming chemistry set. Making smells like rotten eggs, he is."

They turned and sauntered down the garden.

Mothers and grandmothers often wore a pinafore as an apron to protect their normal clothes and Mrs Nelson was no different. The gang had discussed the matter of these ladies who looked so fearsome in their 'pinny', as it was commonly known. Trapdoor it was, of course, who stated that they even had their own section of the Royal Navy under the name HMS Pinafore. He had heard it referred to in assembly when it was announced that there would be a school trip later in the year to go and see it, which puzzled him no end.

A stunned silence spread over them as they arrived at the shed and peered in through the window where the figure inside turned and looked out in its World War Two gas mask and bright yellow Marigold rubber gloves. It held up a hand with all its fingers outstretched and shouted something in a muffled voice.

"What did he say?" asked Balsa.

"Fried midges, it sounded like," laughed Olly. "Perhaps he wants us to wait five minutes."

They wandered to the back-door of the house where each of them then rushed to sit on the metal dustbin and played a short game of push and shove that became 'I'm the king of the castle'. They soon moved away, however, when they noticed the strong rotten eggs smell of the stink bombs that their friend seemed to have been producing again. This was strong competition for the unpopular smells produced by the strangely named Aroma-Free Group and their Light Aroma-Free Fuels (LAFF) and Chemicals From Coal (CFC). Many local people did not trust their claims to being perfectly safe and not at all harmful to man or beast. They pointed to the state of the River Doe lea that flowed through the site.

Babs particularly, was suspicious of them and, with his enthusiasm for chemistry, he knew more than anyone about the dangers of chemicals. This was why he had acquired a large number of gas masks that he would use when performing what he also knew would be dangerous processes and the rest of the family kept out of the garden shed when he went in and put up the 'No Entry' sign. It had become his laboratory. He had worn one of his gas masks, along with some 'borrowed' Aroma Free Group overalls, when he secretly investigated their foul smelling 'Chemicals From Coal' site on several occasions that year. He had walked alongside the River Doe Lea from the bridge on Chesterfield Road, benefiting from the cover of the riverside trees and vegetation that formed the western perimeter of Bolsover Colliery. He collected various samples of water from the river, soil, dust and flora, all of which he labelled with description, date and place. Not for nothing was the River Doe Lea known as the 'Black Waters'. He took photographs using the Minox spy camera that he had borrowed from his friend Nigel. At least the stuff relating to this sample and evidence collecting trip was not taken from his 'lab' when they were burgled as he had hidden it in the shed roof.

He came out of his laboratory and washed his Marigold gloved hands in a bucket of water, then took off the gloves and gas mask as his friends watched in silence, transfixed.

"Hello, what are you lot up to ?" said Babs in his usual friendly manner.

Whereas they would normally have laughed at the sight of their pal in his Marigolds and gas mask there was a serious atmosphere as Olly handed the bullet shell to Babs.

"What's this mean ?" asked the chemist. "Are you going to kill me for making my stinking bombs ?"

"Look inside at the piece of paper," replied Olly. "We saw Wild Bill leave it for Lettuce in a hole he made in the trunk of the Cedar of Lebanon 'Teatime' tree while we were up it."

Babs pulled out the scrap of paper and, as everyone had done, read it aloud, eyes widening.

"Lettuce, Lynda says he will be at Plaza on Fri 9th Aug and she will get him to sit at back and smother him with kisses. Mac will create a diversion in front of stage at 8 o'clock. Ringo and his mates will straight after create second diversion in middle, then use Babs Nelson's hankie and smother him with either kisses and take him out through back exit to where we'll be waiting with a van to take him to …"

He pulled a face to show his confusion.

"And then, when we were hiding up the trees on Port Well

Lane, Lynda Marshall came along and we heard her calling Sneaky Snead 'Mac', which he didn't seem pleased about, cos he likes to be called Mal. And we think they mean 'smother him with ETHER kisses' from your hanky, Babs," said Olly. "Anyway, something's going on. Get ready and meet us on the Rec at 4 o'clock so we can talk it through with everyone. We'll go for Jasper, Micko, Jack, Webby and everybody. The girls as well. Can you nip to Port-ton, Babs and get Trapdoor and The Pope, if he can come ? He might not be able to though cos of cricket practise and jobs on the farm, what with how hard he works and their big cricket match coming up."

Olly walked past the outbuildings with Mac, followed by the others in their usual order of age, with Willie bringing up the rear. Babs went back into the garden shed to tidy up, out of respect for the dangers of his 'chemistry set', which had now outgrown that description to be replaced by his 'laboratory'. He was determined to act responsibly, well, up to a point, to ensure that he caused no ill effects from the chemicals for his family, innocent people or animals, even next door's nosey cats, Radford and Dorothy. They were named after the British 1960 Olympic medallists, Peter Radford and Dorothy Hyman. Radford the cat would often sit on a fence post and howl at Babs for as long as he was in view and if the boy disappeared, the animal would jump down and spray cat pee at any available target, then run like his namesake away from the scene.

Mrs Nelson often blamed that smell on her son's chemistry set and would not listen when he blamed it on next door's cat. Radford's owners knew their pet was to blame but they never spoke up on the matter.

Quite by chance, Constable Stagg's father was third cousin to the head of the King family that lived on the corner of Castle Green and Pleasant Avenue and the PC used this to do some observations of the comings and goings on both streets in general and the Heath, Wood and Nelson houses in particular.

Some of the results he noted and entered on his 'Link Chart'.

Olly and Mac gave everyone various parts of Bolsover and Hillstown to go to. They were to seek out other friends and call them together on Hillstown Rec. Newt and Balsa had written out abridged versions of the note that had been found, but excluding mention of Mac and Babs, with an added note saying what they thought – 'One of our mates is going to be kidnapped. We don't know who or why but we know where, when and how. We have to stop them.'

The six of them ran down Mansfield Road together before dividing into pairs and splitting up at the crossroads. As they were doing so, Babs walked down his garden path and noticed that just across Pleasant Avenue, someone apparently visiting the Kings' house had parked an old but sturdy black bicycle next to the pavement edge. This was just too tempting for Babs to resist and he straddled the bike, kicked up the stand and was off up the street unnoticed by anyone. Although the surface was somewhat uneven he made quick progress along the footpath and across the fields to Palterton. He was just passing into the second field when a familiar figure came along the path.

"Alright Babs, what you doing with Constable Stagg's bike, you idiot ?" asked a shocked Trapdoor. The equally surprised cyclist looked down at his mount and, leaning over to get a better view of it while still riding, he fell off into the cornfield beside the path.

The amused Trapdoor tried very hard to hide his laughter but was unable to resist a jibe.

"That looked as easy as falling off a bike, Babs. What's all the hurry then, mate ?"

"Shut up you," said an unimpressed Babs. "Anyway, Olly and Mac asked me to come and get you and The Pope. I found the bike outside Kings' house and I just borrowed it cos I'd got to come and get you quick. They want everybody on the Rec cos

Lettuce Stuck-up Tightrope is planning to kidnap one of us but we don't know who and I never knew whose bike it was anyway."

Trapdoor shook his head in desperation and sighed at his friend, then pulled him out of the corn. They picked up the bicycle together, only to find that the front wheel had buckled. "Look what you made me do," said Babs, smiling at his attempt to try and deflect a bit of the blame away from himself. "It's all your fault."

"Oh no, you little liar," countered the laughing Trapdoor. "It's all your fault, not mine."

"What about The Pope?" said Babs, remembering that he was supposed to get him as well.

"He won't be able to come," advised Trapdoor. "His dad's got him wrapped in cotton wool till the cricket match on Saturday and you know how hard he works as well. Come on, let's see if we can take the bike back before it's missed. Then we'll get on to the Rec."

As Babs told the story of the note, as far as he knew it, Trapdoor somehow ended up with the bent wheeled bike to pull along, holding the front wheel off the ground. When they reached Pleasant Avenue he furtively propped it up on its stand where Babs said he found it and they sprinted away to Mansfield Road and on to the appointed meeting place. The two boys lay down in the pleasant sunshine beside the football pitch. A group of younger children were playing football but when they saw Babs arrive they moved their goal post jumpers and more crucially, their bikes, further away to the bottom corner of the field. Trapdoor shook his head knowingly and, opening an Oxo cube, he popped it in his mouth and began chewing it, which he often did. Babs watched him and pulled a face, then picked a blade of grass and chewed it.

"I don't know how you can eat that stuff like that Trapdoor. It's disgusting without water."

"Well, I don't know how you can chew that grass Babs,

although at least I suppose it's had some water. Every dog in Hillstown will have pee'd on it."

Babs quickly spat out the grass and pulled even more faces while Trapdoor laughed at him. They were interrupted by the cheerful sound of the jingle-jangling music of a Cherry's Ice Cream van that announced its arrival in the nearby Miners Welfare car park. Just what Babs decided he needed to counter any ill effects he might suffer from dog pee on the grass.

"Want an ice cream?" he shouted cheerily as he ran down the Rec to be the first one there.

"Yeah, go on then, can I have a flake?" said Trapdoor as he got up and followed Babs only to see the small figure of a younger girl skip happily across the road and up to the ice cream van in front of a disappointed Babs. She scanned the board advertising the different selections available and dithered undecidedly as the boy waited patiently.

"Come on Susie Hope, hurry up," said her father approaching from behind her. "Young David's tongue's hanging out from the look of things."

She pointed at the board and said, "Err, that one," which she repeated several times pointing at different parts of the board.

"Quick Susie, before it all melts," said Newt as he turned up with Balsa, Giggsy and Mac. Newt ruffled the girl's hair gently. "Hello, Mr Hope," he added to her father.

"Hello Neville," replied Arthur Hope, who was a local funeral director and lived on Mansfield Road, across from the Rec. "Right, we'll have a large cornet with bits, a flake and raspberry sauce and an orange lolly please," he added, losing patience at this long process of choosing an ice cream by his daughter.

The boys all stood behind Susan, patiently waiting their turn, while the girl and her father were served before they turned and went back across the road and home. Babs got to the front and ordered two flakes as more boys and a few girls began to arrive and most of them joined the queue for ice creams. Cherry's looked like they were going to be busy. Soon all the gang were back and everyone they knew seemed to be in the queue for an ice cream. Olly and Mac stood a few yards from the van discussing how they would next proceed when Steve Maude spoke to them from his position of fourth in the queue, as quietly as he could.

"It's a bit like Harry Lime, this, isn't it ? All this mystery is madness."

"Yeah," laughed Olly. "Don't say any more though Maudey, till we get sat down on the Rec."

Olly and Mac went and sat in the middle of the football pitch and were eventually joined in ones and twos by around sixty of their friends, all eating their ice creams. The two leaders crouched near the centre spot facing everyone else who sat around chattering loudly in a semi circle along the centre circle line.

"Ok," said Mac, standing up. "Here's what we know. We found this note that Lettuce Stubley-Stanhope seemed to have dropped and which Wild Bill Hitchcock appeared to leave for her in, err, a tree trunk near where we were hiding in Scarcliffe Woods. Then we saw Lynda Marshall acting suspiciously on Port Well Lane with Sneaky Snead. Most of you have heard what the note says but I'll read it out again for those that have haven't heard it.

Micko stood up and everyone turned to listen. "We've just heard Willie say that the note mentions someone else that you've left out of your version of events. Who is it and why ?"

Babs stood up and he and Mac said together, "It's me."

Everyone began talking excitedly. Olly stood up and waved his arms to quieten them all down.

"Ok, we left Mac and Babs out because we didn't know if they were the ones being kidnapped or attacked or whatever. We'll read out the original version. Come on Newt, you've got it, stand up and read it out."

Newt did as requested and read the note.

"Lettuce, Lynda says he will be at Plaza on Fri 9th Aug and she will get him to sit at back and smother him with kisses. Mac will create a diversion in front of stage at 8 o'clock. Ringo and his mates will straight after create second diversion in middle, then you use Babs Nelson's hankie to smother him with either kisses and take him out through back exit to where we'll be waiting with a van to take him to ..."

"Right," said Olly. "We heard Lynda Marshall call Mal Snead, 'Mac', so that's obviously not our Mac and Babs' house was burgled a few weeks ago and they took all his underpants, socks and hankies from his bedroom and some bottles of ether from his laboratory. And we think that whoever wrote it meant 'smother him with ether', instead of 'either'. They maybe just got the spelling wrong. So all of this seems to fit together into some kind of cunning plan to kidnap someone at the Plaza on Friday, but who and why, we don't know."

"Perhaps they're going to get rid of that mad usherette who hits you with her big torch," shouted Webby, to howls of laughter.

"Perhaps," said Olly, trying not to laugh himself, "but has anyone been asked about going to the flicks by anybody, especially Lynda Marshall ? We might at least identify their target."

The boys all looked at each other, shook their heads and chorused "Not me", except Webby. "I'll volunteer though if she's desperate," he shouted.

"She's not that desperate," joked Irene Howard and Webby jumped up and chased her, screaming and laughing across the field.

They returned and resumed their places in the semi circle to all round amusement.

"Something is clearly planned for 8 o'clock," resumed Olly. "And it's probably someone we know and it could be one of us. In which case, we have to do something about it. We've got a number of options. We could either turn up in force, like this, and stop them by sheer weight of numbers or we could hand the note to the police, let them deal with it."

"Or, I could blow up the Plaza on Thursday night," said Babs excitedly. "That'd stop 'em."

"Isn't it a film about prisoners of war digging tunnels to escape from the Germans ?" observed Jack Bradshaw. "I think we'd all rather watch it than be part of it, thanks Babs."

"Me and Mac think we'll all be best turning up on Friday and planning a few surprises of our own to coincide with their so called diversions, if we aren't able to identify the target," said Olly. "They surely wouldn't dare take on all of us, it'd be like The Alamo. Mind you, that was a brilliant film, wasn't it ? John Wayne, get off your horse and drink your milk."

"Ok," said Mac, taking over. "We're asking everybody to turn up on Friday at the Hornscroft, by the swings and we'll go over our plan. Basically, we're going to all go dressed more or less the same, which probably means school clothes or something similar and we're all going to have one of Babs' gas masks so that the other mob don't know who we are and we don't get affected by either their ether or Babs' stink bombs. Right, 6 o'clock on the Hornscroft, everybody in grey or black trousers and grey or white shirt, school clothes preferably. See you all on Friday and bring a friend. There'll be fireworks."

"I'll bring a girl but it'll be a bit difficult snogging on the back row with gas masks on," shouted Webby.

"It'll be the only time you'll get a girl to snog you if your face is covered by a gas mask," joked Irene as she jumped up and ran laughing down the field again, away from the pursuing Webby.

"And if you hear anything at all about what's going on," shouted Mac, as everyone was standing up. "Let me or Olly know but don't tell anyone else about this, even if you bring them along on Friday. We don't want it getting out what we're planning. Babs has enough gas masks for everyone and those bags, like him and Newt carry everywhere. Bring a catapult, just in case and some ammo, marbles or pebbles. No weapons though."

The young people of Bolsover and the surrounding villages usually spent most of their days in the summer holidays at the local swimming baths, walking to either Scarcliffe Woods, Hardwick Hall or Sutton Hall, going to either Mansfield or Chesterfield on the bus, getting together with each other, having ice creams from Cherry's, Mr Whippy or Manfredi's from the mobile ice cream vans or listening to some of that Radio Luxembourg pop music at night. Some lucky ones might get taken out for the day by a parent or even taken for a fortnight's holiday in a caravan at Skegness, Mablethorpe, Blackpool or further afield. The Diamond Horseshoe cafe was a favoured location for many, to drink Coca Cola and eat chips while listening to the Juke Box. Of course, for the boys, mostly, there was football and, after his performance in the FA Cup Final that year, everyone wanted to score goals like Denis Law, even if they supported a team other than Manchester United. Another, more local hero, was Joe Payne who had played for the Bolsover Colliery side before he went to Luton Town, where he once scored ten goals in a league game in 1936, still a record. Cricket was less popular, mostly because it was easier to lose the ball but also because the names Brian Bolus, Geoff Boycott, Basil Butcher and Freddie Trueman may have had a poetic ring but the people themselves lacked the pop star image of modern footballers like Law. Other games were sometimes played : hula hoops, tiggy, tin can-a-lurkey, hopscotch, skipping, snobs, marbles. The girls were always better than the boys at hula hoops, skipping and hopscotch which Irene often said was because the boys could not work their bodies in conjunction with their brains, before she ran away laughing. Only if the weather was bad and the film was one they particularly wanted to see would many of them venture to the Plaza Cinema on a Friday night. As had always been the case, it was mostly seven to twelve year olds that went wild at the Saturday Matinee, shouting, booing, cheering at various heroes and villains.

The twelve to sixteen year olds went to see or be seen, with or by, the opposite sex so when they did go, it was usually at night in their smartest, modern clothes. They tried to look cool and relaxed, while underneath the surface most of them were gibbering wrecks when they saw someone they 'fancied'.

Around a hundred local young people therefore surprised their parents by, for once, dressing very smartly and formally to go to the pictures on a Friday night. Although they were pleased to see that their children were now listening to their mothers' and fathers' advice, there was understandably great suspicion as to the motives for all of this and the general view was that they were meeting someone who they were trying to impress. Around a quarter of an hour before 6 o'clock, most of these young people began to arrive at the gates at the north end of the Hornscroft Park, at Town End in Bolsover. They walked over the park towards the playground area in the western corner where a dozen younger kids were playing on the swings, mountain slide, 'bobby's hat' roundabout, bucking bronco and other playground equipment.

As soon as the playground kids who had been happily playing saw this swarm of grey and black clad figures walking silently towards their playground, they jumped off the rides and ran out of the gates at the southern end of the park, screaming as if they had seen a crowd of ghosts. And who should be coming in to the park but the Olly Wood Gang, similarly dressed in black and grey, all carrying large numbers of Babs' gas mask bags.

"Come back," shouted Mac, seeing the eerie looking ghostly battalion of their friends. "Nobody's going to hurt you."

The kids from the playground were not staying around to find out and were gone, to the amusement of most of the gang.

"We can't afford to scare people like that and attract too much attention, can we Mac ?" observed Olly. "When we go in to the pictures we'd better go in small groups, eh ?"

When the gang reached the playground they could not help but laugh at the numbers of their friends that had turned up, mostly boys but many girls as well. It was like a sea of grey in the playground and the waves were still coming.
Soon it became a trickle and then stopped so Olly quietened them all and addressed them loudly as they gathered around.
"Right, thanks for coming. For anyone that doesn't know why we're here, we saw Wild Bill Hitchcock, the gamekeeper from Scarcliffe leave a note hidden in a tree in the woods. Lettuce Stubley-Stanhope collected it but then seemed to drop it and we found it. Lynda Marshall and Sneaky Snead, Mal Snead that is, are involved as well, along with a gang led by someone called Ringo, in a plot to kidnap someone in the Plaza at 8 o'clock."
"How do we know they didn't leave it where they knew you'd find it and are setting a trap for you, well, all of us now ?" asked Barbara Easterman, a girl from Newt's class at school.
"It's a good point Barbara and one we hadn't thought of," admitted Mac, laughing. "Either way, they're still after someone and they won't expect the Cavalry turning up like this."
"Right," said Olly, returning to the Plaza Plan. "Before we go through the plan, has anyone heard anything or any rumours about the plot ?"
"Yes, my dad says the film that's on has had really good reviews," said Irv. "He read in The Times that the plot is about British and Yanky prisoners of war in the second world war who try to escape from their prison camp by digging three tunnels that they call Tom, Dick and Harry."
"Ok Irv," butted in Olly. "But we want to hear what anyone's heard about the kidnapping plot, not the film plot. Anyone else heard anything, then ?"
As there was just shaking of heads, Olly continued.
"Right, here's what we're going to do. Everyone gets a gas mask bag and we walk down to the Plaza in groups of four at two minute intervals and go in at the same intervals in the same groups. Mac, Babs, Newt and me will go first and we all sit as

near the back as possible. If nothing happens before five minutes to eight, we'll give the signal that we're about to start our own diversions before theirs are due to start at eight o'clock. The signal will be 'Geronimo', which I will shout once and our Balsa will repeat once from the end of a row of seats where he'll be sat. If they start anything before we do, we'll use the same signal, which means get your gas mask on because there might be Babs' homemade fireworks, big bangs and stink bombs, ether and possibly other dangerous gases. If any of you see anything starting, shout the signal, get your gas masks on and get stuck in and remember, we're looking at Sneaky Snead, Lynda Marshall, Lettuce Stubley Stanhope, Wild Bill Hitchcock and this Ringo and his gang. We'll all be with you and there's certainly enough of us. Come on, GERONIMO !"

Everyone threw their arms in the air and shouted "GERONIMO" just as the number 8 bus to Glapwell went past on the other side of the park railings. All the passengers were astonished at the sight of over a hundred young people attending some kind of political or religious rally with such fervour and dressed in their uniform, waving their arms and shouting loudly.

"Young people today, eh ?" said one old chap on the bus. "What is the world coming to ?"

The gang handed out the gas mask bags and there were just a handful left over. Babs collected up the left-overs and dropped them over the hedge between the playground and the back of the church hall to hide them.

"Right, we're off," said Olly. "Our Balsa will set everyone off at two minute intervals. Walk, don't run, see you all inside. Operation Light At The End Of The Tunnel is under way."

The first four left the playground and walked down the park to Town End, then to the Plaza. They went straight in as there was no queue and paid the totally disinterested woman in the box office cubicle, passing their money through the hole in the

glass window in return for a ticket and they received a filthy look for good measure. Further along the corridor stood the Plaza's manager in his black suit, white shirt and maroon velvet bow tie, appearing to guard the double swing doors that led through to the auditorium, which was exactly how he viewed his role. The gang had knowingly nicknamed him J. Arthur Rank, after the famous British film producer and founder of the Rank Organisation. The four boys approached him cautiously and handed him their tickets which he tore in two and returned a half of each ticket back to them and they scurried through the door and headed for the back row. The first person they saw was the friendly lady who sold ice creams and sweets and she smiled at them. As they walked up the right hand aisle they were confronted by a fearsome sight – Mrs Lunn, known to young people as 'Torchy', the senior usherette. "Where do you think you're going ?" she demanded. "I tell you where to sit and on a Friday, you sit down the front where there's plenty of empty seats."
She ushered them down to the front of the hall.
"There's no-one in here yet," said Mac in protest. "The whole place has empty seats."
"Don't you cheek your elders Malcolm Heath or I'll tell your mother about it," she chided.
"Sorry, Mrs Lunn," tried Mac in a friendly voice. "Mam said we were to dress smart and sit quietly at the back and not cause you any trouble and she'd send you a magazine on Sunday."
His mother worked at the newsagents at Hillstown that delivered the usherette's newspapers.
"Alright then, of course," relented the torch-bearer at this clear bribery.
Before she could continue with any conditions or threats the double doors swung open and in walked four more boys and Mrs Lunn turned to look and saw a new group of apparent replicas of the first four who had now made a run for it up to the back.

She ignored the newcomers and chased after Mac and his friends. They had found their seats in the middle of the back row but 'Torchy' was so used to them running about that she was surprised to see them sitting quietly.

"Have you worked here long Mrs Lunn ?" asked Olly, trying to distract and occupy the lady.

"Never you mind," she replied. "And why have you ruffians all got those gas mask bags ?"

"It's our Neville," said Mac. "He's started a fashion cos he's always used one, haven't you ?"

"Yes," continued Newt, opening the lid of his bag. "Look, I've got a book I'm reading, 'Brother To The Ox' by Fred Kitchen. He lives in Bolsover, on Mooracre Lane, do you know him ? And I've got a notebook, pencils, bag of sweets, some liquorice, drink, bubblies, string, penknife, snobs, compass and look, I've got a torch like you. It's not as big as yours though." He made as if to show her the contents of the bag, to the horror of the others, but she turned away as he had expected, uninterested in his ramblings and returned to her station. Meanwhile, Webby, Micko, Jonah and Jack dived on to the floor in separate rows of seats near the front and crawled along the length of the rows to the other aisle to avoid Mrs Lunn. They scooted up to the back on all fours, then along the row and suddenly popped up into the seats alongside Olly and the others. Mrs Lunn was about to rush to the back row again when the double doors swung open and four more of the ghostly black and grey figures came in.

The puzzled usherette went to wipe her forehead with the back of her sleeve and only succeeded in hitting herself on the temple with the enormous torch that was the origin of her nickname. Stunned, she stood back against the wall and allowed the boys to pass, then staggered to the front and went through the swing doors to speak to the manager.

"What's going on ... ?" she started to ask the manager but the rest of her question tailed off as she saw another group of dark-clothed boys approach the box office.

"I know," replied the finance-conscious, black suited, swing door guarding, ticket tearer. "We've already got more in than last Friday. It could be a big night. Go back to your post please Mrs Lunn. Hang on though dear, what's happened to your forehead? You've got a lump the size of an egg above your eye brow."

"Oh, shut up," replied the embarrassed lady. "I walked into a door." She angrily swung open the door and strode through to her normal position halfway up the aisle.

As planned, a fresh wave of grey and black arrived just under every two minutes and eventually filled the last four rows and half of the next one of the downstairs section. Behind them was another aisle then ten sets of double seats set into the back wall where 'courting couples' usually sat holding hands and kissing, although Mrs Lunn always kept an eye on these and gave anyone a whack with her torch if they got too amorous. Unbelievably, they all sat really quiet.

The only four other customers in the cinema, two couples, came in intending to go in the courting seats but, when they saw the massed ranks at the back, they thought better of it and sat warily near the front, not daring to walk past them. There was so far no-one on the small upstairs balcony. The cinema lights went down at 6:45 pm and moments afterwards a group of eight young men arrived, most aged between eighteen and twenty-three, led by a long-haired older one in his thirties, and they swept into the auditorium and swaggered up the aisle in the dark. They were also all dressed the same, in ice-blue denim jeans, white t-shirts and black leather jackets, looking like James Dean in the film 'Rebel Without A Cause'. This was all too much for Mrs Lunn who stood back against the side wall and let them go to whichever seats they wanted. They went to the middle of a row in just about the middle of the cinema. At the same time as these eight came through the swing doors on Mrs Lunn's side, three other figures sneaked in on the other side.

One dropped straight on to the front row and slid down in his seat while the other two went straight up the aisle and into the nearest 'courting couple' double seat, unnoticed by the massed ranks of the grey uniformed Confederate Army who were intent on the eight Rockers in the middle seats.

Pathé News was yet again showing Henry Cooper knocking down Cassius Clay on 18th June 1963 at Wembley Stadium which held everyone's attention, except for the young couple in the 'courting couple' seat. He was trying to look at both the Pathé News feature and the surprisingly large number of people occupying the four rows in front of him. She held him close and kissed him passionately and prevented him looking at anything. He did not resist, thinking he would rather kiss the gift horse in the mouth than see whatever else was going on. His brain could not function properly. Hers was working overtime, wondering how they were going to get past the back row boys and girls without being seen. She knew there were some girls there too because she heard and recognised Irene's voice and a boy's laugh.

"Get your hand off my leg, Webby !"

"Hahaha. Owww !" he complained on receiving a hard slap to his face.

Lynda kept up the passionate embrace and kissing with Colwyn Holness 'The Pope' and he did not protest. She had called for him at 5:30 pm to catch the bus into Bolsover for the pictures, as agreed with his mother the previous day. He wasn't going to pass up this opportunity. The main film had now started but the boy could only listen and snatch the occasional view of the excitement.

The Pope, like everyone in Palterton, had a great sense of humour and they all enjoyed telling jokes and he had some new ones to share. He gasped for breath but when Lynda stopped kissing him to give him air, he started telling her jokes.

"What do you call a man with a spade in his mouth? Doug. What do you call a man with no spade in his mouth? Douglas.

What do you call a man with a seagull on his head? Cliff. Confucius, he say, man with one watch always know what time it is, man with two watches never sure.
Five year old Little Johnny was lost, so he went up to a policeman and said, I've lost my dad! The policeman said, What's he like? Little Johnny replied, Beer and women!"
"Shut up and kiss me," said Lynda. She knew she could not afford to let him carry on with the jokes, as for one thing she was beginning to snort loudly at the humour so she resumed the kisses, but not before those on the back row nearest to them recognised the jokes and the voice telling them. Almost everyone was now so interested in the film however, that they paid little attention to the kissing couple. Helen Huckle, universally known to her age group as Honeysuckle, who was sat on the end of the row, glanced around jealously at the young lovers several times but only when the star of the main attraction was not on screen. The boys were just as admiring of him, or of his character, but for different reasons and they could not take their eyes off the film. Until Newt noticed that it was five minutes to eight and urgently hissed at Olly, Mac and Babs, showing them his watch.
"Tell everybody to get their gas masks on," whispered Olly. "Two minutes to Geronimo."
Babs got several handfuls of stink bombs out of his bag and handed them out to his three fellow secret agents. As they were being passed over however, one fell between two hands and dropped towards the floor. It was fortunately cushioned by Newt's shoe, from which it rolled off, still intact, and continued to roll down the sloping cinema floor. Babs got some other 'goodies', as he called them, out of his bag and quickly set one up ready to execute. They looked along the four rows to confirm that everyone else had their gas masks on before donning their own.
Olly, Mac and Newt threw a stink bomb down to the bottom of each aisle, next to the swing doors. Next each of them

launched them straight down the middle, aiming for between the stage and the front row, where they suspected Sneaky Snead was positioned. Then they did a spread bombing around the Leather Jacket mob.

Sneaky and 'the mob' automatically turned around and looked up to the back of the cinema and were shocked to see the next missile, a home-made rocket, beginning its trajectory towards them just above the tops of the seats. They all dived to the floor to get out of its flight path. From there they could not see Babs and his metal tube with which he had launched the rocket and it hit the screen with a thud. The two usherettes and the ice cream lady held their noses and bolted through the swing doors to make good their own escape.

Olly climbed on to the back of the seats, lifted his gas mask slightly and shouted "GERONIMO – OOOOO !!", having previously forgotten his lines. He walked forward and everyone else took his cue and similarly climbed on to the backs of the seats and tottered down the slope of the cinema. Sneaky Snead and the Rockers, on seeing the advancing horde of gas masked acrobats, leaped up and ran for the swing doors and safety. Lynda had now stopped kissing The Pope and they sat open mouthed watching this alternative to the main attraction. She decided she had had enough of all this chaos, danger and distraction.

"They can keep their five pounds," she exclaimed to The Pope's dismay and ran across the rear aisle, up the passage to the fire exit doors, which were open courtesy of the already departed and terrified Projectionist. She ran out of the back of the cinema on to Church Street, round on to Cotton Street and into the Diamond Horseshoe cafe, where she bought a coke and sat in the back, well away from the door to avoid attention. As the grey hordes swept down the auditorium, the leather jacket mob and Sneaky Snead disappeared through the double doors and straight out of the Plaza. The Pope, now sat on his own in a lovers' seat at the back, applauded and cheered at both the film and the gang. In the dark and in their gas masks, none of them, other than Honeysuckle, knew who it was. "GERONIMOOOOOO," shouted Olly again and they ran up on the backs of the seats whooping and shouting different war cries. "Geronimo" had easily the most mentions, followed by "Tecumseh", "A man's gotta do what a man's gotta do", "Get off your horse and drink your milk" and, from Honeysuckle, "Wait, it's The Pope", just as a large part of the row she was standing on collapsed and deposited her, screaming, on the floor.

13

THE MASKED BALL'S UP

Colwyn Holness 'The Pope' did not like the look of the masked and crazed group advancing on him and, like Lynda Marshall earlier, made a run for the rear exit, only to find it had been slammed shut moments earlier by the lovely Lynda as she left. He turned and faced his attackers, only to hear a hundred voices shout as one, as they all took off their gas masks, "The Pope, what are you doing here?"
"I was having a nice evening at the pictures with Lynda Marshall till you lot wrecked it," said the boy, though clearly not too upset. "So, more to the point, what are you lot doing here?"
"We haven't got time to explain now. We need to get out before the cops come," said Olly. "Let's get that door open. Come on, we'll give it a push."
The strongest boys gave it several mighty pushes but without success. Lynda's slam had both locked and broken the door.
"Babs, can you get it open?" asked Mac, knowing what the answer would be as a large circle of space opened up around Babs, although most knew little about his skill to do it.
"How's he going to do what ten of you couldn't manage?" said a sceptical Honeysuckle.
"Everybody get your gas masks back on and go back round the corner into the pictures," said Babs, ignoring Helen's jibes. He would never let anyone see his equipment or how he

achieved his results if it could be avoided. After setting up the apparatus and various substances he banged on the door and shouted.

"If there's anyone on the other side of this door, I suggest you run like hell out of the way unless you want to get blown to smithereens. You've got five seconds. Five. Four. Three ..."

Not being the quickest of boys Babs himself ran and got around the corner just in time before an explosion shook the whole place and scattered clouds of dust and debris into the auditorium as the doors were blown thirty yards into Church Street, narrowly missing two fourteen year olds who had been kissing in the Caledonian Market doorway, the entrance to the indoor market hall.

They nearly had heart attacks when the explosion happened and they blinked at the scene and stared fearfully at the cinema. A black Bedford CA Panel van parked near the Caledonian Market was showered with debris.

The boy fainted when the swarm of grey, dust-covered ghostly figures came walking out of the gaping hole and the girl stood open mouthed and quite still as the figures drifted along Church Street. They turned left and walked quickly up Cotton Street. When they reached the top, they went across High Street and hurried down the jennel, known as Surprise View, leading to the Back Hills which had a long, steep grassy slope. In winter when it snowed, it was a favourite place for sledging and in summer it was also popular for 'grass sledging' on pieces of cardboard. A footpath ran along the top of the slope for the whole length of the Back Hills and near each end of the path were small, stone, cottage-like structures called Conduit Houses (or Cundy House), built in the 1620's as part of the system to carry water to Bolsover Castle along the south western ridge of Bolsover. There was a similar system and another Conduit House to the north east of the castle which gave its name to the nearby Cundy Road.

"Everybody take your gas masks off, put them in your gas

mask bags and stash them in the Cundy House," instructed Olly. "Then get a piece of the cardboard that's stored in there and start grass sledging and we say we've been here all night if anybody asks."

There was a mad dash for the strange little stone hut and the gas masks were quickly removed and exchanged for the bits of cardboard on which they were all soon hurtling down the slope en masse. All except Olly, Mac, Newt and Babs who sat on the grass at the top of the incline and talked to The Pope about what had happened. They told him about the note that they had found in Scarcliffe Woods and Newt fished it out of his gas mask bag, only he and Babs still having them. The Pope sat quietly as he heard and read about the kidnap plot, with his eyes wide in astonishment and disbelief.

"But why would anyone want to kidnap me ?" asked Colwyn. "Mind you, I'd have handed myself over of my own accord for that Lynda Marshall. Crikey she can't half kiss. It was like having your brain sucked out through your tongue. So she was some kind of bait ? And Mal Snead as well, I've never liked him since he moved here with his family from Shrewsbury."

"Yes but we don't know why," said Mac. "Any ideas The Pope, 'cause they might try again ?"

"Only that they might be trying to stop me playing in the village cricket match tomorrow," replied the new bowling sensation for Palterton. "That's all I can think of, to be honest."

"Blooming 'eck," exclaimed Olly. "I never thought of that. They're out to nobble The Pope."

Their conversation was interrupted by screams from the bottom of the slope in a small copse of trees, from which Webby ran laughing, chased by a cursing, red faced Irene. They had slid down the slope together side by side and gone straight into the copse where Webby had rolled over and daringly stole a kiss from her as they lay there laughing.

"Aaargh, help," shouted the boy. "She just kissed me in the

bushes and wants another."

"I'll give you a good smack in the kisser if I ever catch you Webby and for everyone else's information, it was you that kissed me," said his pursuer, to great cheers from everyone.

"I'd better be getting home I think," said The Pope. "My dad won't be very happy if I get kidnapped and nobbed ahead of tomorrow's match. I'm not even supposed to be out."

"You'd better get the word right," said Olly, grinning. "It's nobbled, not nobbed. Anyway, we'll walk home with you, just to make sure you get there safely."

Olly stood up and shouted to all their grass sledging friends that they were leaving to take The Pope home and explained that it appeared to be him that was the target of the kidnap plot because of the cricket match.

"Shouldn't some of us go through the Market Place and see if we can see any sign of Sneaky and Lynda and those rockers and anybody else ?" asked Trapdoor thoughtfully.

"That's a good idea," said Olly. "Me, Mac, Newt, our Balsa, Giggsy and Willie will walk along High Street, round past the Castle and The Angel Hotel into the Market Place. Babs, you take The Pope down on to New Station Road, walk up to the next Cundy House, then over the fence and down the Spring Field, past Pip Hill's place and over the fields to Palterton so that you avoid the roads. Trapdoor, you bring a gang to follow us at a distance to watch our backs. Everybody else stay here."

They all watched Babs and The Pope wander off along the path past the Cundy House and towards New Station Road, looking like they were butterflies in the grass. Then the 'gang of six' set off up Surprise View and reached the High Street in single file, where they all stood up against the wall, as if on a ledge a hundred feet up on a cliff face. Trapdoor stood at the other end of Surprise View and watched as each of the six spies edged around the corner still on their ledge and disappeared on to High Street. He jerked a thumb towards the masses stood behind him and moved forward along the same ledge, up against the wall, followed by 'Trapdoor's Troops' as he called them.

Reaching High Street, he looked right towards the church to reconnoitre, then turned and checked the other way, where he saw Olly and the gang spread out and dashing from one hiding place to another past the Telephone Exchange and heading for the Castle.

Without bothering to glance round at 'his men', Trapdoor motioned for them to follow and he headed along High Street after Olly's forward party. Trevor hid behind walls, the ends of buildings, vehicles and trees as he followed his friends and continued to wave his right arm to prompt his 'forces' to move forwards behind him, like a platoon of commandos.

As he passed the entrance to the Castle, The Sportsdrome and Steinways, the piano shop, he dodged imaginary enemies and their bullets and he saw Olly and his group stop at the petrol pumps in the Market Place. There they captured and interrogated Albert Woodhead, of Castle Coaches, who was filling up his coach, Lady Jane, ready for his trip to the coast the next day. Newt interrogated his daughter, Jane, who he knew and liked from school.

"Ok Jane," said Newt. "Co-operate and tell us what you know or we'll torture you by tickling you until you spill the beans. Have you seen any strange characters in Bolsover tonight ?"

"Neville Heath," laughed the girl, hands on her hips. "Yes, I've seen hundreds of them !"

"You have ?" asked Neville, very puzzled by this information. "Who ? What ? When ? Where ? How ?"

"Look behind you," said Jane. "There, coming down Castle Street following Trapdoor."

The gang all turned and looked back towards The Anchor and The Angel public houses where Trapdoor was still dashing and dodging imaginary bullets and peering around the corners of these old drinking establishments. Behind and unseen by him, walked the whole of the Plaza and Back Hills Platoon, hands in pockets, 'slouching', as all their fathers called it.

"Trapdoor," Olly half shouted, half whispered. "You weren't supposed to bring everybody. This is supposed to be a secret mission, not an announcement with a megaphone !"
The platoon commander spun round as his troops jumped into doorways and behind buildings and vehicles to hide from him. Captain Trapdoor laughed and shouted.
"What are you tailing me for ? Come on out, Come out, come out, whoever you are."
Even Trapdoor was surprised however as everyone who had been in the Plaza and on the Back Hills as part of Operation Light At The End Of The Tunnel came out of their hiding places and stood there in front of him, over a hundred of them.
"For goodness sake," shouted Trapdoor in a sort of half-whisper. "Why have all of you followed me ? I asked for a dozen of you to come and watch the gang's backs, not a hundred of you."
"We all came," shouted the crowd. "Cos you never said who you wanted to come." They all sniggered at their response and Trapdoor waved them to follow as he shook his head in despair and walked towards the Market Place.
As Trapdoor's Trackers passed the Cenotaph War Memorial, a police car, a 1951 Wolseley 6/80, Winkworth bell clanging to announce its urgency, raced along the bottom of the Market Place towards Town End and screeched to a halt outside The Plaza. In the front passenger seat Sergeant Pyewright did a double take as he caught a brief glimpse of the great crowd of young people, almost matching the report of a marauding mob of five hundred rampaging juvenile delinquents who had terrorised the cinema.
"Reverse back into the Market Place, Constable Stagg," ordered the excitable sergeant. "We're going to arrest that mob." The junior man did as he was instructed and sped backwards with the bell still clanging loudly, alerting everyone

to their return. Ever more practical than his superior, the constable wondered how the two of them would arrest the Olly Wood gang if they were here, never mind a mob, unless the sergeant was exaggerating.

Olly and the gang at first hid behind the bus but Mr Woodhead pushed them up the steps and told them to crawl along the floor to the back and hide behind the seats with his daughters. The bus was now filled up with fuel and the pump attendant wrote down the details for the Castle Coaches account that Albert settled at the end of each month.

Trapdoor and his followers disappeared as quickly as they had appeared moments earlier, so that when the police car pulled into the Market Place opposite Wycherley's Chemists there was no sign of any mob. In fact, there was no-one at all to be seen, only Mr Woodhead pulling away from Eyres' Garage in his coach, 'Lady Jane'.

14

A BIT OF A FUSS ON THE BACK OF A BUS.

Babs and The Pope walked along the Back Hills and down on to New Station Road, which they crossed cautiously, then ran to the next Cundy House and jumped over the railings into the Spring Field.

As far as they were aware no-one saw them. Although the field was slightly boggy when they reached the bottom where the springs appeared, they covered the ground quickly. They were soon through the hedge and across the next field between the Carr Vale end of the disused railway tunnel and Pip Hill's farm. When they got to Darwood Lane they slowed down and, feeling safe, Babs discussed chemistry with The Pope, who was the only other young person he knew that was knowledgeable enough about the subject to join in the discussion. They talked about various chemicals and their properties, stink bombs, explosives, his home made fireworks and the tests being done in the laboratories at the nearby Aroma Free Group of Companies.

They trudged up Polyfields and then walked along the path at the back of the garages that belonged to Castle Green residents. There was a tarmac drive in front of the row of ten individual garages of varying designs and materials, mostly prefabricated, with another two at the bottom end facing up the drive. Behind the row of garages was an eight feet high, thick, privet and hawthorn hedge bordering the footpath to Palterton.

The two boys had just joined the path when they were suddenly jumped from behind and smothered with handkerchiefs soaked in ether. They were both dragged into the back of a black van parked on the drive in front of the garages and it quickly sped away carrying the kidnappers and the kidnapped kids.

There were no witnesses to what happened and the kidnappers left no signs that they had been there. Except for two handkerchiefs, one bearing the letter A, the other the letter M.

Albert Woodhead drove along the top end of the Market Place and across the road into the bus garage at the rear of his house, Dane Bank, which stood between two public houses, the Black Bull and the White Swan.

"Ok boys," said Mr Woodhead in a friendly tone, as the bus came to a halt and he walked down the aisle to the back.

"What's going on ? You're in some kind of trouble again, I can see. What is it this time ?"

Olly nodded to Newt who brought out the note from his own, ever-present gas mask bag. "We found this in the woods after Wild Bill Hitchcock left it for Lettuce Stubley-Stanhope. It shows about their plan to kidnap Holness 'The Pope' in The Plaza tonight."

"Whoa there, who are these people ? Can't you leave out the nicknames for my benefit ?" said Albert laughing. "Right, so has someone been kidnapped ?"

"No sir," said Olly. "We turned up like the cavalry and Trapdoor, sorry, Trevor Appledore and that lot we just saw on Castle Street came as well and we nearly filled The Plaza. Those Indians didn't stand a chance, although we're usually on the side of the Red Indians, aren't we lads ? I mean they owned the land before the Cowboys arrived. Tecumseh !"

"Tecumseh !" shouted the other boys in response, causing Albert and his daughters to nearly jump out of their skin, after which they laughed at this unexpected outburst of Indian hero

worship, although it meant nothing to the three of them.
"Wait there," said Albert and he crept furtively to the end of his drive, just as Fred Kitchen, the local author, and his wife came walking past, having been to the Black Bull for a drink. "Ay up, Albert," greeted Fred. "What yer creepin' about for ? Are y'in trouble wi' t'missis ?"
The proprietor of Castle Coaches saw that Sergeant Pyewright and Constable Stagg were still standing beside the police car. As the Sergeant stood looking around and scratching his head, his Constable stood chewing his finger pensively as he peered towards Albert Woodhead and Mr and Mrs Kitchen. Albert had a sudden thought and grabbed Fred and Elizabeth's arms and led them down the drive and into the house. In the kitchen he found a small map of Filey and stuffed it in an envelope on which he wrote 'Neville Heath' and gave it to Mr Kitchen.
"Fred," said Albert. "Take this home with you and don't let anyone else open it. The gang are in danger and might need it. Someone's tried to kidnap one of them tonight."
"Right," said Fred, his trilby hat perched jauntily at an angle on his head, as always. "But couldn't you give it to 'im y'self. I swear I just saw young Neville and the rest of 'em through yonder window on your bus out there. And what's all this about 'em bein' kidnapped?"
Albert smiled and knew that Fred was far too clever and observant to be told half a story. Born in nearby Edwinstowe, where the 'Major Oak' was said to be a hiding place for Robin Hood and his Merrie Men, Fred Kitchen had been a simple farm labourer in his early working life. Except that he was far from simple and had expanded his knowledge in the 1930's by attending Workers' Education Association classes in literature, music, psychology and economics, before later beginning to write and having several books published. The gang recognised Fred's knowledge and, like themselves, his love of the countryside and shared a mutual respect over this. They would sometimes visit him with questions about wildlife or just life

and he had a lot of time for them.

"Ah see, Albert Woodhead," said Fred sternly. "You want me, a law abiding citizen, to act as a decoy and 'ope them coppers follow me in the discharge of their duties of catching criminals, so you can take them lads 'ome ?"

Albert smiled wryly and shook his head, saying, "You should be a policeman, Fred Kitchen."

"Give us that package," said Fred. "Follow us down yer drive and when we've gone ten yards, shout and tell me to put it in my pocket out of the way. We'll then walk as fast as we can to The Cavendish and break into a run round t' corner and up t' Kitchin Croft."

The couple set off down the drive and Albert walked to the road a few yards behind them. Fred was waving the package around but as they walked past the front door of The White Swan, Albert shouted and told him to put it in his pocket, in a tone reminiscent of "He's behind you" in a pantomime. Equally pantomime, Fred held up the package with his right hand and pointed to it with his left, looked around in an exaggerated manner then stuffed the envelope into his jacket pocket and strode off with Elizabeth as they both tried hard to conceal their laughter. As they neared The Cavendish Hotel, Fred cast an obvious glance across the Market Place towards the two policemen to check that he was being watched.

"Sergeant," said the Constable, pointing across the Market Place. "Fred Kitchen is behaving very oddly." The two policemen both watched open mouthed, hands on hips, as Fred and Elizabeth, sprightly for their ages, began to run and disappeared around the corner towards the Kitchin Croft (named after an 18th Century Bolsover clay pipe maker called John Kitchin.

"Quick, get in the car, lad," ordered Pyewright. "If we hurry we can possibly head them off."

"At the pass !" smirked Stagg, happy to have the thrill of a

chase for a change, even if it was only the normally respectable old couple. They might catch a fugitive for once, he thought. "If you took this job more seriously instead of behaving like some juvenile delinquent," barked the Sergeant, cuffing Stagg's ear. "Then we might stand a chance of preventing the Teddy Boys and layabouts from turning Great Britain into part of the Common Margate." "Common Market sir," replied Stagg. "Margate is a seaside town in Kent. Nice though, I ..."
"Just drive the car to Town End, then proceed up Oxcroft Lane, you big oaf," shouted Pyewright.
The junior officer realised that his Sergeant was not happy so he quickly started the engine and set off as instructed but with a squealing of tyres and brakes that always irritated his superior. As soon as the police car had gone past The Cavendish Hotel, Fred and Elizabeth Kitchen came back out of the side door of the pub through which they had earlier dashed and walked cautiously back into the Market Place, just as a green Corporation bus arrived that was destined for Mooracre Lane. They climbed aboard and sat down chuckling and giggling like teenagers, to the amusement of the bus conductor as he approached them, ticket machine ready.
"Two to Mooracre Lane please," said Fred presenting the correct fare with a broad grin.
"What's amusing you two then ?" enquired the conductor as he set the dial and wound the handle of his machine which produced the required tickets and he dropped the coins into the large leather cash bag slung around his shoulder and hanging by his waste.
Fred and Elizabeth simply laughed some more and shook their heads as they thought about the two policemen on their wild goose chase.

Albert Woodhead left his yard in his 1949 Rover 75 with the red leather seats and drove along the bottom of the Market Place to Town End. As he turned up Hornscroft Road towards the Parish Church he was surprised at the sight before him in the gathering dusk.

"What the heck is going on in Bolsover tonight?" said Albert.

"What's up Mr Woodhead?" chimed the boys as they raised their heads above the blankets under which they had been hiding and squashed in the back seat. Albert pulled over and stopped the car opposite the first house on Hornscroft Road. Around thirty yards further on a gang of ten Teddy Boys, although they would all be considered as grown men rather than boys, had run from the path through the churchyard, straight across the road and down the alley between the houses and on to the Hornscroft. He shook his head and was about to start moving again when he first heard, then saw a column of around a hundred younger teenagers, boys and girls, who charged along the same path and followed the supposed tough guys who were beating a hasty retreat.

"What the ... ?" said the open mouthed and shocked Albert as the boys sat up in the back seat and cheered Trapdoor leading his troops.

"Come on. Thanks Mr Woodhead," shouted Olly and they all leapt out of the back doors of the Rover and ran up the road to join their friends. They disappeared round the back of Hornscroft Terrace and vaulted over the wall into the park, calling after their friends. Albert sat flabbergasted for two minutes before he turned the car around and went home. Olly and Mac shouted to Trapdoor and his army to stop, so the pursuit of the Teddy boys, who had Malcolm 'Sneaky' Snead and Lynda Marshall with them, was halted.

"They're getting away," complained Trapdoor, waving his hand behind him disappointedly.

"Don't worry Trapdoor," said Olly. "We've stopped them getting The Pope, that's all that matters really. Come on everybody, let's doss round the pavilion where we can't be seen."

"How are over a hundred of us going to get anywhere that we

can't be seen?" said Balsa and they all laughed as they walked past the tennis courts to the pavilion. The old men who came to the bowling green during the day had all gone home or to the pub and there was no-one around. It was almost dark. They sat on the walkway and steps of the building and chatted excitedly about never having had such fun as they had enjoyed tonight.

"We'll laugh about this for ages," said Webby. "The Fire Engine was at the back of The Plaza when we came past. And we saw Pyewright and Stagg chasing around like idiots in their police car, probably looking for us. They disappeared up Welbeck Road."

"Mmm," said Olly chewing his finger. "Pyewright might be stupid but that Stagg has his head screwed on right. Never mind them, at least The Pope will have got home safe."

Wilfred Holness worked long hours on Lilac Farm, located on Main Street in Palterton and even the next day's important cricket match did not shorten his day. When he came in from his labours at 9:00 o'clock that evening, his wife, Mary, set a large mug of tea on the big, old farmhouse kitchen table at which he sat and he gratefully quenched his thirst. He raised his eyebrows and looked up at the ceiling at the sound coming from upstairs.

"Him and that blooming devil music. I don't know what they see in that stuff. You can't tell what they're singing and you can't tell the boys from the girls. Give me the Joe Loss Orchestra any day," said Wilfred, which were similar to sentiments voiced by most parents.

On this occasion, since he had made his eldest son stay in to protect him from injury ahead of the cricket match, he did not go upstairs to tell him to 'switch off that terrible racket', which was just as well as The Pope had not yet returned from the pictures. Mrs Holness was beginning to feel a little concerned that their son had still not come home but she decided not to tell her husband yet. He would be on the next bus, she was sure. Mary chewed her lip and wondered what to do while her husband had his bath. She was more than grateful for the time to think things through as she busied herself in the kitchen and had decided to tell him the whole story when he came back downstairs.

Babs and The Pope were both bound and gagged, rope around their ankles and their wrists, hands behind their backs and sticking plaster and bandages over their mouths, laid on their sides in the back of the van. They were accompanied by five men in balaclavas and three more sat in the front with their heads similarly covered.

Babs began to shout, which came out as a loud indistinct mumbo jumbo.

"Hell, I fee ick. I pie o'foyick."

"What should we do Ringo ?" said one of the men in the back to another one in the front.

"Stupid," came an irritated reply. "I told you all not to use names, you idiot. Too late now. Anyway, you can take off their gags now, no-one will hear them. Watch them in case they have something up their sleeve."

'Stupid' took off their gags and they both took in deep breaths and cleared their throats. "More like it's you lot that's got something up your sleeves," shouted The Pope angrily.

"Yes, I've really got something up my sleeve," added Babs sarcastically. "I'm pyrophoric so there's no way I could untie these ropes and anyway, I need a drink, I'm choking."

The kidnappers ignored the word they had not understood and 'Stupid' held a glass pop bottle filled with water in front of Babs so he could have a drink but the van went over a pot hole and the bottle smacked him in the mouth, cutting his lip and gums.

The Pope understood that his friend really did have something up his sleeve that was 'pyrophoric', or self igniting, when the parts in secret compartments in each sleeve were mixed together. Colwyn's suspicions were confirmed when Babs winked at him.

"Can you drop me off in Palterton," said The Pope sarcastically. "I'm playing cricket tomorrow and my dad expects me to have an early night."

"Shut your shine, suntrap," replied 'Stupid', getting his words mixed up and amusing his mates. "I mean shut your trap, sunshine," he blurted angrily, as everyone tried unsuccessfully to hide their laughter.

Ringo climbed into the back of the van and gave The Pope a hard cuff across his face, cutting the second boy's lip badly because of the rings he wore. Babs' cuffs were too hard for him to move his hands as well for now and would have to wait until they were not being watched so closely before he could reach and use his pyrophorics.

15

THE 1812 OVERTHROW BY TCHAIKOVSKY.
(OR A GUARD DOG, A DUCK AND A RAILWAY SLEEPER.)

It was the day after the Plaza Plan had appeared to be so successful. The gang had been round the woods all day and were returning along Gang Lane. As they peered over the hedge at the Annual Scarcliffe versus Palterton cricket match, they looked for their friend, The Pope.
"All that fun, I mean trouble, we had last night," said Balsa. "And he isn't even playing, eh ?"
"Shhh," whispered Mac. "What the heck is going on here ? Down the end of the lane, look." He threw his arms out to stop everyone then jumped to the side and pointed towards the road, where a police car was parked across the lane end like a road block.
Two policemen they did not know, not Pyewright and Stagg, were patrolling the road, apparently watching Main Street in both directions, as well as Budget Lane, and Manor Lodge, where Rothschild was staying, but ignoring Gang Lane where the boys were hiding.
Four of the gang crouched low beside the hedge of the Vicarage while the other three were on the opposite side of the lane, behind Bathurst Cottage and Stone Row. Mac on the Vicarage side whispered to Willie and Newt to go through into the Vicarage garden and then crawl through the field above the

tunnel to reconnoitre Main Street downhill from Gang Lane. Olly, on the other side of the lane, then told Balsa and Trapdoor to get through their hedge into the field and crawl along the garden of Bathurst Cottage to get a look at the uphill part of Main Street.

Behind them along Gang Lane, the sounds of the game of village cricket echoed from the field between the Vicarage, the Railway Cutting, the Little Wood and the lane itself. The big game of every summer between Scarcliffe and their rival village of Palterton continued, the players and large crowd oblivious to the unfolding scene on Main Street. Scarcliffe were demolishing Palterton yet again, in the absence of their star, Colwyn Holness. Willie stayed as low as a snake and pushed himself through the bottom of the hedge with a struggle, crawling through nettles and thorny branches. Newt meanwhile simply stood up and quietly walked a few yards forward, then turned and sauntered through the gate into the Vicarage grounds. Willie shook his head and laughed as he followed Newt into the adjacent field where they both commando-crawled across towards Main Street. As the two boys hid and watched they were shocked to see Rothschild brought out of the cottage in handcuffs by a man not in uniform and placed in the police car at the entrance to Gang Lane. This man spoke to the two uniformed men then went back into the cottage. After ten minutes the four spies returned and reported their findings. Two Police Cars were parked across Main Street, blocking the road either side of Gang Lane. An unmarked car similarly blocked Budget Lane leading up to Bolsover Road, effectively sealing off Manor Lodge. Two officers stood guard by each vehicle and more seemed to be in the cottage. Newt told how he had found that morning that he still had some of Babs' bombs in his gas mask bag – stink, smoke and exploding varieties so Olly divided them up and planned a diversion. He gave everyone a job to do and when they were all in position he gave a signal.

Mac first threw a bomb which set off an explosion outside the front door to the cottage and Olly immediately did the same at the back door, to make the police officers inside the property remain there. As one of the two police officers on Gang Lane ran to investigate, Newt made a dash to the cottage gate shouting that he had to rescue Tchaikovsky the cat. When the remaining police officer chased and grabbed Newt, the rest of the boys arrived and 'helped', while Olly pulled Rothschild, still handcuffed, out of the car and away up Gang Lane. In the mêlée, one of the boys snatched the keys from the police officer without him realising and he told them all to go away and not get in the way. They did just that and melted away, running off in different directions as pre-planned, with Newt sprinting up Gang Lane as fast as he could with the key to the handcuffs. He did not dare to be seen by the cricketers and spectators so he too was taking a long route to their destination of the tunnel.

The others sauntered away, all making a point of saying goodbye to the officers, then once out of sight ran as fast as they could go without arousing suspicion but, in any case, most people were at the cricket match. Each of them headed by different routes to Wood Lane at the bottom end of the village. Balsa knew that, on this occasion, he was unable to go to the tunnel here in Scarcliffe as he had reluctantly agreed to stand in for Babs, the master bike thief and cyclist. He was therefore to steal a bike and race by road to Bolsover and the other end of the tunnel at Carr Vale, and to pick up everyone from last night along the way.

All the police officers had now managed to escape from the house, no more bombs having gone off. They rushed out of the front gate and gathered beside the police car opposite, away from the stinking smoke and gas.

After looking into the car an Inspector addressed the two officers who had stayed outside supposedly guarding Rothschild.

"Where's the bloody prisoner, you useless pair of halfwits ?"
"He was here when the bangs started at 18:12 precisely, sir and those boys came to rescue Tchaikovsky," said one fearfully.
"What the hell are you talking about Constable ? This isn't the 18 blooming 12 Overthrow" shouted his superior. "And it was 16:12, not 18:12. Can't you even tell the time ?"
"Overture sir, you mean the 1812 Overture, sir, by Tchaikovsky, sir. Oh yeah, 16:12, sir,"
The now beetroot faced Inspector grabbed the Constable by the neck and shook him.
"What boys ? And where's our prisoner ? And what's Tchaikovsky got to do with it ? Find those boys ! Find him ! Check every house in the village ! Now !!"

Once all the boys arrived on Wood Lane they carried on without a backward glance up the lane and over the style into the first field, then on towards the dangerously steep railway cutting. A few weeks earlier, when they had brought Joss, the Woods' family dog, he had chased a rabbit down the embankment and they realised, on closer inspection, that they had found a quick and only slightly dangerous way down the steep sides. As one by one they reached this point they appeared to jump into the cutting and collected and hid in the overgrown and flooded part of the cutting just outside of the tunnel doors. Willie, the last one to arrive, was enjoying the chase so much that he threw himself down the steep embankment excitedly instead of sliding down carefully as the others had done.
He realised his mistake when he hit a block of concrete at the bottom and everyone heard his leg break with a loud crack which sent a searing pain through his lower leg. They all instantly knew that they had a problem and Willie knew that he was the problem.
"Cut me two branches that I can use as crutches," he said with an air of sadness as he knew that he would hold them back.

"And I'll go back along the cutting and up Station Road back into the village. Then I can perhaps get someone to take me home or to the hospital."

Giggsy and Trapdoor used their machetes to cut and fashion a pair of crutches for Willie. Trapdoor tested them before presenting them to the boy who seemed strangely pleased with his new toy as he set off back along the cutting.

"See you at home," he whispered.

Seconds later Olly and Newt slid down the steep sided cutting, while the Baron descended in both comparative slow motion and awe of his young rescuers.

"What's happened to our Will and why's he saying he'll see us all at home ?" asked Olly.

"He's broke his leg jumping down the cutting too fast," replied Giggsy.

"We made him some crutches and he's hobbled off up Station Road to look for help." added Trapdoor.

"Well, he'd better be alright or you're all for it. You should have looked after him better. What's our mam going to say ? Come on, let's get into the tunnel quick," urged Olly.

Giggsy grabbed what seemed to be two branches from within a tree that grew near the tunnel doors but on being pulled out was clearly visible as a roughly hewn wooden ladder made from branches. One by one they climbed up and through the metal window at the top of the doors and Newt, as last man, pulled the ladder through too. Victor Rothschild was ever more impressed by this strange gang of heroes.

"No messing about this time and no talking," ordered Olly seriously, "We have to be quick and careful, especially when we get to the roof fall."

Newt drew out four torches from his gas mask bag and handed out three of them to Olly, Mac and Giggsy, keeping one himself. "Don't switch yours on yet, our Newt and Giggsy, till we're past the mound," said Olly. "Me and Mac will light the way at the front."

The two oldest boys went side by side at the front and lit up their path ahead while Newt and Giggsy waited to be told to switch on their torches. As they were about to set off Giggsy got a bag of sweets out of his pocket.

"Bullseye, Mr Baron?"

"Yes, thankyou, errr," replied the man, unsure in the darkness who it was offering them.

"It's Giggsy, Mr Baron," he said, switching on his torch and lighting up his face scarily.

Not wanting to be outdone, Newt retrieved his own bag of sweets from his pocket. "Flying saucer, Baron?"

"Err thankyou, is it Neville?"

"Yes sir, Baron, there you go." He offered his bag and the man took a sweet.

Trapdoor pulled a packet from his pocket.

"Oxo cube, Mr Baron? I like them better than spice."

Olly turned angrily on those behind him.

"Look you lot, this isn't a party or a picnic. We're being chased by the cops because we've liberated Mr Baron here so we're in big trouble if we get caught. So keep quiet."

Willie was hobbling up Station Road towards the village on his makeshift crutches as fast as his little legs, or at least, one of them, would carry him when he suddenly got the urge to have some of the Barley Sugar Twists he had in his pocket.

"Energy," he thought. "All this Hopalong Cassidy hobbling and not much Speedy Gonzales, I need some energy."

He stopped at the side of the road and hovered on his one good leg, supported by his crutches held in one hand, as he attempted to use his other hand to get his Barley Sugar Twists out of his pocket. He wobbled for a few seconds and then he toppled over.

"Willie, hobble, hover, wibble, wobble, topple, nettles, ouch ..." he said to himself after he hit the ground.

They say that every cloud has a silver lining and, moments after he toppled over and fell into a bed of two foot high nettles, the cloud appeared in the shape of two people coming along the lane towards where Willie had just been standing. As the men passed him, nestling unseen in the nettles, Willie heard two voices that he recognised as Hector Stubley-Stanhope and William "Wild Bill" Hitchcock.

"They'll have headed for the tunnel, I'm sure," said Hector Stubley-Stanhope. "We can shoot them all in there and no-one will know. What weapons have you brought ?"

"I've got the two rifles and three handguns, the SIG, the Ruger and the Smith and Wesson," replied the Gamekeeper, not even appearing to flinch about killing the boys.

Willie froze on hearing these words which he thought seemed a bit extreme just because they caused him a few problems in the woods. Still, the men had not seen him, so he must be well hidden. The men strode purposefully along the lane to the station and then turned up the cutting. Willie tried to pull himself up using a branch but found he was unable to because of his badly injured leg. He was astonished to feel a soft, fragrant hand placed over his mouth from behind although he was even more shocked when he turned around and saw Mrs Scholes, his school deputy headmistress. The lady had her finger to her lips telling him to keep quiet, then she leaned back and looked along the lane to make sure the men had really gone. She looked back up Station Road towards the village and whispered, "Come on, quick."

"I can't Miss, I think I've broke my leg and you're standing on my crutch," replied Willie as quietly as possible.

Mrs Scholes at first was puzzled but, on moving aside, saw that she had indeed been standing on a roughly cut wooden crutch and that there was another one nearby. She managed to pull him up and placed them under his arms whereupon he set off up the road with the Deputy Headmistress hovering in close attendance. As they reached houses, Mrs Scholes dashed into the drive of the first property, Jasmine Cottage, where she lived. Willie felt a little wary but relaxed when she came out of the front door and helped him into the big 1939 Rover 12 on the drive. The car itself was a definite attraction for him at any time, and especially now with a broken leg.

"Let's get you to hospital," said the lady, smiling as she set off up Station Road much faster than Willie expected a schoolteacher would drive.

"Please miss, don't go up Main Street because ..." Willie tailed off his warning about the police as the officer standing in the middle of the junction signalled them to stop.

"Leave this to me," whispered the teacher before she wound down the window.

"Hello, Officer, how may I help you ? I'm Mrs Scholes, the village school Deputy Headmistress."

"Sorry to trouble you Madam but we've had some trouble in the village and a gang of boys are involved. Can I ask you who the lad is and where you're going?" enquired the policeman.

"Of course," replied the lady convincingly, "This is my son, William, and I'm taking him to Drama School in Chesterfield. Break a leg and all that, as they say in the theatre."

The Officer looked up the street uncertainly, searching for inspiration. "Err, alright Madam, you can carry on and, yes, break a leg, William," said the smiling but nervous PC Marsh. As the car headed up Fox's Hill and out of the village Mrs Scholes was already persuading William to tell her the truth about what had happened and he felt unable to resist, so he told her everything, almost. He deliberately made no mention of Babs whose reputation and scientific knowledge, particularly of explosives, did not endear him to teachers, when his performance and behaviour in class, even in science, did not match that knowledge.

"It's complicated Miss," began Willie and he did not finish the story until they were near the hospital in Chesterfield.

Mrs Scholes became increasingly wide eyed, with a mixture of alarm, humour, intrigue, and suspicion at the story she was

told, especially when he related the details of the guns that
'Wild Bill' Hitchcock was alleged to have spoken of having in
his possession, which she had been too far away to hear.
On their arrival at the hospital the concerned teacher explained
the background to William's injury to the reception staff and
asked to use a telephone to contact the police.

When Balsa reached Wood Lane he sneaked into the large
workshop of the first house on the lane, where he knew several
bikes would be attached to brackets on the wall. He also knew
that he had to make as little noise as possible so he wrapped
some rags around the bracket which he then gave a hefty
whack with a lump hammer he found. The bracket came out of
the wall and he caught it to avoid being heard. He grabbed a
hacksaw from the work bench in case he needed it later, then
ran the bike out of the workshop and down the lane. He was
about to jump on and peddle out of Wood Lane when he first
heard, then saw, Mrs Scholes come roaring out of Station Road
in her old Rover with, to his shock and amazement, his brother
Willie sat in the passenger seat.
Hearing PC Marsh's footsteps running back on to Main Street,
he went back up Wood Lane and hid in Kilroys' yard.
"Bring it back when you've finished with it, Balsa," whispered
the familiar voice of Johnnie Kilroy from behind him.
"Thanks Johnnie," said the relieved Balsa and, seeing the police
officer walk past the end of the lane and head back up Main
Street, he sneaked across the road.
Once out of sight he jumped on his borrowed getaway vehicle
and pedalled towards Fox's Hill. As he left the village, a motor
cycle gang of around fifteen motor bikes passed him coming
the other way into the village – it was the Rockers from The
Plaza, even more of them this time.

The gang in the tunnel had quietened down on Olly's
instruction, even the Baron, and they were about to try again to
set off towards the light at the end of the tunnel at the Carr

Vale end when they heard adult voices outside in the cutting. Olly silently put his finger to his lips in a sign to everyone in the half light to be quiet.

"We'll never get up there and into the tunnel Hector," Wild Bill was heard to say, "Not carrying these guns anyway but ******** said we have to get rid of that bunch of rats."

The name he had said was garbled to the tunnel occupants, as in the background the nearby thwack of willow on leather from the village cricket match, to accompanying cheers, happened at the same time. William "Welly It" Elliott had just hit another six to win the match for Scarcliffe. Moments later there was the distinctive sound of the cricket ball travelling into the cutting like a missile, followed by a sickening thud, a moan and a clearly shocked reaction from Wild Bill as Hector slumped to the ground, stunned and bleeding from a nasty head wound.

"Damn bloody villagers and their cricket," observed Hitchcock as he knelt and tended to Mr Stubley-Stanhope, the injured party.

Taking advantage of the distraction, Olly signalled to his men to follow him as he tiptoed away from the mouth of the tunnel into the darkness but without switching on their torches. Victor marvelled again at their intelligence and organisation but said nothing.

Within minutes of setting off they arrived at the roof fall that Olly had caused the last time they walked through the tunnel. He and Mac said at the time that it was too dangerous to attempt it again but on this occasion they felt they had no choice. Now it seemed more dangerous than ever as they were pursued by policemen who they did not know, a gamekeeper who had been told by someone to kill them all and Hector the cricket ball deflector. At least their eyes had adjusted to the darkness, allowing them to see better.

The group became silent in awe of the enormous pile of bricks, concrete, wood and earth piled up against one side of the tunnel. They stood and stared, with the frightening image in their minds of how they might have been buried and killed. Now they scrambled past the other side in single file, all the time looking at the six feet high and twelve feet across, mountain of rubble and wreckage that seemed to be trying to grab and consume them.

When they reached the other side of the mound there was clear and universal relief which was instantly replaced by shock at the sight that appeared in front of them as the torches were switched on.

Their friends Babs and The Pope sat back to back on the floor, gagged and heavily bound together with thick rope.

"What have you two been up to?" Olly said to them in disbelief as he attacked the ropes with his sharp Bowie knife which quickly freed the pair.

He pulled Babs to his feet while Mac similarly helped up The Pope. Both of them wobbled and staggered as if they had just stepped off a ship that had crossed a storm lashed Bay of Biscay.

At the same time, Balsa was two miles away on Johnnie's bike, approaching Hillstown crossroads, in the shadow of the concrete water tower at the junction of Langwith Road and Portland Avenue. A group of six boys crossing the road had to dash out of his way and he skidded to a halt.

"Micko, it's carrying on from The Plaza last night," shouted Balsa, without giving away what was carrying on, which he was unsure of anyway. "Our Olly says to get as many together as possible again and meet at the entrance to the tunnel down Carr Vale. They're on their way through the tunnel from Scarcliffe now, being chased by that gang of Rockers and there's lots more of them. I saw them on their motor bikes heading for the tunnel as I was leaving the village." He'd made up half of this but it could be true and it had the required effect.

"Ok, we'll get everybody," shouted the six boys excitedly and they divided up Hillstown and Bolsover between them and ran off in various directions to round up the Cavalry and Red Indians from the previous night. They succeeded in getting almost everyone, plus a few new faces and soon amassed around a hundred and forty young people - boys and girls - who made their way noisily to the cutting at the big metal doors that barred the disused tunnel.

The cycling, winged messenger, Balsa, set off once more, pedalling furiously down New Station Road in Bolsover, not far from the end of the tunnel where he would, hopefully, be joined by enough of his comrades to help the gang to escape both any pursuers and the tunnel itself. Why he was still pedalling so fast when going down such a steep road was anyone's guess but he was, like all the gang, confident in his ability to ride a bike.

The Olly Wood Gang were mostly principled bicycle thieves for they always returned any bikes they had borrowed to either their owners or where they 'found' them. Not only that, Babs always repaired and cleaned them. 'Gave them a good service' as he called it. Balsa finally came to a halt fifty yards after he began braking and some distance past the entrance to the footpath leading to the bridge over the railway cutting. The boy was quick though and soon reached the footbridge. In his haste however he took the route down into the cutting that they usually took on foot. Balsa clung on for dear life when the bike shook violently as it careered down a well-used but steep and bumpy path to the floor of the old railway cutting. To his great surprise, when he reached the bottom he was still upright and sitting on the saddle with both feet on the pedals. He resumed pedalling and despite rough ground and undergrowth he soon arrived at the tunnel and its great big metal doors.

Within minutes the reinforcements began to arrive in groups of ever increasing numbers and they congregated in front of the doors. Balsa hushed them to be quiet, without much success, so Irene shouted, "Shut Uuuuppp !" to enable him to speak.

He told them what had happened and how Babs and The Pope had disappeared, probably kidnapped. Balsa announced their plan every few minutes, for the benefit of every group of new arrivals, so some of them heard it at least five times. The floor of the cutting was not as flooded here as it was at the Scarcliffe end but there were still some large puddles of water, in places over two inches deep, where the sun did not reach. This was just too much for Webby to resist on such a hot summer evening and he kicked at a puddle, sending a large spray over everyone within his range, but mostly over Irene, Annie and Jessie James. The three girls stretched their arms out wide and took sharp breaths in shock and anger at being soaked by their frequent tormentor. Irene kicked back at her own puddle, sending her spray off at right angles and totally soaking Paul Morley, Micko and Jasper and these three laughed with everyone else. A kick-water fight took place, lasting several minutes, as it spread through the crowd until Balsa insisted that they concentrated on getting into the tunnel and helping the gang.

The fight subsided and Irene suggested that the strongest boys should form a human pyramid against the outside of the giant metal doors to let everyone climb up, starting with herself first. She was surprised when Balsa agreed to the idea and the human pyramid was quickly started amid much laughter and a certain amount of chaos. Irene climbed on to the first bent leg, then up a variety of sturdy limbs and shoulders and even a head on one occasion to reach the hinged window which easily opened and through which she swung and disappeared inside. Dropping to the ground she turned and saw a succession of heads, each followed by its body come through as they began to join her one by one. Soon there were over fifty when the procession seemed to stop and an argument began outside.

"What's happening?" asked Irene but her words struggled to be heard above the din. After several minutes of shouting something heavy seemed to be thrown against the outside of the doors, which was followed by loud cheering.

"One at a time," instructed Balsa loudly. "We don't want to break it."

Moments later he popped his head through the window and announced with a laugh to those already inside, "I forgot there was a big wooden ladder hidden in the bushes."

He turned to those outside and said, "The last person to come in will have to pull the ladder up and bring it into the tunnel so we can do without having to build stupid human pyramids in the dark."

Police Constable Marsh, who hadn't let Mrs Scholes and Willie go up Main Street, started to go back up that street himself. He had just passed the village Post Office when he heard the roar of numerous motor bikes so he turned to stop them coming up Main Street. It was a great surprise to him when they went down Station Road, since there was no longer a station and the only other thing down there of any note was the sewage treatment plant. Rather than follow and confront them himself he decided it would be best to report their arrival to his superiors back at the junction of Gang Lane with Main Street. As he hurried past the church, then the Manor House, he remembered his conversation with his friend, Constable Ian Stagg and the constantly interrupting Sergeant Pyewright. It was the sergeant who had gone to Inspector Spector with Stagg's roll of wallpaper, which Pyewright said showed that a Mr Hector Stubley-Stanhope of Manor HOUSE, instead of Manor LODGE, was to be arrested there although he now seemed to have been freed by a bunch of kids. Passing Wildgooses' Scarcliffe Hall Farm and Wigleys' Manor Farm, PC Marsh wondered how he should break this news about their mistake to his sergeant and even worse, to Inspector Spector, known to his men as Phil. He was lucky, he thought, when it was Sergeant Mills that approached him as he neared the cottage.

"Anything to report, constable ?"

"Yes sarge," said the young officer nervously. "First I encountered a school teacher lady, Mrs Scholes, the Headmistress, taking her son, William to his drama school in Chesterfield."

Sergeant Mills raised his eyebrows. "I know Mrs Scholes, who doesn't have a son called William," commented the sergeant, deflating the PC. "Carry on constable. Anything else ?"

"Yes sarge," resumed the young man with a sigh. "After they'd left and I'd begun walking back up Main Street, I heard the roar of a large number of motor cycles and turned to see around twenty of them come from the Shirebrook direction and head straight down Station Road. As this leads only to a disused railway station, disused railway line and disused railway tunnel, also a sewerage works, plus a farm and a couple of houses, I thought it was strange and I should report these facts to you. And finally sarge, as I was walking, I mean hurrying, back up Main Street, I noticed a sign for Manor House, near the church, then further up a sign for Manor Farm and, on the cottage we raided, a sign saying Manor Lodge, sarge and I remembered we were supposed to be raiding the Manor House address, sarge sir."

"Damn !!" exclaimed Sergeant Mills at this last part of the report. "Damn !!" he repeated.

The Inspector was meekly informed of all of these developments and he predictably exploded with anger and demanded to know who was to blame for the targeting of the wrong address and the resulting wrongful arrest, even though the suspect, suspiciously, had escaped. And he, the Inspector, would be a laughing stock at the Lodge (Mason's, not Manor).

The whole of the operation moved two hundred yards down Main Street, fifty officers and three road blocks, but there proved to be no-one in at the Manor House. None of the police seemed to be aware that almost the whole village was at the cricket match up Gang Lane. Forty-five of the officers and two of the road blocks moved further down Main Street to Station Road.

Balsa's boys and girls were making progress through the tunnel while trying to make as little noise as possible, which was not easy for a hundred and forty pairs of footsteps marching in the echoing underground chamber. The leader voiced his concern by saying "Shhhhh !" to those immediately behind him, who repeated the sound to those in the next row until it spread right through the column like a steam engine. Balsa liked the atmosphere that this created and began making the noise rhythmically and it was quickly picked up by everyone.
The rest of the gang, the Baron and the now liberated Babs and The Pope were still over a mile away from the oncoming 'train' and its sound had not yet become obvious to them.
Outside the thick, iron doors of the Scarcliffe end of the tunnel Hector angrily got to his feet.
"Shoot at the lock of the access door and blast our way in, Hitchcock. I've had enough of this being messed about by a bunch of kids and stupid villagers playing their game of cricket."
The gamekeeper unzipped his padded, canvas gun bag and took out the frightening, Magnum 44-firing, Smith and Wesson Model 29 and the SIG P210 Swiss Army Pistol. Two shots were fired that saw the lock shatter in the small door but alerted the whole village, cricket fans, police, rockers and the Olly Wood gang, that someone meant mean business.
The cricket match had just ended and rival fans swarmed on to the pitch amid accusations from the Palterton people that Colwyn Holness had been kidnapped by the Scarcliffe people to safeguard their winning streak. Even the visiting dignitary, Andrew, the Duke of Devonshire, tried to pacify everyone but arguments were breaking out and fights were about to start when the first, unmistakeable shot was heard from yards away

in the cutting. Half of the crowd ran away from the railway like an express train on the 'up Gang Lane' line, around fifty stood rooted to the spot on the cricket pitch, scared out of their wits, while the rest, led bravely by the Duke, rushed to the edge and peered down the steep drop into the cutting, just as the second shot was fired into the door and finally shattered the lock.

"I say, Hector and Hitchcock, what the heck is going on down there, dammit ?" asked Andrew Cavendish, the 11th Duke. Wild Bill Hitchcock spun round and fired another shot, this time with the other handgun, the Ruger Blackhawk, over the heads of the watching crowd, causing them all to dive to the ground and crawl quickly away.

"Shot at by my own gamekeeper ! Right. Listen everyone," said the Duke quietly, taking charge. "No-one will get hurt so long as we don't put our heads above the parapet. Someone high tail it to the vicarage and telephone for the police."

A man stood up and said, "It might be best if I go, sir."

"Ah, yes, well done, vicar. Good man," observed a slightly embarrassed Andrew Cavendish. "You'll be the right man for that job, knowing where your telephone is and all that."

The 'revved up Reverend' sprinted across the cricket field and hurdled the vicarage fence to the astonishment of those present.

"Crikey," said the Duke. "I'd back the vicar over fences. Come on you chaps, let's collect sticks and stones to throw into the cutting at Hector and Hitchcock to keep them penned in until the constabulary arrive. They don't shoot at Scarcliffe and Palterton men and get away with it, do they, chaps ?"

Everyone set to and scrambled around finding suitable missiles to hurl down on their armed attackers. They assembled in front of the Duke looking like a platoon of the Home Guard.

"Excuse me, captain, err, Sir Duke, sir," said one fellow. "Wouldn't it be a good idea for some of our troops to take that footpath across the top of the tunnel and go around to the other side of the cutting so that we can launch a second offensive from the other side, sir?"

"Good idea. What's your name, that man?"

"Elliot, sir. William 'Welly it' Elliot, sir. I hit the winning six in the match, sir," came the reply. "Splendid, Elliot, you take your chaps and on a count of three we bombard the blighters." 'Welly it' led a group of men and children round to the other side of the cutting, then he waved a stick with his hankie tied to it to indicate that they were ready. The duke counted down, "Three, two, one …"

All hell rained down on Hector Stubley-Stanhope and 'Wild Bill' Hitchcock from their unseen assailants and they were shocked when it became clear that they were being attacked from both sides.

"Hurry up and get that door open, Hitchcock," urged Hector. Wild Bill took a step back and launched the sole of his boot just below the half mutilated lock area of the access door. It flew inwards with a loud echoing bang and the two targets disappeared into the tunnel while at the top of the cutting the stone-throwers continued hurling their missiles towards the big metal doors.

The gang of leather-jacketed rockers walked along the cutting from the station and were puzzled by the sticks and stones that were raining down from above on both sides as they neared the tunnel.

"Come on," said their leader making a snap decision. "Something's going on. We'd better make ourselves scarce. Sticks and stones may break our bones and all that."

They turned and ran back to the station where they had hidden their motorcycles round the back of the old platform and were about to kick-start the bikes when they heard footsteps. Leader-man raised a finger to his lips to urge quiet and they were relieved to hear a voice say,

"This way. That noise sounds like it's coming from the cutting leading to the tunnel."

Inspector Spector led his policemen up the cutting and the

Rockers kicked their bikes off their stands and pushed them along the trail that had once been the railway line heading in the opposite direction towards Shirebrook. Although it was hard work to push their machines the leader would not allow anyone to start up their engines until they reached Langwith Junction to avoid attracting unwanted attention from the 'Rozzers', as the police were known.

The Olly Wood Gang plus the Baron had heard the gunshots and turned to face eastwards, towards Langwith Junction, Shirebrook and Lincoln along the one-time Lancashire, Derbyshire & East Coast Railway. There followed apparent peppershots sprayed at the big doors, interrupted by a loud echoing clang that sounded to them like someone had kicked open the small access door, which they thought must be true when an even bigger light at the end of the tunnel suddenly shone from the door. The peppershots continued.

"Listen, what's that noise?" whispered Olly, as he turned an ear to each end of the tunnel.

"Sounds like loads of twelve-bores being fired at the doors," suggested The Pope helpfully.

"No, not the noise from the Scarcliffe end," said Olly quietly, pointing towards Carr Vale.

Everyone leaned and stuck out an ear in the direction indicated but they all scratched their heads while their eyebrows and mouths were screwed up to show that they heard nothing.

"What can you hear?" asked Mac, knowing his friend had better hearing than anyone.

"Couldn't be certain," replied Olly, concentrating. "But it sounds like a train's coming."

The boys all laughed knowingly, whereas Victor Rothschild wondered how this could be so.

16

EYE OF NEWT AND TOE OF FROG – DOUBLE TROUBLE PILE OF RUBBLE

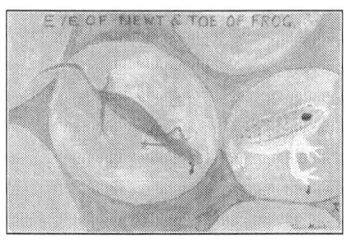

On approaching the tunnel and the hail of missiles from both sides Inspector Spector suddenly stopped and held out his arms to halt his men, who clumsily bumped into him.
"Stop," shouted Derek Spector upwards through cupped hands. "This is the police. We have you surrounded. Now stop throwing stones and give yourselves up. You're under arrest."
The missiles stopped raining down into the cutting and a head appeared, then many others.
"Hello Specky," said the duke. "I didn't think you would get here so quickly or with so many men but where are Hector and Hitchcock ? They are armed, old chap. Shot at us in fact."
Several police hands pointed towards the open door to the tunnel and all eyes followed.
"Come on men," boomed Inspector Spector and he stooped to pick up some handy stones. "Weapons at the ready."
No-one seemed too keen to face guns with stones until PC Marsh stepped forward, picked up his weapons and stood by the Inspector. All the other officers joined them, if somewhat cautiously and stayed behind the crazy Inspector.
Inside the tunnel Hector and Hitchcock heard the whole of this hullabaloo and ran away into the darkness as fast as they could. As they reached the mound of rubble that was deposited on the gang's previous visit, the two men stood still and listened

when they saw the boys and heard a strange shunting sort of noise.

"Fire a shot to scare those ruffians, Hitchcock," instructed Hector. "Then we can move on."

"What, shoot AT them?"

"No, you fool, up above," replied the bossy one curtly. The gamekeeper did as he thought he was told and fired one shot.

"This is the police," shouted Inspector Spector. "Put your hands down and your guns up."

Before he had chance to correct himself there was a loud rumble as the roof caved in where it had been shot by Hitchcock.

"Run for it!" went up a shout further into the tunnel as bricks, mortar, metal, wood and earth, assorted debris and a cloud of dust descended from the roof and the walls.

The gang and the baron raced away for a hundred yards but then Olly stopped them.

"Listen, it's not falling now. We can't just leave them back there. They might still be alive."

He began walking back and switched on his torch but could see little because of the dust. The others all followed him, as they always did wherever he led them. When they reached the start of the new mound of debris Olly put out his arms and they all stood still and listened again.

Behind them, they could hear the rhythmic sound of the steam train coming through the tunnel. In front of them, the mound, beyond which could be heard Inspector Spector shouting.

"Can you hear me? This is the police. Is anyone there?"

"Yes," replied Olly. "Stop shouting and get out of the tunnel. It isn't safe. We'll see if we can get them out and get them to the Carr Vale end. Get a doctor to come there. We're safe."

Olly then turned around, walked away a few paces and shouted at the oncoming train.

"Balsa, stop that noise and get here quickly and quietly but don't run."

When the train arrived there were so many there that it was like a crowd waiting to enter a football match.

"Right everybody, two blokes are buried under this lot but not far away," said Olly. "Get in, say, six lines stretching down the tunnel and all of you pull out your shirts. We'll pick up the rubble and debris and you catch it in your upturned shirt or jumper and carry it past the end of the line and dump it, then join the queue again. Any questions?"

"How do you know they're not far away?" asked Jack who always asked good questions.

"Because there's the gun," replied Olly, shining his torch at the floor nearby to illustrate. "Let's get on with it and no more noise."

He pulled the weapon out and handed it to the Baron, before ushering him to one side as the six lines formed of boys and girls holding up the fronts of their shirts to catch rubbish. The main gang members took up positions.

"Remember only lift from the top," said Mac. "Don't pull anything from underneath."

They began picking up rubble and placing it in upturned shirt fronts and it was carried away into the darkness and deposited past the end of the queue at the sides of the tunnel. After several minutes a hand was discovered and concentrating on its position they quickly unearthed 'Wild Bill' Hitchcock. Soon afterwards his gun bag was found and this and its owner were laid down next to Victor Rothschild who examined the man.

"Come on everybody," urged Mac. "The other one must be close." They renewed their frantic work and were rewarded with the discovery of Hector Stubley-Stanhope.

They quickly lifted and carried him away along the tunnel.

"Get the other bloke and hurry up before the roof collapses on us altogether," shouted Mac and another group did as they were told as more debris began falling from above them and they ran away in panic from another deluge.

When Constable Ian Stagg spent time spying on Pleasant Avenue he was looking for any activity involving, by or against, the Olly Wood Gang but he noted down all the comings and goings of people and vehicles on the street, to later enter them on his charts.

What a busy street it was, he thought and not even a through road. Still, he managed to write down the times and their names when he observed the boys and the times and vehicle registration numbers and descriptions of all the vehicles that drove up or down the avenue and where they went; cars, vans and motor cycles, most of which seemed to go to Mrs Roberts' bungalow at Number 8.

The next day he called at each of the old people's bungalows on Pleasant Avenue and as these pensioners loved to talk, he came away with lots of information. Mrs Heath gave him a good telling off for coming round and spying on everyone when that was something she did. She further told him off when he asked if she knew when Mrs Roberts would be in and she told him that the old lady had gone to stay at her daughter's the previous weekend.

Apparently, the daughter's husband had run off with the barmaid from the Black Bull and the daughter had taken to drinking.

"To celebrate him going, probably," said Mrs Heath.

And she told him about events from the day before. She claimed that various people went down Mrs Roberts' path, stayed a few minutes each and left to the same strange comments from her next door neighbour, whose name she could not pronounce so she never tried. She insisted that Frankenstein had told two callers as they left, Hector and Hitchcock,

"Remember, you have your cigs. Use them."

"Oh boy," Stagg said to Sergeant Pyewright. "It will take a long time to process all the detail I've collected and put it on the chart." He summarised the main points to his boss who listened with a serious look on his face.

"That's an odd thing to say about cigs," said the sergeant. "When those two don't even smoke as far as I'm aware. Mind you, they seem to have a number of things they are keeping quiet about so maybe they are secret smokers as well. I bet Lettuce doesn't know."

While his junior officer began 'drawing patterns on his wallpaper', as Pyewright called it, the sergeant left without saying where he was going and headed to Chesterfield to outline what he suspected to Inspector Spector, his own boss. This was what prompted Operation Manor.

They ran for their lives along the tunnel, a hundred and fifty filthy ragamuffins, a Baron, two casualties and tons of rubble and clouds of dust chasing the extended gang. Newt was at the back, where he and Froggy each carried a leg of Wild Bill Hitchcock, while two others carried his arms and two supported his middle. Running was awkward and after thirty yards Froggy stubbed his toe on some of the rubble they had earlier carried away from the mound.

'Stumble on rubble, double trouble', it would later be called by Babs.

Froggy tripped and fell, having broken his big toe, bringing down Newt and both of them dropped Wild Bill's legs which caused the front end carriers to come to a shuddering halt.

"Oww, I've broke me toe," yelled Froggy, as his good foot shot out and accidentally kicked Newt in the face, drawing blood from a cut and a swelling below his eye, like a boxer. Mac, Olly and the Baron appeared beside the new casualties and pulled them both up as the roof collapse came towards them. The two boys then lifted Froggy up for a piggy-back ride on Victor, who galloped off down the tunnel like a racehorse with its jockey. The two boys ran after them leading Newt who was temporarily blinded by blood, dust and a swollen eye. The roof collapse either stopped or they simply outran it but no-one turned to look back. When the first ones reached the doors at the Carr Vale end of the tunnel they immediately began to climb the ladder to get up and out of the dark tomb.

It took over forty-five minutes for the last stragglers to arrive and these predictably included the six casualties; Hector, Hitchcock, The Pope, Babs, Newt and Froggy and their rescuers and helpers.

Half of the crowd had climbed the ladder on the inside and dropped to the ground outside, while after the first one, each of them had their drop cushioned by those already out. Then everyone heard the Winkworth Bell announcing the imminent arrival of a police car, then another, then a fire engine, an ambulance, more police cars, another ambulance and two doctors. It was like the parade at Bolsover Illuminations. When they heard a police car some of the kids did not hang around for the grand switch on and scaled the cutting and ran off. The fire engine was allowed up to the doors and their Chief addressed Irene who had stepped forward confidently.

"Alright, young lass, I thought there were supposed to be lots of kids trapped in the tunnel. Are you them or are they still inside ?"

"There's about a hundred still inside and lots of them are injured so they can't get up the ladder that's leaning up against the window inside," she replied convincingly. "Babs and The Pope were kidnapped last night and kept prisoner in the tunnel. The two blokes, Wild Bill and SS fired a shot that brought the tunnel roof down on them but we dug them out, Froggy says he's broke his toe and Newt looks like he's just gone ten rounds with Sonny Liston."

While this exchange was going on, more able-bodied tunnel inhabitants continued to climb out through the window.

Babs quietly suggested to the gang members still inside that he could easily blow the access door off with a 'little something' he had sewn into his sleeve.

"Better not to, Babs," said Olly. "We can't afford any more accidents and we don't want them knowing about your bombs and chemistry set. Let's see if they can get us all out first."

After discussing the problems with the Police Inspector, the doctors, the ambulance-men and Irene, the Chief Fireman said they would make a platform to stand beside the window to bring out the injured. While this was begun the doctors and an ambulance-man climbed a ladder and disappeared into the tunnel to make initial examinations and begin treatment.

As always in such situations a large crowd quickly gathered and rumours were soon voiced.

Nuclear weapons being stored inside had exploded and killed some kids playing in the tunnel.

The Blue Banks had collapsed into the ventilation shaft there, taking kids down to the bottom who had been playing on the surface.

A giant worm had sucked some kids into the tunnel and was just about to eat them when Babs Nelson had farted and killed it.

And finally, this was a community of tunnel dwellers and some of the kids had been found when they came out at night scavenging for food and stealing clothes from people's washing lines.

A tower and platform were constructed and the two men who had been buried came out first, unconscious, unrecognisable and strapped to stretchers, to rounds of applause from the onlookers, who cheered unwittingly. Next, Newt appeared under his own steam but when he stepped on to the platform, he was also unrecognisable. He promptly threw up over the two waiting firemen, then fainted and collapsed into their arms. They lowered him down carefully, to gasps and cries of concern from everyone, especially his friends. Then it was the turn of The Pope who climbed out and waved to the crowd. They were so relieved that someone looked relatively unhurt and able to walk unaided that a loud cheer went up and they applauded wildly. The boy took a victory pose to emphasize his muscles, took a step forward and slipped on some sick and fell off the platform.

Thankfully, his fall was broken by waiting firemen and policemen, to another worried gasp from everyone. The firemen hosed down the platform to avoid a repeat of The Pope's slip but Babs got a soaking when he poked his head through the window at the worst possible time and lost his footing on the rung of the ladder. He slid down to the ground on the inside, holding the sides of the old wooden structure and his feet demolished some of the rungs as he crashed into them. There were yelps of pain and harsh words as he also crashed into some of his friends at the bottom who had been holding the ladder.

"Are you alright ?" shouted a concerned fireman. "Has anyone been hurt ?"

"Yes, I'm fine," replied the rogue, Babs. "But there now seem to be some kids in here with broken fingers and other injuries. Have you got another ladder ?"

One person had earlier heard the events at the end of the cricket match with particular dismay that was different to that felt by all the other spectators. He was especially interested when he was told that Hector and Hitchcock had shot at the crowd and had been pursued into the tunnel by enough policemen to fill the double decker number 3 bus that passed through the top end of the village. The man waited a while before moving away quietly with a disinterested look on his face. He walked up Main Street and arrived at the deserted bus stop a few minutes before the bus was due. No-one else had left the cricket field because of all the excitement. As the bus arrived and he got on, the first of many police cars came roaring up Main Street, like something from a nightmare, causing other passengers and the driver to stare out of the window to watch these unusual events. They asked him if he knew what was happening but he simply shrugged and stared out of the window to appear like the other passengers. Within fifteen minutes he was back home after making a quick call from the nearby telephone box on Mansfield Road, Hillstown.

While Sergeant Pyewright was required by Inspector Spector to attend the tunnel rescue to ensure that no local villains escaped, Constable Stagg re-examined his intelligence charts for at least the twentieth time. He decided that, although there was plenty of useful information, something was missing that required further investigation so he changed into his uniform, locked up and headed off in the car.

Parking around the corner from his destination Stagg made his way quickly to the house, up the garden path and round to the back, where he knocked on the door without hesitation. He saw the occupant through the frosted glass as the man approached but when he opened the door it appeared that he had been expecting someone else from his look of surprise.

"Good evening, sir," said the officer politely. "May I come in to ask you a few questions ?"

"Err well, I was just going out. It's not convenient," replied the man nervously.

Stagg pushed his size twelve right foot into the gap of the slightly open door and smiled.

"It will only take a moment, sir and then I can give you a lift to wherever you need to go as I'll be done for the day."

The man let go of the door and disappeared into the living room so the constable went in, closed the door behind him and followed into the living room where he was shocked to be confronted by a smiling Mr Finkelstein who shot him in the shoulder, knocking the officer to the floor. He then shot him again in the stomach, picked up the small suitcase he had already packed, stepped over the prone and badly bleeding young man and left his bungalow with the gun in his jacket pocket. He had been expecting someone else coming to pick him up so he walked along Mansfield Road towards Bolsover, hoping his lift would come along soon and meet him. Finkelstein did not notice that Mrs Heath watched him from her kitchen window, having seen the policeman arrive earlier and then being alerted by the distinct sound of gunshots. And now he was leaving in both a hat and a hurry and with a suitcase. She waited a few seconds before going to her front gate and looked along Mansfield Road where she thought that she could see him going away past the Miners' Welfare Club. When she thought it was safe she went round to his bungalow and peered through the living room window where she could see a blood soaked body on the floor. The frightened old lady screamed and shouted for help and a few people came out of their houses, including her own daughter and son-in-law, who had just left their house round the corner on their way to the Miners' Welfare for a Saturday night drink.

"What's the matter, mam ? What's happened ?" asked the younger Mrs Heath, who had not needed to change her name when she married George Heath, her distant cousin.

"That young Constable Stagg has been shot dead in Frankenstein's living room," reported the shaking pensioner. "You'd better ask Georgie to go and telephone the police and tell them one of their men has been killed by that man."

Jack and Mary Wood, Kath and George's next door neighbours, came along, also on their way out for a drink and joined the swelling crowd.

"Has anyone tried the doors to see if they can help the lad ?" asked Jack, having a go at the front door which he found to be locked. He went round the bungalow but found the back door was locked too. He returned frustrated.

"Go and telephone for the police, George, or an ambulance, or both. I'll nip round home and fetch my sledgehammer so we can break the door down."

Jack ran in one direction towards Castle Green while George went the other way to the telephone box on Mansfield Road.

Mr Wood came back with his sledgehammer, with which the public telephone looked as though it had been smashed, as Frankenstein had deliberately broken it on his way past earlier. George Heath ran to Lawman's Newsagents and went round the back to ask Mrs Lawman to dial 999. He explained what was thought to have happened and the shop owner hurriedly rang for the emergency services. Meanwhile Jack Wood swung the enormous hammer at Finkelstein's back door, aiming at the lock area. The door flew open and he ran in and stared anxiously at Ian Stagg and all the blood on his body. The young man was laid motionless on his back, staring up at the ceiling.

After the worst tunnel casualties were taken to hospital, Inspector Spector had to decide who needed to be interviewed about the sequence of events. The well-spoken man who they had wrongly arrested at Manor Lodge had emerged from the tunnel with the horde of unruly children, some of whom Pyewright thought, as usual, must be guilty of something. The local sergeant was his normal self, claiming credit with a smile where things went right and, with a frown, blaming anyone else where things went wrong.

All of this changed and his colour drained when word was received on a police car radio that his constable, Ian Stagg had been shot dead by persons unknown while he was conducting some enquiries at Hillstown. Pyewright left immediately on hearing the news and went to the scene of the shooting, shocked and distraught, as were all the police officers at the tunnel, at such a thing happening to the young officer. Spector sent two of his own officers to assist.

Another surprise came when Andrew Cavendish, the Duke of Devonshire, turned up with his driver, having been involved in earlier events at the Scarcliffe end of the tunnel. As he approached Spector, he recognised the Manor Lodge occupant and spoke to him like an old friend.

"Hello Victor, old chap. What the devil are you doing here?"

"Andrew, how are you? What a pleasant surprise in trying circumstances," replied the Baron. "Have you heard that a police officer has been shot? We don't know if he's alive."

"What? By those two chaps that we had cornered till they went into the tunnel?" asked the Duke.

"No, they were buried when one of them shot at the roof of the tunnel and these heroic boys dug them out with their bare hands while at great risk of further collapse," explained Victor.

Spector shifted uncomfortably and coughed politely before speaking.

"Excuse me, your Grace, can I presume that you know this gentleman who came through the tunnel with those boys? They were all being chased by the two gentlemen who shot at you, sir."

The duke raised one eyebrow and smiled.

"Yes, of course I do," he replied. "Inspector Spector, allow me to introduce Baron Victor Rothschild from the …"

"From the House of Lords," interrupted the Baron, "which is how Andrew and I know each other and I'm here doing some work for Her Majesty's Government. At least I was until the Inspector and his men knocked on my door just as I was about to catch the end of that cricket match in Scarcliffe. You know how much I enjoy a game of cricket, Andrew but we've more important things to sort out. Come on Inspector, shall we go to your police station?"

17

WILLIE WOOD IN EASTWOOD WARD.

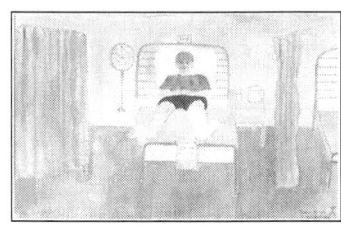

It being a Saturday evening, the hospital was not that busy and Willie was x-rayed, had a plaster cast put on his broken leg and was fairly quickly admitted to a ward where he would have to stay for a few days. Mrs Scholes had spent much time in discussion with the police concerning what William had told her, in which they were very interested, since most of the local force had gone out on Operation Scarcliffe and the boy's story might be linked to it.

She also managed to keep checking on Willie and the doctors and nurses accepted that she was acting 'in loco parentis', as some knew her position as Deputy Headmistress at Scarcliffe School. She promised to call on her way home and let his parents know what had happened to him. Moments after Mrs Scholes had left, Willie was surprised when first Babs and then The Pope were brought into the ward in wheelchairs and looking pale and ashen-faced.

Both of them seemed to perk up when they saw Willie sat up on his bed, his leg newly encased in a pot.

"Alright Will," said Babs. "What's happened to you?"

"Well obviously, I've got a bad case of chicken pox," said the lad. "So they've put me in pot. No, I jumped down the cutting at Scarcliffe and broke my leg. What are you doing here?"

The pair began telling their own story and had got most of the details out and that they were both being kept in overnight for observation when Willie pulled himself up on his bed. He looked down the ward in astonishment as he saw Froggy being brought in a wheelchair, followed by the bloodied and swollen-faced Newt laid on a trolley. The broken-toed Froggy did the talking for these two as Newt had bit his own tongue and talking was too painful.

Four nurses lifted Froggy and Newt on to their beds, while Babs and The Pope climbed on theirs unaided and the boys continued excitedly, but quietly, discussing the events of the evening.

Except Newt, who could not talk so he just nodded and grunted his contributions.

The atmosphere changed abruptly when the double doors at the other end of the ward opened and a porter came in with a trolley bearing another patient. It stopped beside the nurses' station and the five boys were shocked when the porter announced to the nurses,

"Police Constable Ian Stagg, gunshot victim, for a side room apparently, plus bodyguards."

He pointed his thumb over his shoulder at two armed policemen and raised his eyebrows. The porter, the trolley, the two policemen and two nurses disappeared into the side room. After five minutes, one policeman and one nurse came out and went to the nurses' station, while the porter left with his trolley. Moments later another porter pushed a trolley into the ward and announced to the nurses' station,

"William Hitchcock", leaving Willie, at least, stunned.

While the Duke, the Baron and the Inspector had been holding court Olly whispered to Mac, "Let's climb out of the cutting and get away from this lot. Why are we being kept here ?"

"Yeah, come on," agreed his friend. "Get Balsa up the cutting with the rope."

The side of the cutting posed no problem for Balsa, the best climber anyone had ever seen, as he virtually ran up it, grabbing the bull rope that was attached to a tree halfway up. At the top he looped the rope around the trunk of another tree, threw the end down and a hundred and forty plus tunnel kids ascended the steep wall of the cutting in no time at all. They all raised their index finger to their lips get the crowd to keep quiet about their escape and the crowd obliged by not breathing a word. When the last one reached the top, most of the others had already sneaked away up the fields to Darwood Lane and past Pip Hill's farm. Sneaked and snaked as there was a line of them almost a hundred yards long.

As he often did, Pip Hill came out to shout at the Olly Wood Gang which was usually six to twelve strong but today he just stood and stared, took off his flat cap and scratched his head in disbelief. Some stared back, others said hello, a few waved to him and everyone, bar Olly and Mac, quietly sang the First World War song, Goodbye-ee[vii], as they walked past him.

Goodbye-ee, goodbye-ee, Wipe the tear, baby dear, from your eye-ee,
Tho' it's hard to part I know, I'll be tickled to death to go.
Don't cry-ee, dont sigh-ee, there's a silver lining in the sky-ee,
Bonsoir, old thing, cheer-i-o, chin, chin, Nah-poo, toodle-oo,
Goodbye-ee.

Although they were all by now really tired, this lightened the mood and they carried on singing as they walked through the garages and on to Castle Green. The singing stopped as they saw everyone angrily coming out of their houses armed with knives, scythes, cricket bats, hammers, bows and arrows – obviously to use as weapons.

"What's going on here ?" asked Mac. "Have the Russians landed ?"

"Frankenstein has shot and killed that nice PC Stagg, so we're going to wreck his house," said Mrs Launders.

"Come on everybody," said Olly quietly to Mac and the others. "We've got to stop them."

The two boys began running towards Pleasant Avenue, immediately followed by a hundred and fifty foot soldiers, although those at the back did not have a clue about where or why they were suddenly running. Outside Frankenstein's place were hundreds of local people, waving their weapons above their heads like an out of control mob and they were indeed threatening to ransack and set fire to the little bungalow. Two frightened policemen were trying to keep them back.
"Lift me on to Mac's shoulders," said Olly to Micko and Webby and he was hoisted up there.
"Listen everybody," he shouted. "We've been shot at as well in the tunnel by Wild Bill Hitchcock and Hector Stubley-Stanhope and they're now dead cos the roof fell in on them.. Something funny is going on here and there are probably other people involved in this and we might all be in danger of being shot. You should all go home and stay in and let the police search the house for clues."
The mob was silenced for a moment before a shout went up, "He's right, I'm going home."
Mad panic broke out and the mob stampeded away in all directions, leaving just a cloud of dust and a hundred and fifty loyal, unlikely and dirty looking rescuers.
"Phew, thanks," said one of the police officers. "That was good thinking. We were worried."
"We know them all," said Mac. "Anyway, what's happened to Ian Stagg and Finkelstein ?"
"Well, Ian's been taken to hospital in a very bad way after being shot twice but I can't tell you any more than that, only that one of his neighbours saw Mr Frankelstein, or whatever he's called, leaving the scene."
Another policeman came round the corner from Mansfield Road, where his police car was parked and whispered to the sergeant who scowled at this message.
"Has something happened ?" asked Mac. "What's going on ?"
"Well, nothing's happened," he replied. "It's just that my

Inspector has sent instructions to arrest a gang of young tearaways, which is you I presume, but I don't see how I can do that given what's just happened and how many there are of you. If I could just take the names of you two who seem to be in charge ?"

"Don't give them your name Andy," blurted out Mac in a pre-arranged practise that they had, which let the questioner think that his friend had accidentally given the game away.

"Mmmm, I guess your name is Andy then," said the sergeant, looking round to assess things. "Alright young man, I'm arresting you and your fellow leader."

"No you're not," said the small but determined voice of Kate Heath, Mac's grandma, as the crowd parted to reveal a tiny lady pointing a twelve bore shotgun at the shaken policeman.

"If they're more interested in arresting children who've done nothing than someone who's shot a police officer, then I think I'll have a go at it as well. I've always wanted to say this - get your hands up mister."

The large gang all smiled at this intervention. The two lawmen threw their hands up in the air.

"Be sensible, grandma, don't do anything you might regret," said the senior officer.

"And don't you call me grandma, you cheeky young devil. It's Mrs Heath to you," said the lady, jabbing the shotgun at him. "Like I said, you should be concentrating on Frankenstein, not these young people. Our Neville even sings in the church choir. Where is he Malcolm ?"

"He's gone to hospital, grandma, but he's alright," said Mac, unsure how much to tell her.

"See, sergeant, my grandson has risked his life fighting for your freedom while you're trying to take away their freedom. You can tell your Sergeant-Major that I said so and don't think of following me or I'll lump you full of lead. Come on boys."

She strode away with the twelve bore stock under her armpit like an experienced shooter.

"You mean pump him full of lead, grandma," said Mac and she slapped him for his trouble.
"Don't be cheeky, our Malcolm," she replied.
The officers took off their helmets and wiped their sweat away in relief.

Inspector Spector was driven with his two 'guests' to Bolsover Police Station, where they met up with a distraught Sergeant Pyewright. The Inspector told his sergeant that since the Duke was a Minister in Her Majesty's Government and the Baron was a Lord and worked for the Government, they both had security clearance and could view operational materials. Pyewright showed them the 'link chart' and the note that Stagg had left on his desk saying that his enquiries and the link chart indicated that Finkelstein was somehow linked to both Hitchcock and Stubley-Stanhope from the number of visits that they made to his bungalow.
"Alright, that seems to confirm that the three of them are associated then," said Spector. "What we need to find out is why, where and when and with what result, they have acted and associated with each other and where Finkelstein is now. One presumes that he has now taken steps to leave the area by catching a bus in Bolsover to either Chesterfield, Sheffield, Mansfield or Shirebrook, all of which would enable access to the railways to travel further afield."
"Or he could also have other associates," added Rothschild. "And they came to collect him in Bolsover to take him somewhere by private vehicle to either a safe hiding place that we would not suspect or to a safe place further afield, a port or an airport perhaps."
"Hang on a minute, Rockswild," said the Inspector. "What do you mean, 'we would not suspect' ? What is this work that you do for the Government ?"
"I'm working on issues of national security," replied the Baron, ignoring the mis-pronunciation of his name. "I will give you

more details as may be necessary in due course but for now you should accept that we have to work together to locate and detain Mr Frankenstein before he attempts to leave the country when he gets the chance."
The Duke nodded his agreement and Spector did likewise but wondered what was going on.

Kate Heath beckoned them into her bungalow after her, ten getting into her living room, five in the kitchen, three in the hall, the rest snaked down the path and out onto the pavement. She searched for something on the old sideboard, muttering all the while. "Damn glasses, where did I put them ?"
"You've got them on, grandma," said Mac helpfully and the others shook with laughter.
"Oh yes," she smirked. "I'm a silly old devil. Now, where's that notebook, our Malcolm ?"
"Do you mean that blue one on the sideboard, grandma, that you lifted up while you were searching for your glasses ?"
"Oh, I'd lose my head if it wasn't fastened on," Kate laughed. "Now, unlike Miss Marple, my favourite detective, I'm not in any way nosey but I've been watching old Thimblefull because I've always thought he was very odd. And I wrote down the days, dates and times whenever somebody visited him and I worked out that people had set days and times when they came."
"Blimey, grandma, you should be careful," said Mac. "Spying on someone who's shot a copper, then threatening to do the same yourself. Something could have happened to you."
"Oh, don't be silly, our Allan, err, I mean Charlie, no, Lawrence, no Malcolm," replied Kate. "I've survived two world wars and I live here, so I'm going to look out of my own windows and your Uncle Allan left his twelve bore here but I've never bothered loading it. Anyway, about the person who I didn't know, that visited Mr Finkelstein on a motor bike. When I realised which days he came and from which direction on

Mansfield Road, the next time I waited at the crossroads to see which direction again, then the next, next time, I got Mr Battersby to take me on his motor bike and sidecar and we followed him to Shirebrook."

The boys and girls all laughed at the thought of Mac's grandma, in her 'pinny', riding on the back of a motor bike. She had even obtained the man's name and address which she pointed to in the notebook and showed it to her grandson.

"It's a big house on Sookholme Road but he seems to be the only person living there," she said. "He has several motor cycles and several disguises for some reason, including a long dark wig that makes him look like the one that hit young Barry that time out here. Now I think you'll find Mr Finkelstein there but as they've got guns, you should tell the police."

She sat down with a smile in her old armchair as Mac and his friends watched open-mouthed.

"You can say that it was your idea for me to watch him and then you can take the credit."

They still all just stood there staring in disbelief at Mrs Heath, who closed her eyes and went to sleep with that smile fixed on her face. It had been a long and tiring day for her. Mac signalled to everyone to quietly leave and he picked up the notebook and took it with him as they left, closing the door behind them. The stunned silence and looks of the ones coming out of the bungalow produced many questions from those that had been left outside but Olly just told them all to go home and they could get together again tomorrow.

18

GET ME THREE JETS AND SEND THREE AND FOURPENCE, WE'RE GOING TO A DANCE.

Willie kept trying to attract the attention of the nurses but they were working their way along the ward, settling down the patients ready for bedtime and told him to be patient.
Newt had injuries to his face and mouth so he made no attempt to speak and instead was trying to listen under the bedclothes to Radio Luxembourg on his tiny transistor radio that he always carried in his gas mask bag. He was having trouble, as many similar teenagers did, in locating and keeping the tuning dial on 208 metres, Medium Wave, and the crackling, hissing and interference sometimes made it difficult to hear his favourite radio station.
Even more irritating to them were some of the adverts, particularly Ovaltine and Horace Batchelor's 'famous Infra-Draw Method' of football pools forecasts. Babs and The Pope sat discussing chemical reactions and watching the approaching nurses. Froggy daydreamed about kissing one of them, the lovely young dark-haired Jennifer.
Wild Bill Hitchcock had been asleep since he was brought into the ward but he now seemed to be stirring and began to mumble. Newt switched off his transistor with a click and they all leaned towards the mumbling man in an attempt to hear what he was saying. Jennifer arrived at his bedside and

straightened his bedclothes and tidied his bedside table, then checked the patient himself. He was clearly repeating the same few words but she could not make them out properly.

"What's he saying, nurse?" whispered Froggy, taking the opportunity to address her. "It was us that rescued him and Mr Stubley-Stanhope. That's how we got our injuries, isn't it everybody?" The others all nodded as Jennifer herself leaned closer to him to listen.

"It's alright, Mr Hitchcock, you're in hospital now. Did you want something?" she said softly.

He murmured the same thing again but she was not sure what he had said. "It sounded like 'get them, it's three jets' or something like that, I think," she whispered to the boys.

They pulled faces in confusion as to what it could possibly mean as they repeated the words out loud, except Newt who only said them in his head. Eager to continue talking to the lovely nurse, Froggy spoke to her again.

"What's happened to the other one, Mr Stubley-Stanhope? Has he survived as well, nurse?"

"Yes, but he's very poorly and was being operated on," said Jennifer. "But I didn't say that."

"Blimey, we saved both their lives then," exclaimed Babs. "And I thought there was more chance of me making an atom bomb with my chemistry set."

"Chemistry set ..." repeated Wild Bill and they all raised their eyebrows as they now realised what he had said and they all looked at Babs. "Get me three jets ..." murmured the man again.

There was great relief when the news broke that Stagg had survived. He was still in some danger however so Pyewright was also relieved when Inspector Spector suggested that the 'lad', who the sergeant loved like a son, should have a couple of coppers to watch over him at the hospital. Until they knew why he had been shot, the Inspector meant that he would have

armed guards to prevent further shooting attempts, not extra support for the nurses as the sergeant had thought he meant. Rothschild made three telephone calls from a private room to Peter Wright, Roger Hollis, Director General of MI5, and the Metropolitan Police Special Branch. Fifteen minutes later, Spector's Chief Constable telephoned the Inspector and instructed him to retain control of the operation in name but to allow Rothschild to make all the decisions.
He did not like this.

Olly and Mac decided that if the crowd with them agreed, they would go to Shirebrook.
"Right," shouted Olly. "Mac's grandma has proof that Frankenstein will have gone to a house on Sookholme Road in Shirebrook so we are going to catch the 28 bus now and follow him. If you want to come, you can, but remember, he's armed with a gun so we're going to get our own weapons; catapults, baseball bats, throwing arrows, pellet guns and the like."
"Those things against a gun?" said Webby. "I'm not sure that I like the sound of that, Olly."
"We could get some of Babs' bad bombs," added Mac. "He gave me his lab key just in case."
"Alright," whooped Webby. "You can count me in if I can lob a few bombs at Frankenstein."
"Right, everybody who wants to come, go home and get whatever weapons you can and meet at Town End in twenty-five minutes in time to catch the bus. Bring three and fourpence, we're going to a dance," said Olly to puzzled, enquiring looks from everyone. "Bring reinforcements, we're going to advance," he explained, laughing. "We'll get all the bus fares from the money we've got from the odd jobs we've done, won't we Mac?" His friend nodded.
There was a mad dash in all directions as they ran off to get 'tooled up'. Balsa was asked to take Mrs Heath's notebook to the police station and tell them what the old lady had found, so

he too set off towards Bolsover. Trapdoor 'borrowed' a bicycle parked with its pedal against the kerb, halfway up Pleasant Avenue and he pedalled furiously to Palterton to fetch his older brother's crossbow.

Everyone did the same and either ignored or mislead their parents over their intentions.

When Balsa arrived at the police station, he banged the door with his fist to ensure that he was heard. A constable came to the door and Balsa briefly explained the reason for his visit.

"Come in," invited the officer. "They're in a room upstairs." The man led the way to the first floor, opened a door and held it for Balsa to enter, closed the door behind him and locked the boy inside which he realised immediately. He didn't waste time trying the door but went straight to the desk in the corner and wrote a note in large printed letters.

COPS, READ THIS NOTEBOOK, WE'RE GOING TO SOOKHOLME LANE, SHIREBROOK TO CATCH FRANKENSTEIN, SEEING AS YOU LOT CAN'T.

He added the sarcasm for them attempting to capture him and lock him up. The room was not a cell and had an ordinary window which easily opened. He climbed out but instead of dropping to the floor, Balsa scaled the nearby drainpipe up to the roof, where he lay out of sight listening to conversations through various open windows, it being a warm evening. Within moments he heard the man return, accompanied by other officers and then,

"Damn, he's escaped through the window. Sorry sir, I didn't expect that, Inspector Spector. It's such a long way down sir, I wouldn't think of trying that. I mean there's no footholds."

"Get out of the way boy, let me see," boomed the irate senior officer. "Criminals are getting cleverer and the police are getting stupider. Heaven knows how we ever won the war!"

Balsa shook with laughter but did not make a sound for fear of being found up on the roof.

"Sir, I think he's left a suicide note for us, look," said the constable, pointing to the desk.

"How can he have left a suicide note, you stupid boy ?" replied Spector, tiring of police work. "Where's the body ? A suicide is where someone kills themselves, whereas murder is what I'm going to be driven to do to you if I have to work with you lot for much longer."

Balsa was by now shaking uncontrollably and almost fell off the roof at all of this. He heard Spector and the constable reporting to Baron Rothschild in another room what had happened as though he was in charge of everything, and he fired questions at the officers.

"Have you searched the building if no-one actually saw him climb out of the window ?"

Balsa laughed and crawled across the roof, climbed down a drainpipe at the back of the building, scaled the fence and reached Town End in minutes, while the police searched their own station for him and Rothschild read the scrawled handwriting in the notebook from beginning to end. If he had had a quick look at the final pages, he would have been better. When the crowds of mostly eleven to fifteen year olds began arriving at Town End, Olly and Mac decided it would be best if just six of them stood at the bus-stop while the rest hid behind the wall of the Hornscroft, across the road, until the bus arrived. Although some found it difficult, they also told them all to hide their weapons. It's hard to hide a crossbow or an air rifle in your trousers, said several.

Balsa told Olly about his visit to the police station and the leader shrugged his shoulders.

"Don't worry, it's too late now anyway. We'll sort this out ourselves."

The bus arrived and four older Teddy Boys, all aged about twenty, got off on their way to the pubs in Bolsover. Olly climbed on to the bus and said to the driver and conductor that he had the money and would get everyone's fare and the others began streaming on and they counted them in. Two of the

Teddy Boys grabbed Mac and were about to start hitting him when the first of the crowd came round the bus, to the astonishment of the Teds.

"Come on Mac, we've got a bus to catch," said Micko, grabbing his friend from the Teddy Boys who stood rooted to the spot when they saw the apparently endless line of youths.

"Listen, I don't want any trouble," said the worried driver after fifty kids got on to his bus. "But what's going on here? How many of you are there and have you got enough money?"

"There won't be any trouble," said Olly. "Here's ten pounds for the fares for us all to Shirebrook, ten pounds for a tip for you both and there's another fifty pounds as a deposit."

"What if we don't want your tip?" The bus driver shook his head in disbelief and said warily.

"We've all seen the news about the Bristol Bus Boycott on the television," said Mac. "So we'll start a Bolsover Bus Boycott and name you as the reason for it."

He took his family's new Kodak Instamatic 100 camera out of his pocket and took a photograph of the driver who waved them on the bus and the conductor took the money. Olly went upstairs and delivered the same speech to their followers as Mac did downstairs.

"No trouble, shouting or mess on here as we've given the driver a deposit to let us travel. And the same thing goes when we get to Shirebrook. We'll all get off at the stop before the Market Place, six of us will go round there while the rest of you wait five minutes before coming round, unless you hear us shouting you to come straight away. Keep quiet now."

The journey was sort of quiet and uneventful, if you did not count Trapdoor telling jokes all the way and having everyone laughing so much that they nearly wet themselves. When the bus reached Carter Lane, Olly rang the bell to 'request stop' by the school and the bus duly came to a halt. The large crowd got off and stood along the pavement while Olly and Mac collected their deposit.

"Right, we need three couples to go into the Market Place first," said Olly to the throng. "Me, Mac and Trapdoor with Irene, Maxine and Honeysuckle. We've got to make sure we're alright with the locals before we invade. Just think how we'd feel if they came to our patch."

They hid their weapons again before the six of them set off and walked round the corner into the Market Place which was busy on a warm, Saturday evening. Lots of young people were about and the cafe was full, with the door propped open and the juke box blaring out. As they had expected they were soon recognised and a crowd gathered, including their friend Mick Furness, who had been through the tunnel with the gang earlier in the year.

"Alright Olly, Mac, Trapdoor. We don't see Boser folk very often on a Saturday night," said 'Flyer' Kyte, a youth that the three boys knew. "Hope you haven't brought your gang to cause trouble." The swelling numbers of Shirebrook's finest youngsters laughed. "What brings you lot here ?"

"Babs and another lad were kidnapped on Friday night," said Mac to a sharp intake of breath as everyone knew the likeable rogue Babs. "We rescued them from the tunnel today but then the kidnappers started shooting at us and Babs, our Newt, Froggy Frost, The Pope, and little Willie have all ended up in hospital, along with the two that shot at us, Wild Bill Hitchcock, the gamekeeper and Hector Stubley-Stanhope. And somebody else connected with the kidnappers has shot and nearly killed that copper, Ian Stagg, and they're now hiding in a house on Sookholme Road."

There was stunned silence.

"So we wondered if you'd like to help us storm the house," continued Olly. "Or if you'd let us come into your town and we'll do it with just our gang ?"

"Well, I'd join in if there were more of you and half of you weren't girls," said Flyer Kyte and the locals all began to murmur agreement. "That's not a gang. You're on your own mate."

"This isn't our gang," said Mac. "That's our gang coming down Victoria Street over there." He pointed to the other side of the Market Place and the locals turned to look as the 'gang' started to appear and just kept coming in their droves.

"Stop there," shouted Mac. "We don't want to cause any trouble." The massed ranks obeyed and stood still once they had all entered the square.

"I'm in," said Mick. "And me," said his friend Max, followed by a loud chorus of the same.

"Come over here," shouted Mac, waving across the square. "This is brilliant, and just how we should be," he said to the joint hordes who shook hands and embraced emotionally. "If someone had told me we'd ever get together like this, I'd never have believed it. We've got the same principles and the same enemies. We should fight them, not each other."

Everyone cheered Mac's magnificent speech, though many understood not a word of it.

Finally, Baron Rothschild reached the important part in Kate Heath's notebook and asked Spector to order all available officers to Bolsover police station and to have as many armed as possible. Finkelstein was thought to be in hiding at a property on Sookholme Road in Shirebrook and he showed the relevant entries in the notes to the Inspector to justify the action, if evidence was required. They should all report here for orders and they would then proceed in convoy to the address in Shirebrook.

19

GUNFIGHT AT THE SOOKHOLME CORRAL.

Following Mac's stirring speech, Olly gave some more practical instructions about how they would proceed and, as he always had a lot to say, 'Flyer' Kyte was chosen from the Shirebrook contingent to be their co-commandant.
They had decided that they had better draft in one of the locals so they did not feel ignored when orders had to be given. Olly and Flyer led half of the young rebel army across the Market Place, heading for Victoria Street and Sookholme Road, while Mac, Mick and Max took the others along Market Street and over to Portland Drive to set up a pincer movement towards Sookholme Road.
Olly had deliberately told Mac that he should have Mick and Max with him at the front of their column for the fun of their names. All of them laughed at that although their fear and uncertainty about what they were going to face was obvious. Frankenstein with a gun.

Spector gathered his men at the police station in Bolsover and passed on the instructions agreed with Rothschild.
The Inspector read from Balsa's hurriedly printed note and waved Kate Heath's notebook to show where the information had originally been recorded. One of his men was delegated to use the station wall map in Pyewright and Stagg's office to confirm where they were going. He checked their destination

but took the map down from the notice board and took it with him to confirm the location. They set off towards Sookholme Lane near Shirebrook, between Sookholme and Warsop.

When they reached Sookholme Road, Olly and Flyer Kyte stopped their Battalion and sent Balsa along the road to similarly halt Mac, Mick and Max's mob, to get some of Bab's bombs from Mac and to advise them to wait for Geronimo, as he was going to climb on to the roof of the property and drop some bombs down the chimney (Balsa, that is, not Geronimo). Mac gave him the gas mask bag containing Babs' bombs and Balsa slung it over his right shoulder and round his neck. The twelve feet high chain link fencing that surrounded the bungalow was no barrier to Balsa. He seemed to run up it and straight over the top and on to the roof.
"How did he do that ?" enquired Flyer Kyte, envious of such an ability to scale anything.
"Levitation," replied Olly, as Balsa stood by the chimney pot and waved across at them.
Olly raised his arm towards Mac, Mick and Max. Mac signalled their readiness with a thumbs up sign. Countless catapults and two crossbows were held ready, aiming at the house. Battalion Commander Olly Wood dropped his arm as a sign to Balsa to drop Babs' bombs down the chimney. Immediately, a loud bang could be heard all the way to the Market Place and the shock caused Balsa to lose his footing and he slid down the roof to the side of the house. He was going too fast to stop and when he reached the edge he launched himself at the chain link fence which broke his fall as he clung on. When two guard dogs appeared as if from nowhere, he climbed over and dropped to the ground on the outside of the fence. Olly and Mac ordered fire by the catapults and a hail of large pebbles and stones hit the property and the dogs, which ran off round the back of the house, whining and yelping.
As the catapults continued, the smashing of glass in the front

windows was the main sound that could be heard. They had expected a reply of gunshots but the occupants must have been taken by surprise and were waiting for the opportunity to return fire, it was presumed. Olly signalled for the catapulting to stop and everything was quiet, save for the noise of a motor cycle accelerating in the distance and the sound from nearby pubs, the drinkers ignorant of the goings on in their neighbourhood. The guard dogs had fallen silent.

The convoy of cops drove up and down Sookholme Lane several times between Sookholme and Warsop but found no sign of either the Olly Wood Gang or anywhere that Finkelstein could be hiding. They went to all the farms in the area and on nearby Sookholme Road.
"Inspector, could we just have another look at the address given in the notebook?" said Rothschild. "Are we sure that we have come to the right place?"
Examination of the notebook and the map brought from Bolsover police station confirmed that they had indeed come to the wrong place, a mile from where they should have been. Spector sighed heavily and glared at Constable Chapman (the Mapman) as if it was his fault. They left Sookholme Lane and headed back into Shirebrook to Sookholme <u>Road</u>.

Balsa stumbled back to Olly's battalion and reported to his commander, Colonel Olly Wood.
"That was some explosion that Babs' bombs made," said Olly. "How many did you drop in?"
"I'm fairly sure it was a gunshot, not an explosion," replied Balsa. "And I reckon I could hear someone moving about inside before it went off but it made me jump and I lost my balance and fell off the roof. And after the dogs went round the back I didn't hear them again at all."
Olly ran along the street to Mac, Mick and Max's battalion to get some more of Babs' bombs. He explained what Balsa had said and suggested to Mac that they should catapult bombs

through the smashed windows into the property which should flush out anyone still inside. Mac agreed and handed bombs to some of his catapulters to await a signal from Olly who ran back to his own troops. The Colonel waved and shot a stink bomb through the broken downstairs window that started a barrage of bombs that lasted only a matter of seconds before the leaders called a halt.

Everyone stood watching the house but there was neither movement nor sound, of humans or dogs. After several minutes both battalions cautiously advanced to the fence. Olly and Mac climbed over with instructions to their men to shoot with the crossbows anyone or anything that attacked them. When they reached the window they both hesitated in shock at what they saw.

Frankenstein lay on the floor, gun in hand, brains blown out but it was clearly him. They turned and climbed back over the fence.

Marked and unmarked police cars and vans screeched to a halt further up the street, unable to get closer due to the sheer numbers occupying Sookholme Road.

"What's going on here ? This is an unlawful and riotous assembly in a public place or private property, whichever it is," shouted Spector, leaping out of one of the lead cars as four armed policemen, though dressed like soldiers, took aim at the defiant teenaged battalions.

"Look, I'm getting fed up of folk aiming their guns at us and moaning about their property," said Mac angrily. "And then there's property. Who originally said 'property is theft' ? Because that's what's happened round here; round everywhere, in fact. The Dukes of Devonshire and the Earls of Bathurst claimed Scarcliffe Woods or were given them by some dodgy French king, while the Enclosure Acts stole the land from ordinary people like us."

Mac took a piece of paper from his pocket and read from it.

"George Orwell, who wrote the book '1984', also wrote - Stop to consider how the so-called owners of the land got hold of it. They simply seized it by force, afterwards hiring lawyers to provide them with title-deeds. In the case of the enclosure of the common lands, which was going on from about 1600 to 1850, the land-grabbers did not even have the excuse of being foreign conquerors; they were taking the heritage of their own countrymen, upon no sort of pretext except that they had the power to do so.[viii]"

"Either put down your pop-guns or you'll have to shoot me in the back as I walk away. Then you can climb over the fence and go and look through the window at Frankenstein's body. He's inside with a gun in his hand and his brains blown out and we've not seen or heard anyone else."

There were now around seven hundred and fifty young people in the crowd and they once again cheered and applauded Mac so much that it truly became a riotous assembly. Rothschild got out of the lead car and whispered to the Inspector who passed on the order.

"Train your guns on the property, men. These boys and girls are not under suspicion at all."

The police had equipment and tools that allowed them to break down the gates. The armed officers entered the compound and found that both the back door and the back gate into the field were open and there was no sign of the dogs. Their sweep of the house revealed one fatality, an elderly male who had been shot in the head, possibly a suicide, and no other persons. They found evidence of burns from explosions and a disgusting stench in the living room and one of the bedrooms. Spector and Rothschild entered the property once it had been confirmed safe and the Baron ordered that nothing be touched while the armed officers stand guard outside in case the property owner or an accomplice returned. The Inspector wanted to have the body removed and the place secured but he was overruled as Rothschild insisted on having the whole place examined by a forensic scientist who would also conduct a post mortem on the deceased, to Spector's obvious irritation.

"What is the point of that ?" he asked. "We've got the body of the man responsible for shooting my constable, we've got the men who shot at the Duke and at those hooligans who were trespassing anyway. Surely the matter can be closed."

"Not only was I with those boys and I was shot at too, my good man," said Rothschild calmly. "But, as you know, I shall be reporting back to the Prime Minister, the Home Secretary, Roger Hollis, head of MI5 and your Chief Constable, all of whom may wish to speak to you."

"Right, yes, of course," stammered Spector. "We'll keep the case ongoing and arrange for a forensics man first thing on Monday morning."

"No, I'll arrange for Professor Keith Simpson to come. He's the leading forensic pathologist in the country and regularly works for Scotland Yard and lectures at several universities. Now, you stay here with ten of your men to secure the property. No-one comes in and none of you touch anything. Get a shop to open up in the Market Place and buy enough Marigold rubber gloves for everyone who stays inside the fence, you included and no exceptions. I want a driver to take me to Scarcliffe in a van and Olly Wood and Mac Heath and any of their brothers and close associates can come with me. Start your men interviewing local people about this place and its occupants, especially asking all the local youths who appear to be more observant than adults. Make full notes so that nothing is missed. Understood ?"

Rothschild walked outside followed by Spector and they both spoke to various people. Then the Baron thanked the large crowd before he and eight of the gang walked along Sookholme Road, got into a 'Black Maria' and drove away, as people watched open-mouthed.

While the Baron and his guests went to the house he occupied in Scarcliffe, Manor Lodge, the rest of the Bolsover youngsters were ferried back home in groups of up to ten at a time in the three Black Maria's.

Being dropped outside their homes, as some of them were, caused near heart failure in their parents when they saw them getting out of a police van and saying thank you. Whether it was the police van or the thank you's that were the cause may be debateable but twenty questions and twenty unbelievable answers undoubtedly followed. In Manor Lodge, Rothschild made a number of telephone calls and set in motion an invasion of the area by 'associates' of his, doing 'investigations'. The boys were then called into the study and he would not go into detail about this, not even to the gang, saying only that they were criminal investigations. One of his calls after they came in had been to the hospital where their friends were all on the same ward. He was told that they were fine, if a little noisy, especially Babs and Willie, which made the gang laugh. They might all hopefully be discharged the next day, the nurse had said, in fact, following his request.

Rothschild supplied them with tea, cakes and biscuits and they discussed the events of the day and what had led up to them. Without Newt there they could not be sure what he had told the Baron so Mac and Olly quietly signalled to everyone to tell the man everything. He had already heard most of what they told him from their informant, Neville Newton Heath. The driver of the 'Black Maria' had taken his refreshments in the kitchen with Mrs White, the housekeeper, and when the boys were ready, he drove them home, one to Palterton, five to Hillstown and two to Bolsover. They were bursting with excitement but said nothing in front of the police officer driver.

The initial inquiries by Inspector Spector and his officers revealed that people in the neighbourhood of Sookholme Road, Shirebrook thought that there were more than ten young men in their twenties or thirties living in the house who only ever went out individually, never more than one at a time. They were said to have just one high powered motor cycle between them that they all seemed to use, a Norton Dominator 650SS, but that had disappeared along with all the occupants of the house. They were all said to have nodded to people in the same friendly fashion but never stopped and joined in conversation or answered people's questions when out at the shops. None of them ever went in a public house although all of them occasionally bought Vodka from an off-licence. They would always look smart and often wore a suit to go shopping. The local barber had never known any of them visit him for a haircut, even though they all wore it stylishly long and people thought they must have it cut sometimes in Mansfield and they might be in a pop group like that 'Terry & The Lacemakers', as one person said. Not much information was obtained about them at all, or at least very little that was of any use or interest to Victor Rothschild and his associate, Peter Wright, who returned and took over from the Baron. No-one who came across him seemed to like the new man very much, saying that he was an ignorant pig and his nickname of Mr Wrong soon spread throughout the area.

The day after the night of the shootings of the Olly Wood All Stars and the 'Shirebrook Shenanigans', the talk was all about the events of the weekend; the rescue of the Baron of Victor Rothschild, the journey through the tunnel, the attempted murder of the brave Stagg, the raising of a posse of hundreds of boys and girls from Bolsover who caught the bus to Shirebrook on the trail of Frankenstein, Mac's speech that rallied their traditional enemies, the local young people. So much had happened in one weekend.

Word spread around Bolsover that Willie, Newt, Froggy, The Pope and Babs were all being discharged from the hospital at 12 noon on Sunday, which was unusual but had been requested by both Baron Rothschild and Inspector Spector. Everyone

decided that they would catch the bus to Chesterfield to be there when their friends came out of the hospital. Even more than the number that made the trip to Shirebrook went into town to welcome their injured friends. Over two hundred of them travelled on three separate corporation buses with Olly, Mac and Balsa on each bus to pay the fares from their 'savings'. The seventy-six led by Olly that travelled on the first bus were mostly dressed in their Sunday best and well behaved but nevertheless half scared the bus driver and conductor to death. When they streamed off the bus on Vicar Lane two passing police officers walking the beat nearly choked on their Fruit Gums. They had been told about the events of yesterday.
"What the heck is going on here ?" asked one, thinking if he should send them all home.
"We're going to the hospital to cheer our friends coming out," said Olly calmly but firmly.
"I'm sure you won't all be allowed in," said the very tall one, six feet five in his 'Bobby's Hat'. "Two of you can go to the hospital. All the rest can go back to Bolsover on the same bus." Just then, another, older bus arrived on Vicar Lane and its seventy-five young occupants began jumping off the platform at the rear which had no doors, before the bus had even stopped. The newcomers shouted and cheered as they ran past The Red Lion public house and came to a halt in front of the two police officers, for whom this seemed to be too much.
"Come on," shouted Balsa, full of excitement. "Let's go to Newbold Road to the hospital."
"No, we've got to wait here for Mac and the other buses," replied Olly.
The two officers looked at each other fearfully, pushed their way through the crowd and ran off down Vicar Lane, round St Mary's Gate and along Beetwell Street back to the police station.
They were so intent on their return to the safety of the station that they did not see the third bus make its way to Vicar Lane,

where the final seventy-two laughing, cheering boys and girls joined their friends to march and skip happily across town to the hospital.

From John Turner's corner on Vicar Lane they went up Packer's Row and turned right on to Burlington Street, heading towards the Crooked Spire of St Mary and All Saints' Church. When they reached 'Woolies', the Woolworths store at the top of Burlington Street, they turned left and headed down Cavendish Street past the ABC Cinema. At the end of the street they ignored Salter Gate, the first left, and took the second, Holywell Street which led to the Royal Hospital where their five friends had been kept overnight.

They marched down the middle of the roads singing pop music songs at the top of their voices and it was as well that it was a Sunday morning with not much motor traffic about.

Occasionally they passed families on their way to church who stood and stared at this unusual sight. All of the parents made disapproving comments and some of their teenagers joined in with the singing but they were quickly stopped by their angry mothers and fathers. "If young people can sing that loud they should be in the church choir, not in the streets," was a typical comment.

They began singing 'Mack The Knife'[ix] for their own Mac Heath as they approached Holywell Cross Methodist Church and people came out of both the church and the houses opposite to stare in wonderment and disbelief at this strange, large throng.

"It's like the 'Pied Piper of Hamelin' but without the piper," said the visiting Methodist preacher, Donald Soper, known as 'Doctor Soapbox' after his use of a soapbox when preaching to the crowd's at London's Hyde Park Corner. "What a congregation !" he added.

They were about to cross Durrant Road and enter the concourse at the front of the hospital when Olly turned and faced them all and shouted, "Stop, quiet !. That was a gunshot."

In quick succession, four more shots were heard, followed by screams from in the building. Moments later they watched a figure, dressed all in black and gun in hand, run out of the main entrance and jump on the back of a waiting motor cycle, a Norton Dominator 650SS. Another shot rang out and the fugitive threw the dead rider to the ground, having shot him in the back. He then rode out on to the main road and disappeared up the A61, Sheffield Road. Olly and Mac ran across Durrant Road followed by everyone else and up to the hospital doors as people came running out and screaming hysterically.
"He's killed our Will and the others," said Olly to Mac gravely. "There were five gun shots."
"Well, if he has," came a voice of someone else coming out of the hospital. "He's going to be scared when he sees five dead kids chasing him. 'Night of The Ghouls' are after you, mister." Newt emerged pushing Willie in a wheelchair, followed by Babs, The Pope and Mrs Scholes pushing Froggy in a wheelchair as well.
"It sounds as though he has shot people in the ward we were in," continued Newt. "But it doesn't seem as though he was after us and anyway, we'd already left the ward with Mrs Scholes who has very kindly come to take us all home."
A loud cheer went up from the large crowd of friends and, unable to think of a more appropriate song, they began singing 'When You're Smiling'[x]. The school teacher smiled at them all and wheeled Froggy to her car and Newt did the same with Willie. The two invalids were helped in with their crutches, Willie in the front and Froggy in the back with Newt beside him. Olly and Mac moved the wheelchairs to the wall of the building. Babs and The Pope decided that they would travel back to Bolsover on the bus and, in any case, it would have been cramped in the car, especially for the broken toe'd Froggy. Mrs Scholes drove away to resounding cheers and singing. The fun and excitement continued as Olly and Mac led

the surge out of the hospital grounds and past the Holywell Cross Methodist Church, from which the congregation had just emerged, looking awestruck at the crowd, especially the radical preacher, Doctor Soapbox. To Soper's delight, Mac started the gang singing 'Onward Christian Soldiers' and they skipped and danced along Holywell Street.

"There goes our future in front of our very eyes, the youth of today," shouted the visionary Donald Soper as he applauded loudly and was hesitantly joined by the rest of the church-goers.

When the young people began singing 'Jerusalem', old Sopey could not help himself and joined in, singing and dancing up Cavendish Street.

"We'll not be inviting Mr Soper again," said a Church Steward quietly to the Local Preacher.

"From the look of him, we won't even see him again," came the smiling reply.

All the way back to Vicar Lane, they gained more support as people joined in the singing and dancing. When they reached the bus station the conquering heroes queued for, then boarded, their buses with their fares paid again by Olly, Mac or Balsa, leaving the local kids who had joined in feeling empty after the excitement.

20

Join The Navy And See The World – What If You Can't Swim – It Doesn't Matter, They Give You A Ship

Baron Rothschild's collection of forensic scientists took over examination of the scene of the murder of Hector Stubley-Stanhope and William Hitchcock and the attempted murder of the two armed police officers, all of which occurred in Eastwood Ward of Chesterfield and North Derbyshire Royal Hospital. The officers came out of a small side room, where they were guarding Police Constable Ian Stagg, to investigate the shots that killed the two fatalities. Fortunately they were both wearing the bullet proof body armour that had recently been introduced for armed officers and this undoubtedly saved their lives, as well as them diving to the floor and their assailant making his escape.

The forensic science team had already established at the other death scene at Sookholme Road, Shirebrook that Mr Finkelstein had most probably not committed suicide, after examination of his height, the angle of entry of the bullet and the location of his blood and brain splatters. More tests were being conducted that would conclude this particular case.

After visiting the hospital on Sunday afternoon, Rothschild returned to Bolsover in the 'Black Maria' that had transported him and the forensic science team into Chesterfield. He called to see Olly Wood and the gang and found them sat on 'the

Green', the grassed area at the centre of Castle Green, where they lived. At the Baron's request they collected Willie and his crutches, Babs with a bacon and brown sauce sandwich, then The Pope and Trapdoor from Palterton in the police vehicle, which took them all to Manor Lodge for 'a chat'.

He told them full details of everything that had happened, beginning at the first indication from a Russian double-agent that someone local, either codenamed, or located in, 'Scarcliffe Wood', was supplying secret information to Moscow about the development of chemicals in Bolsover for use in warfare. They all looked totally shocked, except Babs who nodded.

Rothschild continued by saying that further messages from 'Scarcliffe Wood' said that local communist sympathisers, under the control of a spymaster, were to mount a clandestine operation to steal or copy secret chemical formulae and information with military uses. A later message stated that this plan appeared to have been thwarted by a group of people who called themselves 'The Chemistry Set' and appeared expert in industrial espionage. They all looked at Babs and laughed and the boy nearly coughed up his bacon sandwich.

Even the Baron smiled at him knowingly but carried on, telling them that Stagg had worked out that Finkelstein, Stubley-Stanhope, Hitchcock and the mystery man from Shirebrook were involved in criminal activity, namely espionage for a foreign power. It was thought likely that this other man was a Russian 'sleeper', a spy who had probably been here for many years and had killed the other three to ensure both their silence and his getaway, even though they had been on his side and he was now thought to have fled the country. He said that Stagg was now out of danger but would be in hospital for a while to recover and that the young man was destined for a bright future if he got the credit he deserved.

"I have to ask you," said Rothschild seriously, "Not to make any comment to anyone, neither your families nor your friends nor the press, about any of these matters. Some of it may get into the newspapers anyway but it is best if we protect your identities, as far as possible."

"Moreover," he told them, "PC Stagg went to great lengths to confirm your story about having gone to Dudley on the very same day that Hitchcock and Stubley-Stanhope were apprehended on private property belonging to the Aroma-Free Group and maintained that they were chasing you boys for trespass and theft. They were released on the instruction of Sergeant Pyewright, who does not appear to trust you quite as much as his Constable does. Hector and Hitchcock being heavily armed with both handguns and shotguns was not questioned by the sergeant."

The boys all laughed loudly at the thought of Sergeant Pyewright's obvious attitude towards them.

"Now, as I have said," continued the Baron. "We are convinced that the Russian will have fled the country but of course, we cannot be certain that there are not other agents or sympathisers who might cause problems for us or for you. For that reason, we shall provide four people who will move into the area to keep an eye on things for a while. They will make themselves known to you by saying that 'Ian Stagg sent them' and you will be able to contact them and me for assistance or advice. Here are the telephone numbers you would need and their cover details. Note down the telephone numbers and memorize the names."

Mrs White, the housekeeper, brought in tea, coffee, squash, biscuits and cakes which interrupted the questions that they had all planned to ask and they concentrated on the refreshments instead. Babs did try to voice a question but it was so jumbled up with his munching of a large piece of chocolate cake that no-one could understand what he had said. The Baron asked them all what they were interested in and what they wanted to be when they grew up, starting with the oldest and working down.

Mac said that he liked football and he wanted to join the Royal

Navy and travel the world.

"But you can't swim," said Newt. "That doesn't matter, they give you a ship," replied Mac.

Olly said he liked football as well but that he would like to be a gamekeeper in the woods.

"You'd have to catch yourself poaching," laughed Babs through a second helping of cake.

The Pope followed next and said that he too liked football but he would like to be a cricketer or, having seen the young Mademoiselle student teacher, he would like to teach French. This final part produced howls of laughter as French wasn't one of his strengths.

Newt liked football as well but wanted to be either a writer or a teacher and a youth leader like Ernie Smith at the Youth Club at Moorfield School.

Balsa also said that he liked football and would like to be either a gamekeeper like Olly or a football referee. "Boo," said the others, surprised at this ambition.

Trapdoor said that he liked football, pop music, catapults, going to the pictures, swimming, girls, reading, arguing, chewing Oxo cubes, going on the rides at the funfair, going to the seaside, going in the Miners Welfare, roast beef and Yorkshire pudding and that day when they all went to Hardwick ponds and Babs was 'Boss of Hardwick'.

"Blimey, Trapper, you'll need a rest after your long list," said Balsa, to great laughter.

Babs said that he could not stand football and wanted to make foul smells, fireworks and explosives with his chemistry set. "You already do," said The Pope and they all agreed.

When it came to Giggsy's turn he began to laugh uncontrollably and they all joined in. Everyone so far, except for Babs of course, had said that they liked football, which they all loved and the two older Wood brothers had both said they wanted to be gamekeepers. Eventually he managed to blurt out, "I like football as well but I'd like to be a gamekeeper."

They all looked expectantly at Willie. Although frustrated at having to wait so long, he at least had worked out exactly what he was going to say. "I like football and driving cars, tractors and JCB's but Mrs Scholes has offered to let me play the pirate in the school play."

"She only said that because you've got a pair of crutches so you can be Long John Silver," quipped The Pope.

"No, it's not just that," replied Willie. "She said something about me being a natural actor so she reckoned I could be something she called a lesbian." They all collapsed with laughter.

"Are you sure she didn't say that she thought you could be a thespian ?" asked Rothschild. "Yes, that was it," said a puzzled Willie.

"Alright everyone, calm down," Rothschild came to the boy's rescue. "Let's call it a day now but I would like to see you all again at the same time next Sunday afternoon. The police van will come to Castle Green for you again. The officer will take you home now. No talking to anyone about any of this and telephone me here if you need any assistance. Goodbye."

21

ON THE SLOPES ABOVE THE SHEEPWASH IN SCARCLIFFE WOOD.

Here come Woody and Wally !!

The following week dragged for them, largely because their mums and dads would not let them go out of Hillstown or Bolsover without prior approval and all the local teenagers were 'bored stiff'. The parents of the Heaths and Woods promised their children a treat on the Saturday of a supervised walk to Scarcliffe and a picnic and games in the field above the Sheepwash.

The whole of the area was still full of gossip and rumour about the events of the previous weekend but the boys would not discuss them, as instructed by Rothschild. The only exception to that was when the Smith family from 3, Castle Green suddenly moved out on Monday and another Smith family moved in on Tuesday; a man and a woman in their forties and their two sons in their twenties who told the boys that' Ian Stagg had sent them'.

When Saturday came the two families gathered outside their houses. Babs had been invited, as long as he brought his own picnic and his 'super trolley' to transport Willie and the food and drink. As Babs arrived from Pleasant Avenue, pulling his trolley carrying his picnic and his little sister, from the opposite direction of the bottom end of Castle Green came Jasper and his sister, then Irene with her little sister and Ann, Alan, Edna and half of the street. The road was beginning to look a little full when the ring of bicycle bells was heard and Trapdoor and The Pope raced neck and neck round the corner on their bikes to cheers from the watching gang who parted to allow them through. Trapdoor just edged in front to win.

"Had we better set off before the Dagenham Girl Pipers turn up ?" asked the bemused Jack Wood. The two boy racers parked their bikes behind the wall of the Heath's front garden and the picnic party began walking to Pleasant Avenue and on to Mansfield Road.

As they proceeded down Mansfield Road to join up with Newt and Mac's Uncle Allan and Auntie Pam, pushing their baby daughter in a pram, more picnickers joined along the route and many of them made a temporary diversion to buy sweets and crisps from Lawman's shop.

When they neared the Miners' Welfare car park Uncle Alan shook his head and said, "Let's hope you've brought enough loaves and fishes to feed the five thousand, our Kath."

"Oh, a few extra doesn't hurt, Allan," replied his sister, looking around at the twenty or so extra that had joined since the start. "And anyway, they've all brought their own food."

"Maybe a few extra doesn't hurt," he said, waving his arm up the Rec behind the big wall. "But even Scarcliffe Woods aren't big enough to accommodate a jamboree this size."

The Castle Green party peered around the wall and there was a mixture of shock and laughter at the sight of the hundreds of cheering families sat on the grass in the middle of the Rec.

"Oh well," said Kathleen, paraphrasing St Francis. "Where there is patience and humility, there is neither anger nor vexation. Where there is poverty and joy, there is neither greed nor avarice. Where there is charity and wisdom, we can all have a good picnic. Come on."

They marched across the dry and dusty fields to the Blue Banks in a column stretched out like a biblical procession, with over twenty prams containing babies and Babs' super trolley containing Willie bringing up the rear. It wasn't long however before Willie and the pram pushers began complaining about the smells being caused by Babs' breakfast of egg and bacon doorstep sandwiches that he was eating on the move.

Babs was sent to the front and was replaced by a team of boys who took it in turns to pull the trolley containing Willie, his crutches and a variety of containers of food and drink. The uneven surfaces over which the trolley and the twenty-odd prams travelled meant that all their contents and occupants were shaken and almost thrown out repeatedly. This slowed down the tail-enders considerably until Babs was sent back to the rear again.

By the time the prams and the trolley reached the field above the Sheepwash, the first arrivals had already staked their places, the most popular spots being at the top end where the slope levelled out a little.

One group built a large dam in the stream between the Sheepwash and the wooden bridge. It quickly created a three foot deep pool big enough for many to swim in.

Another group erected two new rope swings on strong branches above the created pool and one swing was already in place anyway. A third group marked out a rounders pitch. Two more bull ropes were tied together to make a tug-of-war rope. On Olly's instructions, Balsa and Irene climbed the Cedar of Lebanon that was at the edge of the wood bordering the field. The platform at the top of its branches allowed someone to keep lookout in all directions and the gang had decided that this was needed, 'just in case'.

When finally the prams and Willie on a trolley arrived they were all hauled, with some difficulty, to the top of the sloping field where their families had grabbed the best land.

Willie was pulled from his transporter by Babs and Giggsy who gave him his crutches and urged him to go and play rounders as he could use one of his crutches as an oversized bat.

"Mam, our Steven's making fun, saying I could use one of my crutches as a rounders bat."

"Take no notice of him son, go and play on a rope swing instead," said Jack, his dad.

The games were in full swing and players regularly swapped or dropped out, tired, bored or injured. When Newt decided that he needed a drink of limeade, he announced his intention and was followed up the slope by over a hundred similarly thirsty, happy kids.

"Neville, just rock our Catherine's pram a bit for me, would you please, dear ?" asked his Auntie Pam when he had finished his drink and the boy duly obliged, producing happy squeals from his baby cousin as he rocked and made goo-goo sounds to her.

Meanwhile, on 'Lookout Lebanon', as the boys had long ago christened their favourite tree, Balsa put a hand on Irene's arm, a hushing finger to his lips and pointed into the woods, where he saw someone creeping towards the picnic field and holding a shotgun. The figure reached the edge of the wood, laid down and levelled the gun through the undergrowth towards the field, appearing to take aim. Balsa jumped up and shouted from the platform.

"Get down, he's got a gun. Olly, Mac, get everyone down, he's going to shoot at you."

Virtually everyone in the field threw themselves to the ground and when Newt let go of the handle of his cousin's pram, it began to slowly roll down the slope as he had taken the brake off. It picked up speed and fairly flew down to the bottom of the field, narrowly missing everyone and came to an abrupt halt as it crashed into a bush. Newt's auntie screamed when her baby shot out of the pram and landed in some long grass. All of the adults and a large number of children jumped up and ran down the slope shouting hysterically.

Seeing this, the gunman stood up and peered into the treetops but he could not see anyone up there due to the position of the platform and the thickness of the Cedar of Lebanon's branches and greenery. Nevertheless he shot up at the platform with

both barrels of his twelve bore shotgun which he then threw down and he ran away into the wood. The platform blocked most of the cartridge pellets but some did get through and hit both Balsa and Irene. As he was stood up, the boy was knocked off balance and fell off the platform and his feet got caught in the V of a branch, leaving him hanging upside down.
"Quick Olly, help," shouted Irene. "Balsa's hurt and whoever's shot us has run off."
"I'm not hurt, I'm stuck upside down with my legs trapped," added Balsa but then changed his mind. "Quick, I am hurt." Baby Catherine was found to have slept soundly through her own dangerous adventure, thanks to the cushioning of both her blanket and the long grass that she landed in, so the attention shifted to the Cedar of Lebanon tree.
Olly and Mac were the first there, followed by the massed ranks of the running picnic panic, minus Auntie Pam left holding the baby, Uncle Allan, his sister Kathleen and a distraught Newt, upset at having caused the incident of the runaway pram that nearly killed his cousin.
"Quick, I think he might have broken his ankle or something," said the worried Irene. "I heard a crack and I don't think it was a branch."
"Somebody get the tug-of-war rope," said Mac urgently. "We need to be able to lift him either up or down once we've freed him. Hang on a bit Balsa, we'll soon have you down."
"I'm definitely hanging on, but by my feet," replied the boy wryly.
Mac and Olly devised a plan to create a spider's web of support around him that would be held by six boys standing on the platform while Olly cut the branch with Willie's small saw that he always carried in his gas mask bag. This worked perfectly and they soon had the casualty up on the platform.
"If anybody had wandered past, they'd have thought it was a lynching, not a lunching, and we were hanging Balsa," said The Pope, as they lowered the injured party to the ground and Irene

climbed down after him. Both the lookouts had visible pellet wounds and blood on their arms, legs, neck and face but Irene appeared correct that Balsa had also broken his ankle, which had swollen up like a giant marrow.

"We'd better get you two to a doctor," sighed Jack Wood, looking closely at their injuries.

"Dad, can we have our picnic first? I'm famished," pleaded Balsa, pale with the pain of it all.

"Alright, but then we have to get you two seen to," conceded his father, prompting cheers of appreciation from most of the other children gathered around the edge of the wood. They made their way back to their places in the field and Uncle Allan pulled the pram back up the slope while Auntie Pam carried their daughter, refusing to risk her going back in it. Olly picked up the twelve bore shotgun and quietly showed Mac the initials stamped on a small silver oval on the stock, 'H S-S'.

"It must be Stubley-Stanhope's," said Mac, surprised. "Perhaps it was that brat, Peter, blaming us for his dad getting killed and wanting revenge."

"Yes, I think you could be right," agreed Olly. "I think we should call and see Rothschild on the way home and tell him about this." He checked that it was unloaded and shoved the barrel down his trouser leg and hid the butt under his shirt. The pair walked over to their families' picnic position where Olly had to remain standing, so Mac and Giggsy passed him sandwiches, cake, fruit and a drink of lemonade. When everyone's hunger and thirst had been satisfied, they all began to pack up and left together. Olly suggested that Balsa should be carried back to Main Street, Scarcliffe and then they try to get a lift from someone to take the two casualties home or to the doctors.

Balsa refused to travel in Babs' trolley as he wanted his little brother to still use it, so Mac suggested that some of them follow him into Little Wood where he knew of some ideal materials for making a really good stretcher. Within minutes they had demolished part of the fence that was erected for the scouts' clearing, took the 'Keep Out' sign boards and lashed it all together with string to produce a perfect stretcher. And he just loved doing it.

"Just let anybody complain," said Mac, joyfully. "And I'll set my Grandma on to them."

When they neared Main Street, Newt was sent ahead to tell the Baron what had happened and he was so shocked that he came out to meet them and was even more shocked at the size of the crowd which absolutely filled the road.

He told Olly and Mac to have Balsa and Irene brought inside and he would arrange for transport and medical attention for them both and call the police about the incident. Rothschild smiled at the 'Keep Out' signs that he recognised when Balsa was lifted off the stretcher.

The picnic crowd went up Budget Lane and over the fields to Hillstown and then on to Bolsover or Palterton, having mostly enjoyed their brief day out, cut short by some unfortunate and unwanted incidents that would see the gang the talk of the town once more and two of them taken to hospital for a second weekend.

"I'm mad," Mac told Rothschild. "We get shot at while those bodyguards you sent to look after us might as well be on holiday with you aristocrats. We fight your wars to protect your freedoms while we don't have any. And your sort gets medals and knighthoods and stuff."

Despite his outburst at the Baron the day before, Mac was still happy to go and see him on Sunday with the rest of the gang as planned. Balsa was unable to attend as he was in hospital with a badly broken ankle, while Irene had been allowed home after treatment of her wounds from the pellets of a twelve bore cartridge. The gang had to promise their parents that, other than travelling in the Black Maria to and from the Baron's cottage, they would not go anywhere else unless accompanied by the police officers or the 'Smiths'. This was similar to the usual promises they made not to get into trouble but it was always other people's fault, not theirs, when things went wrong. The van arrived and they helped Willie into the front seat and took his crutches into the back as they all piled in and went to Palterton to pick up Trapdoor and Holness The Pope. Colwyn had only just finished his jobs on the family farm but his hard-working father urged him to go because of his private chat with the Baron who had visited all the boys' parents. On arrival at the Baron's house, they were met at the door by the housekeeper and shown into the kitchen where biscuits, cakes and snacks were set out on the large table and Mrs White made them drinks to order as they sat around the table. Rothschild came in and exchanged greetings with everyone as he helped with placing the drinks in front of them. Mac had taken the Baron's best seat at the head of the table but Victor took the one remaining chair instead, which he had intended for Willie as it was the smallest one he had. And William, of course, was perched on an enormous kitchen stool, on to which he had been lifted by the others. He towered above everyone else like a judge. Rothschild looked around and was not happy that all of his guests were higher than him so he stood up to speak. "Thank you all for coming once again, especially after the unfortunate incidents that affected your picnic in the woods yesterday and the injuries that were caused. And I must pay tribute to your actions, especially by your brave friend and brother, Balsa Wood, in the face of great danger. I would also like to pay tribute to Mac Heath for his brave words afterwards when he voiced his understandable feelings concerning the situation."

Mac smiled, a little embarrassed, as the others all cheered or jeered him.

"Now," continued the Baron. "I've been in contact with people that I know from university, government and my friends and relations to arrange some of the things that you spoke about last week, as rewards for what you have done. Starting with Mac Heath, then."

"No, can you start with our Will this time and work upwards in ages for a change?" interrupted Olly to nods of approval from everyone. "He's always last and it isn't fair."

"Of course," said Rothschild, wondering if Mac's speech had made an impression on them. "First then, William. I have arranged with my friend Dame Sybil Thorndike, a famous actress, that you will receive acting and voice coaching within the coming weeks and your teacher, Mrs Scholes, will join her for those sessions to ensure that it meets the requirements of your role. When your leg is better we shall look to give you some dance training too."

The rest of the group were stunned by this, while Willie had a big smile on his face.

"Giggsy, I have arranged with my friend Andrew, Duke of Devonshire, for you to spend a few days straight away with a gamekeeper at the Chatsworth Estate and this can be followed up by other sessions if you wish. I have spoken to some other friends who have some influence in the Football Association – the Duke of Gloucester and the Earl of Harewood – and they have pulled some strings for me. Tickets for the Directors' Box, refreshments and transport will be provided for games at the Manchester United football stadium."

All of the boys raised their eyebrows in shock and delight at Giggsy's reward.

"Now Babs, I hope that you will allow me to join you in what I have in store for you as I have arranged for you to spend some time in a laboratory at Cambridge University, where I studied many years ago. And if that goes satisfactorily, we may supply and equip you with your own laboratory to enable the work to continue." They all smiled and Babs beamed.

"Trapdoor, you are a much more difficult proposition than everyone else and I would prefer to speak to you privately before agreeing your own rewards." The Trapper simply nodded.

"Although he is absent through the injury suffered while showing great bravery yesterday, I will announce the rewards for Balsa. He will receive the same as Giggsy – the gamekeeping and the Manchester United football match tickets – plus he will also have football refereeing training and spend some time with Mr Kenneth Aston, a Headmaster and prominent International Football referee, who also officiated at this year's FA Cup Final, again courtesy of my friends, the Duke and Earl."

"Neville, I mean Newt, I have spoken to my friend Graham Greene, a famous author, who is very interested in providing you with some guidance on writing. He also has a knowledge of politics of all shades and social justice and the two of you should get on very well."

"The Pope, I hear that your ambition to be a cricketer is founded on an outstanding ability. Cliff Gladwin, as you know was born at nearby Doe Lea and played for both Derbyshire and England and was a fearsome bowler, and Charlie Elliott, a Scarcliffe man, who also played for Derbyshire and is now a First Class Umpire, and myself, having played cricket for Cambridge University and Northamptonshire, will all visit your family and arrange specialist training sessions for you. I have already agreed this with your father." The boy was speechless.

"Olly, you are a born leader and, I understand, a superb woodsman. Andrew Cavendish, the Duke of Devonshire himself, wants you to spend some time with his head gamekeeper and with Andrew himself, with a view to you eventually working for the Chatsworth Estate. Oh, and tickets for Manchester United football too."

"And last, but not least, Mac. Once again, I have spoken to a friend, Earl Mountbatten of Burma, a Navy man, who is now Chief of the Defence Staff, a very high office. Now Dickie …" Mac stood up and looked around like some serious French actor before he began to speak.

"Thank you Mr Rothschild but I don't need any help or advice from your posh friends. Me mam says everybody is equal but some people get a leg up, which she says is something called nepotism. Anyway, I've already applied to join the Navy and I've been accepted. I start my training four weeks tomorrow. I'm not saying we shouldn't accept the other things you've offered us all but you Barons, Dukes and Earls should realise that there are millions like us around the country and there were at least nine hundred of us that surrounded that house in Shirebrook to catch whoever shot PC Stagg. They all deserve rewards and medals."

Once again there was a stunned silence at this latest speech by Mac and they were all full of admiration for him, none more so than the Baron, who agreed with every word that he had said. He struggled however to come up with a satisfactory response but felt he must speak.

"You are absolutely correct Mac and I feel that you are representative of a new generation of those millions of young people that are changing the world. You will meet resistance from people who want to keep the old order and increase what they have inherited or awarded themselves. Land, titles, woods and forests, rewards and recognition should all be yours. You've seen the light at the end of the tunnel and you're all part of the movement heading towards it. Let us sort out the things that I can deliver for you. The rest is up to you."

In the following weeks they all began their various activities. On some days important people visited them and on others, cars came to collect them. They enjoyed themselves and the opportunities they had been given. Then came the day when Mac went away to HMS Ganges at Shotley near Ipswich to start his training in the Royal Navy. His departure was a sad occasion for everyone but also a source of pride in their outspoken friend.

Meanwhile, Rothschild advised them that the Shirebrook

shooter had been identified by their sources as a Russian agent known as Ivan Valery Ivanovich, although this was, he said, a false name for Major Valentin Petrovsky, a specialist in espionage and disguise. He was now in Russia.

The Scarcliffe shooter who injured Balsa and Irene while they were on 'Lebanon Lookout' was identified as Peter Stubley-Stanhope. He had blamed the boys for the death of his father, Hector, with whose twelve bore shotgun he had tried to shoot the gang. Letitia Stubley-Stanhope and her two children and several other local people had been taken into custody and questioned about their role in the events.

22

WICKED WILLIAM, THE PIRATE CAPTAIN, BRINGS THE HOUSE DOWN.

Scarcliffe School's annual Christmas play was to be a pirate story this year, The Jolly Roger. Willie had been really happy to be told by Mrs Scholes that she wanted him to take the part of the Pirate Captain. The Olly Wood Gang had never before been shown such kindness or gratitude or whatever it really was as they were now.

Willie was the youngest in the gang as well as in his family so entertaining, singing and dancing were popular past-times for him and also he was really good at them. His class and the teachers however were unaware of his talents and there was therefore both surprise and laughter when he his name had been announced as the lead role in the school play. Of course, no-one else knew that he was receiving personal training from stars of the West End and the 'silver screen'.

Aside from the boy's obvious talent, further secret weapons had been used to help prepare their shining-star-to-be for the play.

First there was Newt's experience in having had singing lessons for the church choir and he agreed to join in with Willie's own singing lessons to assist.

Second, there was Newt and Mac's Uncle Harry, known as 'Flash Harry' for his extravagant and virtuoso ability on the piano and he also read music, having had piano lessons as a child. Flash was 'persuaded' (or rather, instructed) by his mother, 'don't mess with me' Kate Heath, to attend Mac and Newt's house where the upright piano was to be used for Willie's lessons.

Then there were the acting and singing teachers who turned up with Dame Sybil Thorndike.

Finally, everyone in the two adjacent houses of the Heath and Wood families gave full support and help to Willie, including Balsa, so that he trained and practised whenever possible.

These two both had a plaster cast on a broken leg and each would have them on until at least October so, initially at least, there could be no dance teaching or practise. They made great strides, at least in their recovery.

It was not long before Willie began taking part in rehearsals with his fellow actors, if only from a sitting position, when he went back to school. It was not so much the being at school that was a problem but the getting there and back as the bus stop was at the top of the village, on Rotherham Road and the school was at the bottom of the village, over half a mile away. One of his friends had a home-made wooden trolley which they tried to make use of but the downhill trip was too dangerous as it flew down too fast and the uphill trip was much too hard for children to pull it up to the bus stop.

Eventually Mrs Scholes decided that she would transport him to and from school every day.

All the gang and their parents and the variety of acting and singing teachers joined in with rehearsing all of the lines of the play and the songs which were learned by the boy very quickly, though poor Willie received a hefty slap from his brothers if he got anything wrong.

Willie became so accomplished that he could easily win the part of either Oliver or the Artful Dodger in the West End, according to his three coaches and their audience of the two families and the visitors who were allowed to hear, but not watch, the rehearsals.

He learned how to breathe correctly, practice and sing scales

and record and listen back to the songs on 'Flash' Harry's
Philips Starmaker EL3514 Reel to Reel tape recorder.

Fifteen men on a Dead Man's Chest [vii]
Yo ho ho and a bottle of rum
Drink and the devil had done for the rest
Yo ho ho and a bottle of rum.
The mate was fixed by the bosun's pike
The bosun brained with a marlinspike
And cookey's throat was marked belike
It had been gripped by fingers ten;
And there they lay, all good dead men
Like break o'day in a boozing ken
Yo ho ho and a bottle of rum.

Newt wrote a letter to Mac on behalf of the gang every week to tell him their own and local news and they usually got a reply three or four days later. Everyone except Balsa had begun their activities that Rothschild had arranged and he had returned to London although he too wrote some letters to the gang. Mac wrote about his adventures which he said were just like being at home but in a uniform and he had not yet been given a ship. He thought he would be able to come home for Christmas unless he was given a ship and he sailed away.
When Willie's pot was removed it was such a relief to him as his leg had begun to itch and drive him mad. He had tried all manner of things to poke down his pot to scratch himself – knitting needles, wooden rulers, sticks, the long thin poker from the fireplace. Now it was a joy to be able to have a bath properly and wash his scaly, numb, limp leg. Within a few days he was able to jump around like a baby deer but the hospital had advised him not to put too much strain on it. No football and no dancing for at least a week.
By the time a week had passed, William was becoming ever more frustrated and impatient. He wanted to take part in a full

rehearsal and also to receive some of the planned dance training from the choreographer who had been chosen and who had worked on some Stage Musicals and various projects involving both Cliff Richard and Tommy Steele.

Once he started his dance classes, he showed good promise, learned quickly and soon began to impress Mrs Scholes, the other teachers and his fellow actors with his newly refined skills of acting, singing and dancing.

"I always knew he had it in him," said the many that had been shocked at Mrs Scholes' insistence on him being given the lead role but they still held secret doubts about him.

The play was performed for three nights from Wednesday the 11th till Friday the 13th of December. Some people said that it was inviting disaster to have one of the Olly Wood Gang as a pirate on Friday the 13th but Mrs Scholes would not listen to such talk and pointed out how well he had done in rehearsals. Since Mac had told the gang that he would be home around 3 o'clock on the Friday, they had all decided to get tickets for that night's performance. Two of Mac's fellow Navy trainees were breaking their journey home to Glasgow so they were also included in their party to attend the school play.

On Wednesday the 11th, most of the cast were as nervous as hell. Not Willie, who simply continued to practise his lines, dances, songs and bows with great confidence, poise, ability and cheekiness. The boy carried and stole the show and clearly inspired the rest of the cast. The audience went wild, especially the guest of honour, PC Ian Stagg, who was given a hero's welcome on his first night out since leaving hospital two weeks earlier.

Perhaps the only unsatisfactory part of the evening was when the National Anthem was played by the pianist, Miss Sally Birmingham and there was an unfortunate atmosphere between the right-hand side of the hall and the left-hand side as local people thought they were still fighting the Civil War. The Royalists, or Cavaliers, always sat on the right, while the

Parliamentarians, or Roundheads, occupied the left and when the National Anthem began, the right-hand side sang loudly but the left-hand side sat down or remained seated and refused to sing a word.

Mrs Scholes wisely brought the anthem to a halt after one verse and climbed on the stage. "Ladies and gentlemen, boys and girls, let's give another hearty round of applause to everyone that has contributed to such a wonderful evening's entertainment," she said, successfully changing the focus.

'Three Cheers' were shouted and people either went home or went to the pub happy. Thursday night's performance was even better and the deputy headmistress managed to avoid any unpleasantness over the National Anthem by the same tactic, for which she was now prepared.

Mac and his two friends arrived home on Friday afternoon and before long the rest of the gang descended on his house, except for Willie who had to stay at school to get ready. The two Glaswegian sailors chatted to them for a while but then both took up the suggestion of having a nap before they went out to watch the play. After they had left the room, there was much discussion of the events of the summer, which the gang avoided speaking about to anyone else.

After the excited chat they decided to start and get themselves ready to go and see their youngest gang member in his chosen activity. Mac woke up his friends and they took it in turns to use the bathroom and then got dressed in their uniforms to impress any young ladies. They then met up with the others and caught the bus to Scarcliffe.

On entering the school hall the three sailors were asked to sit on the back row, as they were all quite tall, while the rest were shown to the front row but all of them on the left-hand side, being bolshie roundheads. The sailors sat next to three men in suits, possibly teachers or reporters, Mac thought.

The anticipation was increased by Willie peeking from behind the stage curtain and waving and shouting to his family and friends, especially Mac, who he hadn't seen for three months. Mrs Scholes introduced Miss Sally Birmingham, the young teacher who was the pianist accompaniment and asked her to 'take it away' and the play was under way.

The black clad menacing looking pirate captain had undergone a remarkable change from rogue to 'good guy'. He vowed to the Queen to renounce his wicked ways and defend his country and the high seas against evil, which didn't go down too well with the bolshies on the left. His strong clear voice boomed out to the assembled audience as he took four great strides forward as if to confront his enemies.

"I will stand firm", he declared but his last word tailed off as his gaze went to the rear of the hall, as required at this point. Puzzled by what he thought he saw, one of the men in suits loading a handgun, he whistled a blackbird alarm call, first at Olly and the others on the front row, then at Mac and his mates at the back. The gang all realised that something was wrong.

Then, through not concentrating on what he was doing, Willie fell off the stage and over the top of the upright piano, which gave a mighty clatter of keys hitting all the wrong notes. He hurtled on, into the lap of Miss Sally Birmingham and he ended up astride her as she fell backwards off her stool. They landed at the feet of Mrs Scholes, the deputy headmistress.

Scarcliffe School hall erupted in uncontrollable laughter at the timing of this piece of slapstick in the Christmas musical which had turned into a pantomime. Mrs Scholes turned on the audience angrily.

"Will you show some decency", she shouted, "Miss Birmingham is unconscious. Mr Madin, can you help please?" she asked of the local Captain of the St John's Ambulance Brigade. The young teacher was brought round but was clearly dazed and confused.

"It's alright Sally, William decided he'd rather be a pilot than a pirate and crashed into you when he overshot the stage," said

Mr Madin. "She shouldn't carry on," he added quietly.
Willie got to his feet and shook himself down, indicated that he could continue, while the young teacher was taken into the head's study.
Seeing that Miss Birmingham was being taken care of, Mrs Scholes returned to the hall.
"Sally is unable to carry on," she announced to the audience, to groans of disappointment. "So I am going to ask Mr Heath to provide the accompaniment for the finale."
A round of applause went around the hall.
Newt and Mac's uncle, Allan Heath stood up and took out his mouth organ. "Alright, I'll do the finale but I'm not doing the National Anthem," he said from the left-hand side of the hall, prompting boos from the right.
"Not that Mr Heath," responded an amused Mrs Scholes. "I mean, err, 'Flash' Harry Heath who plays the piano and has been helping William rehearse at home." Allan sat back down, smiling as he had known that it wasn't him that was being asked.
'Flash' Harry Heath was there in a second. He made most of the hall cringe when he cracked his knuckles several times to demonstrate his readiness. He had played with numerous local bands and often sat in for sing-songs at both the Horse and Groom public house, the 'Top Pub' as it was known from being at the top of the hill and the Elm Tree Inn or 'Bottom Pub', which was of course at the bottom of the hill, near the school.
Flash played remarkably well and to the great enjoyment of everyone in the audience and on stage. William particularly enjoyed his playing because he knew it so well from their rehearsals and he was able to express himself very well. Mrs Scholes was pleasantly surprised at the accomplished performances and seamless piano playing. The whole audience was impressed but from his vantage point at the front of the five foot high stage, Willie saw the three men in suits, who he

had forgotten about, acting very strangely again.

Instead of the proper ending where he stood and took a bow, Willie threw himself to the floor of the stage and propped himself up on one elbow, to thunderous applause. Under cover of the noise he said to Olly sat directly below him.

"Something funny about those three blokes in suits sat next to Mac. I tried to tell you before, I'm sure I saw one of them loading a gun earlier. What if it's Igor ? Come on, let's sneak out under the stage."

The pirate captain rolled off the front of the stage and disappeared under it through a little door, followed by his brothers and friends, unnoticed by most of the audience who were giving a noisy standing ovation. When they reached the rear door of the stage they climbed out and locked it with the external locking bar.

Babs had undertaken the job of car park and traffic control and bicycle shed attendant, which Mac unfairly said was like putting the fox in charge of the chicken coop. He had left the hall and returned to his post just before the finale.

The car park attendant watched the gang emerge from the back of the building.

"What's going on here then ?", making them jump with surprise.

As if on cue, Flash played the National Anthem which often caused fights between the loyal farming and business community and the rebel, republican, council house and working class tenants.

When the first bars of the anthem started and the right-hand side began singing loudly, Mac dragged his two fellow sailors off their chairs and they went outside quickly, as he explained the local history that made for problems between the rival factions of the village. They lit up fags to avoid any trouble involved in Her Majesty's Forces not singing Her Majesty's song.

Inside however, the three men in new suits, standing at the

back on the left-hand side and unaware of the local convention, knew only that in Great Britain, it was customary to sing the National Anthem at the end of the night in cinemas, theatres and other events. The three therefore sang it with great gusto, making almost everyone else in the audience turn and stare at them in shock. People in the left-hand side just did not sing the National Anthem.

Olly and Willie explained what the pirate thought he had seen and the gang then heard the strange events surrounding the National Anthem, which the three men ended up singing on their own. Allan Heath hit one of the three men with his harmonica to start the fight.

As they peered in through the hall windows, the boys saw one of the men take out a handgun which he shot into the air, causing widespread fear and panic.

"Quiet everybody," shouted the shooter. "Where did that Olly Wood gang disappear to ?" No-one spoke but the men noticed the open door leading under the stage.

"No-one move or I'll shoot you. Come on," he said to the others. "We have to catch them."

They ran to the front, all pointing their guns at the terrified audience, then they disappeared under the stage.

"Quick," said Babs to the gang outside. "I've got some new bombs we can use – 'Earsplitters', 'Headbangers' and 'Thunderblunders'. We've got to hurry and throw them under the stage."

He led them all to the main door of the hall, where Mac and his friends were about to go in.

"Let me go first," he said without breaking stride and ran straight in and down the central aisle to the front, taking things out of his haversack as he went.

When they reached the open door to the stage he threw his handful of small missiles through the opening and yelled to the others. "Get the piano to stop them coming out." They shoved it quickly in front of the now closed door and he shouted again.

"Get out, we've only got five seconds." It was, in fact, seven and a half seconds before a series of bangs was heard that deafened everyone within a hundred yards and seriously injured the three men trapped under the stage, knocking them out cold.

The two supposed bodyguards took over at the school, which had been badly damaged. They first sent for Rothschild and his men who were back in London, then for the local police, ambulance and fire service. The audience, staff and cast were all accounted for and sent home although many went to either the top or the bottom pub.

The gang were reluctant to go but they eventually left and caught the East Midland number 28 bus back to Bolsover. The two Glaswegian sailors said they had never enjoyed a trip to the theatre so much. They had to be persuaded to continue their journey home the next day and Mac had to promise to let them come back another time.

The three men in suits would later be identified as Russian spies, led by Major Valentin Petrovsky, who would admit to the murder of his fellow agent, Leo Finkelstein. It also came out that they had found out the identities of the group of young people who called themselves 'The Chemistry Set' who they believed had stolen the formula and other information about a chemical produced by the 'Aroma Free Group' for use in chemical warfare. Their intention had been to kidnap 'The Chemistry Set', obtain their secrets by whatever means were required, then kill them. The three men were taken to London where they were treated for their injuries and locked up before being tried and found guilty of spying and murder but were subsequently exchanged for British agents locked away in Russian prisons.

The Olly Wood Gang all continued to pursue the activities that the Baron had arranged for them but for now they simply enjoyed some fun over the Christmas holidays and talked and laughed about the adventures they had in 1963 and what they hoped for in 1964. They wondered if they would all have as much success as Willie did in his chosen pursuit.

23

READY, STEADY, GO !

Over the Christmas holidays they all gathered several times in the Heaths' living room and watched their favourite television programmes – ATV's 'Espionage', BBC's 'Doctor Who' and Rediffusion's 'Ready Steady Go' among them. There were not enough seats for everyone, so some always had to sit on the floor.

On Friday 27th December 1963, they were squashed in the living room waiting for the 'Ready, Steady, Go!' Christmas show with The Rolling Stones and a scrawny kid only a month older than Newt, called Little Stevie Wonder, who played harmonica nearly as good as Newt and Mac's Uncle Allan but was a much better singer than their uncle.

"What you writing about, Newt ?" asked Willie, peering over his friend's shoulder to look.

"Well, I might write a book in the future about all the things that have happened so I always write the important stuff in a notebook. It's not a diary, just a note of our adventures."

"What will it be then Newt, a thriller or a comedy ?" enquired his older brother, interested.

"No, a whodiddit, I reckon," replied the would-be author, to laughter from Olly and Mac.

"You mean a whodunnit, I think," said Mac.

As they awaited the beginning of the programme, Mac and Olly gave out drinks of pop, bags of crisps and Kate Heath's lovely homemade mince pies and Christmas cake.

Mac took up a position standing in front of the mantelpiece which meant he was going to speak and they all hushed and looked at him.

"I'm the oldest and the first to go away and out into the big world," he said. "We've already started moving in different directions and doing different things - as a sailor, an actor, a cricketer, a gamekeeper, a chemist, a writer, a football referee and a mystery man, in Trapdoor's case. Our lives have changed massively this year with all that's happened and who knows where we'll all end up. But just remember this. The Baron said that we were representative of a new generation of millions of young people that are changing the world. He said that we should all have land, titles, woods and forests, rewards and recognition for what we've done. Trouble is, when they talk about defending Queen and Country, they're on about US defending THEIR lifestyle, with their palaces, mansions, big houses, cars and land. Rothschild might have given us all some treats as rewards cos they needed our help to sort out the threat to them from the Russians but we still live in council houses, while they still live in luxury. Whatever we get, they'll want to take off us. They're just using us and they'll continue to use us, making more money out of our work than we will, whether it's from writing a book, acting in a play or ..."

Keith Fordyce on the television announced the start of the programme he presented.

"Shut up Mac, 'Ready, Steady, Go!' is on now," they chorused. Part way through the show, Mrs Heath entered the kitchen to make a pot of tea and popped her head into the living room to check on the boys and in curiosity at the strange noise.

"SWITCH IT OFF," she screamed when she saw and heard it. "IT'S THE DEVIL'S MUSIC !"

[i] 'O For The Wings Of A Dove', a passage from 'Hear My Prayer' by Felix Mendelssohn (1844)
[ii] 'The Canoe Song', a traditional African tribal song sung by Paul Robeson in Sanders Of The River, 1935
[iii] 'Song To The Men Of England' by Percy Bysshe Shelley, 1819
[iv] 'Leviathan' by Thomas Hobbes, a book of political philosophy published in 1651
[v] 'You dirty rat', the saying often attributed to James Cagney, was never said by him or anyone else in a film in those exact words.
[vi] '4ft 8½ And All That – For Maniacs Only: A Sort of Railway History' is a humorous book about the history of British Railways by W Mills, published 1964.
[vii] 'Goodbye-ee' was a First World War song composed by R.P. Weston and Bert Lee in 1915.
[viii] 'Land Grabbers' was an article by written by George Orwell in 1944, for Tribune magazine.
[ix] 'Mack The Knife' is a song written by Kurt Weill and Bertolt Brecht for 'The Threepenny Opera' which premiered in 1928.
[x] 'When You're Smiling' is a song written in 1929 by Larry Shay, Mark Fisher and Joe Goodwin.

Made in the USA
Charleston, SC
06 December 2013